A RIGHTEOUS KILLER

BLOOD MURDER BETRAYAL

ELLACE JAMES

authorHOUSE

AuthorHouse™ UK
1663 Liberty Drive
Bloomington, IN 47403 USA
www.authorhouse.co.uk
Phone: 0800.197.4150

© 2018 ELLACE JAMES. All rights reserved.

No part of this book may be reproduced, stored in a retrieval system, or transmitted by any means without the written permission of the author.

Published by AuthorHouse 12/28/2017

ISBN: 978-1-5462-8673-8 (sc)
ISBN: 978-1-5462-8674-5 (hc)
ISBN: 978-1-5462-8672-1 (e)

Print information available on the last page.

Any people depicted in stock imagery provided by Thinkstock are models, and such images are being used for illustrative purposes only.
Certain stock imagery © Thinkstock.

This book is printed on acid-free paper.

Because of the dynamic nature of the Internet, any web addresses or links contained in this book may have changed since publication and may no longer be valid. The views expressed in this work are solely those of the author and do not necessarily reflect the views of the publisher, and the publisher hereby disclaims any responsibility for them.

CHAPTER 1

Blood was seeping from beneath the curtain of the confessional. Inside, fragments of brain were smeared on the wooden walls, and blood ran like a leaking tap from the partly dismantled head of a priest who had met his fate. In the other half of the box, I sat with a demonic expression, chopped and screwed two revolvers resting in my lap with my head tucked against the lattice.

No, I was not a murderer, a killer, or a saint. I was none of those. I was just a man named Arthur Brown, who was doing the wrong things for the right reasons.

Months earlier, I was in Carol City, my home town. Some refer to it as a drug capital for every dealer looking to make a name for himself. It had been this way for as long as I could remember. The streets were home to every low life, slime, and scumbag who infested the sidewalks and the street corners, with the wicked constantly preying on the weak. Dirty cops were on the biggest drug lord's payroll. Crime was at its peak.

No justice, no peace, and no hope. All the city had was its prayers—prayers that needed answers, prayers that could be heard. That was where I came in. It took a lot to make me what I was now.

Carol City Pentecostal Church, Sunday morning, on the edge of town near the capital: Lismore. The church was filled, and the members were singing songs of praise. I stood at the altar, just an average-looking man, six feet tall. I was in my forties with a shade of grey hair and was always smiling.

I proudly looked at my family sitting in the front row. My wife, Lauren Brown, had recently turned forty. She was brunette, slim, and five foot five. She was my world. And both my sons were beside her:

Charles, who was eight, and Andy, who was ten. Both had dark hair and took after their mother. Both were my pride and joy.

I live for three things: God, my church, and my family. I am a very devoted husband and father, faithful to my religion. Or so I thought.

The choir finished their hymns, and I stepped forward to the podium to deliver my morning sermon. I said to the warm audience, 'Welcome to another blessed day of worship, my people! Please turn to the book of Psalms!'

I was about to begin my sermon.

Things weren't so pleasant on the other side of town—at Carol City's old dockyard. It was quiet and deserted that day, until a black Lincoln saloon pulled up in a hurry between a set of old salvage trawlers.

The front doors swung wide open, and two men with pistols in their hands emerged. Joe Harris was casual, with slick, shiny, combed-back hair. Rick Lawson had half the side of his head shaven and a big beard. They appeared to be in their mid-forties, had average height, and were well built. They opened the boot and dragged out two men in beach shorts and holiday shirts.

'Get out! Fucking pieces of shit!' Rick shouted. *'You think you can steal from us? Do you?'* He and Joe were pressing their pistols to their victims' heads.

Rick Lawson. A nasty piece of work. Also a yes-man, an associate and loyal companion to crime and notorious drug cartel boss Richard Sullivan and his son, Paul. Rick was paid to clean up their dirty work.

Both of their victims, Martin Redding and Stuart Randle, were men in their early forties with average height. They were dragged aggressively towards the edge of an old wooden jetty at gunpoint, thrashed around a few times, booted in the gut, punched, gun butted, and knocked to their knees.

'Where's the fucking money you stole from the casino?' Rick yelled, scuffing Stuart Randle by the throat while his partner watched.

'We don't have it, Rick! You got to believe me!' Stuart cried, with blood dripping from his busted mouth.

'He's right, Rick. We don't have the money! You got to believe us!' Martin pleaded as Joe pressed his gun to his neck.

Rick started yelling at Martin. 'Shut the fuck up! I'll get to you next, dipshit!'

Rick put his pistol to Stuart's head, between his eyes. 'I'm going to ask you one last time. *Where's Mr Sullivan's fucking money?*'

'Please, Rick! We don't have it! We never took the money!' Stuart continued to deny the accusations.

'We'll see about that, Stuart! We'll fucking see!' Rick replied in a threatening tone.

'Get him up!' Rick indicated to Joe, pointing his pistol at Martin.

Joe heaved Martin to his feet, standing him upright. Joe pointed his pistol at Martin.

'*What're you doing?* Don't, Rick! I'm begging you! Don't! We don't know where the money is!' Martin cried his eyes out.

Rick put a bullet in each of Martin's kneecaps, dropping him to the ground. Another bullet in both of his arms rendered Martin helpless as he screamed his lungs out on the jetty.

Rick was then about to finish Martin off when Stuart decided to squeal. 'Don't shoot! I'll talk! I'll fucking tell you where the money is!' He cried helplessly, throwing his dignity out the window.

Rick then turned his attention towards Stuart. 'Go on, then! Talk before I lose my fucking patience!'

Stuart stalled for a while before he spilled the beans. 'We hid the money!'

'*Where? Where have you hid the money?*' Rick demanded, holding his pistol over Stuart's head.

'Martin and I hid the cash in some guy's house!' Stuart answered.

Rick was angry, annoyed. He cocked the hammer, ready to put an end to Stuart. '*You fucking did what?*'

'Wait! Wait! The money is safe! I promise!' Stuart flinched at the sight of Rick's gun at his head.

Rick hurled Stuart to his feet. With a foul tone he said, 'You fucking hope it is! Because you are going to take me there!'

'Come on! Let's get out of here!' Rick said to Joe, hauling Stuart up by the back of his collar.

'What about this piece of crap here, Rick?' Joe asked with his foot on the chest of Martin, who lay there bleeding out.

'Put him on the news! Show Mr Randle we mean business!' Rick said to Joe as he shoved Stuart back to the Lincoln.

'No! Please! You got to let me go! Please!' Martin pleaded as he bled from his knees and arms.

Joe emptied a full clip of ammunition into Martin and walked away.

Stuart was rammed into the boot of the Lincoln. Rick and Joe drove away, leaving Martin's body on the jetty—soaking in blood.

At Carol City Pentecostal Church later that morning, my sermon was just about wrapped up and a closing prayer was being offered before the service ended.

'Heavenly Father, we pray for your loving mercy. We pray that you restore upon us your blessings. Guide us to the path of righteousness that we may not stray. Deliver us from the hands of the wicked and the foulness of the city. Amen!'

I finished the prayer, shook a few hands, and shared brotherly hugs with a few of my church colleagues as they exited down the aisle. After that, I joined my family, and we made our way out of the church.

Outside, I stumbled upon a homeless man named Jack Wielder. He was six foot two and in his late fifties. He had rough grey hair and ripped clothing and was hanging around the churchyard. He came here every Sunday. Never had he entered, though I tried to persuade him many times.

'Father Brown! Interesting sermon today! I sat out front and listened to the whole darn thing! Very moving', Jack said, coughing his lungs up. He had a bottle wrapped in a brown paper bag.

I patted him on the shoulder with a sign of goodwill. 'Thanks, Jack. Maybe you will find yourself inside one day!'

Jack took a long, sharp swig of the bottle. 'Maybe! Just maybe, Father!'

'You should put the bottle down. Don't want to find you dead outside God's house!' I said to Jack, showing my deepest concern for his well-being.

With a chuckle, Jack replied, 'Don't worry about me, Father. There's more ways to die than one!'

Lauren and the kids had already sat down in the car and were waiting for me to finish my usual chat. Suddenly there was a scream. An old church lady was being mugged by a drug addict. He was fighting for her purse, and the lady fought back. I rushed to her aid.

'Hey! Get your hands off her!' I shouted as I stormed the steps onto the sidewalk.

The drug addict fought harder, dragging the old lady to the ground. She fell hard, hitting her head on the pavement and passing out. I was too late. The drug addict made off with her purse. I picked her up, making sure she was still breathing and alive.

Lauren came to assist, calling the ambulance for immediate attention. The incident captured the attention of the surrounding people. The ambulance came, I explained what had happened, and they took the old lady away.

Over at the dockyard, blue lights were flickering and reporters were probing to get the latest scoop. Martin Redding had been discovered by a local boatman named Bennie Brickworth, a middle-aged labourer who salvaged ships for repairs.

The cops cordoned the scene, whilst the forensics team investigated the crime. Bennie was in the middle of giving a statement when a silver Ford Crown Victoria pulled up in the boatyard.

Detective Carl Brooks was African American, clean-shaven, tall, and very loud, the kind of guy who told it like it was and took his job seriously. He exited his cruiser with his rookie partner, Craig Bollington. Bollington was an average-looking guy with dark hair and blue eyes.

'*What the hell is going on here?* This isn't a fashion show, people! Stand the hell back! Get back!' Carl shouted at the reporters and the onlookers with cameras. He ordered them to stay clear as he tried to enter the crime scene.

Carl made contact with a male officer on the scene and asked for an update. 'What we got here? Talk to me!'

'We got a homicide', the officer replied. 'White male, age forty.

Victim died from a series of gunshots to the abdomen. Body was discovered by a local labourer early this afternoon',

'Sounds like someone was really pissed off,' said Carl as he approached the body. He lifted the drape and had a look at the victim. 'Any witnesses?'

'None so far', the officer replied.

'Looks like we got another drug-related crime on our hands', Carl muttered. Then he started barking orders. 'Okay! I want a look at any surveillance feeds in and around the area. Craig! See if any of these locals knows anything. Make it happen!'

Craig went off seeking answers with the officer on the scene. Carl walked over towards the local boatman, Bennie, for further questioning.

Uptown Carol City, busy street with a lot of shouting and horn blaring. Paul Sullivan's penthouse. Paul, son of Richard: slim, average height, dark hair with facials.

In his open-planned living space, pearl white walls with expensive portraits, sculptures of naked women, a large wall-recessed fish tank filled with piranhas.

Paul sat on an all-white leather sofa in an Italian robe, in front of a black glass centrepiece, music blaring, dragging cocaine from his centrepiece. Two misguided females, early twenties, half-naked, one rubbing his shoulders, the other on her knees, head deep in his crotch, each playing her part.

The doorbell rang. Paul tossed the girls aside onto the sofa like rag dolls. 'Get the fuck off me!' He scrambled to pull himself together and answer the door.

Three men stood waiting, semi-casual clothing. Two big guys with straight faces, side by side. In front of them stood a man of medium height with short curly hair, a beer belly, and a goatee, an old associate of Richard Sullivan.

Paul was surprised. 'Oh, shit! Mr Donavon, I wasn't expecting you. Come on in.'

Paul waved the three men into his humble abode. Mr Donavon walked in accompanied by his muscle. Had a slow and suspicious gander around the living area with his hands in his pockets. His gazed settled on traces of cocaine on the centrepiece, and the girls looked at him funny

Mr Donavon shook his head disappointedly. 'So this is what you up to, huh? Fucking this pair of nobodies and blowing cocaine!

'Get the fuck out of here! Go!' Mr Donavon scared the girls off, forcing them out the door half naked.

Paul tried to justify himself. 'It's not what it looks like, all right?'

'It's exactly what it fucking looks like. You supposed to be getting your father's cash back into his casino!'

Paul walked to his minibar and poured himself a drink. 'I am handling it. My men are on it. Dad's cash be in his pocket by sundown!'

Mr Donavon wasn't so easily reassured. 'Oh yeah? What makes you so sure, Paul?'

'Because Rick always comes through.'

Helping himself to a drink, Mr Donavon replied, 'You want to hope he does. You know what happens if you fail.'

Unhappy about Mr Donavon, Paul poked his finger at Donavon's chest. 'Is that some sort of threat, Mr Donavon?'

Mr Donavon's hired muscles gave Paul a funny look. Paul got the hint and calmed down.

Mr Donavon downed his drink and straightened his blazer. 'Don't forget to show up tomorrow night. Follow the money!' Mr Donavon said as he and his hired muscles saw themselves out.

Paul picked up his phone and called Rick for an update on the missing cash. As soon as Rick picked up, he shouted, 'What the fuck is taking you so long, Rick?'

'I am handling it as we speak! We know where the money is', Rick replied, calm and collected, from the Lincoln parked outside a local shop.

'Get the money and get the job done. Don't give a fuck how you get it done—just get it done!' Paul hung up.

Rick paid no attention to the shouting. His loyalty surpassing his own anger, he carried on with the job. Stuart began banging around in the boot, begging to be set free.

Joe: 'Sounds like someone is awake.'

'Shut him up! But quietly', Rick replied.

Joe got out of the car and went round to the boot. When he raised the lid, he saw Stuart rustling around, still trying to free himself. Joe punched his face in, breaking his nose and knocking him cold. Then he closed the boot and got back into the car, and they drove away.

Later that afternoon I was in the kitchen helping my wife with the afternoon lunch. The television was on in the living room where the boys sat playing together. A news broadcast was overheard that got both Lauren's and my attention.

'Local church lady, Maggie Watson, was pronounced dead as a result of a serious mugging incident earlier outside the Carol City Pentecostal Church. Suspects have been released on bail.' The female reporter announced, 'In another story, two men have been discovered dead at the old Carol City dockyard. The CCPD is treating the incident as a drug-related murder.'

The reporter continued. 'Good news for the people of Carol City. Police have raided the home of small-time drug dealer Aron Carter. He was said to be smuggling an unknown quantity of drugs inside the capital, Lismore. Footage of the raid was released by CCPD. Warning! Footage may contain graphic imagery.' The reporter's picture gave way to a video clip of the raid.

A SWAT team of four stacked up outside Aron Carter's house. A battering ram smashed the door open to show three men in pyjama bottoms and white stained vest tops, perhaps in their late thirties, counting money with bricks of cocaine stacked on a nearby table.

They sprang to their feet reaching for their shotguns. The SWAT team opened fire, and all three men went down. Another came storming from a side door carrying an assault rifle, and he too was shot dead. The SWAT team moved into the bedroom only to find Aron Carter with his hands up and quickly surrounded him.

'Get down! Keep your hands up! Face the floor!' the lead officer shouted. Then he slapped the cuffs on and took Carter away-

I was upset that it took the cops that long to track down the likes of Aron Carter. Mostly it was because I felt that I could have done more to help Maggie, a faithful and loyal servant of God. She didn't deserve to go out like that, not after a church service, and certainly not by the hands of the wicked. I caught myself brooding over it.

'Don't beat yourself up about it, Arthur', Lauren said, resting her warm hands upon my shoulder. 'You did all you could.'

'Someone needs to do something about this city! How long must drugs and crime flood the streets before we see change? When will the police wake up and do the job the city pays them to do?' Angry and disappointed, I excused myself back into the kitchen and made myself a cup of coffee.

Lauren approached me and reassuringly took my hand. 'I think we should launch an anti-drug crime campaign outside the church tomorrow morning. Get the church members involved to honour Maggie!'

I was pleased at what seemed a brilliant idea. I smiled. 'You know what? I think you might be onto something here, honey. I'll send an email!' I gulped my coffee down in a hurry.

Outside the city hall in Lismore, there was a mass. A crowd of locals and news broadcasters was gathered in front Mayor Ronald Reed for a live feed. He was a slim-looking grey-haired man of average height and smartly dressed.

'Mayor Ronald? What do you plan on doing to keep drugs out of the city?' asked a young reporter, nudging her specs upwards.

The mayor cleared his throat. 'The CCPD is working around the clock cracking down on every drug operation there is. I assure you that crime will be eradicated with zero tolerance', he claimed openly over the live broadcast.

Across town, in the suburbs outside Carol City, Richard Sullivan's mansion sat on an estate of many acres with fancy cars parked on the drive.

Inside, in Richard Sullivan's room, a man in smart trousers and suspenders, about six foot three, in his forties, and clean-shaven, Richard Sullivan's personal bodyguard, was ruthless and cold with a killer's instinct. Maxwell Stein was his name.

With the remote in his hand, he stood before the television watching Mayor Reed address the mass. He switched the television off and informed his boss about the news report. 'Sounds like the mayor plans on shutting us down.'

Sullivan, aged sixty-three, a slightly built grey-haired crime lord, master of his drug empire, was coughing his lungs out. Dying from lung disease, he was connected to an oxygen tank by his side. 'No one is going to stop us, even if I'm on my deathbed! I didn't build this empire to be thrown drown by some infidel in a cheap suit. I think it's time we sent the mayor a message!'

Mr Sullivan coughed some more, but Maxwell got the message. 'I'll make sure of it, sir!' He slipped into his blazer, ready to fulfil his boss's request.

Late afternoon at the Carol City Police Department, Lismore. The officers were busy, Cops wrangling files and rushing about various cases and paperwork on their desks. The entire department was like Wall Street, a congested zone, a zoo. Detective Carl Brooks sat behind his desk making calls and following up on leads on the recent murder case. A male officer approached his desk.

'Carl, I've got some good news that will help with your case.'

'Talk to me. What you got?' Carl sat back in his chair, arms folded.

'I examined the CCTV feeds around the docks. There was nothing covering the jetty. But I've got a Lincoln driving into the docks. Guess whose it was.' The officer laid a printout copy of the feed onto Carl's desk.

Detective Craig Bollington was fetching water from the dispenser when he overheard the officer talking with Carl. Craig stood and listened from afar, seemingly minding his own business.

'Motherfuckers! Looks like we got a new development.' Excited, Carl sprang to his feet and slipped on his overcoat. 'Run me the plates on the Lincoln!'

'I did. The car is registered to Richard Sullivan's private fleet.'

'Good job. You done well.' Carl thanked the officer and waved his partner over. 'Hey, Craig. Let's go. We got a lead.'

Early that evening, Rushmore Street, 53rd Grand Avenue. Two blocks from my house a Lincoln pulled up and parked between two cars on the side road. Ricky and Joe had arrived on my street. They sat in the car and waited. Stuart was now in the back seat, half beaten and busted up.

Rick looked back at Stuart with a straight-looking mean mug. 'Is this the place?'

'Yeah, that's it, all right.' Stuart confirmed the house address.

Three days ago, 2030 hours: The Diamond Chip Casino, situated on Greenwood Street, downtown Carol City, Lismore. Owned by crime lord Richard Sullivan, amongst numerous venues dotted about the city. Outside, the queue stretched from the front door around back—busy. Inside, the sound of the rich upper class lifted the atmosphere inside the casino, everybody who was anybody was gambling the night away.

Then shrieks and screams audible outside. The casino doors slammed open, and six armed men, smartly dressed with black gloves and machine guns stormed the casino, firing bullets into the ceiling, and everybody panicked.

'Everybody get the fuck down! Get on the floor! Now!' yelled a masked man, firing another burst into the ceiling.

Everyone dropped to their knees, and three gunmen secured the entry and exit points. The other three proceeded upstairs to clean out the casino vault. They shot through the office door lock and entered. Four of Richard Sullivan's loyal employees were waiting, armed to the teeth. Fire erupted through the office door. One masked man went down, a bullet to the chest. Two of the employees were shot dead, and the other two were overrun, disarmed, and held at gunpoint.

One of the gunmen barked, 'You! Open the fucking vault now!'

Downstairs a croupier laying face down under the craps table quietly reached up to the edge and activated the silent alarm. Then another gunman on the scene spotted him and grabbed him by the collar. He shouted in his face, prodding his gun at his neck, 'What the fuck did you just do, huh? What the fuck did you do?'

Hearing no answer, he shot the croupier in the head. Then he rushed up towards the office, calling, 'Get the SUV ready! We got to move now!'

'I don't have the combination! I can't!' the employee explained.

A masked gunman grabbed another employee and put his gun to his head, insisting that he open the safe.

Another gunman showed up bearing bad news. 'We've been compromised! The alarm was set off. Let's go!' Then he took off back down the stairs.

'You heard him. Let's go!'

As they were about to leave, one of them saw a briefcase behind an office desk. One of the gunmen grabbed it on his way out. Then, following his partner, he stopped, looked back, and emptied his pistol into both the employees. Then he exited the office and joined the others outside, where all six masked gunmen saddled up into their Lincoln Navigator and took off.

The driver noticed the briefcase. 'What's that you're carrying?'

They removed their masks. 'We are about to find out!' one of them replied.

Stuart opened the briefcase, finding cold hard cash. Martin looked into the case and smiled. 'Looks like we didn't lose after all, huh?'

Stuart peeled off a few notes and flipped through them. 'Must be at least two mill right here!'

CHAPTER 2

Not long after, two muscle cars, a '69 Chevy and a '68 Dodge Charger, began tailing the Lincoln. Rick drove the Charger, flanked by Joe. The Chevy was manned the same way. They have been dispatched by Paul Sullivan on behalf of his father after the alarm was triggered.

'We got company!' A gunman had spotted the cars at the rear.

Stuart panicked. 'Let's lose them. Let's go!'

With Rick driving the Charger, Joe opened fire on the Lincoln, supported by a partner from the Chevy. The night streets of Carol City were now a battleground. The three men in the back of the Lincoln returned fire, one standing in the sunroof and two of them reaching out the windows. The gunman topside in the Lincoln was shot dead and sprawled face down on the roof.

The vehicles barrelled through the streets aimlessly, running red lights and trashing the sidewalks, forcing the pedestrians to take evasive action.

Rick was annoyed, 'Joe, if you don't shoot these guys, I'll have to shoot you myself!'

'I'm working on it! Hold steady, will you?' Joe kept on shooting.

Stuart and Martin were running low on ammunition and ideas. The two gunmen in the back were out of ammunition and lying low.

'We're out!' one of them shouted, closing his window.

'You going to have to shake these guys, Martin!' said Stuart, clutching the money.

Soon a police cruiser on patrol joined the chase. Sirens echoed along the streets. The officers issued an order. 'This is the CCPD. Cease fire and pull over!'

Rick and Joe along with their partners split up, heading into an alleyway. The cops pursued the Lincoln, calling for backup.

'Dispatch! This is 419, requesting backup. We are currently involved in a high-speed chase moving north on Third Avenue. Suspects are travelling in a black Lincoln Navigator and considered dangerous. Over!'

'This whole thing went downhill pretty fast', Stuart said. 'We need to stash the money. Take a left here!'

Martin pulled into a backstreet heading into the Carol City scrapyard, and the cops followed. Martin tucked the Lincoln behind a pile of scrap metal and killed the headlights. The cops drove by with their mounted floodlights scanning around, barely missing the Lincoln. Martin then quietly rolled the Lincoln out of the scrapyard and headed into the night.

Later they drove slowly along Grand Avenue, a residential street on the outskirts of Lismore. They were looking for a place to stash the stolen cash.

'We should have hid the money back at the scrapyard. This is fucking crazy! No way we'll find somewhere around here.' Martin was unhappy about Stuart's decision.

'It was a fucking scrapyard! If we hid the money there, it'd be gone by morning.' Then Stuart noticed an ideal place to dump the cash. 'Pull over here!'

Martin pulled to the roadside. Stuart saw an open basement window. He smirked and shook his head suspiciously.

The men sitting in the back seat were curious. 'What now?'

'Look over there. A basement window!' Stuart said, indicating with his finger.

'Are you outta your fucking mind?' Martin retorted. 'This is a bad idea!'

'Listen, this is the best chance we've got', Stuart explained. 'The plan is simple. I take the money into the basement and stash it in the vents. Then we lie low for a few days and come back for the money!'

'I hope you know what you're doing!' Martin was worried and uncertain but leaning in favour.

'Do you have a better idea, wise guy, huh?' Stuart looked at him for a second opinion.

'No, I don't. Let's get it over with.' Short on time, Martin went along with the plan.

Stuart exited the Lincoln with the briefcase in one hand and a nine millimetre in the other. He quietly slipped across the front lawn, keeping low, and slid into the narrow open window. Soon he was back at the Lincoln, and they fled the residential area.

Now, outside 53 Grand Avenue: 'Let's get this over with. Mr Sullivan is running low on patience!' Rick checked his pistol over, making sure it was loaded.

Just as he and Joe were about to exit the car, a police cruiser pulled up outside the house where the money was claimed to be. Rick and Joe held back and watched two officers emerge from the cruiser and proceed towards a house across the road onto the front porch.

Joe was already having second thoughts. 'Maybe we should call it a day. Don't think the mayor was lying in his speech.'

'No! We're going to wait this out. Do you want to be the one breaking the bad news to Mr Sullivan?' Rick was frustrated but wanted to see it through.

Joe kept his mouth shut, saying nothing more as a sign that he understood the complexity of the situation.

'That's what I thought.' Rick made himself comfortable, sinking back in his seat.

Same day, in the suburbs, at Richard Sullivan's mansion. Detectives Brooks and Bollington pulled up at the front gate and flashed their badges at the gate camera. Inside the mansion's CCTV room, Maxwell Stein was looking at the security cameras with a handful of armed security men smartly dressed.

Maxwell contacted Richard Sullivan via an intercom. 'Sir, we got cops at the front gate. What are your orders?'

'Let them in', Richard Sullivan acknowledged from his bedroom, coughing down the line. 'See what they want.'

Maxwell ordered the security team to open the gate. Carl proceeded up the drive, around a Greek god Apollo fountain, and parked in front of the mansion. A pair of security men stood at the front door. Carl flashed his badge once more to satisfy their curiosity. The men let them inside, where they were greeted by Maxwell. The interior was expensively decorated, clean, vast, and highly polished.

Carl introduced himself with his badge. 'I am Detective Carl Brooks, and this is my partner, Detective Craig Bollington.'

'What can I do for you, Detective?' Maxwell, with his hands crossed in front of his body, looked rather unimpressed.

Carl's response triggered a change in the atmosphere. 'Nothing! Not yet at least. We are here on a routine murder investigation. We need to speak with Mr Sullivan.'

'Right this way.' Maxwell escorted both Carl and Craig to Mr Sullivan's room.

Richard Sullivan was being treated with his prescription medicines by a female nurse, his carer. She was in her mid-twenties, a slender, average-height woman with blonde hair, wearing a little nurse outfit for Mr Sullivan's own personal satisfaction.

Maxwell diverted Mr Sullivan's attention from the nurse's miniskirt. 'Sir, these men are here to see you.'

Mr Sullivan dismissed his carer with a flick of his chin. 'What is it you want with a dying man?'

Carl explained his reason for an unexpected visit. 'We are investigating a murder case, and we think a few of your men may be involved.'

Craig took off to have a look around the mansion under Maxwell's supervision.

Mr Sullivan seemed unfazed by Carl's unexpected visit. He plucked a cigar from his bedside table and lit it, despite his dying lungs. 'What? You suddenly think my men were involved, is that it?'

Carl passed Richard Sullivan the photo from the CCTV. Sullivan took a close look at the photo and then passed it back to Carl. He gnawed on his cigar whilst he inhaled from his oxygen mask. 'I am sorry, Detective. Those aren't my men.'

'They might not have been your men, Mr Sullivan, but the car is. Don't play games with me. This is a serious matter.' His tone was rising as Craig returned after his tour with Maxwell.

Mr Sullivan's temper was then provoked. 'Are you implying that I have something to do with all this?'

'Not likely. But I am sure you know something, and I'll find out what you're hiding.' He replaced the photo in his coat pocket.

'I suggest you get the fuck out of my house, detective! Don't come back without a warrant!' Sullivan's pique shortened his breath, and he drew for more oxygen.

'You heard Mr Sullivan. Am I going to have to ask you to leave?' With that, Maxwell saw Carl and Craig out of the mansion.

Both detectives left the mansion and got in their cruiser. Carl had his suspicions and wasn't about to leave any stone unturned. 'You find anything around the mansion?'

Craig had nothing to offer during his quick gander. 'Nothing. Place was as clean as a whistle.'

'Maybe we're barking up the wrong tree.'

Carl thought otherwise. 'He knows something. We are going to find out what it is.' He fired up the cruiser and took off.

Inside, Mr Sullivan had other ideas. 'Take care of this. Last thing I want is a curious detective nosing around my home, especially when I have the shipment coming in.'

'I'll handle it', Maxwell said, standing at his bedside. 'He won't know what's coming.'

Mr Sullivan had a few daring requests for Maxwell. 'First, you're going to do two things. Get my son over here. He needs to answer for his incompetence. Then you're going to teach Ricky and Joe a lesson.'

Later that day, Rick and Joe were still sitting outside the street waiting for a chance to move on the money. The officer on the front porch was having a social moment with an old lady regarding a domestic affair.

'Maybe we should forget the money', Stuart boldly offered from the back seat.

'You shut the fuck up! Remember, this is your fucking mess.' Rick, waving his gun about into Stuart's face, reminded him where he stood.

As the day drew close to an end. I was in my office at the church, preparing next week's sermon. I called my wife Lauren to check that they were OK. The city can be a hostile place; I always make sure they are well and OK when I'm out.

The phone rang, and Lauren answered. 'Hello, honey. How's your sermon coming along?' She was sitting with the boys, reading the Bible on the living room sofa.

'It's coming along just fine. How are you and the boys?' I placed my palm on my forehead in exhaustion.

'We are just fine. Hurry up and make it home.' I could hear her smile.

'Won't be long. I am just about finished.'

Then I heard a noise. Someone was stumbling outside, in the seating area. 'Honey, I have to go now. I'll see you and the boys at home. Love you.' Cutting my call short, I headed out of the office.

I proceeded carefully into the seating area. There he was, sitting peacefully at the back of the church, with his head hung low, his hands clasped in humility: Jack Wielder. He somehow found the courage to take a seat in God's house.

I walked down the aisle unnoticed and sat calmly next to him, facing forward. 'Peaceful, isn't it?'

'It sure is.' A peaceful response from Jack, who gave a sign of relief.

I tried engaging Jack in a religious conversation. 'Have you thought about doing something more with your life?'

'There's no place in heaven for the likes of me, Father. Don't get your hopes up about me.' Jack wasn't interested; he was far from being reached.

I tried some more to soften his heart. 'There's a place for everyone, Jack. Believe in the Lord, and thou shalt be saved. Thus said the Bible.'

'I believe, all right. Thing is, Father … I've done a lot of things. There's no saving me.' With little faith, Jack doubted himself.

'God forgives. You need to have faith, my friend.' I could only offer hope with a bit of reassurance.

Jack stood up, braced his arms on the seat back before us, hanging his head, and then breathed a sigh of dissatisfaction.

'I'm not the man I used to be, Father. I've done a lot, and I've lost a lot. I'm just riding the wave till it drags me down.' Jack turned to leave, having given me something to think about.

Early that evening, Rick's and Joe's patience paid off. With daylight already fading, the officer across the road got into his cruiser and drove away. Not long after, I pulled up outside my house onto my drive and entre my home.

Rick's interest was roused. 'This must be the man of the house.'

'What do you reckon he does?' Joe asked.

Rick didn't care at all; he had his priority. 'It doesn't matter what he does! Let's hope he doesn't create a problem retrieving the money.'

'You got a plan? How are we gonna get inside?'

Rick gave Joe a simple order, nothing too farfetched. 'I've got a plan. Just follow my lead. We move in five minutes.'

Over at the CCPD headquarters that same evening, Carl Brooks and his partner, Craig, sat behind their desks. They were busy filling out reports and chopping down a mountain of paperwork before their shift ended.

Then an office door swung open. Police Captain Chris Walter, African American, five-ten and slightly built, with a moustache, poked his head out his door and bellowed across the squad room.

'Brooks! Get the hell in my office, now!' The entire department stood still, focusing on Carl.

Carl walked towards the captain's office, everyone watching as he strolled across the floor, puzzled and confused.

'What the hell are you trying to pull? Are you trying to get yourself suspended?' Captain Walter, bent over, was pounding his desk in anger.

Carl sat down, still confused about the yelling. 'What the hell are you talking about, Captain?'

The captain continued yelling, with many eyes peering through his office window. 'I'm talking about you and your partner with your unauthorized visit to Sullivan's place! You don't just walk into a man's home and snoop around without a warrant!'

The captain took a sip of his coffee and grimaced. He tossed it into the bin at his feet. 'Damn it, Carl! Get a hold of yourself!'

'I was following a lead. Questions needed to be asked.' Carl stood his ground, defending his purpose.

The captain wasn't having it. 'Not according to Sullivan. Way I see it, you and Detective No-Brains over there were a complete nuisance!'

Carl sat back in annoyance and straightened his coat. 'Is that right? Don't you see what this man is doing, Captain? He's playing the system because he knows I'm going to bust his ass!'

'No one's playing the system, Carl. From now on, Sullivan's mansion is off limits, you hear me? I've got the mayor breathing down my neck. Last thing I need is you and your partner embarrassing this department!'

Dissatisfied, Carl sprang to his feet. 'Damn it, Captain! Whose side are you on? This man's been involved in drug running in the city, organized crime, murders—you name it. I have no intention of letting him win!'

The captain thought otherwise and stuck to his guns. 'You will do as you're told, Detective! Now get the hell out of my office!'

Carl exited his office unhappy and frustrated, finding everyone staring as he walked across the room. 'What the hell are you all staring at? Get back to work!' he shouted, grabbing his coat and leaving the room. Craig sat, nervously scratching the back of his ear.

At home, early evening, I was sitting at the dinner table with my family about to say grace when the doorbell rang. Not planning on visitors, Lauren was a bit puzzled. 'You expecting anyone?'

'Not that I can recall. I'll see who it is.' I excused myself from the table and headed for the door.

'Hey, Dad. Maybe it's someone from the church.' Charles gave me a huge grin, happy boy that he was.

Andy wasn't too keen about having an unexpected guest and frowned. 'I hope not. They talk a lot.'

'It's all right, boys. I'll take care of it.'

I opened the door. Two men stood there, backs to the door. They turned around and looked at me with a tough expression.

My approach was as nice as they come. 'Can I help you gentlemen?'

With a snide look on his face, Rick answered. 'I do believe you can. You got something of ours, and we are here to take it.'

'I am afraid you might have the wrong house.' I slammed the door and ended our talk on that note.

'Is everything OK, honey?' Lauren called from the dinner table as she passed the mash around to the boys.

Before I could answer, the front door was kicked in, and both men burst in armed with pistols. Rick held me by the neck against the hallway and held his gun to my head.

'Lauren! Take the kids and hide!' I cried out in panic, fearing for their safety.

She knew something was dead wrong. She tried gathering the kids. Confused and terrified, they froze. Joe stormed the dining room to hold my family at gunpoint before they could get away to safety. I was gun butted to the head, dragged into the dining room, and tossed to the floor at my family's feet.

I tried to soften the situation with a kind gesture. 'Just take whatever you want! We don't want any trouble!'

'Shut the fuck up! Now!' Rick yelled. He waved his gun in our direction, causing a scare, and the kids shrieked.

'Joe! Get the money!' Rick demanded, keeping a close eye on my family and me.

'What money? We don't have any money!'

Rick insisted he had money somewhere in my home. 'You don't, but we do!'

'What's going on, Arthur?!' Lauren was petrified not sure what to do with herself.

'I don't know, honey! Stay calm! "We shall not fall by the hands of the wicked!" It's in God's hands now!' I was trying to put my family at ease with my religious ordeal.

Rick had other plans. 'Oh, I am far from wicked! Your religious nonsense won't save you!'

'I have faith. We all do in this house.' I spoke confidently showing that his gun antics weren't about to shake me.

Rick grabbed me by the scruff of my neck and stuffed his gun in my mouth. My wife and kids screamed; he made them watch as he tried to prove a point. 'Look at him! Look!'

He pulled the gun out and smashed his fist into my face. On the floor he planted a knee in my chest and delivered a couple more punches. I had no idea what money they were after; all I knew was the man wouldn't leave quietly before terrorizing my home and my family.

'I'll blow your fucking head all over your tidy walls! Your wife and kids will watch!' Rick sinks his pistol deep into my mouth.

'Please, mister, don't hurt my dad!' Don't kill us!' Charles pleaded with Rick in the most pitiful tone.

It hurt me to see my family at the mercy of the wicked. My son pleading for my pardon was not something I wanted. I held firmly to my faith, believing that all would be well.

'No, boys! No! Never beg for your life! Don't you ever! '. I cried out to my sons with teary eyes, whilst Lauren cried into the boys' shoulders.

Rick was stunned by my performance. He paced about my floor dangling his gun. 'You're a very interesting man. Men like you … so self-righteous with your religious lifestyle!' He preached at me with hatred and anger written all over his face. 'You think you're better than everyone else out there, passing judgement, influencing the system with your so-called ministry. Well, guess what: I'm going to give you a chance to save yourself and your family. Let's see how much God loves you!'

Boldly I rose to my feet to defend my honour. 'Don't you dare hurt my family!'

Rick knocked me back to my knees, booting me repeatedly, fracturing my ribs. I was being made a fool in my own house and in front my family. *Where is God in all this?* I began to wonder.

'Stop! You're hurting him!' Lauren shouted with tears dripping down her cheeks.

'I am just getting started!' Rick was about to deliver another punch to my face when Joe returned with the briefcase of cash.

'Got the money! Let's get out of here!' Joe was happy, pleased, and keen to leave things as they were. But Rick still wanted blood.

'Where did that came from? Whose money is it?' I had to have some answers.

'This money is the least of your concern!' Rick was still hovering over me with his gun. 'Go on, Joe. Get out of here. I'll be out. This won't take long.' He looked down at me with piercing eyes, a cruel intention at the back of his mind.

He grabbed me by the hair and dragged me out of the dining room into the living room. I could hear Lauren and the kids screaming. He then knocked me cold with a single blow to the head.

I later learned that Lauren took the chance of getting herself and the kids to safety, but Rick was too fast. He returned to the dining room just as they were fleeing out the front door. He shot them down without hesitation, my wife and my sons … he took them away, just like that.

Rick returned to the living room where I lay unconscious. He slapped my face till I regained consciousness. I woke in a rage, paranoid and confused. I swung a punch that grazed Rick's jaw. He retaliated, trashing me about my home.

'Where's my family! Where are they? What have you done?!' Battered and broken, I was stumbling for words.

I was heaved from the floor by my chin, and Rick looked at me with hateful eyes. 'If I were you, Father, I'd worry about what's about to happen to you!'

He put away his gun and took a knife from his waist. I was exhausted from the beating, and he overpowered me with his blade and made a mess of my face. Slowly and painfully I suffered at Rick's cruelty. Eventually I stop struggling, and my body collapsed; it all went quiet. He stopped, stood up, and looked down at me. He wiped his blade clean on my body and spat on me.

'Let's see you come back from this.' He put his knife away and left the house.

Rick shuffled across the street casually, carefully looking around. Into the Lincoln he climbed, blowing a sigh of satisfaction with a deadly smirk on his face.

Joe looked at him. 'Everyone all right back there?'

'It's all taken care of.' Rick switched the engine on and pulled away, ignoring the banging noise in the boot.

Hours later, the following morning. The phone started ringing. This incoming call wouldn't be answered. It was my work colleague and dear friend, Mr Lenard Franklin, the old priest that I succeeded. He was bald, of average height, and rather stocky, and he was calling from the church office.

I was due in church that morning to rehearse my sermon. Franklin was now concerned, and his curiosity was aroused. Having not received an answer, he put the phone down gently, eased back into his office chair carefully and thought for a moment.

He's never been late for a service, a rehearsal, or any church-related matter. Why now, what could have happened? What's his excuse? There must be a logical explanation. I need to know. Then Father Franklin grabbed his coat and left the office in a hurry.

Early morning, Richard Sullivan's mansion. Two lavish automobiles—a Maybach and a Phantom—pulled up outside the entrance to the mansion.

Outside the mansion gates, was Detectives Carl Brooks and Craig Bollington sat in their unmarked cruiser, out of sight, observing.

'Remind me again why we are here.' Craig seemed uninterested, sipping a coffee and pretending to care.

Carl gazed into his binoculars trying to get eyes on the premises. 'Something is going on, and we are going to find out what.'

He looked across at Craig and noticed his lack of interest and enthusiasm. Carl shook his head in disappointment followed by a sigh of dissatisfaction. 'Am I the only one playing cop? Are you the least bit interested in what's going on?'

'I'm just thinking about the captain. Maybe we shouldn't be doing this.'

Craig aggravated Carl, and he raised his tone. 'The captain doesn't have a clue what the hell is going on. Show some enthusiasm!'

Inside the mansion gates, the drivers of both lavish cars synchronized their deliveries in a clean, professional manner.

'Looks like we got activity!' Carl's long-nursed anticipation was paying off.

A man emerged from each car: Gosnell and Johnathon Logan.

Brothers, they were rivals of Mr Sullivan in the drug trade. Smartly dressed, of average build with dark hair, approximately five ten, in their forties, and looking highly important.

Carl struggled to get a facial recognition. 'Can't seem to get a facial ID on those two.'

The mansion doors opened, and Maxwell greeted the men. They straightened their jacks pompously and entered the mansion.

Craig pretended to take a sudden interest in what was going on. 'Looks like it's a waiting game from here on.'

Inside the mansion, in Richard Sullivan's room, both Gosnell and Johnathon stood in his presence, standing casually before the foot of his bed under Maxwell's supervision.

Gosnell greeted him with a businesslike attitude. 'Good to see you again, Mr Sullivan. How's business?'

'Business is as good as it's ever been and getting better', Mr Sullivan replied, poorly with his chronic cough and fading health.

'Interesting. I suppose your son must be heading all operations now?' Gosnell inquired, digging his nose into Mr Sullivan's family affairs.

'I'm afraid that's none of your business.' Mr Sullivan coughed yet maintained his composure.

Johnathon raised his shoulders. 'I am afraid it is, Mr Sullivan. Besides, you don't look too good. You're on your last string. How do you plan on keeping your business afloat against our blooming empire?' He inflated his chest as he boasted about their success.

'My brother is right. Face it. You're done, washed up, finished!' Gosnell commented with an evil smirk.

Mr Sullivan felt ashamed and insulted by their remarks. He knew they were right, yet he somehow refused to admit it—no humility whatsoever.

He cleared his throat thoroughly. *Time to get serious*, he thought. 'Enough about me. You're here on business. Let's get to it.'

'If you insist. We have a proposal for you, Mr Sullivan.' Gosnell was ready to place an interesting offer on the table.

'I'm listening.'

Gosnell began his pitch. 'Two cargoes. Fully loaded with a million in cocaine.'

'Sounds like a hit.' But Mr Sullivan frowned sceptically.

'It is. Which is why we need your help', Johnathon pointed out.

'Why should I help you ship drugs into my city? What's in it for me?'

Gosnell laid out the heart of the deal. 'You guarantee safe passage for my drivers, and you will be rewarded.'

Mr Sullivan wasn't too certain. 'I'll think about it.'

'No disrespect, Mr Sullivan, but you do not have time to think.' Johnathon insulted Sullivan while trying to be persistent.

Mr Sullivan grew annoyed and irritated by the brothers' presence. 'Like I said, I'll think about it. Now, get the fuck out!'

'All right, you think about it. Remember, there's always a second option.' Gosnell was trying to reel Mr Sullivan in on his offer.

Both brothers left the room and saw themselves out of the mansion. Carl and his partner still sat outside waiting for a clear visual on both men as they left the mansion.

Through his binoculars, Carl ID'd both men as they ducked into their luxury cars and drove away. Carl and Craig sank their heads behind the window as the brothers drove past their cruiser. A call came through on the radio.

'Notification of a 419, 420 at 53 Grand Avenue. All units in area please respond.'

'Let's go! Let's go!' Craig was excited and chucked his coffee out the window as they took off.

Same day, 53 Grand Avenue, Carl and Craig arrived on the scene. Cops, ambulances, a few neighbours and onlookers dotted about behind the yellow tapes.

Carl look around as he and Craig weaved through the crowd. 'Looks like the whole street is out.

'All right, people! Nothing to see here! Stand back, clear the area!' Carl tried his best to keep the crowd under control.

A male officer on scene approached the detectives and briefed them as he escorted them through the front door. 'Thank God you guys are here. It's not looking good inside. We got four victims: a mother, father, and two children, both males, dead.'

He goes on, 'Victims were identified to be Mr Arthur Brown. Father and head of the Carol City Church. Wife Lauren. Lying next to her body are their sons. The mother and both kids took single shots to the abdominal area. The father … hmm. That's another story', said the officer, with a strange, worried look on his face.

'Something wrong?' Craig asked, standing next to the bodies draped with white sheets.

'See for yourself.'

The forensics techs stood aside as Carl stooped and peeled the sheets back: my wife, Lauren, and my two boys, dead, murdered for nothing, in cold blood.

Carl and Craig then proceeded to examine my body. Lying there on a stretcher with no pulse, presumably dead … I was shunned. They turned away, petrified at the sight of my mangled face.

'What the fuck happened? What monster would do something like this?' Carl was disgusted by what he saw.

'That's what I thought when I saw the body', the officer commented, with a foul look on his face staring down at me.

'Looks like someone got really pissed off!' Craig pointed out the obvious.

The officer went on explaining the incident before us. 'Father Brown was barely alive when the ambulance arrived. Barely had a pulse. The paramedics did what they could to save him. Sadly, it was too late.'

The officer signed the cross over my head. 'He passed on just before you guys showed up.'

'Who called for help?' Craig asked, with his hands on both hips, spreading his coat with his badge in plain sight.

'A family friend, Father Franklin. He got worried. Decided to drop by, and there they were. Poor fella is more shaken up than a rattlesnake's tail.' The officer hung his head in obvious sympathy.

'Thanks for your time, Officer! We'll take it from here!' Carl dismissed the officer to carry on his investigation. He turned to Craig. 'See if Father Franklin has anything else to tell us. I'll have a look around the house, see what else I can find.'

Carl wondered off. Craig stood at the front door looking across at Farther Franklin, who sat on the back of the ambulance with a blanket and a cup of hot cocoa gibbering, shaken by the horrible incident and being reassured by a medic-Craig walked over and introduced himself.

'Father Franklin, I am Detective Bollington. May I ask you a few questions?' Craig extended his badge to put the poor priest at ease.

Father Franklin became hysterical. 'Please! You got to find whoever did this! Please, I'm begging you! These were good people! They didn't do anything to deserve this!' Father Franklin pleaded, weeping his eyes out.

'It's OK, Father. We will. We will'. Craig patted Father Franklin's shoulder, hoping to ease his troubled mind. Then he went to work on his questions. 'Did Father Brown have any enemies? Anyone who might have a grudge against him?'

'No. Not one. He got along fine with everyone he knew', Father Franklin replied with a sad, hurtful tune.

Inside, Carl was looking around the house. He looked at a few family photos, checked for anything around the home that seemed out of place, anything that might highlight a clue. He then made his way into the basement and flipped the light switch. He scanned around carefully, looking at every detail. He noticed a broken vent. He inspected it but found nothing much to look at. Then he turned around and stepped on something. He looked down to see a cigarette lighter, silver with red dice imprinted on it. Carl retrieved the lighter, looking at it in an unusual way.

Upstairs the coroner was just about to wheel my body out the front door when a slight movement was detected by a female officer standing out front as my body wheeled on by.

'Hold on! I think I saw something!' she cried out, unzipping the body bag and placing her head near my mangled face. Then she straighted up, calling, 'Somebody get me a medic! This man's alive! We got a pulse!'

Everyone on scene rushed to my side. The paramedics re-examined my pulse, confirming life. Father Franklin was overwhelmed with joy, calling it a miracle. For some miraculous reason, I had pulled through—barely. But I wondered why.

'Thank you, Lord!' Father Franklin shouted in excitement.

'Well, I'll be damned', Craig said in disbelief. 'Not every day do you see something like this.' He stood among the medics in astonishment.

'He's alive! Looks like this man went into a coma', a male medic informed his colleagues and the nearby officers.

Carl was just returning from the basement when he stumbled into Craig out front. I was being loaded on the back of an ambulance, with Father Franklin along for the ride.

'What's going on?' Carl looked confused, wondering about all the commotion.

'Father Brown pulled through. That's what happened', Craig explained, watching the ambulance.

'You got to be kidding me. How? How in God's name did that happen?' Carl, swung his coat back, hands on hips in disbelief.

'In God's name. That's how.' Craig seemed pleased with his irony.

'Don't be a wise-ass, Craig.' Carl did not find it funny.

As they both walked towards their cruiser, Craig asked, 'Find anything interesting inside?'

'Let's just say I don't think Father Brown is the type to light a cigar. We need to talk with him soon as possible.' Carl had a hunch he was onto something.

Later the same day, down a narrow country lane into the sticks outside Carol City, Rick and Joe turned up at an old remote cabin on the edge of a cliff overlooking a rift valley. They stopped, looked at each other silently. Joe grabbed the money, and both exited the car and headed towards the boot and opened it. Both aimed their guns in at Stuart, who was gagged, tied up, and mumbling aggressively.

'Sorry, pal, can't hear you.' Joe refused to sympathize

'Your ride ends here.' Rick stated the obvious whilst he cocked his hammer and stroked the trigger, ready to blow Stuart away.

Without hesitation, both emptied their guns into the boot, killing Stuart—a cold-blooded move. They rolled the car off the cliff, and it crashed into the jagged rocks below. Rick and Joe then made their way around to the back of the cabin, where an empty 1972 Monte Carlo was waiting. They got in, Rick behind the wheel with Joe sitting shotgun. Rick got on the phone and made a call.

Paul Sullivan answered, sitting at his father's bedside sipping whiskey. 'It's about fucking time you checked in! Tell me you got that fucking money, Rick!' Paul angrily rose to his feet, on edge and impatient.

'Yeah, I got the money. Had to take care of a little problem, but we got it', Rick answered.

'Good! Now get your fucking asses back here!' Paul growled down the phone line and hung up.

Personal matters were about to be discussed. Richard Sullivan was making sure his son Paul understood his role as future heir to his empire. He turned his attention towards his son.

'Tonight's deal must go according to plan. No screw-ups. No cops. You make sure my money gets there.' Mr Sullivan forewarned his son about the urgent matters at hand.

'I can handle it. No need to worry.' Paul was keen and looked forward to proving himself to his father.

'Until you show me you got the balls to fill my shoes after I'm gone. Until then I'll keep worrying'.' Mr Sullivan thought otherwise, gulping oxygen, coughing away.

Paul became annoyed and aggressive, rejecting his father's claim. 'You know I've got the fucking balls, Pop! Stop with the bullshit and let me do my job.'

'You watch your fucking mouth, son! You want to prove you got the fucking balls to fill my pants? Here's what you're going to do.'

'I'm listening. Enlighten me.' Paul couldn't be any more intrigued by his father's response.

'When those two scumbags get here with the money, you're going to teach them a lesson. In fact, you're going to make an example out of them. Do that, and you might just have some balls after all.'

'If that's what it takes. Then I guess I've got no choice, do I, Pop?'

Paul then left the suite in a hurry. As he left, his father called. 'It's a cold game, son! Remember who you are!'

Maxwell came to the suite just as Paul disappeared. 'Keep an eye on him', Richard said. 'Make sure he gets the job done.'

'I will, sir. I'll see to it that your son does exactly what's expected of him.' Maxwell immediately set out after Paul, acting on Mr Sullivan's orders.

At the Carol City General Hospital that night, there I lay in my coma, lifeless. Bandages around my entire head, plugged up to just about every medical machine the doctors could fashion—heart monitor, drip, ventilator … the works, you name it.

Father Franklin sat by my side keeping the faith, hoping and praying that I would pull out of the coma. Then the detectives walked in, Carl and his partner, Craig, looking for answers, trying to make sense of things.

Carl made a professional approach with a token show of sympathy. 'Father Franklin! A pleasant surprise. How's he doing? Any progress?'

Father Franklin wasn't feeling quite himself, bearing a sad face and a sunken heart. 'No, Detective. No progress at all.'

'Looks like Father Brown won't be telling tales anytime soon.' Craig stood over my fading body, gazing down at my face with little regard for my health.

Carl took his notepad from his coat pocket. 'We have some questions, Father. Would you mind answering on your friend's behalf?'

'Anything to help find the monster who did this.' Father Franklin was willing to cooperate by any means.

'Hey, Craig? Get the man a coffee.' Carl grabbed a seat, Craig disappeared for the coffee, and Carl got to the point. 'Was Father Brown involved in anything contrary to his work?'

'If you're asking if he's been doing wrong, then you got the wrong idea, Detective'. Father Franklin was certain that I wasn't on the wrong side of the law and gave the detective his honest word.

'Just had to ask, Father. That's all. I looked around the house. It was clean; nothing was taken. Could not have been a robbery.' Carl ruled out a few options.

'The basement had a broken vent. Was Father Brown in the middle of any repairs?' Carl thought he'd ask before making an irrational decision.

Just then Craig returned with the coffee, he passed one to Father Franklin to soothe his discomfort.

'Thank you, Detective.' Father Franklin took a gentle sip from the cup and then resumed the conversation.

'The only handiwork Father Brown did was the work of God. Why do you ask?'

'Whoever did this—whoever murdered his family came looking for something.'

'What do you mean? What are you implying, Detective?'

'Father Brown might have had something in his basement that contributed to the loss of his family. Does this look familiar to you?' Carl took the lighter from his coat pocket and showed it to Father Franklin.

Father Franklin took a close look at the lighter. 'No, it doesn't. Father Brown never smoked.'

Craig got a look at the lighter, and his eyes widened at the sight. Father Franklin was curious as to where the lighter had came from. 'Who does it belong to?'

'Not sure, but I'm going to find out.' Carl slipped the lighter back into his pocket as a female nurse entered the room.

'I am afraid I have to ask you gentlemen to leave. Visiting hours are over. The patient needs to be re-examined.'

'Just on our way, ma'am.' Carl cut the visit short, folding his pad away in his coat pocket.

'How long before the patient starts showing signs of recovery?' Craig took an interest for unknown reasons.

The nurse tried her best to give a suitable answer. 'It's hard to say, sir. The patient's vitals are critical. We are doing all we can. Even if he does pull through, I'm afraid he won't be the same.'

'Now, why's that?' Carl interjected.

'His insurance didn't cover his injury. The doctors did what they could to repair some of the damage.'

'That's a shame. We'll be in touch, Father Franklin.' Carl and Craig exited the hospital room, leaving the nurse to her duty.

Late afternoon at the Moon Walk hotel, a ten-floor five-star luxury hotel in the heart of Carol City. Inside at the hotel bar the atmosphere was moderate, visitors adding life to the surroundings. Gosnell and his brother Johnathon sat at a window view table nursing martinis.

'What are we going to do about Mr Sullivan?' Johnathon wanted to know. 'He's clearly not willing to assist in any way.'

'Don't worry about Mr Sullivan. Just like him, his empire is dying.

I've got something in mind.' Gosnell had a far-reaching plan and was willing to do what it took to topple Sullivan's empire.

'What is it you have in mind? I'm rather intrigued to know.' Johnathon casually sipped his drink, but his interest was roused by his brother's response.

'Mr Sullivan has a deal going down tonight. We are going to put a dent in his plans. I've already emailed Lady Casandra. It's time we take this city.' Gosnell then drained his martini and threw his coat on, ready to leave.

'I like the way you think', Johnathon said. 'I'll make sure Lady Casandra is ready to move.'

CHAPTER 3

In the kitchen at Sullivan's mansion, Joe and Rick were strapped to chairs and being hammered with fists in every way possible, by Maxwell himself, his sleeves rolled back and his knuckles glazed with blood. Paul was calling the shots.

'You know how important this money is to my father!' Paul ranted. 'Still, you've wasted valuable time and effort retrieving it!' He circled the chairs where they sat like a lion circling its prey.

'My father is under the impression I don't have the balls to fill his pants! So here's what I'm going to do. One of you motherfuckers is going to pay the price!' Paul slipped a knife from the kitchen worktop and teased the blade at each man's cheeks.

Rick and Joe did not utter a single word the whole time. They were accepting their fate, showing humility and pride between themselves despite what had happened. Paul looked at both men, shaking his head, astonished by their firm attitude.

'So! You two think you got some balls, huh? sitting there! Acting tough Practically laughing at me!' Says beckons his knife at the pair sitting query.

Paul nudged his head at Maxwell and passed the knife on to him. Maxwell cut Joe's legs free from the chair. He then sliced Joe's belt from his waist.

'Whoa! What the fuck, man? What the fuck!' Joe yelled, shaking all over, terrified.

Maxwell dragged Joe's pants to his knees. Rick sat beside him and began to quake quietly in fear of what was about to happen.

'Come on, Paul!' Joe pleaded 'Don't do this! We got the money like you asked! The job's done! Right, Rick?!' He was seeking Rick's support for his mercy pleas.

Paul showed no hesitation. He had his priorities—to satisfy his father's doubts. 'You got it done, all right. Just not quick enough for the old man. Go on, Max! Finish this asshole. We got a job to do.'

Maxwell stuffed his hand into Joe's boxers, slipped the blade between his legs, and severed his ball sac. Joe screamed in agony and immediately vomited blood. Maxwell stuffed his balls down his throat. Joe choked on his own balls and passed out. Rick became petrified, wondering if he would suffer the same fate.

Then Paul grabbed the knife from Maxwell and sliced Joe's neck open. Then he turned to Rick. 'See what happens when you fuck me about? Do you? Huh?!' He was spraying saliva in Rick's face.

Then he lowered his tone reasonably. 'I am not going to kill you, Rick. Your loyalty towards me just saved your worthless life! Joe is dead. No one's left to hold you back. You're going to go out there tonight and do your fucking job, right? Got that?' Though angry and frustrated, Paul was still partially reasonable towards Rick.

'Clean up this piece of shit, will you?' Paul left his mess to Maxwell on his way out of the kitchen after cutting Rick loose.

Late that afternoon at the CCPD, Carl and Craig sat in the captain's office discussing their homicide cases.

'I am sorry, Captain', Carl insisted, 'but I can't run with the Father Brown case. I am already swimming in shit trying to solve the case we're working on down the docks!' He hoped his honesty would cut the mustard with the captain.

'Oh, is that how you feel? What about you, Craig? What do you think?' The captain, shocked by Carl's comments, raised his tone.

'Your call, Captain. Your call.' Craig was a pushover, not wanting to challenge the captain.

Carl looked at him with a sad expression. 'Would you have some balls about yourself?'

The captain was decisive: 'You're running this case, and that's final! Get the hell out of my office!'

As they left, a disappointed Carl let Craig have it. 'Next time, I'll do the talking. Remember that!'

It was early evening in my ward at Carol City General Hospital. I was still unconscious, with no sign of cutting loose. The door slid open, and a man entered and approached my bedside. Dirty shoes, ragged clothing, and dirty nails—Jack Wielder had found his way to me. He stood and watched for a moment, pondering, and then took a seat. He signed, crouched forward, and looked at me.

'I told you, Father … you can't save us all. Look what it got you. If you pull through, you're going to understand. You'll see things a lot different.'

Jack stood up, wandered about my bed space in the shadows, and then leaned in to whisper more daring words. 'You're going to change … you're going to change for good. See you soon, Father … see you soon.' He then suddenly hurried from the room.

A few days later, on Sunday morning, outside my house everything seemed peaceful, tranquil, and blissful. I stood on the front lawn admiring the weather. I heard a voice calling to me from behind. I turned. There was my wife, with both my sons beside her, standing at the front door. I smiled; all was perfect.

'Come inside', she called to me with a sweet smile. 'Dinner is ready.'

I followed her inside. We sat down for dinner and joined hands. Charles said grace. Lauren looked at me and smiled. I smiled back but with a hint of scepticism. I suddenly felt something was wrong, missing.

Lauren reached for my hands across the table. 'It's going to be all right, Arthur.'

'I am not sure. I don't know if I'll be.' I worried deeply, with a troubled heart.

She walked me to the living room sofa where she sat me down, holding my hands in hers as she reassured me that we'd always be together, even when apart. She gently massaged my shoulders in this fictional reality. 'Have faith, my love … it's all you need.'

It was early evening at the Moon Walk Hotel, in the top floor presidential suite, room 88. Johnathon sat on the leather sofa sipping expensive red wine, with the Bose radio tuned to classical music. His laptop sat open on the coffee table before him. Johnathon sipped his wine, set the glass next to the computer, and then dispatched a confirmation email.

Somewhere in the sky at that very moment, a red private jet nosed through the overcast. On board three men sat at a table with a briefcase, notepad, and champagne. Mr Raymond Conwell, a business tycoon, was an average-looking man in his late forties, smartly dressed. Next to him sat his business aide, Benjamin Greyham, also in his forties and average in appearance, in businesslike attire. In the corner was their hired muscle, Rosco Jenkins, smartly dressed, with a pistol peeking from his waistband.

Raymond, flipping the briefcase open, acknowledged the woman sitting before him. 'I'm pleased to have you on board, Lady Casandra. This meeting has proven to be worth every penny.'

Casandra Roswell—Lady Casandra by profession—was tall, with long blonde hair and blue eyes, in her late thirties. She was as beautiful as she was deadly. Skilful and unpredictable, she was a freelancer and con artist, available to the highest bidder. She sat facing Raymond with her legs crossed in an all-black business suit, a short black wig, and glasses. She was in character; this was strictly business.

She acknowledged an email on her smartphone and then tucked it away into the handbag at her feet. 'The feeling is mutual, Mr Conwell.' She reached for a briefcase under the table before her.

'Shall we commence with our business?' Raymond asked.

'Ten kilos of pure grade A cocaine, as promised.' Benjamin recited the contents, exchanging a satisfied smile with Raymond.

Casandra took a pen from Raymond's pocket. She poked a hole in the package of cocaine and had a taste.

'Hmm. I see you're a man of your word.' She gave a killer smirk, sat back, and folded her arms.

'Now that you are happy, show us the money?' Raymond leaned forward on the table with a straight-faced, businesslike attitude, looking to seal the deal.

Casandra placed her briefcase on the table and popped it open, revealing a large sum of money. She spun the case around to face Raymond and Benjamin. 'Half a million. As promised.'

Raymond smiled in excitement. 'I love this lady! What did I tell you? Good as gold!'

He clapped to gain Rosco's attention, 'A toast? It's time to celebrate!'

Casandra could not agree more. 'Thought you'd never ask.'

Rosco stood up and poured glasses of champagne for Raymond, Benjamin, and Casandra. Then he quietly sat down. Casandra picked up her smartphone, scanning the email she'd received, which stated a clear and precise order: 'Pick up in 10 minutes.' Then she set the phone down on the table.

'Cheers to a deal well done—to Lady Casandra.' Raymond smiled happily as they raised their glasses to another successful deal.

Raymond and Benjamin sipped their champagne, while Casandra bluffed, passing the glass close to her lips but only pretending to drink whilst faking a smile. Suddenly, Raymond and Benjamin began to react in an unusual manner. They dropped their champagne glasses, began trembling, and their eyes bled as they fell back into their seats. Rosco stood up immediately, not sure what was going on. He drew his pistol but too slowly: Casandra pulled a silenced pistol from her bag and dropped him with a bullet to the head.

'You fucking bitch! You'll pay for this!' Raymond fell to mumbling, as blood began to gush from his mouth.

'I already have', Casandra replied, packing the cocaine and money into a single case.

Benjamin protested, 'You can't do this! My people will come for you!' He was coughing blood on his last breath of air.

'I can do whatever I want. There's no stopping me.' Casandra leant into Benjamin's face boldly savouring their last moment. 'If you gentlemen will excuse me, I have a ride to catch.'

She stripped her wig and business outfit off, revealing her undergarments and her true features and long, dark hair. She then grabbed a bag from beneath her seat and dumped its contents on the table. She slipped into cargo trousers, a skintight tank top, and ankle boots. She then shrugged into a parachute pack.

She approached Benjamin and Raymond, still dying from the

poisoned champagne. 'I hate to leave on such short notice.' She playfully pinched Raymond's cheek.

'Oh, why so grumpy? You're going to die a slow, painful death. You should be happy', she mocked in a singsong voice, making fools of the pair. She then made her way to the door of the aircraft, lifted the hatch, and opened the door.

The pilot began to panic at the roar of wind. 'What the hell is going on back there?' he yelled, fighting the controls to keep the jet on course.

Casandra leapt from the jet into mid-air. Behind her, inside her bag a countdown began. Casandra have left another surprise. Raymond and Benjamin stared at the bag, terrified at the continuous beeping. Then the explosive went, blowing the jet to pieces.

Casandra glided safely down onto a speedboat waiting in the sea below and unclipped her parachute as she nailed her landing. On the boat was a girl in her mid twenties, slim, with dark hair and average height in swimming gear, waiting to take her away. 'It's about time you got here!' She grabbed Casandra by the butt cheeks copping a feel as they both kissed on the lips.

Casandra was preoccupied. 'Let's get the hell out of here!' The girl fired up the speedboat and took off across the wide open sea.

Early that night, a ten-story building, the old Carol City Car Park, stood deserted, in the far side of the city on 44 East Street avenue. It was scheduled for demolition for a new police department, as promised by Mayor Reed. The entire area was in shambles; grasses and wild bushes had claimed the concrete walls and building surrounding a perfect hideaway from the city cops.

On the ground floor Rick and four armed men stood next to a Lincoln Navigator, waiting for their guest. Inside, on the top floor of the car park stood three pickups and two cars. Mr Donavon had come semi-casual in a black blazer with a holiday shirt beneath. His pair of hired muscle, sporting neat slacks and bowling shirts, stood around the cars. Four armed men were posted to all corners of the top floor.

In the car's back seat sat Paul Sullivan with a black leather jacket, a necklace, red button-down shirt, and jeans. Maxwell sat with him flaunting a three-piece suit.

Paul quietly asked Maxwell, 'Are the cops taken care of?'

'Mayor Reed got the message', Maxwell answered calmly, head straight, chin up.

'You want to make sure he fucking does. If shit goes sideways and cops get involved, you'll answer to me.' Paul's usual blunt, obnoxious manner, avoiding eye contact, was on full display.

Two days ago at city hall, Mayor Reed's office, early evening, the mayor had been tied up in paperwork He sat behind his mahogany desk going through some files when a knock came at the office door.

'Who the hell could this be?' the mayor muttered to himself as he rose from his seat to investigate. 'Angela! That better not be you! I've told you to go home!' he called out as he approached the door.

He opened the door, and a gun was put to his head. 'Who the hell are you? Look, if it's money you're after, I've got lots of it! Just don't hurt me, please!' The mayor trembled, holding his hands high in submission.

The pistol nudged up and down, indicating that the mayor should recede into his office. He backed into his office towards his desk with his hands up, the pistol stuck to his forehead.

'Wh-what is it you want?' he stuttered.

'We need to talk … and you're going to listen.' The man holding the gun calmly spoke to the mayor.

'I guess I have no choice. What is it you wish to talk about?' Mayor Reed was curious.

'Sit down. Take the load off', Maxwell said, pointing his gun at the mayor.

Mayor Reed was much obliged to cooperate. He noticed his handgun strapped underneath his desk, and as he sat down, he began to feel confident.

Maxwell pulled up a chair, sat down before Mayor Reed, and put his pistol away, sliding it into his suit and folding his arms peacefully. Mayor Reed saw this as a chance to turn the tables. He sat back and crossed his legs, waiting for the right moment.

'You comfortable, Mr Mayor? You look comfortable.'

'Yes ... yes I am. Let's talk', Mayor Reed responded as calmly as possible, trying not to break character.

Maxwell began to lay out his demands. 'Good. Now, here's what you're going to do. In two days' time, you're going to have every cop in the city clear of East Avenue. Don't ask why. Get it done.'

'And if I don't?' the mayor asked, raising his chest in confidence.

'Then I'll have to persuade you.'

'I'm afraid I can't do that', the mayor said, pulling the handgun from under his desk. 'I will not allow scumbags like yourselves to infest my city. It all ends now!' Mayor Reed stood up, pointing his gun resolutely.

Maxwell remained poised, chuckling at the mayor for a few seconds. He fiddled with his cufflinks and stood up boldly seemingly unfazed by the mayor's sudden reaction. 'On the contrary, Mayor. It's just beginning.'

'I don't think so!' The steeled himself to pull the trigger.

The gun clicked; the shot failed. Mayor Reed was frightened and confused and tried the trigger twice more; still nothing. Maxwell chuckled and shook his head in disappointment. Mayor Reed dropped the gun, stepping away from his desk slowly, worried, with his back towards the wall.

'Well, Mayor. You have just made things a bit more difficult. I think I'll have to convince you the hard way.' Maxwell slowly and intimidatingly approached the mayor.

Mayor Reed, terrified, glued himself to the wall. 'What are you going to do to me?'

Maxwell swung his fist and knocked Mayor Reed to the floor. Then he reached for the mayor to lift him by the neck and hit him hard in the gut, knocking him back into his seat.

'Now that I've got your attention, I suggest you cooperate.' Maxwell stood over the mayor and gripped his shoulders.

'You don't scare me! I will not help you!' The Mayor resisted arrogantly.

Maxwell was running out of patience and growing annoyed. He hooked his arms around the mayor's neck, fastening his hold as the mayor struggled to break free.

'You won't kill me! You need me!' The mayor grunted, gasping for words.

'You're right. But I will hurt you.'

Maxwell knocked the mayor about his office. Then he reached into his pocket whilst the mayor sprawled helplessly on his desk. He grabbed a cigar cutter from his pocket, placed it around the mayor's right middle finger, and clipped it clean from his hand. The mayor screamed in pain.

'Next will be your wedding finger. I suggest you cooperate.'

'The answer is no!' The mayor held his ground despite the pain and a missing finger.

Maxwell clipped his wedding finger and then his little finger. The mayor wailed in agony, barely hanging on to his dignity.

'I am not going to stop, Mayor. I'm going to cut every last one of your fingers, then I'll move on to your toes—and if that doesn't work, you don't want to know where I'm going next. If you ever want to cut bad checks and write love notes to your little secretary, Angela, you'll do as I say!'

'All right, I'll do it!' The mayor caved, finally and yielding to Maxwell's demands.

Maxwell relaxed his hold on the mayor. That's what I thought.'

The mayor crawled back to his chair like a helpless child, each hand clutching the other, and planted himself in his seat. He sat down, trying to catch his breath, holding his fingers in agony as he tried to lessen the pain.

'I am waiting, Mayor. I don't have all night.' Maxwell was impatiently waiting for the mayor to fulfil his end of the deal.

The mayor picked up his phone and made a call to CCPD Captain Walter. The captain answered on his way to his car parked outside the CCPD premises.

'Talk to me, Mayor!' he answered, standing at his car door.

'I need you to do something very important.'

'Anything, Mayor!' You name it!' Captain Walter was keen to assist if not to please the mayor at any cost.

'I need all your units to patrol Western Avenue within the next two days.' The mayor was diverting the patrol routes to draw the cops away from the eastern side of town.

'Why? What's this about? What about the rest of the city?' Clearly Captain Walter was concerned.

'The rest of the city will be fine! Just get it done!' Mayor Reed replied urgently, biting back his pain.

'OK, Mayor! Your call!' Captain Walter agreed, hanging up. He pondered the call whilst getting into his car.

'It's done! Are you happy?'

'Not happy, Mayor. Pleased.' Maxwell straightened his suit and turned towards the door. 'Just stick to the plan.' He saw himself out the door, leaving the mayor to pick up the pieces.

Outside the mayor's office, he made a call of his own. Richard Sullivan answered his bedside telephone wrapped up in sheets with his carer led on his bare chest.

'It's done, sir.'

Mr Sullivan cleared his throat. 'Excellent, Maxwell. We can proceed with our plans.'

Now, Paul Sullivan and Maxwell sat waiting in the old Carol City Car Park. Finally they saw headlights, as two grey transit vans approached.

An armed watchman looking out from the top floor spotted movement. 'Heads up! They're here.'

Both vans stopped at the entrance of the ground floor. The men identified themselves to Rick and his armed colleague.

'I'm Raoul. Some call me The Man.' Raoul had a smug look on his face. He was a big, bearded man with dark hair in his late forties, well built, and of average height, wearing a jet black blazer with a smart shirt. Most hated to cross paths with this dangerous man, who was also a top associate of Richard Sullivan, helping to keep his empire afloat. Rick and his colleague waved him into the parking lot with a clear thumbs up.

Nearby, in an old burnt-out twenty-two-story building, Lady Casandra lay prone in cover, dressed in all black latex oddly paired with ankle-strapped heels. Through a rifle scope she was tracking both vans as they headed into the parking structure.

Inside, the vans pulled up. Raoul and three men dismounted the vans, Paul, Maxwell, Mr Donavon, and his heavies gathered around to greet their associate.

Raoul smiled at the sight of his long-expected partners. 'So Mr Sullivan has sent his little son to do his bidding. Can't blame him. After all, he's not in the best of shape.'

'My father sends his regards.' Paul ignored the sarcasm, getting straight down to business. 'Now if you don't mind, let's get on with it.' H was dead serious, keen to close the deal successfully, with his father counting on his leadership.

Raoul was struck by Paul's deadpan approach. 'You got balls, kid! You really do, talking to me like that. I see you mean business. Your father was the same.' He looked at Paul and the others sceptically, taking careful note of his surroundings.

Then he tapped the van on the side, and the back doors flew open on both vans. Four men emerged with guns. Paul and Maxwell placed their hands on their guns, anticipating foul play.

'Don't be alarmed', Raoul assured the others. 'They're here for extra security. It's a risky business; you understand'.

From the burnt building, Casandra was still observing what was happening. 'Come on, you dipshits', she muttered impatiently. 'Show me the goods.' She was keen to react at a moment's notice.

In the back of the vans were cocaine bundles filling half of both vans, millions worth, which Richard Sullivan planned to sell at a profit three times over to stabilize his empire and maintain good partnerships with his associates.

'What do you think? Beautiful, huh?' Raoul laughed, pleased with himself.

'I see you came through like my father said.' Paul was glad to have a look at the mountain of cocaine, making sure the sum was right.

Mr Donavon, nosing around the van, admired the heap tucked away inside it. 'Mr Sullivan is going to be well-pleased.'

'There it is', Casandra whispered, more impatient than ever for the perfect moment to strike. 'Enough blow to paint the city white. Now let's see the green.'

Raoul straightened, suddenly eager to leave. 'Let's see the fucking money so I can get the fuck out of here!'

Paul nudged his chin at Maxwell. Maxwell opened the boot of the car and grabbed a briefcase. He held it up whilst Paul unclipped the locks to reveal a large quantity of cold hard cash.

Casandra saw the cash and was ready to react instantaneously. She put a finger to her ear and made the call to her team on standby through her radio comm. 'The money and the package are ready. Move on my command.' Outside the burnt-out building, two motorcyclists, armed and clothed in black leather, waited to move on Casandra's command.

Raoul, smiling, picked up a stack of cash from the case, flicked through it, and replaced it in the case.

'It's all there. Ten mil, every last dollar', said Paul.

'I'll take your word for it, only because I trust your father', said Raoul with a serious look on his face.

Casandra took a shot, putting a bullet through the eye of a man standing out in plain sight. Everyone scattered, drawing their guns. Paul and his men took cover behind their vehicles; Raoul and the rest of his men occupied the rear of the vans.

'You trying to double-cross me, Paul?' Raoul called across the floor. 'You trying to fuck with me?'

'I don't know what the fuck is going on!' Paul shouted back, keeping his head down. 'This is not on me!'

'Move now!' Casandra ordered. 'Clear the building!' She abandoned her rifle for the guns strapped to her waist.

The two motorcyclists rode into the front of the parking structure, machine guns blazing. Rick with his associates took cover, returning fire but missing their targets as the bikes zoomed past into the structure. Paul, Raoul, and their men heard the gunshots quickly dispersed in firing position holding firm.

'Who the hell are these people?' Paul shouted, waving his gun in anger.

'Don't worry. I'll handle it', said Maxwell calmly, covering the entrance of the tenth floor with his gun.

The riders stopped on the third floor. They fitted their gas masks and then began to disperse tear gas floor by floor, shooting their way to the tenth floor. Casandra slipped her mask on and fired a grappling hook from the burnt building to the parking structure's tenth floor. The bikers launched multiple teargas canisters before entering the tenth floor.

'Take cover! Take cover!' Maxwell shouted.

Everyone began opening fire onto the entry point to the tenth floor, holding their noses, firing blind as the gas built up. The two riders moved in firing, keeping everyone suppressed and pinned down as they spun around on their bikes, spraying fire. Casandra swung in from the burnt building into the tenth floor, opening fire with her pistol as her feet touched down, killing a handful of men.

Paul grabbed Maxwell by the collar and shouted into his face, both of them coughing. 'Do something before we all die!'

'I am getting the fuck out of here!' Mr Donavon yelled, scurrying away. He called to his heavies, 'Come on, you two! I'm not paying you to die just yet!'

Donavon and his men headed for their vehicle. The riders sprayed a burst of shots at them, forcing them back into hiding. Everyone kept on choking on the gas. Maxwell saw a rider about to take a shot and took aim, but Casandra shot the gun from his hand, and a spin kick to the head knocked Maxwell cold.

Finally all coughing and shooting ceased. Paul and his team, along with Raoul and his men, were all out cold, passed out from the gas. The riders ditched their bikes and took their seats at the controls of the vans. Casandra pried the money from Paul's hand and boarded one of the vehicles.

Tyres screaming, Rick raced in, heading towards the van, his gun blazing. The van stopped, and Casandra stepped out boldly and emptied her gun into the car's grill, blowing the bonnet open. The car swerved and crashed into a wall.

Casandra returned to the van and took off with the drugs and the money. 'Thanks for the snow and the dough … mwah!' She blew a cheeky kiss at Rick as they drove past.

Later that night at an old warehouse on the far side of Carol City, the two vans arrived and pulled indoors, where a limousine, a transit van, and two SUVs were parked, waiting.

The vans stopped, facing the waiting vehicles with the lights on. Casandra ordered the van drivers still to flash their headlights. The doors of the waiting vehicles were flung open, and the Logan brothers,

Gosnell and Johnathon, emerged from the limousine. A group of four men appeared from the transit and eight men from the SUV, all casually dressed except for the Logan brothers, who were both smartly dressed as normal.

Casandra and her two riders exited the vans and approached the Logan brothers. 'What's this, the welcoming party?' she asked sarcastically as she dismounted the van to greet the brothers.

'Haven't you heard? There's safety in numbers!' Gosnell responded with some excitement.

'Are you saying you're a coward?' she asked lightly.

'Don't make me shoot you in the mouth', Gosnell replied, unimpressed.

'Once again, Lady Casandra', Johnathon said, 'you have proven your worth.'

'I always deliver. It's a habit!' she replied.

Gosnell snapped his fingers, and his men took the briefcase from Casandra and placed it onto the bonnet of the limousine, ready to undo the clips.

'Get that briefcase off the God-darn car before I shoot you in the face!' Gosnell said aggressively, feeling touchy about their car.

The man placed the briefcase in another man's hands and opened it. Gosnell and Johnathon confirmed it was all there.

'That's ten mil, all right? It's all there!' said the man with the briefcase.

'Check the vans out', Gosnell ordered his men. 'Make sure the stash is all there.'

Casandra looked surprised and even insulted by Gosnell's suspicion. 'What? Don't you trust me?'

'I like to be very certain. I'm a curious man', Gosnell replied.

The men confirmed the contents of both vans, indicating to the Logan brothers that the cocaine was all present and accounted for.

'Guess it's time to talk money.' Johnathon walked Casandra to the boot of their limousine. 'Half a million, as promised!' he said as he pulled out another briefcase and handed it to her.

Casandra checked the money with her two partners and was satisfied. 'Pleasure doing business with you, gentlemen.' She closed the briefcase. 'Don't hesitate if you need me', she said, hurrying from the warehouse.

The Logans watched as Casandra and her partners left. Johnathon gave a loud whistle. Footsteps echoed in the dark of the warehouse, and Raoul emerged, joining the Logan brothers.

'It's done … the drugs the money … all here', said Gosnell.

'By the time that dying old fool realizes what happened … this city will be ours', Johnathon declared.

'He had it coming', Raoul commented. 'He needs to realize his son is dead weight.'

I was tucking my boys in bed, kissing them good night. I froze, staring at a man standing in my sons' room. I felt rage, anger, and hatred towards the man—that man who took them, the man who'd left me for dead, the man who took everything I stood for …. I grabbed my hair in frustration and yelled in rage, 'Arrrrgh!'

The boys got scared, and I snapped out of it, assuring them everything was all right. Lauren put her arms around me, comforting me.

'Get out of here!' I yelled, as the man taunted me with his presence. Leave us alone!'

Lauren was shaken. She looked at me, terrified. I left the room shamefully, retreating to the kitchen where I trashed a few appliances.

'Why? Why?' I sobbed, covering my face hiding my tears from a man I had come to despise.

I wiped my face clean of the bitter tears and returned to the kids. The room was empty, bare. I panicked and went looking around the rooms, seeking the kids and my wife, who were still nowhere to be found. Out the front door I ran, onto the front lawn, screaming their names.

'Lauren! … Kids! … Where are you?!' I shouted in despair.

Dr. Ramrod, a tall skinny grey-haired man in his fifties, was at my bedside on night duty, checking my vitals. The doctor saw my index finger twitch.

'Shari!' he called out to his assistant, 'get in here now!'

He immediately checked my heart rate, which seemed to have elevated. Shari rushed into the room. 'The patient's vitals are off the charts! We're going to need to run further tests!' said Dr. Ramrod as he and his assistant prepared to re-examine me. Everything went calm, I was sedated and now at ease.

'Keep a close eye on him, and inform me of any changes', the doctor ordered.

'Will do, doctor. Take the load off', Shari said, peering at him closely; 'you look like you could use some rest.'

'I do believe you're right. I'll see you in the morning'. Dr. Ramrod saw himself out of the room, leaving Shari, his assistant, to care take for the rest of the night.

CHAPTER 4

The next day, Mr Sullivan's yacht stood off the coast of Carol City bay. Inside the yacht the atmosphere was tense: Paul, Maxwell, Rick, Mr Donavon with his heavies, and four other men on Mr Sullivan's payroll stood out on the lower deck waiting anxiously.

Mr Sullivan, dressed in a gentleman's robe, appeared in his wheelchair. He was hooked up to his oxygen and carrying a drip bag. His beautiful carer was pushing him along when he threw his hand up, and she stopped.

'Tell me. Which one of you pieces of shit is going to answer me? Which of you's got the balls to step forward and take the fall?!' Mr Sullivan's foul mood was unmistakable. 'Huh? Anyone? No one man enough around here?' Mr Sullivan shouted angrily followed by an unhealthy cough.

Everyone stood wordless, afraid of what might happen. Then his son spoke. 'Listen, Pop! We didn't know this would happen!'

Mr Sullivan cut him short. 'Shut the fuck up, Paul! Don't make me do something I'll regret! I've just lost a shitload of cash and a whole lot of fucking blow! Heck! I even lost a valuable associate, all because you bunch of nincompoops could not do a simple job!' Mr Sullivan's rant broke into coughing, and his carer fed him oxygen.

'We'll get your money back, sir', Maxwell calmly assured his boss.

'Damn right you will. And someone is going to pay for this fuckup of a job!'

All faces went pale with fear. Someone was about to be cut from Mr Sullivan's payroll in a very gruesome manner. Mr Sullivan wiggled his finger at his carer, and she leant down. He whispered something to her, and she shouted, 'Chen Wang!'

A Chinese man wearing a chef's outfit appeared from inside the yacht. He was Mr Sullivan's personal chef, in his late thirties. His thin moustache fitted his nature: dangerous, sly, and cunning.

Mr Sullivan announced, 'Mr Chen here will see to it that one of you dipshits never fucks up again! Paul! Maxwell! Rick! Get your asses over here!' Mr Sullivan isolated a select few to stand at his side.

'Whoa now! I'm not taking the fall for this screw-up!' Mr Donavon cried.

'I'd shut the fuck up if I were you!' Mr Sullivan grunted.

Chen walked over towards Mr Donavon, his hired heavies, and the four men on Mr Sullivan's payroll. Chen paced up and down slowly with a Chinese chopper in his waistband, his hands behind his back, spreading an uncomfortable atmosphere amongst Mr Donavon and the others. Chen began speaking Chinese, telling the men that he'd feed them to the sharks, chop their balls off, and make mincemeat of their livers—but not today.

Chen drew his blade, and with a quick clean swipe, he sliced open a man's neck. The others watched as he bled heavily, falling face down to his death. The others were terrified, shaking in their pants. Then Chen tossed his blade into the air with everyone looking up as the spinning blade came back down. Chen caught the blade expertly and threw it into the head of another standing beside Mr Donavon, splitting his skull.

He walked over to the dead man, pulled his blade from the skull, wiped it clean on the dead man's shirt, and casually strolled inside the yacht. Mr Donavon and his men breathed a sigh of relief.

'Now you understand the consequences if you fail me again!' Mr Sullivan warned.

'Now! My money and Raoul's stash is out there somewhere, and you pieces of shit are going to find it!' Mr Sullivan's emphasis on the urgency of the situation clashed with the sight of him gasping into his oxygen mask.

'Maxwell?!' Mr Sullivan called.

'Sir?'

'Get me the mayor! He's the only loose end in all this. No one else knew what we were up to that night!' Mr Sullivan's tone is ominous. 'Bring him to me!'

'Right away, sir!' Maxwell replied. Then he boarded a speedboat, cast off from the yacht, and raced away.

Chen reappeared and dragged the dead bodies inside the yacht whilst the others stood by and watched. He took them below into the storage compartment, where he hacked them to pieces with a cutlass. Then he dumped them in a plastic tub and dissolved them with hydrochloric acid.

Early that day, Carl and his partner Craig were already at the hospital in my room being briefed about my recent medical condition.

'The patient has been experiencing a slight acute bodily dysfunction', Dr. Ramrod explained. 'It appears that he's in some sort of dream state that seems to be triggering a traumatic response. Whoever did this to him has caused a lot of permanent damage … physical and psychological.' Dr. Ramrod delivered this news with a sympathetic look on his face.

'It's a shame. Don't think he's going to be the same', Carl sais, looking down at me lying helplessly on the bed.

'Whatever he's experiencing, he's not going to wake quietly', the doctor said. 'He's going to have to keep his face bandaged.'

'Why's that?' Craig asked in surprise.

'Well, Detective, the damage done to his face could not be fully repaired, even with our most advanced medical procedures. Any exposure to light and air will cause serious damage.'

'Thanks for your help, Doctor. We'll be in touch!' Carl said, and the detectives excused themselves and left. 'We've got some people to question', Carl said to Craig. 'Let's head uptown! I have a feeling this case is going to be blown wide open.' Craig got into the cruiser with a sceptical demeanour.

Soon the detectives sat outside a liquor store in their cruiser, each with a drink of coffee. Rick emerged from the front door of the liquor store wearing jeans, a smart shirt, and leather boots, carrying a case of champagne to the boot of a Land Rover parked three cars in front of

Carl. Just as Rick was about to place the box into the boot, Carl and Craig came up, and Carl flashed his badge.

'Can I help you?' Rick asked coldly, scanning Craig with a very peculiar look.

'We're going to have to ask you to come with us! Got some questions need answering regarding the murder of Mr Martin Redding', Carl said with a straight look on his face.

'Whatever you think you know, I assure you that you're dead wrong', says Rick with high confidence.

'Let's hope for your sake you're right, but either way, you're coming with us!' Carl said firmly.

Rick thought about it for a moment. He had his eyes on an automatic weapon in his boot that it seemed Carl had not noticed. Craig saw it, though, and nudged his head quietly at Rick, deflecting him from his plan.

Carl was losing patience. 'Listen, asshole, we don't have all day!'

'Sure, why not? Got nothing to hide!' Rick decided to cooperate, and the detectives escorted him to the back of their cruiser and drove away.

Back at the city hall the same day, Maxwell entered the ground floor smartly dressed with a mean expression. He headed towards the lift, purposely slipping past security.

'Excuse me, sir!' a security officer called. 'Can't let you any further without clearance.' He hurried towards Maxwell.

Maxwell ignored the officer and stepped into the lift, which was empty.

The security officer slipped into the lift just as the door was closing. 'Sir, I'm afraid I'll have to escort you from the building!'

'I can't let you do that!' Maxwell replied calmly, his back to the officer.

'You have no choice! You're leaving!' the officer insisted, hitting the button to the ground floor.

'You're very determined. You must take your job seriously', Maxwell commented, still not offering eye contact.

'You bet your sorry ass I do!' the security officer replied aggressively.

'So do I', Maxwell responded, quickly pulling a knife from inside his jacket and driving it through the officer's eye socket. The knife penetrated the eyeball and killed him instantly.

The lift door opened on the fifteenth floor, where several employees were waiting to enter. Maxwell straightened his suit and walked out of the lift and across the open hall past the secretary's desk, towards Mayor Reed's office. Inside the lift the employees stood quietly together, as the lift closes. A woman hit the button for the twenty-second floor and relaxed as the lift ascended.

Soon a spot of red dripped onto one man's shoulder. He didn't notice, but then another and another drew the attention of another man standing at the rear, who rubbed his finger into the red patch on his colleague's shoulder. His colleague looked at him and then at the red patch on his shoulder, and they looked at each other with a disturbed expression. Then everyone looked up and saw blood seeping through the top of the lift, and the sound of panicked screams echoed within the elevator shaft.

Meanwhile, Maxwell entered the mayor's office. The secretary, Angela, called after him, 'Hello, sir? Hello?' trying to get his attention.

Maxwell ignored Angela's calls and kept going. She scampered from her desk and grabbed his arm. Maxwell stopped and turned with a threatening look on his face.

Frightened, Angela let him resume his walk. 'Sorry, sir … go on in.'

Maxwell opened the door and let himself into the mayor's office.

Mayor Reed sat facing out the window, fiddling with his missing finger. The door slammed shut, and Reed twitched and turned around. 'What are you doing here? I've done what you asked of me!' The mayor was uninterested and annoyed.

'Someone knew what we were up to', Maxwell replied calmly, locking the door behind him. 'Someone found us out.' He slowly approached the mayor. 'So, Mr Mayor … here I am.' He calmly laid his palms on the mayor's shoulders, and Reed was terrified.

'Tell me, how did they know?' Maxwell demanded, pressing down on the other man's shoulder for emphasis.

'What? No, you got it all wrong! I have no idea what you're talking about, I swear!'

'That's not good enough, Mayor. Do not make me take another finger', Maxwell warned.

'I'm telling you the truth! For God's sake!' Mayor Reed, angry and agitated, accidentally knocked his desk lamp to the floor.

'I am a very sincere man, Mr Reed, and I don't like being lied to—and neither does Mr Sullivan.'

Mayor Reed broke down in tears, pleading his innocence and trying to convince Maxwell he was totally honest. 'You got to believe me! Please, I'm begging you! I had nothing to do with what happened! Please!' Mayor Reed, in tears, knew what would become of him should he lie.

Maxwell was surprised by the mayor's behaviour. 'Well, look at that. These must be the tears of an honest man! Tell you what, Mayor … you carry on with your day.' Maxwell seemed to be letting the mayor off lightly.

'You sure? You're not going to kill me?' Mayor Reed was stammering in shock.

'*Kill* is such a strong word, Mr Mayor', said Maxwell with a smooth smile. 'Like I said, Mayor, I'm a sincere man. You enjoy what's left of your day.' And he left.

Across town at the Carol City Police Department, Rick sat in an interrogation room at a bare table with Carl screaming down his face and Craig standing quietly to one side, playing good cop.

'What the hell were you and your partner doing around the docks at the time of the murder?' Carl placed photos before Rick of him and Joe within the area.

'Like I said, Detective, I wasn't there.' Rick was playing it cool.

'You listen to me, you scum-sucking piece of shit!' Carl grabbed Rick by the collar. 'You know something, and you're going to tell me!'

'I am not saying a word without my lawyer, got that?' Rick refused to crack.

'The only lawyer you're going to have is my foot up your ass!' Carl slammed his fist on the table. 'Now start talking!'

'I'll handle this, Carl', Craig broke in, trying to soften the mood. 'Let me have a crack.'

'You think you can get this scumbag talking? Be my guest.' Angry and annoyed, Carl left the room.

Craig sat down at the table, facing the other man. 'Listen here, Rick. You better start playing the game. The sooner you start cooperating, the sooner you're out of here.' Craig spoke quietly, urging Rick.

'I am trying my best. Your partner here needs to be taught a lesson', Rick replied as calmly as he could.

'You let me worry about my partner. You worry about keeping your nose clean. Last thing Mr Sullivan needs is another screw-up', Craig whispered, edging forward and invading Rick's personal space.

The door was flung open, and Carl returned after cooling his temper. Rick took a pack of cigarettes from his jacket looking to smoke.

'Still can't get a word out of him', Craig lied.

'Did I say you can smoke?' Carl grunted, ignoring Craig. With his hands on his hips, his badge was on display.

'It's a free country. I do whatever the fuck I want', Rick snapped, sticking a cigarette between his lips.

Carl snatched the cigarette pack and stuck it in his pocket. Then he felt his pockets and thought for a second, and his face brightened. 'You know what? I think we got off on the wrong foot. Have yourself a cigarette … smoke to your heart's content.' He placed the cigarettes back on the table.

Craig looked at Carl, confused about what he might be up to, what stunt he might be pulling. Rick took the cigarettes and placed a fresh one between his lips. Then he dug in his pocket for a lighter. Carl watched and waited until Rick pulled it from his pocket. There it was, a lighter just like the one Carl had found at my house with a dice imprint. Carl played it cool: he sat down in front Rick and shook his head in mock disappointment.

'Got a problem?' Rick asked, blowing his smoke into Carl's face, rudely.

'Yeah, I do,' Carl replied, boldly tossing the lighter from his pocket onto the table. 'Does this look familiar to you?'

Rick looked a little worried and spooked but somehow kept a straight face. He looked at Craig and then at the lighter. Then he picked it up and tossed it back onto the table. 'Looks just like mine. So what?' He had another puff at his cigarette.

'This was found at the crime scene of the family you and your partner murdered!' Carl alleged, landing his fist on the table.

'Hold on, Carl. We don't know that yet!' Craig interjected.

'We will! … soon as Forensics gets us a match on the prints left at the scene!' Carl replied loudly. He turned on Rick and punctuated his answer with his fist against the table. 'You were at the docks! You were at that home! You murdered that family! Worse, you murdered those kids!'

'Fuck you, asshole! You don't have proof! You don't have anything!' Rick stood up, yelling back at Carl.

'You're not going anywhere. I'm arresting you on suspicion of murder!' Carl replied, screaming across the room. 'Read him his rights, Craig!' He walked away from the table, fuming in anger.

Craig read Rick his rights, slapped the cuffs on, and escorted him out of the room.

'You're making a big mistake, asshole! You can't hold me!' Rick yells on his way out of the room, fighting against the cuffs on his wrists.

Captain Walter walked into the interrogation room once all the commotion had blown over. 'Any progress, Detective?' He was loud as usual, with a stern manner.

'He's not cracking', Carl muttered, still fuming. 'He knows something! He's linked to the Brown family murder … I just know it!'

'You want to hurry and wrap this up', Captain Walter said. 'He'll be out of here as soon as he makes his call, so be quick!'

'I'll chase the forensics, see what they found', Carl replied.

Craig took Rick to a holding cell. He took the cuffs off and then looked around carefully to make sure no one would hear what he was about to say. Then he said, 'I suggest you make use of your call. Sullivan's lawyer will get you out of here.'

'You'd better remember your place', Rick said; 'your partner is getting too persistent.'

'Like I said … I'll handle him.' Craig closed the cell door, leaving Rick to ponder his actions.

Late that afternoon at the Carol City General Hospital, Father Franklin sat beside my bed in my ward whispering the twenty-third Psalm quietly to himself. He fluffed my pillows and replaced the dead flowers beside my bed. Then he began talking to me, assuring me there was still hope.

'Keep holding on, my friend … I have faith in you, and your church needs you … the people need you; they send their regards.' Father Franklin fed me hope from outside the coma.

'We are all praying for you, Arthur. We all are.' Father Franklin looked upwards for inspiration.

Inside I was fighting hard to overcome the monster tearing my family apart. I was afraid … afraid to confront that inner nightmare and come to terms with what I'd lost and face the reality on the other side. Rick had me by the neck, his blade scarring my forehead. He was killing me slowly, and I was too afraid to fight back, just as I was before he took my family away. Still trapped, I began to shake in fear as Rick's blade sank into my face, drawing blood.

'Hold on, Arthur! Help is coming!' Father Franklin, very frightened, decided to call for help. 'Somebody get me a doctor!' he cried aloud into the corridor.

Dr. Ramrod came racing down the corridor into the room.

'Is he going to be all right?' Father Franklin asked worriedly.

'He's going to be fine', Dr. Ramrod replied calmly and professionally as he stabilized me.

'What just happened?' Father Franklin asked.

'Father Brown is experiencing a post traumatic reaction', said Dr. Ramrod.

'The condition is involuntary', the doctor explained. 'It will keep recurring until he wakes up.'

Overwhelmed by the doctor's statement, Father Franklin sat down in despair, as he tried carefully to make sense of the situation.

'He's going to wake … he has to', Father said, worried.

'He's going to need your prayers, Father', the doctor said nicely as he left the room.

Late evening, few hours after the sun had set, Mayor Reed was leaving for home, strutting along in the City Hall parking lot. He unlocked his car a few feet short of the door using his immobilizer. Just as he was about to grasp the door handle, a black van sped to a stop, a door slid open, and the mayor was pulled inside by Mr Donavon's pair of hired thugs and taken away. The van tyres screeched as they disappeared out of the parking lot.

Later, at the Montgomery Funeral Parlour in the City's Capital, Lismore, in the arrangement room, Mayor Reed woke up in the dark in a very confined space, lying down. He panicked, yelling for help and tapping senselessly on the padded wood above his face. He was locked inside a coffin.

'Help! Somebody, anybody? Please!' Mayor Reed cried out hopelessly.

'Save it, Mayor. No one will hear your', came a voice from outside the coffin.

'Who the hell are you?!' the mayor cried out loud.

'By the time you are found, you'll be long dead', the voice continued, calmly threatening. 'That is, if you do not tell us what we need to know. The ball is in your court'. Mr Donovan opened the coffin.

Mayor Reed wailed, 'I already told you people! I don't know anything!'

'Hello, Mayor. Nice seeing you again.' Maxwell came into view. Accompanying Maxwell was Mr Montgomery Daniels, the owner and proprietor of the funeral establishment. He seemed timid, hairy and of average height, slightly built, and in his late fifties.

'I trust that you enjoyed what was left of your day', said Maxwell, standing over the coffin.

'You can't do this to me!' Mayor Reed yelled rustling around the coffin. 'You won't get away with this!'

'Wrong, Mayor! I just did, in case you haven't noticed!' Then Maxwell punched the mayor back into the coffin.

'I don't think this is the right place to be doing this', Montgomery Daniels pleaded, frightened.

'Don't you forget who got you this place!' Maxwell said, reminding Daniels where his loyalty lay.

Daniels went silent. Ashamed and afraid to challenge Maxwell, he backed away.

'That's what I thought.' Maxwell turned his attention away from Montgomery towards the mayor. 'Now, where were we?'

'Just let me go', the mayor pleaded, 'I'm begging you.'

'I'm afraid it's too late for that', Maxwell replied calmly yet ominously. 'Mr Sullivan lost a lot that night, truth be told. He's not a happy man.' He walked casually around the coffin, pacing the mayor.

'Look, I don't know anything!' the mayor ranted on. 'Maybe the captain screwed up! I don't know, okay?'

Maxwell glared down into Reed's face. 'This one is on you, Mayor. You're going to help Mr Sullivan get his money!'

'How am I going to do that?' Mayor Reed asked, squirming in the coffin.

Mr Donavon and his hired thugs laughed suspiciously, making the Mayor even more uncomfortable.

'By volunteering, of course!' Maxwell exclaimed.

'I am not volunteering for shit!' Mayor Reed retorted. 'Tell Mr Sullivan he can fuck himself!'

'In case you haven't noticed, you're already volunteering', Maxwell replied calmly. 'Mr Daniels here is going to take real good care of you.' With that, Maxwell turned and left the room.

Mr Donavon snapped his fingers, and his men held the mayor down, keeping him still in the coffin. The mayor screamed in growing terror as Daniels walked up to him, a surgical knife in his trembling hand.

'I'm sorry! I am really sorry!' Daniels said, sobbing his eyes out.

'Get it over with, you coward!' Donavon shouted impatiently.

Daniels leant over the coffin and jabbed the knife into the mayor's heart, killing him where he lay. The body was then taken from the coffin by Donavon's men and placed onto an operating table in the preparation room in parlour's basement. After Donavon and his heavies left the basement, Daniels removed the mayor's clothing, leaving the body completely naked. Slowly and carefully he began to dissect the mayor by cutting his abdomen open and removing his organs, placing them into a metal tray.

Then he opened the cranium and carefully extracted the mayor's brain. He removed a big holdall bag from a locker and placed it next to the operating table. The bag was full of cocaine and cannabis neatly wrapped in plastic. Daniels began to stack the packets in Mayor Reed's abdomen and cranium, filling them with cocaine and cannabis. Then he stitched the mayor's body back together and dressed him smartly.

He wheeled a coffin next to the operating table and rolled the mayor's body into the coffin, laying him neatly on his back.

Finally he sealed the coffin with a combination lock, wiped his forehead in exhaustion, and made a call.

Maxwell answered from the balcony of Mr Sullivan's mansion. 'You'd better have good news, Mr Daniels!'

'It's done. The body is ready', Montgomery replied.

Maxwell was pleased. 'Good. You've done well; we'll supply you with more bodies. See you in a few hours' time.' He hung up and rejoined Mr Sullivan in the study.

Mr Sullivan sat in a cosy chair in front a fireplace. He wore a robe, with an oxygen tank and mask at arm's length, drinking belvedere on the rocks.

Maxwell walked into the study to report. As the door shut, Mr Sullivan asked, 'What is it?'

'It's done. Mr Daniels came through. But he's going to need more bodies. There's still a large amount left to be stored. Then we'll be ready to move the package on your orders.'

Mr Sullivan replied, 'That shouldn't be a problem. Take a look out the window.'

Maxwell drew a crack into the curtains and had a close look outside the mansion gates. On the side road was a parked ice cream van; inside were two male CCPD officers on surveillance, eating donuts, drinking coffee, and keeping tabs on the mansion.

'No one here eats ice cream. You know what to do', Mr Sullivan said faintly, gasping on his oxygen. 'Have the package ready to move tomorrow … early morning; that way the cops won't be as suspicious.'

'I'll inform the others', Maxwell replied and saw himself out.

Outside the mansion, the officers on surveillance received a call from the department. Carl was calling for an update, hoping for good news.

An officer picked up the phone and muttered, 'Talk to me.'

'What you got for me?' Carl asked, sitting at his desk in the busy squad room.

The officer rubbed his eyes. 'Quiet on our side, Detective. Maybe we should call it a day.'

'You're not moving till you get me something. Radio me when you've got it.' Disgruntled, Carl ended the call.

Craig walked in. 'Anything?'

'We got nothing.' Carl changed the subject. 'How's that scumbag Lawson holding up?'

'He's had his phone call. He's a happy man', Craig replied.

'Not for long. Not when he sees the evidence we've got against him.'

Just then, a tall female lawyer in her late 40s, smartly dressed, walked in, striding in heels across the hard floor towards the captain's office. Carl and Craig looked on as she marched past their desk.

'Just who in God's name are you?' Captain Walter asked as she entered his office.

'Captain, I'm here to authorize the release of my client, Rick Lawson', the lawyer announced.

'Now why would I do such a thing?' Captain Walter said, getting to his feet.

'You don't have enough evidence to start. My client hasn't been charged. Have him released immediately!'

Captain Walter stuck his head out the door. 'Brooks? Get your ass in here. Now!'

'What is it, Captain?!' Carl answered, stepping into the office.

'Get that scumbag out of lockdown!' the captain ordered whilst the lawyer smiled.

'You can't be serious, Captain!'

'My hands are tied! Besides, his lawyer is right! we don't have evidence against him!'

Carl refused, he rages against the captain. 'I'm not having this! No way am I letting that slime walk!'

'Darn it, Detective! Do as you're told! Get that piece of crap out of my precinct!'

Soon Rick's cell door unlocked. Rick gave Carl a cocky smile as he exited the cell to join his lawyer.

'I'll be seeing you again … real soon.' Carl was still keen to get his man.

'I wouldn't be too sure, Detective', Rick replied, strolling past. He avoided eye contact with Craig as he left the holding facility.

'You'd best hope to God Father Brown wakes up!' Carl said to Craig. 'He's our only chance of putting this scum away.'

'For now he's got to stay dead for his own safety.'

'Let's hope Father Brown has a memory when he wakes … *if* he wakes'. Craig had a suspicious look as Carl watched Rick leave the building.

Early that evening, in the woods near their recently acquired mansion, the Logan brothers in their outdoor gear were shooting pheasants for sport or possibly dinner. The place was situated in the heart of the countryside in a small town called Everwood. Raoul and a handful of men casually dressed came by, rendezvousing with the brothers.

'Heard you need to see me, urgently', Raoul said as he approached the brothers.

'You're right!' Gosnell replied, squeezing the trigger and dropping a pheasant from mid-air. 'It's time we started shaking things up!'

'I'm listening.' Raoul was interested.

'My brother's and my plans for taking over this city have just expanded', said Gosnell.

'What you saying?' Raoul asked.

'What we are saying is that we need more clients, and you're going to help us get them', Johnathon said, shouldering his shotgun.

'I would … but you're forgetting something', Raoul replied.

'What might that be?' Johnathon asked.

'This is already Mr Sullivan's city. He owns most of the successful venues around, and those he doesn't own, he controls. You've got your work cut out for you.'

Gosnell chuckled, as confident as ever. 'You seem to have forgotten who we are, Raoul. We take what we want, when we want. We have the resources to handle situations like these. I assure you Mr Sullivan won't pose a single threat!'

'You have already proven your loyalty', Johnathon said, studying Raoul. 'Why not continue to do so?'

'What's the plan?' Raoul asked, climbing aboard.

'Follow me!' Gosnell said with a smile, setting off to lead them into the mansion.

Still afraid and still holding on by a thread, this time I found myself locked away in my basement, scrunched up quaking in a lonely corner, tormented by the sound of a knife scraping and digging against the basement door.

'Come out and face me! Let's finish what I've started!' Rick taunted me over and over.

'Go away!' I called, between sobs. 'Go away! Go away!'

'We both know I'm not leaving here! Not until you face me!' Rick shouted back.

'You took my family away! You've taken everything! Everything!' I cried out in grief.

'I did! It didn't have to be that way. Maybe you could have saved them … if you weren't such a coward. If you ask me, Father, I say it's all your fault!'

I wiped my drenched face. Thinking he was right, blaming myself, I punched the wall behind me in anger and went on trashing the basement. He could hear me and laughed.

Jack walked in and returned to my bedside. He took a close look at me and somehow knew what was going on. He sat down beside me in his rags and sighed, studying me.

'Don't do this to yourself, Father. Don't give in; keep on fighting.' His voice was quiet and reassuring. 'We both know you're not a quitter. Don't let it end like this', he went on, quietly motivating me from the other side.

I was trying very hard to find the courage to face my fears—to open that door and confront the man behind it. After trashing the basement, I crumpled to my knees in despair.

'This isn't the time to quit, Father', a voice whispered quietly.

I stopped crying and tried to make sense of what I'd just heard. I didn't question who or what the voice was; I only knew it was the voice of reason, the voice of faith and hope, trying to get me out that door for the right reasons.

'Hey! You there!' A nurse called to Jack as she walked by the open door to my room.

Jack hid his face with the collar of his dirty old trench coat. The nurse came in to look at him closely. 'Visiting hours are over … you shouldn't be here! Who are you anyway?'

Jack scuttled out of the room without an answer. Shoving past her and into the corridor he hustled, shielding his face all the way, and disappeared out of the building.

CHAPTER 5

At nightfall, the two officers inside the surveillance van were sharp at work trying to get the drop on Mr Sullivan. Then came a tapping sound on the side door, and the officers looked at each other. Bullets burst along the paint job of the ice-cream van, and the officers hit the deck—but too late. The bullets made mincemeat of the van along with their bodies. The door slid open, and four of Sullivan's men lugged the dead officers away into the trunk of a '72 Monte Carlo, which then took off into the night.

Later the bodies were offloaded behind the Montgomery Funeral Parlour. Montgomery Daniels himself assisted the four-man effort, under strict orders to move the bodies to the basement and get them loaded onto operating tables. Montgomery stood steering helplessly at the dead cops, unwilling to proceed with the grim task.

'Hey!' came a barked order. 'Get working, all right?'

Montgomery swallowed his pride and dignity and began stripping the bodies down for dissection. One by one, he worked professionally on the dead officers, storing the drugs in the officers' corpses. After hours of bloody work, he was finished, with both officers neatly dressed in coffins and set beside the mayor's coffin.

Next day the mayor's secretary, Angela, was alarmed at his absence from work. She rang his phone repeatedly without an answer. Not taking any chances, she then called the police, who responded immediately. Two male officers in uniform came to look around the mayor's office and ask questions.

Angela, worried, feared the worst. 'The mayor never misses a day at work. It's not like him. Something is wrong, I just know it.'

'Who was the last person to see the mayor?' one officer asked.

After careful thought, Angela replied, 'Well, there was this guy. Very scary-looking. He barged into the mayor's officer despite my efforts to stop him.'

'What did he look like?' the officer inquired.

'He was tall, smartly dressed', she answered. 'I won't forget his face. Very intimidating.'

'Thanks for your time, ma'am. We'll be in touch.' The officers saw themselves into the elevator, where one said to the other, 'Let's hope he doesn't end up like that body in the elevator shaft. There's enough bodies out there already.'

That afternoon, at the CCPD building, Captain Walter hung up the phone in a frenzy. He pushed the office door wide and yelled into the busy squad room.

'Everyone shut the hell up! We got a problem. The mayor has gone AWOL! I want him found! I want him found now! Someone out there knows something, and you're going to get some answers!

'And another thing: this stays strictly within the department! No public statement until I say so! I want this city turned upside down! I want every goddamned shithole in this city wiped clean!'

The captain carried on, bringing the room to a standstill with his demands. 'I want every vehicle into and out of the city checked! This city doesn't sleep until the mayor is back at his desk drinking his coffee. Get your asses out there now!'

Like a herd of buffalo, the patrol cops immediately scattered from the room. Walter slammed his door and dropped like a brick into his seat, pondering the phone call.

Early that afternoon at Carol City General Hospital, Carl and his partner, Craig, stood in my room having a chat with the nurse who had grown concerned about Jack's visit.

'Nice of you to give us a call, ma'am. What did this mysterious man look like?' Carl asked.

'He was a bit rough and quite hairy. My guess would be that he's living on the streets', the nurse replied.

Craig pulled Carl aside. 'You don't think this guy is trying to finish the job, whoever it is, do you?'

'No one knows he's alive at the moment, but I don't want to take any chances. Get an officer on the door in case this guy comes back.' Carl refused to take any chances.

'I'll get on it.' Craig left the room, pulling out his phone.

'Ma'am,' Carl said to the nurse, 'I need to have a look at the CCTV.'

'Right this way, sir.' She escorted him to the CCTV room.

Out in the hallway, Craig was speaking urgently into his phone. 'I'm going to need to see you, it's urgent … Yes, tonight, at the old factory.' He ended the call abruptly.

Then he returned to my room. All alone he stuck his hands into his coat pockets, sighed, looked at me, and shook his head.

'You know, I could finish this right now, or … or I can have someone else finish the job. I think you should just let go … just let go, Father … let go. You pull out of this coma, you're as good as dead'.

After a tap on the door, a uniformed female officer appeared. Craig went quiet, acting normal and greeting the officer politely with a smile. 'Thanks for getting here on such short notice.'

She smiled. 'No problem, Detective. Just following orders.'

He took a serious tone. 'No one from outside the hospital gets in this room without my knowledge.'

'Not to worry, Detective. I'll make sure of it.'

Carl was observing the footage from the CCTV. He saw Jack entering the hospital with his face directed away from the cameras, slipping past Reception and down the corridors with his shaggy hair shielding his face.

Craig walked in to join Carl in front of the CCTV. 'Any development on the mystery character?' he asked, adjusting his coat.

'Wish I could say yes. Whoever it was knew exactly where to go and how to cover his tracks. All we got is a shady character without a face.'

'Whoever it was, he'll be back', Craig replied.

Carl's phone began to ring in his coat pocket. Captain Walter was on the line. Carl swung his coat aside, hand on hip. 'Talk to me, Captain. What you got for us?'

'Get down to the station right away! It's urgent!' the captain growled.

'We got to go, now', Carl said to the nurse, putting away his phone. 'Thanks for your time, ma'am.

As the afternoon went on, Mr Sullivan, along with eight others, including his son, Paul, and Maxwell, stood waiting behind the funeral parlour, waiting on Montgomery Daniels to wheel the coffins out and load them into the back of the hearse. Mr Sullivan had alternative plans to move his drugs before dark. Finally, the back doors to the funeral parlour opened, and Montgomery wheeled the coffins out.

'It's about time! I don't like to be kept waiting, as you must know!' Mr Sullivan was impatient, sitting restless in his wheelchair.

'Sorry. I needed time', Daniels replied timidly.

'You two!' Sullivan said, pointing. 'Help him load the coffins!'

One by one, the men loaded the remaining two coffins into the hearse. The bodies and the drugs were finally ready for transit.

Mr Sullivan then briefed his men on the spot. 'Remember! No screw-ups this time! The cops are already vigilant with the mayor out of the way. Each of you will travel separate routes. You will then meet at the delivery rendezvous. Don't screw this up for me. Now get moving!' In pairs, the men boarded the hearses and set off on their separate routes out of the city.

Mr Sullivan ordered his son to reward Daniels's mammoth effort by placing a full bundle of cash into his hand. 'Here's your commission. Remember your place. Your effort will continue to be rewarded', Mr Sullivan said as Maxwell wheeled him into his car.

Carl and Craig reported to Captain Walter's office as ordered. Now they stood receiving the bad news.

'What do you mean the mayor is missing?!' Carl looked puzzled, unable to take in the news.

'The mayor haven't been seen for two days. Something isn't right, and you two are going to get to the bottom of it!'

'Don't you think we're jumping to conclusions here?' Craig wasn't too keen about what was going on and had other ideas.

'The Mayor never misses work, Detective! Last time I spoke with the mayor, he wanted all units clear of Western Avenue. Then this guy visited him before he went missing.' The captain laid a photo of Maxwell where the detectives could see it.

'Son of a bitch!' was Carl's immediate response.

'You know this guy?' the captain asked.

'He's one of Sullivan's associates', Carl answered.

'You bring this bastard in immediately! And have a look around Western Avenue, and see what you can find'. Captain Walter ordered.

Meanwhile, the hearses where travelling on their separate routes out of the city—one heading north the others pushing northwest and east in the form of a crow's foot. However, a challenging situation lies ahead. Checkpoints were established, and lines of vehicles heading in and out of the city were being examined by the police, with sniffer dogs being led up and down the lanes.

'Remember, keep your cool', the driver said to his partner beside him as they approached the officers.

'Afternoon, gentlemen. Where are you heading?' a male officer asked.

'Upstate. Body needs to be there by sundown', the driver replied.

'Oh yeah? Why's that?' The officer looked intrigued, placing his arm on the hearse's door.

'Gotta keep on schedule with a service up there', the driver answered.

'You'll be on your way soon as we have a walk-around', the officer replied, whistling for the dog handlers.

A female officer appeared with her sniffer dog-and started slowly around the hearse. The dog stood up on its hind legs, sniffed at the coffin, and then sat back, staring.

'You got something inside we should know about?' The male officer was now concerned.

'Nothing but the dead. Why?' the driver replied calmly.

'Mind if we take a look?' the female officer asked.

'You don't really want to disrespect the dead now, do you, Officer?' the driver replied politely.

The officers looked at each other for a moment. Then, shrugging, they decided to let the hearse through. 'All right, get it out of here!' the first officer called out and gave a friendly slap to the hearse's roof.

The driver had a safe passage. He and his partner were free to leave the city. In fact, all coffins on either route somehow managed to be granted a clean passage without drawing police attention.

Later that afternoon, Carl and Craig were out on Western Avenue, following up on the captain's orders. Their search led them to the old Carol City Car Park, and they drove in for a closer look. As they entered, Carl noticed tyre tracks along the ground floor concrete.

'Guess the captain wasn't wrong about his hunch.' Carl continued to trail the tyre tracks floor to floor.

'This could be anyone, Carl—kids, squatters, drifters. Anyone!'

'Let's hope you're right about that', Carl replied, looking doubtful.

At last they made it to the top floor and immediately had a gander. Within seconds, they found shell casings on the floor. Carl took a knee, and picking a few shells off the floor, he examined them and nodded grimly towards Craig. 'Does this answer your question? In fact, we got two different calibres here. Something tells me there was a standoff!'

'You might be on to something', Craig said, taking a wider look around and deciding on a more professional demeanour. 'Looks like they put on a heck of a show!'

'I'm guessing a deal gone wrong. Let's get out of here!' After having a wander around the top floor but finding nothing more to be done, Carl led them on the long hike back to the cruiser.

I was still at the mercy of the man who'd taken everything I cared about. Outside the basement, he banged the door savagely, eager to finish the job. The walls of the basement were my safe house. I was scrunched up in a cold solitary corner when a voice whispered.

'It's OK, Arthur, it's OK. You don't have to be afraid', the voice whispered softly, lifting the grim atmosphere.

The voice was soothing, filling me with hope, nostalgia, and complete joy. Recognizing the voice, I called out, 'Lauren! Is that you?!'

'No one here but me, Father', growled Rick, stabbing the door with his knife. 'You're running out of time. Show yourself!'

I was running short on time, delaying the inevitable, buying time that would soon transpire. I rose to my feet with my hands on my head, agonized and stymied by confusion; something had to give. That voice, those words, had awakened a sudden profound realization within me. Lauren wanted me to move on. I perceived it as a sign from above.

What is it going to be, Arthur? Die a coward or fight like a man? I asked myself, weighing the options.

It was time, time to do what I should have done from the beginning. I swallowed my pride, embraced the reality, and stood firm, suddenly filled with that courageous spark.

'You coming out, or am I coming to get you?' Rick sounded angry and impatient, banging the door once again.

I stared at the door, hearing his blade scrape the wood. His methods no longer cowered me; everything I'd feared was now behind me. I took aim and charged the door with high momentum, knocking it down with my shoulder. Rick took the brunt of the impact, crashing against the wall behind him as the door flew open. He was disorientated and confused, and his blade fell from his hand. I seized him by the throat and with my fist delivered a jaw-shattering blow. He fell and groped for his blade. Not today, not this time. I crushed his palm with a nearby photo frame, knocked down by the impact of the broken door.

Rick groaned in agony, too thrashed and battered to stand. 'Let's see what you're made of!,' he grunted, spitting blood. 'Go ahead! Finish me if you got the balls!'

I grabbed him by the throat and raised my arm to strike him down. Rage shrouded my mind, anger blinded my faith, and pain drowned my heart. Part of me pondered, *Who am I? What have I become?* I yelled in anger and woke at once from my coma, enraged, confused, paranoid, and in shock.

The female officer outside my door overheard the commotion and immediately alerted a doctor.

'Where am I? What's going on?' I yelled in my confusion. 'Why can't I see? I can't see!' I went on yelling, deeply paranoid.

'It's OK! It's OK, Father Brown! You're just wearing a bandage!' Dr. Ramrod reassured me with the help of the officer on duty.

'No … no! What's wrong with me? What's wrong with me?' Now I was fighting to escape from my bed.

'Calm down, Father Brown! Calm down. You're not going anywhere. We are here to help!' Dr. Ramrod shouted out to me as he held me firmly in the bed.

'Quickly! Get me a nurse in here!' Dr. Ramrod asked the officer urgently. 'This patient is completely disorientated and confused!'

The officer quickly retrieved a nurse. With help from the nurse and the officer, the doctor was finally able to restrain me-Then he injected me with a sedative drug that soon had me unconscious.

'Patient is sedated. He'll be fine, but give him some time to recover; he may still be in shock', said Doctor Ramrod as he left the room.

At the Sullivan mansion, late in the evening, Mr Sullivan sat quietly by himself in his wheelchair in the back garden, staring into the colourful roses. Rick showed up, looking quite pleased with himself.

'You asked to see me, sir?' he said, calm and confident.

'Do you know why I asked you here?' Mr Sullivan replied faintly.

'I have not the slightest idea as to why, sir', Rick answered.

'I'll tell you why … and it will be for the last time!' Mr Sullivan gave way to a spasm of, coughing, as he struggled with his dying lungs. 'Once again you have brought shame to me. My lawyer had to clean up your mess! You seem to have a problem keeping things quiet!'

'Sir?' Rick tried getting a word in, but Sullivan cut him off.

'Shut the fuck up! I'm talking here! I've had cops outside my home. You aroused the interest of a nosy and determined detective. I cannot allow that.' Sullivan was not pleased about Rick's selfish antics and would hold him to covering his tracks and silencing his loose ends.

'Detective Carl Brooks! Shut him down, and this time keep it quiet!' Mr Sullivan demanded.

'As you wish, sir! Consider it done!' Rick answered, happily obliged.

'You screw this up, and you won't have a leg to stand on!' He softened his tone. 'And when were you planning to tell me about the family murder? Don't think you can keep secrets from me! I know everything!'

'They got in the way, sir! I was just doing the right thing', Rick answered, but a bit hesitantly.

'And that you did!' Sullivan said, placing a cigar in his mouth.

'You should quit those things', Rick said with concern, yet he drew a cigar from his pocket and struck a light.

'Why? I'm already dead!' Sullivan replied proudly, unconcerned about his health.

Late that evening, in downtown Carol City, Lismore the capital, near a local corner store, Mr Donavon sat in the back of his SUV waiting, alone except for the driver behind the wheel. Two vehicles pulled up at the rear undetected, a car joined by a van. Four men in each vehicle sat quietly observing Mr Donavon.

Inside the shop, both of Mr Donavon's hired goons were collecting Mr Sullivan's commission from shopkeeper Pablo, a forty-four-year-old humble Dominican looking to protect his assets from outside competitors and crime rivals. Pablo paid in full, with cash in a briefcase, and the deed was done. Mr Donavon's men exited the shop, got into the SUV, and then headed into traffic. The car followed the SUV, leaving the van behind.

Two men exited the van and entered the shop, casually looking around like interested customers. Pablo knew it all too well; he'd dealt with false nonchalance one too many times. He pulled out his shotgun and chambered a cartridge. 'Start talking before I blow your motherfucking heads all over them wines!' He was loud, angry, and short on patience.

'Whoa! We don't want any trouble!'—'Just looking to buy some nuts, that's all!' The men innocently raised their hands high towards the ceiling.

'Don't bullshit me! I've seen your kind before!' Pablo replied, uneasy and trigger-happy.

'You really want to do this, right here?' one of the men asked calmly.

'You bet your sorry asses I do!' Pablo replied holding his shotgun ready to plug both men at short notice.

The shop door swung open, and two more men appeared. Pablo got distracted. Both men already in the shop took the opportunity to draw their guns. Now Pablo was outgunned and out of options.

'I think you know where this is going!' said one of the men holding Pablo at gunpoint.

Pablo lowered his shotgun. A blow to the head rendered him unconscious.

'Load him up with the others!' Two men dragged Pablo out the door and took him away.

CHAPTER 6

Heading down the street. Mr Donavon and his hired thugs took a left up the back street between Fourth and Third, Cedar Wood Street, as a shortcut to their next rendezvous. It was a bitter mistake. There was an obstruction waiting, a garbage truck reversed into the street ahead, cutting Mr Donavon's journey short.

The driver slowed down to a stop and honked his horn sharply in annoyance. Mr Donavon stuck his head out the window. 'Come on! Get this pile of junk out of here!' he shouted.

The car following closed in behind them. The four men exited with automatic weapons, and bystanders scattered at the sight of guns. Mr Donavon then saw the men closing in from the rear.

'It's an ambush! Get us out of here!' he shouted, hysterical.

The driver reversed at high speed. The men opened fire, blowing the tyres out. Another group of eight men climbed out of the garbage truck armed with automatic guns. They opened fire, tearing the vehicle apart and killing the driver.

Outnumbered and outflanked, Mr Donavon and his two men surrendered. Mr Donavon called out, 'Hold your fire! We're coming out! We're unarmed!'

The dozen men surrounded the SUV. Mr Donavon and his thugs were placed inside the car, at the rear, with black sacks covering their heads, and then taken away.

Later that evening, in a deserted factory in downtown Lismore, on the far side of Ivory Street, the sacks were removed from their heads. Mr Donavon and his men found themselves strapped to a set of chairs in the dark. Then the lights were switched on. Standing before them were the Logan brothers, Gosnell and Johnathon, smartly dressed as usual, surrounded by their gang of followers, a twelve-man total.

'What the fuck is this, the welcome party?' Mr Donavon shouted boastfully.

'On the contrary, Mr Donavon. This is your funeral—if you refuse to cooperate, that is', Gosnell replied with a snide look on his face.

'Listen, you lime! Whatever you're selling, I'm not buying!' Mr Donavon replied.

'Maybe I can persuade you!' Gosnell responded calmly, tilting his head at his brother.

Johnathon whistled. Raoul and two others came in dragging Pablo along, on his feet, badly beaten and limping. They sat Pablo down on a chair not too close to Mr Donavon and tied him to it.

'You working for this pair of scumbags?!' Mr Donavon asked Raoul, very surprised to see him.

'Let's just say the grass is greener on the other side, much greener!' Raoul replied proudly.

'You double-crossing snake! Mr Sullivan will have your head!' Mr Donavon shouted.

'By the time he catches on, he be long dead!' Raoul responded with a chuckle.

Johnathon interrupted. 'Enough small talk! Let's get on with it! As you can probably tell, Mr Donavon, we are taking over! This city is now ours! All of Mr Sullivan's clients will be ours!' He smiled right though this, pleased with himself.

'For those who refuse to cooperate, an example will be made!' Gosnell quickly emphasized, looking crossed at Pablo.

'What the hell you want from me?' Mr Donavon asked, at last growing concerned.

'Glad you asked!' Gosnell came straight to the point. 'Mr Sullivan possesses a journal, and we need it!'

'You'll never have his clients!' Mr Donavon protested.

'We were afraid you might say that!' Gosnell replied in mock disappointment.

With a nudge of the head, Gosnell signalled to Raoul, who opened the back of a van and brought out two large, fierce Rottweilers on a chain leash. The dogs barked and growled, wrestling the chains as Raoul fought to keep them at bay. Mr Donavon, his men, and Pablo were now greatly intimidated.

'What the hell you plan on doing?' Mr Donavon stuttered, secretly afraid.

'Last chance, Mr Donavon! These dogs are yet to be fed!' Gosnell forewarned his attack.

'I don't know! I don't know anything about the journal!' Mr Donavon cried out.

'Wrong answer!' Gosnell replied angrily.

Raoul released the dogs, setting them first on Pablo. The dogs instantly charged towards him, throat first and then his limbs, tearing Pablo apart beyond recognition. Then he whistled for them and with difficulty got them back on their chain.

'You and your men are next!' Gosnell was thirsty for blood, no matter the cost.

'Damn it, I'll talk!' Mr Donavon yelled. 'I'll talk. Just call the bloody dogs off!'

'Go ahead! We're listening. Talk!' Gosnell grunted.

'Mr Sullivan does have a journal, but the truth is, I don't know where he keeps it!' claimed Mr Donavon.

'Is this your idea of a joke?' Johnathon replied, frustrated, and short of patience. 'Somebody shoot this low life!'

'No, no! Wait. His son, Paul! He has the journal! He keeps the records, I swear!' Mr Donavon began to spill the beans on his colleagues.

'Thanks for your cooperation, Mr Donavon!' Johnathon replied with a sly look on his face. 'Consider this meeting adjourned!' He turned and walked away.

Everyone began to clear the warehouse, leaving Mr Donavon and his thugs still strapped to the chairs.

'Hey! What about us?' Mr Donavon called out in desperation.

'Oh, right! Thought maybe I'd forgotten something!' Johnathon turned around and addressed Raoul. 'Release the dogs!'

'You fucking piece of crap!' Mr Donavon shrieked as the dogs raced towards him. 'I've told you everything! You'll pay for this! You hear me?

You'll pay!' Then he roared in agony as the dogs tore him and his men apart. Johnathon and his brother watched as the dogs satisfied their ferocious appetites.

Back at the Carol City hospital, I had reawakened from my critical slumber and sat with my head wrapped in bandages peeping through a pair of spy holes. Dr. Ramrod was in the middle of his routine checks, doing his civic duty.

'Right, Father Brown. Everything seems perfectly in order. You should be ready for discharge in a couple days.' Dr. Ramrod delivered the good news with a few kind words.

'When will I see my face? How bad is it?' I asked the first of my burning questions.

Dr. Ramrod hesitated, as if trying hard not to spoil the good news with the bad.

'Tell it to me straight!' I insisted, though I was deeply worried.

Dr. Ramrod sighed. 'I'm afraid you be keeping the bandages on for a while, Father', he said with a sympathetic tone.

'What? What are you saying, Doctor?' Now I was terrified. 'I have a life to live. Hope got me out of that sleeping hell. This right here, Doctor!—this is hell!' I was furious and disappointed, in my frenzy knocking a flower vase to the floor.

'Please, Father! You have to understand we did all we could to repair some of the damage. You can still continue a normal life. This is just a minor setback!' Dr. Ramrod tried to reassure me, but his words weren't enough to comfort my disturbed emotions.

'You call this normal?' I yelled some more, thrashing in the bed.

'Father Brown, please calm down! You must understand there's risk involved in removing the bandages!'

Full of rage and confusion. I snatched Dr. Ramrod by the neck, holding him against the wall. 'Explain, Doctor!' I growled.

'Father Brown, think about what you're doing!'

'I am thinking!' I was shouting in his face, refusing to calm down.

'You're confused and paranoid! Don't do anything crazy!' he pleaded as he struggled to peel my fingers from his neck.

'I'm already insane, doctor!! Thanks to the monster that did this! Now explain!'

The female officer on watch had already been discharged from her duties. Fortunately for Dr. Ramrod, a female nurse on duty overheard the commotion and appeared in the room. 'Sir! You must calm down! We are here to help!' she said as she grabbed my wrists, trying to release Dr. Ramrod's neck from my grip.

'No!! I said explain!! Tell me why?!' I continued to yell, refusing to let go.

By a stroke of luck, just then, Detective Carl Brooks entered the room. 'What the hell is going on here?' He was clearly shocked at the scene he had stumbled into. He immediately reacted, helping the nurse calm the situation. Within seconds I was off Dr. Ramrod and sitting peacefully on the bed. Brooks had come outside of duty, seeking clarity on his case.

'Father Brown, I'm Detective Carl Brooks. My partner and I are working on your case.'

'So you haven't found the man that is responsible? Why am I not surprised, Detective?' I turned my back, giving him the cold shoulder.

'Father Brown, with all due respect, we are handling the case as effectively as we can. It's not exactly easy bouncing between two cases!' Carl replied defensively, trying to explain his situation.

'What the hell is the city paying you for? This man is out there doing God knows what! I'd appreciate it if you do your job and find him, now!'

'I'd appreciate it if you lower your tone, please!' Carl replied as professionally as possible, trying to carry on a peaceful conversation.

Craig walked in with some urgency and flashed his badge to introduce himself. 'I'm detective Bollington. Sorry I'm late. Had to make an important call.' Then he blended into the background, standing idle.

His voice was familiar. I wasn't sure why. I looked at him with an immediate feeling of distrust.

'Do me a favour and bring the man responsible to justice! It's all I'm asking!' I said to the carefree Detective Bollington, who seemed disinclined to assist with my troubles.

'We'll do that as soon as we can get you to ID the suspect. It's our only chance of bringing him down.' Carl was highly agitated, eager to get his man at any cost.

'My partner is right, it's your call', Craig said dismissively.

'Anything to see this man rot behind bars!' I replied, returning to my bed and taking a seat.

'Don't worry, Father Brown. You'll get the justice you deserve.' Bollington's attempt at a sincere smile was a failure. 'We'll see you again soon. Think about your statement while you recover.'

'Get some rest, Father. We'll be in touch', Brooks said and saw himself out the door, leaving me to contemplate my life-changing affair.

Not long after they left, I began to ponder the voices I heard. Actually they were whispers, some of which provided me with hope, others with courage. The voices got louder … Lauren, Father Franklin, Jack, and then another that remained anonymously obscure. That one voice kept on repeating itself: 'Stay dead! Let go!' The voice echoed in my head like church bells.

I lay down to ease the piercing headache brought on by the voices in my head whilst I tried making sense of this new mystery.

'Who the hell are you? Who?' I whispered to myself in agony, clenching my fists, gripping the sheets, trying to subdue the headache that hammered my mind endlessly.

Late that night, Craig Bollington walked into the study of Mr Sullivan's mansion, off duty and casual. Rick, Maxwell, Mr Sullivan himself, and four other employees were waiting, all present and accounted for, in the midst of more foul scheming.

'You're late, Detective!' Mr Sullivan said faintly, hanging on to his oxygen mask.

'My apologies, sir. Had an urgent matter to attend to', Craig replied.

'All I keep hearing is apologies! Results is what I'm after!' Mr Sullivan replied, very displeased. 'What was so urgent that you kept me waiting?'

'I'm afraid I've got some bad news, sir', Craig answered, avoiding eye contact.

'Look me in the eyes and tell me, you worthless shit!' Mr Sullivan was plainly angry and impatient.

'Rick here didn't finish the job like he thought he did!' Craig replied.

'What the fuck is this?' Rick was surprised and confused.

'Shut the hell up! Let the detective speak!' Mr Sullivan insisted on hearing it all.

'The priest is alive. You fucked up, Rick.' Craig let the cat out of the bag.

'What the hell you mean, he's alive?!' Rick asked. 'I watched him die—right before my eyes!'

'Obviously you failed to finish the job', Mr Sullivan said. 'Another screw-up. Why am I not surprised?'

'And you know this how?' Rick asked Craig. He wanted answers, had honest doubts.

Craig stuck his hands in his pockets and began to pace about the room, explaining. He was in his element. 'I wasn't aware he was your victim at the beginning of the my investigation. My partner's persistent instincts led us to you. and that's when it all added up.'

'Why now, Detective? Why tell us now?' Mr Sullivan demanded.

'Trust me, Mr Sullivan, it wasn't that easy. Not with my partner sniffing around!'

'Then I suggest you take care of your partner before it's too late.' Even when Mr Sullivan was coughing his lungs up, he could be very persuasive. Then he turned on Rick. 'As for you, I suggest you finish what you started!'

Early the next morning, I was awakened by the face of the man who took everything I've lived for. I fled the dream shaken and paranoid.

'Looks like a nightmare!' Father Franklin sat by my side reading the daily newspaper.

'How long have you been sitting here?' I asked, trying to catch my breath.

'Long enough to watch you toss and turn', Father Franklin said.

He cleared his throat and laid the folded newspaper down at my bedside, about to speak. 'God has been good to you, my friend. You've been given a second chance at life.'

'Indeed he has, Father', I replied sadly.

'You don't seem too happy about it. Is something bothering you, my friend?!' Father Franklin became worried.

'Believe me, I am. I'll be a lot happier once the man responsible is locked away for good', I replied, glimpsing the headline on the paper next to me: LOCAL PRIEST AND FAMILY MURDERED?

Father Franklin noticed that I'd observed the headline, and he smiled. 'The entire town mourned your loss. Have faith, my friend. It will all work out!'

'Faith seems to be the only thing I've got left. Let's hope I don't lose that too.' This lame comeback was all I had to offer.

The news broadcast from the CCNN (Carol City News Network) interrupted our conversation. Anchor Daisy Whitmore was about to read the daily report and caught in our attention.

'It's been days since the city heard from the mayor. The mayor reportedly went missing not long after police recovered the body of a male security officer in the elevator shaft inside City Hall. Questions are being raised about the mayor's recent absence and whether or not the body recovered is somehow linked to his disappearance. We're told that Police Captain Chris Walter is about to make a statement.'

The news switched to a live feed from outside the CCPD. As Captain Walter trotted down the stairs from the police department entrance, a female news correspondent in the crowd asked, 'Captain Walter, is there any news on the mayor? Is the mayor alive?'

'The mayor is alive; that's all the people need to know!' he replied reassuringly as he parted the audience below the stairs, heading towards his cruiser at the sidewalk. He pulled away without answering any further questions.

'There you have it. According to the police, the mayor is alive!' the correspondent declared. 'Back to you in the studio, Daisy!'

Daisy Whitmore then turned to another report. 'In other news, small-time drug dealer Aron Carter was released from jail earlier today, after the jury voted to acquit him.'

I switched off the television and tossed the remote onto the bed angrily. 'Is this what I've awakened to? Has this city gone mad?' The news report had disappointed me about the city's judiciary system.

Dr. Ramrod entered the room in the middle of my rant. He had come to change my head bandage and not a moment too soon. I was afraid of my own face; for the first time in a long time I was about see myself in a different light.

Father Franklin excused himself. 'I'll see you soon, Arthur. Take care of yourself, and God be with you.'

'I'll try, Father', I replied with a low, sad hum as I seated myself on the bed.

I sat down and anxiously waited for Dr. Ramrod to start the process of removing my bandage. As he prepared to snip through the bandage, I became uneasy. 'It's OK, Father Brown. You don't have to look at your face. I understand how hard this may be for you'. Dr. Ramrod sounded sympathetic, as if he wanted to minimize my pain.

I sighed a sign of discomfort. 'I … I'll take my chance, Doctor.'

Dr. Ramrod began peeling the bandages away, working slowly from the back of my head towards my face. It was a dramatic moment, and I panicked, stalling the procedure. 'Wait! Wait, Doctor! I … I changed my mind!'

'It's OK, Father, It has to be done. You don't have to look; take your time. But we do have to change this dressing.'

'Thanks for understanding, Doctor.' I was relieved to delay the inevitable.

Carefully, Dr. Ramrod went on to remove the old bandages from my head. Then he polished my mangled face with special ointment from the trolley at my bedside. 'This will help aid the healing process.' Then he carefully applied a fresh dressing.

The trauma was now over, finally. I stood up and looked at my face in the mirror, gently touching and feeling the indents of the scars through the bandage. I felt sick, angry, disgusted, and afraid of what I could not see there.

'It will take some getting used to when you're ready', said Dr. Ramrod, offering some comfort. 'Take your time, Father Brown. Don't let this change hinder your progress.' Then he left me to ponder a mammoth decision.

Angry, with a brick like stomach, and a river of pain behind my concealed emotions, I flipped the bed, breaking a few unimportant items lying around the room. Then I sat down in the corner at my bedside, shedding unseen tears.

The Logan brothers sat before the television in the living room of their mansion. They had just witnessed the news report, learning of the mayor's disappearance, and were ready to exploit the opportunity.

'So! The mayor has gone under the radar. Interesting!' Gosnell mused, rubbing his chin suspiciously.

'You know what this means, don't you?' Johnathon asked his older brother.

'I do indeed, my brother. It's time we make an impact. Let's start with something a bit explosive … if you know what I mean', Gosnell replied. He was on his feet, hands clasped behind his back, wandering the living space thoughtfully.

'I know exactly what you mean. The idea is rather malicious … I like it!' Johnathon replied, taking a gentle sip from a wine glass set at arm's length.

Early afternoon, at the Carol City Boneyard, so-called, Mr Sullivan sat in the back of his limousine, accompanied by his son, Paul, and Maxwell. With him were two SUVs stocked with eight men, waiting. The three hearses appeared, and the drivers got out. Maxwell carefully assisted Mr Sullivan from the limousine with his walking stick as they all gathered around the hearses.

'It's done, sir! The exchange was successful', one of the drivers reported.

'Good! I trust that the money is where it should be?!' Mr Sullivan asked.

'All within our catered guests!' the driver answered and opened the backs of the hearses. There, inside the coffins, were the mayor and the officers, still neatly dressed, this time stuffed with millions of cash inside their sewn bodies.

'Excellent! All that's lacking is my royalties!' Mr Sullivan said. 'Mr Donavon is testing my patience! He should be here by now.'

Maxwell calmly assured him that all was well.

'Paul? Find him now!' Mr Sullivan ordered.

Without a word. Paul rounded up a few of the men and took off in an SUV.

'What shall we do with the bodies, sir?' a driver asked.

'After the money is extracted, dump the bodies!' Mr Sullivan replied, as he was wheeled away into the limousine.

Outside Carol City General Hospital that afternoon, a car came to a stop just outside the visitors' car park. Rick Lawson, there by himself, stepped out of the car and entered the hospital. Inside, he managed to slip past a few doctors and the main reception area. He carefully navigated the hallways towards my ward. He then cautiously approached the door to my room and let himself in.

Rick played it safe, blocking the door with a nearby chair, checking around the room for any unwanted guests, and then focusing his attention towards the bed before him.

'So here we are once again, you and I', he said, quietly approaching my bed. 'This time, Father, it will be quick and simple … I promise.' He then attached a suppressor to his 9mm pistol, ready to finish the job.

'I'm surprised you made it this far. You should have stayed dead.' He raised the gun. Then he pulled back the sheet and saw a pistol was already waiting to greet him. He was stunned, disappointed with what he had found waiting under my sheets.

Carl stepped in from the bathroom, where he was waiting in cover, expecting Rick to return to finish the job.

'You? … How?' Rick asked, fumbling for words.

'It doesn't matter. Drop the weapon and place your hands on your head!' Carl replied with a straight look on his face.

'I'm afraid I can't do that!' Rick replied, holding his loaded pistol steady.

A team of four officers already on standby stormed through the door, forcing their way into the room and distracting Rick's attention. Carl immediately seized his firearm and tackled him to the ground, with the help of the supporting officers, Then he slapped on the cuffs and began reciting the Miranda rights. 'You have the right to remain silent, asshole! Anything you do or say will be held you in a court of law!'

'You're wasting your time. You're looking at a free man!' Rick cried out as the officers escorted him out of the hospital.

'Tell it to the judge!' Carl shouted down the hallway whilst the patients and staff looked on in curiosity.

'How did you know he'd show up?' a male officer asked, standing at Carl's side, hands on his proudly tilted hips.

'Just an anonymous tip', Carl replied with an air of satisfaction.

Late the previous night, I had lain awake, eyes closed, with the sound of the unknown voice whispering in my head. After my last encounter with the detectives, my immediate distrust for detective Craig cradled me anxiously, plaguing my vulnerable mind. Somehow I knew his voice, and I was bent on remembering those profound words that haunted my mind.

My eyes flicked wide open, and I sprang from my bed as quickly as the thought came. The voice suddenly became clear, and I remembered Detective Craig! I called for help. 'Nurse? Nurse?'

The nurse on duty came as soon as she heard my loud bellow. 'Is everything OK, Father Brown?'

'Get me Detective Carl Brooks on the phone!' I demanded. 'This is his card. Hurry! It's important!' I said, passing Carl's contact card on to the nurse.

'It's late, Father Brown. You should get some rest. I'm sure it can wait', said the nurse, trying to tuck me back into bed.

'Get the detective on the phone, now!' I wasn't taking no for an answer. 'This is important! Do it now!' I yelled, holding on to the nurse's arms like a deranged psychopath.

'I'll do it! Just let go, please!' she said. Scared and shaken, she left and soon returned with a phone.

'Thank you! Thank you!' I said, taking the phone and dialling the detective's number.

That night at Detective Brooks's home, a nice house just outside the capital on Highwood Boulevard. Carl was in bed sleeping with his wife, Miranda, a tall, slender, dark-haired college professor in her early forties. His bedside phone began ringing. He woke, looked at the phone, sat up bare-assed, and answered the call. 'This better be good', he said, rubbing his weary eyes.

'Listen, Detective! I'm going to need your help!' By now I was wandering around the room.

'With all due respect, Father Brown, it's rather late', Carl said quietly, trying not to wake his wife.

'Who are you talking to?' Miranda asked, awakened by the conversation.

'It's work, honey. Go back to sleep', Carl answered as she snuggled back under his arm.

'You need to hear me right now, Detective! Your partner is dirty! You hear me? Dirty!' I stressed, anxiously rubbing my head.

'Whoa! Whoa! Did I hear you correctly?' Carl replied, astonished by my remark.

'Yes, you did, Detective! You need to be careful!'

'That's a huge accusation right there, Father. What makes you think my partner is dirty?' Carl asked, climbing out of bed and taking the call outside his bedroom.

'I think he knows the man that murdered my family. Or worse, he may be involved on the wrong side of the law!'

'You know what I think, Father? I think you need to get some rest. Good night!' he said, about to end the call and clearly not believing a word.

'No! Detective! Do not do this to me. You need to listen! They will come for me!' I pleaded hopelessly.

'Good night, Father Brown!'

'Darn it, Detective!' I said and groaned in disappointment.

Carl hung up and then stood in his hallway with a distant look on his face. He began to ponder my claim towards his partner, reassessing my remark with careful thoughts before making a decision.

In my ward, just after Rick was taken away by the cops, Carl walked in to break the good news, with his coat over his arm and a satisfied look on his face.

'Looks like you were right, Father Brown. We got the bastard! We got him good', he said, pleased with himself.

'What about your partner?!' I asked warily.

'Don't worry about it. I'll be keeping a close eye on him', Carl answered reassuringly.

'You do just that. Thanks for your help', I replied, grateful but somehow doubtful about what lay ahead.

'Just doing my job, Father Brown!' Carl replied as he left the room.

Later that day-afternoon, at the CCPD, Rick was breathing down the phone, making use of his call to try to wangle himself a get-out-of-jail card.

'You get me out of here! You understand me?' he said to his lawyer over the phone.

'It's not looking good, Rick', his lawyer replied, a stern, average-looking dark-haired male in his mid-forties, by the name of Robert Thomas, sitting in his office behind a fancy oak desk decorated with his achievements. 'You'll be lucky if you survive this trial. Lucky for you, I'm one heck of a lawyer!' Robert boasted.

'Don't forget, I'm paying you a lot of money. You better hope this case swings our way!' Rick threatened, hanging up the phone-

Carl was at his desk, swamped in paperwork, scratching his head. Craig walked in, looking puzzled about something. He sat down eagerly at the desk facing Carl, arms out fingers interlocking, staring at Carl mysteriously until he had his attention.

Carl looked at him, annoyed. 'You got something on your mind, Detective?'

'Yeah! Yeah, I do!' Craig replied. He seemed irritated.

'Go on, then. Let's hear what's on your mind!' Carl was in a foul mood. 'Not often you got something to say, Craig. This must be burning on your mind! Go on!' Carl became very intrigued about Craig's new-found interest.

'I was hoping to be there when we caught this guy', Craig said, leaning back into his seat. 'We're supposed to be partners! What the hell, Carl! Making an arrest without me is bad enough, but leaving me in the dark? I'm very disappointed!' Craig pulled a hand through his hair.

Carl slammed his palms against the desk and sprang to his feet. 'Listen here! I did what I had to do to bring that bastard in! Maybe you should show some enthusiasm! How about that?!' he growled angrily.

Everyone sat around, staring, whispering to each other, amused by the commotion.

Disturbed by the noise, Captain Walter came charging from his office. 'What the hell is going on here? What's all this about? Everyone, get back to work!' He turned to Carl and Craig. 'You two lovebirds, get out of here! Take a walk! Cool down!'

'Everything is okay, Captain! ... Just a little misunderstanding, that's all', Carl responded calmly.

'Get your asses out of here! Now! I mean it!' Captain Walter demanded. Carl and Craig grabbed their coats and left the room.

Beside the indoor pool at Mr Sullivan's mansion later that day, Sullivan's carer was applying lotion to his wrinkled body as he lay wearily face down on a pool chair, in his shorts, with his oxygen at arm's length. Paul walked in.

'This better be good', Mr Sullivan groaned.

'I'm afraid it's not. Mr Donavon is nowhere to be found!' Paul said.

'What? Where the fuck is that worthless piece of crap with my money?' Mr Sullivan growled angrily, rolling over onto his back and letting his carer seat him upright.

Paul laid out the situation. 'We searched his apartment, his beach house, his condo. Nothing! He's gone. Not even Maxwell could find him!'

Maxwell walked in and added, 'Your son is right, sir. Mr Donavon is nowhere to be found!'

'I swear, if that no good scumbag crosses me, he's dead!' Mr Sullivan shouted angrily.

'That's not all, sir', Maxwell said.

'What other dreadful news you got, anyway?' Mr Sullivan asked warily.

'It's Rick. He's been arrested', Maxwell said.

'He's the least of our problems', Mr Sullivan replied dismissively. 'His lawyer will handle it! Dig around my clients! See if they know anything about my royalties and Mr Donavon's whereabouts!' Mr Sullivan ordered, leaving his son and Maxwell to handle his matters.

That day at the Carol City seafront, on the western side of the capital city, Lismore, all was quiet. The breeze was moderate, and the seagulls surfed the air currents. Carl and Craig stood in front of their cruiser, parked on the edge of the seafront overlooking the view.

Their coats danced in the breeze. A silent and uncomfortable atmosphere hung between the two. Neither spoke as they stood around, leaning against the bonnet of their cruiser with a dim expression on their faces.

Craig was beginning to suspect Carl of knowing his secrets.

Carl began to wonder how right I was about his partner, still trying hard to deny the deadly truth. He stood and began pacing around in close range, seemingly puzzled.

Craig, unable to bear the tension, decided to speak. 'Go on, Carl. What's on your mind?'

'You really want to know what's on my mind?' Carl asked grimly.

'Yeah, I do! Seems personal', Craig replied, assuming the obvious.

'Personal, huh? Is that what you call it?' Carl responded, staring out to sea with his back turned.

'Isn't that what it is? Or am I mistaken?' Craig asked, trying to draw his partner out.

'No, Craig, you're not mistaken!' Craig said, not hiding his annoyance. 'You're quite right!' He turned and gave Craig a cross look.

'So enlighten me', Craig replied, with an absurd look on his face.

'How about you tell me what you know about Rick?' Carl threw the burning question onto the table.

Craig chose to deny the truth, pretending to be oblivious. 'I don't know what you're talking about, Carl. I know only as much as you do. You're the expert, and I'm the rookie! Remember?'

'I'm the expert, all right. You hit that mark!' Carl said, again staring into the sea trying to making sense of things.

'What made you ask? You think I'm dirty? Do you, Carl?'

'No one knew Father Brown was alive', Carl said. 'Someone must have tipped his killer off!'

'That's a shame. Someone couldn't keep it shut', Craig replied, smirking behind his partner's back.

Carl got straight to the point, tough and direct as he was. 'Cut the crap Craig! How much they paying you? Your whole attitude stinks from the get-go! Your lack of interest, your disappearing acts, the secret phone calls!'

Craig began shouting after realizing his partner was right. 'Don't you talk down to me, Carl! Don't you dare! You have no idea! You don't have a clue what this is about!'

'Why don't you tell me all about it, *partner?*' Carl shouted back in anger.

'This is bigger than me and you, Carl! You should quit while you're ahead!'

'I'm not quitting till these scumbags are off the streets! I've got a job to do, and so do you. At least, that's what I thought!' Carl turned away with disappointment.

'If that's how you feel, Carl, I'm afraid I'm going to have to stop you', Craig said, drawing his pistol from its holster.

'Put the gun down! It doesn't have to be this way', Carl said, feeling for his own gun.

'You brought this on! You dug too deep!' Craig looked ready to pull the trigger.

'Only doing my job, Craig! Just doing my job!' Carl pleaded, trying to talk Craig down.

'Sorry, Carl! No hard feelings!' Craig replied.

Out of options, with no cover and nowhere to go except into the sea. Carl tried for his pistol. Craig, with the advantage, pulled the trigger four times, aiming for Carl's chest. Carl went tumbling over the edge into the sea.

Craig ran towards the edge of the seafront to witness the fall. Carl was gone, nowhere to be seen. He hurried back to the cruiser and took off in a hurry.

Along the way, speeding through the city, Craig made a call. 'It's done! I've handled it like you asked!' Craig fought down his panic as he tore through the capital.

'Good. That's one less problem to worry about!' Mr Sullivan replied from the comfort of his limousine and hung up. His son Paul was driving him and Maxwell to Pablo's corner shop, where they pulled up outside. The street appeared to be quiet with a few vendors lazing on the sidewalk, trying to lure potential customers with slogans and gimmicks.

Mr Sullivan rolled his window down to have a look at the shop before implementing a decision. A male street vendor, not yet thirty years of age, shaggy-looking, with a beanie and a long coat. He displayed a set of watches hanging inside his coat, hoping for a sale.

'Holy shit! Dig the ride!' he shouted, poking his head into the rear window. 'Darn, Gramps! You must be loaded! How about helping a brother out?' he asked boldly.

'Get the fuck away from the vehicle before I blow your fucking head off!' Mr Sullivan's tone was low but steely.

'Whoa! Whoa, Gramps! Take it easy!' the vendor replied, backing to the sidewalk.

Maxwell and Paul exited the vehicle and approached the shop doors. Finding the entrance locked, they headed towards the rear and were surprised to find it hanging open. The shop was trashed, but all seemed quiet inside. The two entered cautiously, pistols in hand.

Paul looked around carefully at every angle. 'Looks like Pablo had some company.'

'He did, al. right. The question is, who?'

They made their way into Pablo's office. The place was in shambles, but still they looked around and found a locker standing tall in one corner.

'This looks like something worth checking out!' Paul was curious as ever.

They pried open the locker, and two dead bodies came tumbling out, falling against each other, mauled and mangled almost beyond recognition.

'Whoa! What the fuck happened here?' Paul shouted. 'Is that Mr D? What the fuck is going on?' He stood clear of the corpses, shaken and confused.

'That's Mr Donavon, all right. This must be Pablo'. Maxwell was unfazed by the horror at their feet.

'What happened? Who could have done this?!' Paul asked worriedly.

'Not just who but what', Maxwell replied suspiciously, looking closely at the marks on the bodies. 'Looks like someone fed them to the dogs.'

'Fuck this shit! We got to find the fuckers that did this!' Paul was irate, anxious, restless and pacing around the office.

'Not to worry. We will', Maxwell replied with conviction.

'Hold on! What's that in his pocket?!' Something had caught Paul's eye as he paced about anxiously. It looked like the corner of a note hanging from Mr Donavon's shirt pocket. Maxwell drew it out. With traces of blood here and there about the note, he read it and looked up at Paul with concern.

Outside, they climbed back into the vehicle quietly. Maxwell had a straight face, calm as ever, but Paul took the wheel with an angry expression, which drew his father's attention.

'What the fuck happened in there? Start talking!' Mr Sullivan demanded.

'Trust me, Dad! You don't want to know!' Paul replied in frustration.

'Someone better start talking! My money is at stake!' Mr Sullivan went on, more angrily.

Maxwell calmly broke the news. 'They're dead, sir. Both of them.'

'What?! How did this happen?' Mr Sullivan grunted furiously.

'Not sure, sir. I think someone fed them to the dogs. We found their bodies crammed into a locker; they may have had some unwanted guests.' Maxwell carefully explained what he thought must have happened. Then he said, 'We found this', and handed the note to Mr Sullivan.

Mr Sullivan opened the note and the words written on the bloody piece of paper. His face immediately twisted in anger, and he tossed the note out the window. 'Let's go. We got business to take care of', he said quietly with a mean-looking expression.

No questions asked, Paul fired up the engine and pulled away. Behind, on the street next to the kerb, the note lay open on top of a manhole cover. It read: "Everything you have is now ours."

CHAPTER 7

At the Carol City seafront, late that afternoon, bathed in sweeping blue lights, gold badges, uniforms, and local news crews stood gathered around the overlook. Detective Carl, barely conscious, was being loaded on a stretcher into the back of an ambulance by the paramedics with wounds to his neck and right arm and two bullets lodged in his chest.

'Don't worry, Detective. You're going to be all right', said the female paramedic in the back of the ambulance, trying to reassure him.

'He's lucky to be alive', another medic remarked after tearing Carl's shirt open and examining his wounds. 'The bullets seem to have missed his vital organs.'

'OK, let's get him out of here!' the female medic shouted at the driver.

A male officer on scene was about to question a few young stoners who had been present at the scene. The male officer, Tom Brussel, in his late thirties, with dark hair, of average height, saw the ambulance off and then approached the group of kids. 'You kids mind telling me what you saw here today?' he asked, tapping his pen against his notepad.

'Yeah, man! No problem! Shane here saw it all!' replied a young male stoner named Ravie, high off his head.

'Which one of you stoneheads is Shane?' Officer Brussel asked.

'Hey, man! That be me! I saw the whole thing, man!' Shane answered. He was a scruffy adolescent with a backpack.

'Go on then, I'm listening.' Officer Brussel flipped his pad open, anxiously waiting for the young stoner to pull himself together.

'Yow, check it! Me and my crew was just chilling to some tunes when I spotted the body on the rocks down there', Shane told the officer.

'What time was this?' Officer Brussel asked, taking notes.

'That was about an hour ago, man! Before you boys in blues showed up', Shane answered with a drowsy tone, wasted and as high as a skylark.

'What did you see? Think carefully now!' Officer Brussel posed a few more questions.

'Like I said, man! I saw the body washed up between the rocks below! I was like, *Hey, dudes! Is that a body?* Ravie here was like, *Yeah, man! I think it is! What do we do?* I was like, *Man, we got to check this shit out!* We ran down the seafront and saw the jacked-up cop!'

Shane's friend Ravie interjected, 'Yeah, man, that shit was fucked up!'

'Ha-ha ... yeah, it was! Someone fucked him up bad!' Shane said, stupidly making light of the incident.

'You think this is funny!!' Officer Brussel shouted, grabbing Shane by the collar.

'Hey, man, I'm sorry! Like, chill the heck out, man!' Shane grunted, weaselling his collar from the officer's grasp.

'You're lucky I'm in a good mood! Now, is there anything important you might want to tell me?'

'No, man! After all that shit, you guys showed up!' Shane answered.

'Get the hell out of here! I'm wasting my time!' Officer Brussel said, dismissing the young stoners.

At the hospital Carl was rushed along the hall on a stretcher towards the emergency room for treatment. Awake and in bad shape, Carl couldn't help hearing the voice of Captain Walter hurrying along his side with the medics.

'Carl, what the heck happened? Who did this? Where the hell is Craig?!' Captain Walter yelled, chasing along the stretcher.

'Sir, the patient is in no condition to talk'. a female medic said. 'We have to get him to the emergency room immediately. He's lost a lot of blood!'

'Craig', Carl mumbled. 'Find Craig.'

'Craig? What are you saying?' Captain Walter asked, puzzled and confused. 'Is he responsible! Tell me, Detective!' Captain Walter was frightened and worried.

'You got to leave, sir!' said a doctor, blocking him from the emergency room door. 'We have to remove the bullets and stop the bleeding!'

What the heck happened? Captain Walter pondered to himself outside the doors. Back in his cruiser, he picked up his radio and issued an all-points bulletin (APB) in an effort to find Craig.

Next day, in the heart of Carol City's capital, Lismore, it was mid-morning at a local butcher's market, trading under the name Butchers Kingdom. It was owned by a man by the name of Maurice Ragan, forty four years old, slightly grey, of average height, making an honest living and paying his dues. Maurice was out front at his counter, chopping slabs of beef, when the Logan brothers entered his establishment accompanied by two tough guys, both casually dressed and clean-shaven with goatees.

'Not interested!' Straight, blunt words from Maurice as he kept on chopping his meat.

'Is that what you tell all your customers?' asked Gosnell in a reasonable tone.

'Didn't you hear me? I'm not interested!' Maurice grunted as he slammed his blade into the meat.

It was clear Maurice knew their intentions and wasn't about to give in to their demands. Johnathon nudged his head, and the two tough guys snatched Maurice from his chopping board, leaving his butcher knife behind.

'What the hell you want from me? You have no business here!' Maurice yelled as the men restrained him face down on his chopping board.

'On the contrary, Maurice. We do have business here!' Gosnell replied pompously.

'Take him around back, out of sight!' Johnathon snarled.

The two men wrestled with Maurice, dragging him to the back of his shop into his office, holding him face down on his desk next to a meat cutter, ready to make a mess of things.

Gosnell took a book from his coat. 'Do you know what this is, Maurice?' he asked with a smirk.

'Fuck you, asshole! You're not going to break me!' Maurice yelled adamantly.

'If I were you, I'd watch my tongue', said Johnathon, nosing around the office.

'This is Mr Sullivan's dear journal!' Gosnell said, flipping the pages. 'His clients, his contacts, his commissions … his entire life's work, if you ask me!' Gosnell looked very impressed with the power he held.

'If it's money you're after! You're not going to get it!' said Maurice.

Gosnell laughs. 'Not money! We want you, Maurice … to pledge your loyalty to us!' Gosnell replied, leaning close into Maurice's face.

'Keep paying your dues, and we keep you in business, simple!' Gosnell said, aimlessly scanning the room.

'What if I don't?!' Maurice replied in a resentful manner.

The Logan brothers did not take too kindly to Maurice's response. It wasn't quite what they hoped for on such short notice on a busy schedule, chasing Mr Sullivan's clients.

'If you don't, then I'm going to have to do something rather drastic!' Gosnell replied, whistling an order to his tough guys.

With joint effort, the men forced Maurice's right hand under the meat slicer and chopped it clean off.

Maurice was in agony as his blood spilled about his office. 'You bastards!! Who do you think you are?' Maurice yelled as the two men held him securely.

'Oh, Maurice, it's not so bad. You can always hire an apprentice', Johnathon said in an offhand tone, mocking Maurice despite the blood works.

'Where's our manners?' Gosnell said, draping his arm over Maurice's shoulder. 'We got so carried away, we forgot to introduce ourselves. We are the Logan brothers. That's all you need to know. Now, have we made ourselves clear? Are you on board?' Gosnell asked, emphasizing his point by applying pressure to the stump of Maurice's missing hand with his finger dug into his wound.

'Yes! Yes! I understand!' Maurice answered, unable to bear the agony and ready to give in to the Logans' demands.

'Good. We be seeing you again soon', Gosnell assured Maurice, leaving him and his shop behind, missing hand and all.

The Logan brothers got into their vehicle. The tough guys opened their doors and seated themselves up front. One them decided to ask an ominous question. 'What you want to do about the rest of the clients who refuse to comply?'

'Let's send them a special treat', said Gosnell. 'Make sure it's done professionally.'

Later that morning, in downtown Carol City, Lismore, Mr O'Brien's was just opening up the Fish Market on 76 Street Maple Road for business. He was one of the city's finest fishmongers, fifty years old, lean and mildly grey. His male colleague, Billy Mason, was forty-four, short and stocky, with a beard. Just as O'Brien inserted and turned his key into the lock, there was a loud *BANG!* A bomb exploded, destroying the shop and killing both men. A few local street vendors were caught in the blast along with a few innocent commuters.

It was a busy morning at Phil's Barber Shop, 54 Billboard Street on Third Avenue. Barbers were giving haircuts and shaves whilst taking in a game on the local television network.

The door opened, and a mail man entered. 'Parcel for Phil Jenkins!' he called aloud.

'Hey, yow? Big Philly? You got mail!' a barber, Danny Howard, shoutedwith his Caribbean accent to draw Phil from the employer's office.

Phil Jenkins, a plump tall man of Afro-Caribbean descent, came from the back room, received the parcel, and placed it on an empty seat next to Danny.

'Pop it open, Phil!' Danny urged him. 'Might be those new clippers!'

'Yeah, man. You could be right', Phil replied, picking up the parcel. He peeled into the parcel, and *BANG!* It exploded, tearing the shop apart and taking everyone with it. Another business at the mercy of the Logan Brothers and their deadly intent.

The Renaissance Restaurant was an outstanding restaurant in the heart of Carol City, Lismore, owned by a humble man by the name Robert Pattinson, in his late forties, slim with short hair and of average height. Robert and his head chef had just turned up to prepare the night's menu. They pulled in and parked at the rear of the restaurant.

They exited the car casually, and Head Chef Rowe Sandler, about thirty-six years of age, tall and lanky, with short hair, waited for Robert to unlock the back door to the kitchen. As they entered,

Rowe took a pack of cigarettes from his pocket. 'Hey, got a light?' he called to Robert.

'Hold on, let me reset the alarm', Robert replied. He smelled something—a very unpleasant smell, which led him to the kitchen where he quickly discovered the gas cocks on the ovens were wide open. Terrified at what he saw, Robert desperately called out to his chef, 'Rowe? No!'

It was too late. Rowe had his lighter in hand and activated it. *BANG!* The restaurant was engulfed in flames, blown apart by a blast which claimed the lives of Robert and Rowe.

At Paul Sullivan's penthouse the same day, Paul rode to his floor in the lift. He unlocked his door, threw his blazer off, poured himself a drink of Belvedere on the rocks, and casually strolled to his Italian leather sofa. He sat down quietly and gazed at the landscape painting on the wall above the television. Paul stood up and approached a photo hanging nearby, which was slightly crooked. He readjusted the photo, suddenly realizing something was wrong. He took the photo from the wall, revealing a wall safe which he then opened.

In it was a box that appeared to have been tampered with. Curious and worried, Paul opened the box. This triggered a timer, set to go off in a matter of seconds. He quickly ran for the door, when *BANG!* The bomb went, and the blast threw Paul out the door, against the lift. He miraculously survived; as for his penthouse, it was consumed in flames, destroyed by the blast.

The explosions around town didn't go unnoticed. The local news was all over the scene behind the yellow crime scene tapes and the fire brigade fighting the powerful blazes around town.

Paul phoned his father, whilst he stumbled down the stairs away from the fire. 'Dad! The journal is missing! Someone took it!'

'I'm well aware. Get here immediately', Mr Sullivan replied from the back of his limousine. Maxwell, at the wheel, was driving past the fiery blaze of the Renaissance Restaurant, one of his customers' establishments.

'Bastards destroyed my penthouse!' Paul moaned to his father.

'That's the least of our concerns. Get here now!' Mr Sullivan growled with a cough and hung up the phone. 'Maxwell, have the men ready. We got business to attend to', he ordered as he watched the burning restaurant from the seat of his limousine.

I stood straightening my tie in the hospital ward, digesting the chaos on the television through the peepholes in my face bandages. I hadn't missed the madness; compared to this, the coma seemed like paradise.

Father Franklin walked into my ward, smartly dressed, ready to accompany me to the county court. 'Straight out of death's arms and into the madness', I said, shaking my head at the news.

'Are you all right, Arthur?!' Father Franklin asked.

'All I need is justice for my loss, Father', I replied sadly, adjusting my tie around my neck. 'This doesn't have to go any other way.'

'What are you saying? What's the meaning of this?' Father Franklin sounded worried and concerned.

'We are running late. We should get going.' I avoided his question, leaving the room.

Outside the Carol City Police Department (CCPD), a mass of unhappy protesters rallied. Among them were the local news crews, looking to scoop the latest. It seemed that the series of bombings had aroused people, sparking this turnout. Signs, placards, and chants filled the atmosphere as Captain Walter turned up in his cruiser. 'Find Mayor Reed! Peace for the city! Is our city safe?' the crowd chanted. Captain Walter shouldered his way through the mass towards the door.

'Captain Walter! Any news on the mayor? Who's responsible for the bombings?' a female reporter asked, storming the captain with her camera crew.

'We are doing the best we can to find the mayor. The bombing is merely an act of terror, nothing more', Captain Walter replied as he forced his way into the building.

Next day, at the Carol City County Court, the honourable Judge Ronald Athens presided. He was a middle-aged man with all-grey hair, average-looking with a black goatee. The bailiff called for all to rise and be seated ready to begin. The judge called the defendant, Rick, to the stand, where he took the oath and sat down with a confident smirk on his face, I clenched my fist in anger at the sight of his face.

Meanwhile, at 22nd Street Fern Avenue, a community of real estate, a strike team of four skilled officers were about to break into a home after discovering Craig's whereabouts. Inside, Craig stood up against a corner wall, peeking out the curtain with his pistol in hand.

'Sir! We have him!' the lead officer said over the radio to Captain Walter, who was inside an armoured command vehicle. 'We are about to break in! What are your orders?!'

'Break it down!' Captain Walter replied. 'I want that scum brought in, now!'

'All right, men! Break it down!' the lead officer ordered.

Two officers knocked the door in with their ram. Tactically they entered the home in search of Craig. 'Shots fired!' came one cry, and 'Officer down!' came another as the officers engaged Craig, who was holding them off from the top of the stairs.

Across town, in the streets, the chaos continued. The Logan brothers and Mr Sullivan's goons were engaging in a rapid shoot-out in the streets, both trying to establish their dominance over the city. The police and innocent bystanders alike were caught in the free-for-all of gunfire.

Over on High Street, not far from the shoot-out, a high-speed chase with heavy gun fire ensued. The Logans and Mr Sullivan's goons were fleeing the pursuing police, and the local news helicopter hovering above caught the latest. The streets were in turmoil.

Whilst the drug lords terrorises the streets and the Officers battle Craig at close quarters, Carl laid asleep in his ward, slowly recovering from his wounds.

My attorney, Mrs. Berwick, a smartly dress middle-aged lady with a striking personality and dazzling character, was doing her utmost best to earn me the justice I deserved.

'Mr Lawson! Did you or did you not brutally murder the wife and children of Father Brown?!' she pressed Rick in the witness box.

'I'm afraid I can't answer that question', Rick replied confidently.

'May I remind you that you're under oath, Mr Lawson?' said Judge Athens, with a powerful glare.

'Objection, Your Honour!' Robert Williams, Rick's lawyer, interjected, rising to his feet. 'Question is intended purely to intimidate the defendant!'

The judge responded, 'Overruled. Mr Lawson, answer the question.'

'No, Your Honour, I did not!' Rick answered with a cruel look on his face.

Over on Fern Avenue, the police weren't having much luck bringing Craig down. Gunshots echoed within the hallways, and Craig changed magazines and continued to engage the officers from above the staircase. Then his phone vibrated in his pocket, and Craig answered.

'Where the hell are you?' Paul Sullivan demanded, sitting in his father's limousine outside the mansion.

'I'm trapped! Get me the fuck out of here!' Craig screamed into the phone.

'We're on our way! Stay put!' Paul replied, hanging up immediately. 'All right, let's go!' Paul shouted to his men lounging around the limousine and the vans parked outside the mansion. Armed to the teeth, they all jumped into the vans and roared out through the mansion gates.

At the court, the trial hadn't yet proven to be hopeful as I took the stand. Rick's lawyer was ferocious and unforgiving with his pros and cons, attacking me with every professional tactic for the good of his client.

'Ladies and gentlemen of the jury! Can we honestly believe that the witness remembers the face of his assailant? A man who has spent a great deal of time inside a coma?' Robert Williams was wooing the jury with his skilful approach.

'Objection, Your Honour!' Mrs. Berwick shouted in disapproval.

'Sustained!' Judge Athens replied.

'Father Brown, just how long were you in a coma?'

'Long enough', I replied calmly.

'Long enough to forget who came to your home that dreadful day!' Robert Williams stated heartlessly with a powerful grunt that said he was right and I was wrong.

Mrs. Berwick sprang to her feet but the judge was quicker: 'The jury will disregard counsel's testimony', he said with a weary sigh.

Across the Carol City capital, Lismore, the chaos between crime rivals had triggered a riot. With the Mayor missing, top detective Carl Brooks in hospital care, and the captain off on a wild goose chase, the rest of the department fought to control the riot and keep the situation under control.

On Fern Avenue, the cops had taken control of the gunfight. Tear gas was used to apprehend Detective Bollington. With no escape from the room and the home surrounded, the gas was overwhelming. Finally, the officers took Craig down with a rubber bullet to the chest.

'We got him, sir! We're coming out!' the lead officer radioed the captain.

'Good job! Get him into custody!' Captain Walter replied.

With Craig passed out and unconscious, the officers slapped on the cuffs and dragged him out of the house towards a secure vehicle. Captain Walter himself oversaw Craig into the back of the secure transport ready to be taken away.

Suddenly there was the loud report of an explosion. A police cruiser went up in flames, and bullets began flying around the officers on the scene as Paul Sullivan and his heavily armed convoy swept into action, pinning down Captain Walter behind his vehicle.

'Secure the prisoner! Do not let anyone near that vehicle!' Captain Walter yelled.

'Get the van! Let's go! Get him out of there!' Paul ordered his men as they suppressed the officers.

Four officers guarding the transport van were shot dead as the gunmen effectively extracted Craig from the transport. They carried Craig from the transport and into a waiting van, driving away right under the captain's nose.

'For God's sake! Can't anybody do anything right?' Captain Walter yelled in outrage. 'I want these slimes found! I want them taken down! I want them prosecuted!'

With all the chaos going wild in the city, Mrs. Berwick was in the middle of fighting vigorously to earn me the justice I deserved. 'Mr Lawson! Where were you at the time that vicious crime was committed?'

'I was nowhere near Father Brown's home, that's for sure!' Rick replied calmly, with a smile on his face.

'Do you mind telling me why your fingerprints were found in his home?' Mrs. Berwick made an interesting approach, highlighting a key point of evidence.

'Objection, Your Honour!' Robert Williams cried, playing hardball in support of his client.

'Sustained. Please continue', said Judge Athens.

The trial was beginning to show its true nature within the courtroom. Rick and his hotshot lawyer were working the system, and the jury were eating right out of their hands. My lack of faith in the justice system belied my false sense of hope. I needed results, and fast. Rick must pay.

'Court is adjourned and will resume in a week's time', the honourable Judge Athens declared, slamming his gavel down in dismissal.

CHAPTER 8

Later, that day as the sun set and the darkness crept in, at the old Carol City bridge that ran from the rear end of the capital city across demolition town, an old abandoned village set to be torn down, as declared by the mayor, both crime lords met, Mr Sullivan and the Logan brothers.

In the pouring rain, Paul, Maxwell, and Mr Sullivan's gang stood underneath their umbrellas before their vehicles, lights on, facing the Logan brothers and their gang some twenty metres away on the opposite side of the bridge. Something was about to happen. Maxwell carefully escorted Mr Sullivan from the vehicle into his wheelchair.

'You sure know how to pick the time and place, Mr Sullivan!' Gosnell growled across the bridge. 'Are you sure you're up for this? You're not exactly in the best of shape!'

'Cut the bullshit! You know why we're here!' Mr Sullivan snapped.

'Oh yes, of course! You need me to leave the city!' Gosnell replied with an obnoxious tone. 'But I'm afraid we can't do that, Mr Sullivan! You are approaching death's door, and your son cannot fill your shoes!'

'You want to watch your mouth, you piece of shit!' Paul yelled, furious.

'I might be dying, but I won't leave this city in your hands!' Mr Sullivan replied and lapsed into a desperate cough. He recovered enough to insist, 'This is my town! I suggest you leave while you can!'

Johnathon chimed in, 'I don't think you got much of a choice! We have the numbers and the resources!' He laughed. 'Face it, Mr Sullivan! You are yesterday's news and about to be history!'

'Listen, Dad!' Paul urged. 'End this right now! Just do it, before it's too late!'

'In time, son, in time', Mr Sullivan replied cautiously.

'I'm afraid you are out of time!' Gosnell shouted, his voice echoing across the bridge.

A voice sounded from the midst of the Logan's gang. 'He's right! Your time in this city is long overdue!'

The door of the Logan brothers' limousine swung open, and a pair of crocodile shoes emerged onto the drenched tarmac. Raoul stood straight. Mr Sullivan and the rest of his gang were surprised by Raoul's sudden appearance.

'Raoul? You traitor! How could you?' Mr Sullivan yelled and fell into another coughing fit.

'You are washed up, Mr Sullivan!' shouted Raoul, tilting his chin high in the pouring rain. 'Your son doesn't have the balls to run this city!'

'You scum! You're going to pay for this!' Paul cried aloud, recklessly pulling his gun from his waist and triggering a gunfight.

A fusillade began from both sides. Trading bullets for bullets, the gangs faced off against each other. Maxwell quickly escorted Mr Sullivan safely back into the vehicle. Casualties on both sides led to an extraction as both gangs took off in the heat of the gunfight, clearing the bridge.

A long week later. The streets were humming as corner-to-corner drug deals, petty crimes, and chaos painted the city red. Both rival gangs competed with each other's deals through the darkest corners of the city. Small businesses loaded drugs in food containers out their back doors into trucks, with others cross-loading from doorsteps to the boots of waiting cars.

Early that afternoon-Carol City County Court. All quiet, seated and waiting. After a long battle to earn me the justice I rightfully deserved- the jury returned to their seats having reached a verdict.

Judge Athens directed his attention to the jury. 'Have the jury reached a verdict?'

'We have, Your Honour!' the foreman replied.

'Will you please read the verdict?' Judge Athens requested.

'We the jury find the defendant, Rick Lawson, not guilty!'

My heart grew both heavy and faint. I felt sorrowful, empty, and lost for words. Weary tears settled behind my tired eyelids, but I held them back, clinging to my pride. Justice was lost, and pain was my only reward.

A gentle palm was laid upon my shoulder. 'I'm sorry, Father Brown. I did my best', Mrs. Berwick humbly apologized.

Rick and his attorney celebrated their foul victory, shaking hands, smiling about the courtroom, rejoicing. Rick looked at me, holding his chest and his head high with a dirty smile painted on his face as he trotted past. Without a word, I grabbed my coat and walked with Father Franklin out of the courtroom. Shamefully humiliated, I emerged from the building into a mass of cameras and reporters hammering me with a barrage of questions.

'Father Brown! Any comment on the outcome of the trial? Father Brown! How do you feel about the verdict?'

'Father Brown! Do you think there's hope for the people of Carol City, as you have failed to receive the justice you hoped for?' a young female journalist asked, gaining my attention.

My response was direct and pointed. 'The justice system is false! Corrupt! Weak! Not even a man of God stands a chance!'

'Is there anything you would like to say to the people of Carol City?!' another journalist cried out loudly.

'Justice will come! One way or another! Keep the faith!' I urged the audience and the city before me.

'There you have it, people! Words from our very own Father Brown!' the journalist signed off, ending her report.

The dreadful day saw me at home, sitting on the living room sofa, my bandaged head in my hands, disappointed, angry, and outraged. All the painful memories and dissatisfaction overwhelmed me. I took my anger out on the living room, the kitchen, and the bedrooms, all ripped apart in anger. At last, shaken, broken down, and drained, I found myself crunched up in the corner of what used to be Lauren's and my bedroom.

I began to plead my case, my sorrow, my pain, my troubles to God. 'Why? Why, O Lord? Why hast thou forsaken me? Why must the wicked continue to thrive? When will there be justice for the weak?

How long must I endure this pain? I've been nothing but faithful! Yet this is my reward!'—and so on, bellowing in my pain.

Feeling distant, betrayed by my faith, I grew angry, curling up on the bedroom floor, soaking my bandages in tears. 'Help! Help, I beg you! Help me!'

Then it hit me as a sudden realization, a sign of hope and willingness, an opportunity. I must not dwell in this discomfort. I needed to help myself; after all, it was God's way of showing me what must be done. This city needed me. My loss was my motive and my source of self-healing. I was at hell's door, my sanctuary lay beyond that door, and it was where I must journey.

After all, why must I trudge through my life in agony? Why should Rick be allowed to roam the streets? I pondered, pacing the room like a madman, feeling locked out of my own mind. The voices of my family screaming at Rick for mercy began to haunt my clouded mind. It was a lot to bear, and again I roared painfully, holding my head and then ripping the bandages from my face. I scrambled to the mirror on the bedroom wall to face at last the man in the mirror. I was repulsed by the foul sight of my mangled face and smashed the mirror with my fist. Then, shrieking in anguish, I trashed the bedroom all over again and finally crumpled to the floor, crying my misery aloud.

In the Carol City Police Department briefing room, early the next afternoon, Captain Walter brought his officers up to date. The city was in turmoil, and the captain was demanding a tight shift with controlled routine patrols.

'I want every corner of this goddamned city patrolled! If you think you'll have a quiet day, you're lying to yourself! We've got the mayor missing and a dirty cop at large! Screw your necks in and clean up these godforsaken streets!' Captain Walter bellowed on top his lungs, emphasising his authority to his subordinates.

The door to the briefing room flew open, and a familiar figure entered—Detective Carl Brooks, fully recovered and back to his civic duties. Everyone cheered, applauding Carl, happy to see him.

'Welcome back, Carl! Good to have you back!' Captain Walter greeted him with a firm handshake.

'Glad to be back, Captain! The streets need me!' Carl replied proudly.

'Damn right the streets need you!' Captain Walter exclaimed. 'We're up to our eyeballs in shit. The city is in total chaos! These scumbags think they own the town, and we need to end this now!' he said, reiterating his points to Carl.

'We'll find them, and we'll stop them—you can count on it!' Carl assured the captain.

The rest of the department stood up applauding, moved by Carl's exchange with the captain and cheering loudly.

Later that night, in the capital city of Lismore. I found myself in an alleyway, standing watch in the windy night at the Aqua Sushi Restaurant, a classy place owned by Mr Sullivan, where only the rich and the most sophisticated dined.

I could hear the laughter and cheer of the self-important snobs from across the street as I approached in silence, holding the black Andre Rogue felt hat on my head as my overcoat swung in the wind. I didn't yet know that back in the alleyway I was already being watched carefully from the shadows by a familiar character: Jack Wielder!

I barged through the front doors of the Aqua Sushi Restaurant. It was beautifully arranged, with magnificent aquarium walls from floor to ceiling and even underfoot, filled with a variety of marine life. Scattered among the tables were the wealthiest upper class Carol City had to offer.

The receptionist grabbed hold of my arm, holding me back at the door to keep me from venturing further. 'And just where do you think you're going?' he growled.

'Let go of me! I've got business here!' I grunted back, fighting for my arm.

The commotion was overheard by the guests. All eyes peered towards the door, where I stood glaring at the table set in the midst of the restaurant. Rick, Mr Sullivan, his son, and Maxwell all sat smartly dressed before a mighty spread, looking at me as if I were an eyesore.

The bandages around my face drew an uncomfortable look from the other clueless guests.

'Who is this piece of trash? Why is he disrupting my business?' Mr Sullivan cried out from his wheelchair.

'Name's Father Brown. I'm here to face the animal who dines with you!' I replied, stating my purpose.

The group looked at me and then at each other. They mumbled and burst into laughter. I was a joke, a laughing stock, and a broken mess that no one took seriously.

'Wait! I know this asswipe. He's all over the news. Yesterday's news', Paul said with evident disgust. He nudged Rick's shoulder. 'Hey, Rick? This asshole doesn't know when to quit.'

'Somebody get this mummy-looking maniac out of here!' Mr Sullivan yelled angrily.

Immediately I was stormed and scuffed up by a group of six smartly dressed men. My Andre Rogue hat hit the floor, and all eyes were feasting on the disturbance.

'Hold on! I'll handle this!' said Rick, standing to his feet. Step by step, he casually strolled towards me. I looked at him, full of rage and uncontrollable thoughts. He stopped to admire the fishes beneath his feet, chuckled, and looked at me in pity, shaking his head.

Angry and outraged, I grabbed for him, but the men held me back. 'You bastard! You need to pay for your sins!' I yelled bitterly.

'Oh, Father. This isn't a church. It's a restaurant. No one here needs to hear you preach about your sad story. Look around. These people are disgusted.' Rick mocked me, belittling me and carefully destroying my morale.

The customers looked at me with foul eyes and a nasty glare that said they were indeed disgusted by my presence.

'Face it, Father. You're done for. You're a mess, Father Brown, and a coward', Rick continued, stripping me of all dignity. 'Your family is dead because you were too weak to save them!'

'You bastard! I'll take you down! You will pay!' I growled at Rick reaching for his throat. Again I was restrained, forced face down to the glass floor like a prey taken by its predator. Rick placed his snakeskin boot against the side of my face, pressing harshly against my bandage hurting wounds. A shark began to snap its jaws at my face. I flinched in terror, but Rick chuckled.

'Sharks we are, Father Brown. You, my friend, are just a bottom feeder', he said, jamming his foot deeper into my face.

'Get this piece of crap out of here', he finally said, lifting his foot from my face, finished with me. 'Next time you won't be so lucky', he said as he resumed his seat.

I was taken to the door with my feet dragging along behind me, shamed, insulted, humiliated, and disgraced. They tossed me out the door onto the kerb like a street rat and my hat after me. I then began to ponder a few embarrassing thoughts: *What happened to me? Who am I? Look at me, I'm a mess, a joke! A man of God reduced to a scum.*

I picked myself up from the kerb, placed my hat on my head, and walked back into the alley like the scum I'd been reduced to. All I wanted was justice for my loss, nothing more. Instead, I'd gained a life of pain and constant disappointment. Fuming, forsaken by my religious faith, I kicked against a trash bin expressing my anger.

'Why? What have I done to deserve this?' I cried out in tears, feeling let down and cast out.

'Hey, buddy! Someone's trying to sleep here. Do you mind?' a vagrant cried out from behind the trash.

I paid him no attention. Then a hand grasped me on the shoulder from behind and pushed me against the alley wall. It was Jack Wielder, a sight for sore eyes but the last face I'd expect to find in this unusual place. Still shaggy, he looked to be living the life of a drifter.

'Jack? What you doing here?!' I stammered, puzzled.

'I've been watching you, Father Brown!' Jack replied suspiciously. 'That was a stupid move back there!' His foul alcohol breath was in my face, his dirty hands resting on my chest.

'I don't know what you're talking about, Jack!' I replied, peeling his hands off my chest and walking away.

'Back there? In the restaurant? That was a stupid move, Father!' Jack cried out as he followed behind me.

'I was doing the right thing, Jack!' I shouted over my shoulder as I continued up the alley.

'You were trying to get yourself killed. That's what you were doing', he told me as I approached the back street. 'I could help you, Father. You can't do this alone!' he shouted along the alley as I disappeared out of sight.

Jack grunted with disappointment as he stood and watched me wander out of sight. He looked across at a homeless man snuggled up under an old blanket, who stared blankly back at him. Jack noticed a pair of snakeskin boots peeping from the bottom end of the dirty blanket. With googly eyes, Jack stared at the snakeskin boots and then looked down at his shredded flat shoes with his toes poking out. The homeless man stared at his own feet, confused, and then looked back at Jack.

'Nice boots', said Jack, taking an interest in the fancy footwear.

Soon after, Jack was seen leaving the alley with the pair of snakeskins on his feet, hurrying into the darkness. Back in the alley, the homeless man lay unconscious, bare feet poking from under his blanket.

That same night around 11:55 p.m., over on Western Avenue, Third Street, outside a liquor store Detective Carl Brooks was slapping the cuffs on a man by the name Gareth Dolling, a tough-looking German black-market drug and arms dealer covered in tattoos with thick, wavy hair, of average height and no older than forty. Carl had reason to believe he was connected to Mr Sullivan's rivals, the Logan brothers.

In the eyes of the night crawlers looking on, Carl yanked Gareth off the bonnet of his cruiser, shoved him into the back seat, and drove away.

As he drove through the city, noises, screams, and violence seemed pervasive. Cops were making arrests on the sidewalks as Carl looked on, shaking his head, disgusted by what he saw. It was quiet in the car; neither man spoke.

Carl swung a left, heading up a back road outside the capital and rousing the interest of Gareth in the back seat. 'What the fuck is this? Where the fuck are you taking me?' Gareth yelled, banging his feet against the wire mesh that separated the two.

Carl kept his a straight face, calm and collected, and drove on. He was tired and unhappy with the changes the drug lords had caused within the city. He started thinking: *Nothing's the same, no one respects the law, so what the hay? Why should I play good cop? What's that ever got me? A vacation in the hospital, that's what. From now on I'm stepping up my game; it's time to play hardball.* He then drove towards a dockyard on the edge of the city.

'Hey, asshole? I'm talking to you!' Gareth continued to shout, angrily banging his head against the safety wire mesh.

Carl flashed his headlights, and two officers in blue appeared in the dark, opening the gates. Carl drove through the dockyard all the way to the end and parked alongside a boathouse guarded by another two officers in blue.

Carl stepped out of the cruiser and approached the officers. 'Thanks for securing the area. I'll take it from here', he said and dismissed them.

Carl opened the door to the shed. He then opened the cruiser door, grabbed Gareth by the collar and dragged him out of the cruiser.

'What are we doing here? You don't scare me!' Gareth yelled as he fought Carl every step of the way.

Annoyed, Carl knocked him cold and dragged him into the board shed. Soon, Gareth was awakened by a splash of water into his face to find himself cuffed to a boat mast under repair. He nudged the cuffs to free himself, but it was a failed attempt.

'I've got some questions, and you've got answers!' Carl was bent on getting what he came for.

Gareth was just a middleman working both rivals—aiding Mr Sullivan and the Logans with the movement of drugs and firearms in and out of the city.

Gareth made an idle threat. 'Listen, you scum. I'd let me go if I were you. You don't know who you're fucking with.'

'I want to know where these drugs are coming from. how they're getting into the city. Most of all, I want to know everything about Mr Sullivan's rivals', Carl insisted in a reasonable tone.

Gareth laughed at Carl, spitting at his feet. 'You can suck my fucking balls if you think I'm going to tell you anything!'

Carl turned around, picked up a two-by-four the size of a baseball bat, and pointed it at Gareth, warning of what would follow if he refused to talk. 'All I need is answers. Nothing more', Carl said calmly, resting the block of wood on his shoulder.

'You can't do this to me! You are a fucking cop!' Gareth raged on.

'And you're just a worthless piece of crap', Carl replied calmly, keeping his cool, playing it safe for a while.

Gareth refused to come clean. 'Like I said, I'm not talking!'

Without warning, Carl began to beat the life out of Gareth's kneecaps. Gareth began screaming in excruciating pain, pleading for Carl to stop, but Carl needed answers, and he was going to get them. The louder Gareth wailed, the harder Carl battered his knees. Soon blood began to drip down Gareth's legs onto his boots. It was personal: Carl was going to do whatever it took to get some answers. He had reached his tipping point.

Eventually Gareth caved in. The pain was too much to bear. He had crumpled over his broken knees in agony and was ready to talk. 'I'll tell you! I'll fucking tell you!'

'I'm listening', Carl said, tapping the wood impatiently on the boathouse deck.

Gareth bit back his pain and began spilling the beans. 'The drugs are being shipped by a supplier outside the city! I don't have a name! I'm just a middleman, that's it, I swear! Mr Sullivan likes to keep his shit private, and so do the Logans.'

'Don't bullshit me! I'm low on patience', Carl replied.

'His son, Paul! He knows more than anyone. He knows the supplier!' Gareth was desperate to avoid losing his legs.

Carl grabbed Gareth by the jaw and looked him dead in the eyes. 'Let's hope for your sake you're right. Now tell me, how are the drugs getting into the City?' For emphasis he leaned the wood against Gareth's crushed kneecaps.

'All right! They're using hearses!' Gareth replied, grinding his teeth in pain.

'What do you mean? Tell me!'

Gareth went on revealing the truth to Carl. 'Hearses! They're shipping the drugs and money in any corpse they can find, dead or alive!'

Carl was stunned at this. He released his grasp, tossed the block of wood aside, and began pondering in silence trying to make sense of everything. 'Son of a bitch. I'll be damned', he muttered in shock. Then he redirected his attention towards Gareth, grabbing him by the neck. 'What about Mr Sullivan's rivals? What's their part in all this?!'

Gareth began talking as if possessed, laying it all out for the angry and determined detective. 'They're the Logan brothers, from out of town!'

'I know who they are! I need specifics, details! Talk!' Carl growled, tightening his grip on Gareth's neck.

'OK! OK! The Logan brothers are here to take over!' Gareth answered, the words tumbling from his mouth.

'What do you mean? Explain!'

'They want to own the city! They want what's Mr Sullivan's!' Gareth explained as thoroughly as he could, fighting hard to endure the pain from his shattered knees.

'This city isn't theirs for the taking!' said Carl resolutely.

'You can't stop the Logans! You're in over your head!' Gareth answered.

Carl turned and left the boat shed in a hurry, with Gareth still cuffed to the boat's mast without a chance of escaping.

'Hey! You can't leave me here!' Gareth cried out in agony.

'It'll be dawn soon! Someone will find you!' Carl replied, refusing to look back, charging out of the docks at high speed.

In a basement somewhere in the city, amid brick walls, murky drains, dripping pipes, and sounds of agony, the Logan brothers had acquired another victim. He was a man named Raphael Timothy, no older than forty-five with dark hair, around five-eleven and slightly built. This man they had strapped to a chair was also CEO of a large land freight conglomerate, who controlled every road movement of goods in and out of Carol City. The Logan brothers needed his full cooperation.

Next to Raphael, also strapped to a chair and being tortured by the Logans' henchman, was his friend and business partner, George Marcus—no older than fifty-five, with curly hair and of average height. Raphael was failing to cooperate, and his friend was paying the price for his lack of effort to reach an agreement with the Logans.

George, bare-chested, had been drenched with a bucket of water. Two wire clips attached to his nipples were powered by a car battery that sat on the concrete floor. Dogs barked at the sound of George shrieking; Raoul had his pair of Rottweilers at his feet on chain leashes, eager for a quick meal.

'Please! Just do whatever the fuck he wants!' George screamed at Raphael, barely hanging on as the electric shock fried the hairs from his chest and roasted his nipples.

'Only you can help him. Just say the word, and it's over', Gosnell said, fiercely staring into Raphael's eyes.

Raphael cringed his face at the sight of George shivering and trembling at the mercy of the Logans. Raphael then looked up at the brothers with a look of disgust and spat in Gosnell's face.

Johnathon retaliated with a punch, breaking Raphael's nose and drawing a stream of blood. 'Last chance, Raphael!' he urged ominously. 'Last chance!'

'Try that again, and you're going to be dog chow!' Gosnell threatened, wiping the spit from his face with his pocket rag.

'This is a waste of time. Let me end this', Raoul suggested, impatient and looking forward to a bloodbath.

'Raoul is right! We're done here!' Gosnell suddenly lost interest and wanted to put an end to both men. He snapped, 'Let his friend fry! Raoul? Take care of Mr Timothy!'

'I'm going to enjoy this!' said Raoul with a sinister look, about to release his dogs.

George, still plugged up to the battery, was waiting to die, flapping about his seat like a fish out of water barely alive. Raoul had his dogs climbing onto Raphael's lap, snapping at his face, ready to attack on Raoul's command.

'Stop! Stop! I'll do it!' Raphael screeched in fear of what was going to happen should he fail to cooperate.

'You'll do what, Mr Timothy?' Gosnell snarled.

'I'll ship the drugs … I'll do whatever you want! Just stop, please!' Raphael begged, ready to save both their lives.

'That's more like it!' Gosnell replied with a businesslike expression. 'Get them out of here! We're done!' He turned away with his brother Johnathon, leaving his men to handle his affairs.

Raphael and George were cut loose and taken away by the Logans' henchmen. Not long after, along the busy streets of Lismore, with a screeching of tyres, a vehicle pulled to the roadside, its doors were flung open, and Raphael and George were dumped in public view, battered, shaken, and bruised.

'Don't forget to play your part!' Raoul shouted out the window as the vehicle drove away.

I was at home, in my living room, sitting in a dark corner, surveying boarded windows, broken family portraits, a smashed vase, a shattered wall mirror, a ransacked sofa, and an overturned television set. In tears, broken-hearted and feeling lost, I gazed at a duffel bag on the carpet. I was empty and without faith, my heart filled with hatred and my deranged mind hell-bent on revenge. Voices filled my head—screams, gunshots—and flashing images of Lauren and the kids, sleeping in a pool of blood, were enough to set me off. Off my sorry ass I rose, draped a long leather jacket from the coat rack onto my shoulders, pulled my felt hat down on my forehead, scooped the duffel bag off the floor, and stormed out the door.

Later that night the cops were busy patrolling the streets; blue lights pulsed and sirens echoed throughout Carol City's capital, Lismore, as the cops rousted the lowest of drug dealers they could find amongst the street corners. Tucked away inside an alleyway, Detective Carl Brooks sat in his cruiser waiting impatiently on a tip he had received from Gareth.

A hearse drove by. Carl pulled out of the alley, switching his siren on as he pursued the hearse. When the hearse pulled over, Carl approached it with caution, gun braced in the firing position. Two well-dressed men in their late forties sat up front, waiting to be confronted.

'Keep your hands where I see them!' Carl ordered them. 'Step out of the vehicle with your hands in the air!'

'Is there a problem, Detective?' the driver asked, sounding concerned.

'Keep your mouth shut! I'm the one asking the questions!' Carl replied imperiously. 'You?' he said, addressing the passenger. 'Stand back with your hands on your head!'

He turned back to the driver. 'You? Open that rear door!'

The driver, completely oblivious, opened the rear door to reveal a white casket tucked neatly in the compartment.

'Stand back! Keep your hands where I can see them!' Carl ordered the driver as he climbed into the back of the hearse. He eagerly opened the casket. Empty, nothing inside except the nicely woven pillow and padded interior. The bust was a failure.

Unimpressed, Carl slammed the casket shut and climbed out. 'Show me your licence! Both of you! Now!'

Both men handed their licences and permits to the detective. Carl checked the documents, and all seemed fine; both men checked out clear.

'Keep it clean! Get out of here!' Carl grunted, sending them on their way.

CHAPTER 9

Later that night, the hearse drove around the back of the Montgomery Daniels's funeral parlour where Paul, Maxwell, and a handful of Mr Sullivan's loyal employees stood waiting. Doors slammed, and both men exited the hearse.

'It's done. The drop was successful', said the driver of the hearse, turning over a briefcase to Maxwell. 'It's all there, every single penny. But the cops are getting suspicious.'

'Why's that? What have you done?' Paul growled at both men.

'Whoa! Nothing happened. Just a routine stop, that's it!'

'The cops aren't stupid! We have to tell your father!' Maxwell was concerned, refusing to ignore the sudden complications.

Paul got worried, he agreed with Maxwell. 'You're right. We can't afford another screw-up. Lock it up. Let's go!'

The hearse was driven into the garage of the funeral parlour, lights switched off, shut down, and locked away. A vehicle pulled up outside. Paul, Maxwell, and the other men squeezed into the vehicle, which disappeared into the night.

Early the next morning, in the garden shed behind Mr Sullivan's luxurious lake house stood Chen, stripped to the waist, doggedly beating their newly acquired victim with brass knuckles. Looking on were Mr Sullivan, his son Paul, Maxwell, and a couple of the hired help. Their victim was a nobody, a slime, a bottom feeder who happened to be in the wrong place at the wrong time. They had caught him on a street corner hours ago pushing drugs on behalf of the Logans and brought him here.

'Where is the Logan brothers' lab? Tell me!' Mr Sullivan yelled from his wheelchair at the man strapped to a garden chair.

'Screw you!' the man mumbled, weary and beaten.

Chen laid in a few more aggressive punches, hoping to get some answers. The man moaned in agony, coughed blood, and spat into Chen's face. hen retaliated with a blow to the gut, and the man curled over onto the ground, still strapped to the chair.

'You better start talking! You know what I'm capable of!' Mr Sullivan shouted, gulping oxygen through his face mask.

'You don't scare me! You dying old scum!' The man gasped, trying to catch his breath where he lay.

Chen kicked the man a few times and then trampled him. Two men then dragged him upright on the seat, and Chen resumed his brutal assaults.

Mr Sullivan nodded his head at Chen, signalling he'd had enough and had grown impatient. 'He's not talking! Take care of him!' Mr Sullivan said to Chen, as Paul wheeled him away back into the lake house.

Chen looked at the man, standing over him with a sinister smirk. The man flinched, stunned by Chen's body language. Chen walked into the shed, picked up an axe, and ran his thumb along the blade, smiling away. Then he walked behind the man and, with a grunt of effort, swung the axe into the man's head, splitting it open with a twist of his wrist.

Moments later came the revving noise of a chainsaw behind the garden shed. Chen was chopping the limbs from the man he had axed to death and feeding them into a wood chipper with the help of another, who found it hard to stomach the grim task.

Days later, a limousine drove into the Carol City Boneyard, a dusty, deserted refuge for retired commercial aircraft on the southern edge of the city. The vehicle stopped alongside one aircraft, the driver opened the door, and the Logan brothers exited in style, buttoning their expensive suits. Next to follow was Raoul, wearing a holiday shirt and smart trousers.

'Are you certain this location is off the radar?' said Johnathon, sceptical as ever.

'I'm certain. I've been using this location for years', Raoul replied pompously.

'What about Mr Sullivan?!' Johnathon asked with concern.

'What about him?' Raoul snapped.

'You did business in the past!' Gosnell pointed out. 'Should we be concerned?'

'I understand your concerns. Mr Sullivan has no idea this place even exits!' Raoul stated with high confidence, assuring all was safe.

'I do hope for your sake you're right!' Johnathon said dubiously.

Raoul whistle, and his two beloved Rottweilers jumped from the limousine and followed on as Raoul guided the Logan brothers up the stairs into the rear of the old commercial aircraft. Inside was Raoul's large-scale drug lab that produced many different commodities for the Logan brothers' drug empire.

'This looks very impressive', Gosnell remarked, nodding as he scanned the surroundings. 'Looks like you have been busy!'

'What can I say? Both your funding and my expertise go hand in hand', Raoul replied proudly.

'Indeed. Show us around!' said Johnathon, eager to see what Raoul had in store.

Raoul left his dogs seated at the rear exit. Inside the aircraft, half-naked girls sat counting money, while men stacked cocaine by the kilo. Marijuana, crystal meth, and heroin, amongst other classes of drugs were being batched up in large quantities by men in lab coats wearing breathing masks. The Logan brothers smiled as they strolled through the aisles.

'This is what I call first-class service!' Gosnell said with smile, placing his palm on Raoul's back as a sign of goodwill.

'I've got something new for you!' said Raoul, clearly excited.

'Go on, enlighten us!' Johnathon exclaimed.

Raoul led the Logan brothers down the aisle, past the busy workers minding their own business, towards the front of the aircraft into an open cabin where two male skilled workers in lab coats were in the process of stacking boxes with prescription labels.

'Welcome to the business class, gents!' said Raoul boldly, spinning with his arms spread wide.

'What exactly are you getting at?' Johnathon asked.

'Hey, Felix? Tell our friends what goes on in business class!' Raoul called to a man stacking boxes onto a conveyor belt.

Felix, a long-haired geeky-looking man in his late twenties with a stubbled face, briefly explained to the brothers what they had to offer their buyers. 'Simple! We produce the finest drugs of the finest quality. That's it!'

'Show our business associates what is going to be making us rich!' Raoul, excited to please the brothers with his brilliant idea.

'This better be good! We can't afford to lose buyers!' Johnathon had yet to be sold on Raoul's scheme.

Felix grabbed a box from his feet labelled SLEEPAIDE and passed it to Gosnell.

Gosnell, puzzled, looked blankly at the box, turning it in his hands. 'What's this?!'

'Open it, man! Have a look!' said Felix in a mellow tone, already wasted on drugs.

Gosnell placed the box on a nearby table and popped it open. Inside were neatly packed trays of tablets and capsules. Johnathon peered into the box, suddenly interested.

'What are we looking at?' Gosnell asked, still looking mystified.

'What you are looking at is the future!' said Raoul with a smile.

'Explain!' Johnathon, running short on patience, was unable to bear the suspense.

Raoul then began to explain their new product. 'You are looking at cocaine, gentlemen! Specifically graded to keep the cops off our backs!'

He picked up a tray from the box along with some capsules. 'With this label, no one will suspect anything. As far as the cops can tell, these are prescription drugs. Running clean right under their noses. It's fucking brilliant!'

'You want to hope you are right about this', Gosnell insisted, all business. 'We have no room for errors. We need every buyer grovelling at our feet!'

'Trust me. This product is the answer to all our problems!' Raoul was full of confidence for the risk he was about to undertake. 'Mr Sullivan won't know what hit him!' He gloated in expectation of toppling the notorious crime lord's drug empire.

Barks echoed from the back of the aircraft; the Rottweilers were loudly on alert. Raoul and the Logans were now worried there might be unwanted visitors. Everyone drew their weapons, and Felix, Raoul, and the entire work force pointed gun barrels out the exits and a few broken windows as the sound of a car approached the yard.

'Who is it?' Gosnell asked, very concerned.

The dogs stormed out towards a black saloon as it braked to a screeching halt. A tall, casually dressed man in alligator boots charged out of the car in a frenzy, looking paranoid.

'It's Ronald! No need to be alarmed!' Raoul assured everyone, and the workers got back to their tasks handling the drugs and money.

The dogs began scratching, whimpering, and growling at the boot of the car. Ronald, a man of average build in his late thirties with a man bun, began struggling against the dogs, peeling them from the boot.

Raoul followed the Logans outside and whistled to silence the restless dogs. 'Heel, boys! Heel!!' Then he turned to the man beside the car. 'Where the fuck have you been?' he demanded. 'And where the fuck is Rick?'

'You're not going to like this. It's bad, real bad!' Ronald stuttered uncontrollably, pacing around with his hands on his head, clearly panicking.

'Start fucking talking!' Raoul yelled, shaking him by the collar.

Ronald began to whimper and pointed towards the boot of the car. Raoul released his grip and walked towards the boot. The dogs began to bark again. Raoul popped the boot and opened it to reveal two large ice coolers, tightly sealed.

'Is this a joke? What the fuck is this?' Raoul demanded.

'What's in there?' Johnathon shouted. 'I'm about out of patience!'

'Open the fucking coolers!' Ronald yelled, banging the fender with his fist. 'Open it!'

Raoul suddenly got worried. To break the suspense, he unclipped the locks on the coolers, releasing a sudden burst of overwhelming stench. Raoul stumbled backwards, gripping his nose. 'What the fuck's in those coolers?' he shouted.

Frightened, Ronald broke down in tears. Johnathon and his brother hurried towards the boot of the car, where they covered their noses and turned away from the stomach-churning smell. The dogs, unable to hold back, jumped at the coolers and tipped them from the boot. A pool of blood, tangled intestines, and body parts tumbled out and splashed across the tarmac.

'What the fuck! What is this? Who did this?' Gosnell roared.

'You! Start talking!' Johnathon yelled at Ronald, smacking the back of his neck.

'It's Rick!' Raoul cried out, pointing to a severed hand bearing a scorpion tattoo. 'They killed him! Mr Sullivan did this!' Ronald cowered against the parked limousine, shivering in tears.

'I'm going to handle this! Don't you worry!' Raoul was enraged and ready for blood.

'You make sure you do!' Gosnell responded. 'But first, get the supplies ready for dispatch!' He and his brother hurried into their own limousine, leaving Raoul to handle the filth behind.

In the Carol City Pentecostal Church, my second home, I stood weary and burdened by my loss before the cross hanging above the altar. My hat was still on my head; my duffle bag was set down before the altar next to my feet, shod in black suede. Despite my angry heart and my troubled soul, I sank to my knees before the man on the cross, Jesus.

Father Franklin noticed me kneeling at the cross as he emerged from the confessional booth. 'Father Brown? Is that you?'

'It's me, Lenard', I replied with a low voice, hanging my head in shame.

Father Franklin noticed the stuffed bag at my side and grew curious. 'You do not plan on leaving town, do you?'

'I'm not leaving town. I just need some time alone', I muttered with my chin on my chest.

'Time for what, Arthur? To discard your godly duties? Is that it?' Father Franklin seemed annoyed by my irrational decision.

'Things aren't the same, Lenard! Look at me! I'm a freak! I've got nothing, they took it all!' I shouted. Then I threw my hat to the floor and tore the bandage from my face, revealing what lay beneath.

Father Franklin flinched, startled by my mangled face. He was speechless for a moment. 'My God, Arthur! What have they done to you?'

'They've murdered me! That's what they did!' I grunted in discomfort as I struggled to my feet. I replaced my felt hat and pulled it down onto my forehead. Then I grasped my bag and turned, heading for the door.

'For God's sake, this isn't you!' Father Franklin began following me up the aisle towards the door.

'This *is* me! Don't you get it, Lenard? I can't live like this! It's not who I am. Look at me! I'm an abomination!'

'Come on, Arthur! Don't turn your back on your church!' Father Franklin pleaded, desperate to talk me down.

I stopped at the door and looked at Father Franklin with a straight undying expression courtesy of my mangled face. 'I'm not turning my back! I'm embracing my fate!' I replied, thrusting the doors open and seeing myself off.

Father Franklin looked at me, bitter disappointment on his face, as I marched down the steps towards my car. Then he ran to me, catching up just as I seated myself in the car.

'Don't think for a minute that I don't know what you're doing Arthur!' He poked his head into my window, holding me off with another suspicious look.

'What exactly do you think I'm doing?' I played the ignorance card, avoiding the blatant truth.

'Don't try and pull the wool over my eyes. You know exactly what I'm getting at. You are going after him, aren't you?' Father Franklin broke the mould, exposing the truth, thumping his fist down on my door angrily.

In utter silence, I fixed my clerical collar beneath my leather coat, nudged my fedora lower on my forehead, and fired up the engine. With one last look at Father Franklin, I pulled out, waving a farewell.

Father Franklin shouted after me, 'Don't do this, Arthur! You're heading down a dangerous path! This isn't God's plan! Listen to me, Arthur, you arrogant fool!'

I watched him through my wing mirror whilst I drove down the street and mumbled to myself, 'You're wrong, Father. This is God's plan.'

'You don't deserve to wear that collar, not anymore!' With that,

Father Franklin washed his hands of me, watching painfully as my car faded into the distance.

That night brought me to the middle of an old campsite at the Carol City County Park. I drove carefully along a dusty trail amongst old burnt and dismantled caravans towards a battered yet somehow hospitable mobile home. I killed the engine, left the headlights on, pulled my hat down over fresh face bandages, and stepped outside the car.

I straightened my leather coat and walked towards the mobile home, looking around the shattered windows and the battered front door. Through a broken window, I could see inside a mess of half eaten takeaways, leftover pizzas, dirty pots, a stained armchair and an overfilled ashtray.

Then I heard a gun cocked and felt a muzzle pressed firmly to the back of my head. Frightened, I threw my arms up high in submission.

'Move, and I'll blow your head off!' said the man holding a shotgun to my head.

I recognized the voice; it could only be one man. 'Jack? It's me. Put the gun down!'

I no sooner had said that then Jack hit me in the back of the head with his shotgun, and I fell face down onto the dusty ground. Soon, I woke in darkness, blindfolded and tied to a chair. A bucket of cold water was dumped over my head, and a few punches to the face brought me fully alert.

'What the fuck are you doing here?' Jack yelled at me.

'It's me, Father Brown! Come on, Jack, you know who I am. Cut the bull!' I cried out in frustration, straining against the zip ties around my wrists.

Jack snatched the blindfold from my face and peered at me. He seemed confused, steaming with alcohol. 'Well, look at what the cat dragged in!' he said with a disturbing voice, drunk and rattled. This was a side of Jack I'd never witnessed.

Inside his mobile home, above traces of old tobacco, a foul stench of last night's hangover stained the atmosphere. Below tinted windows lined with cobwebs, a wooden desk was heaped to the edges with files.

A pin board nailed to the wall bristled with pages of old news articles, headlines, and photos of faces, all of it unfamiliar to me.

'Well, don't you look like shit, Father!' Jack called to me, lively with drink.

'What the hell are you doing, Jack? Untie me this instant!' I yelled angrily. My bandages were soaking up the blood from a busted lip, and my eye socket was swelling.

'Not so fast, Father Brown, my dear friend! Not till you're ready!' Jack replied, talking into my face like a madman.

'What do you mean?' I asked, clueless as to what Jack had in mind.

'All will be revealed in time, my friend!' Jack's response suggested caution. I was having second thoughts about my visit.

Jack shrugged out of his old, filthy jacket, letting it fall on the floor, revealing a ragged coffee-stained T-shirt. He clenched his face at me and pounded a fist in his other hand. I was even more worried. Jack seemed different—crazy, yet with a purpose. Without preamble he began battering me with his fists, snatching me by the neck and pumping my gut with blow after blow, working me over. I scrunched my body in agony as blows to my mangled face painted my bandages red.

I cried out in pain, seeking clarity. 'What are you doing Jack Have you lost it?'

'What are you doing here?' he shouted, pounding his fists against my already battered face.

'I don't know! I don't know!' I shouted, coughing my guts up.

'Wrong answer, Father!' Jack replied as he continued hitting me.

After perhaps five more minutes of hammering my fragile body, Jack stopped. He looked at me, shook his head in disappointment, and held me by my collar, his sour breath in my face gagging me.

'OK, Father. I'm going to ask you one last time. Why are you here?' He seemed calmer but somewhat impatient.

I coughed a few times, taking a moment to pull myself together. Jack got bored and walked across the room. He ripped a piece of paper from the refrigerator and tossed it to the floor at my feet carelessly. It was another old news article headlined 'Carol City kingpin still at large'. He took a good-sized drink straight from a carton of milk.

Then he looked back at me, clearly feeling he was wasting time and effort. He pulled a knife from his pocket and cut me loose. 'Go on, get out of here!' He had suddenly lost interest; I was of no value to him. 'You're wasting my time. I'm done here!' he said, disappointed and angry for reasons I couldn't guess at.

I stood up, barely on my feet, staggering. I straightened my coat, swept my hat from the untidy floor, and settled it on my head. I looked at Jack's turned back and walked towards the door.

Then I stopped, thought for a second, and looked across at Jack, swallowing my pride. 'I'm here because I need your help', I muttered, feeling embarrassed.

'That's not why you're here', Jack replied doubting my honesty.

So I told him the truth. 'I seek justice! Cold, hard justice! That's why I'm here!' I didn't care whether he accepted it or threw it back at me.

'No, Father. Justice isn't what you are seeking', Jack replied, pouring himself a drink of whiskey from his table.

'OK, Jack, you win! This is not about justice!' I was agitated, no longer sure what exactly I was after. My anger and pain began to surface, and I raised my voice. 'This is personal! I want the man that tore my life apart. I want to punish him! I want him to feel the pain he caused me!'

'Now that's what I wanted to hear!' Jack shouted with satisfaction. Suddenly I saw that he had succeeded in triggering my rage, thus bringing out my darker half. 'This is why you're here! This is your calling!' he said excitedly, patting me on the back.

I felt sick about myself, a mood change, having second thoughts about myself. 'I'm ashamed of myself. Father Franklin was right. This isn't what God wants. In fact, this isn't who I am.'

Realizing what I was about to get into, I marched for the door, taking my sorrows elsewhere. 'Sorry I've wasted your time, Jack. I'd best be going.'

Jack suddenly looked stunned, unimpressed with my change of heart. I said no more, having spoken my piece. Jack hurled his drink through a window.

I took my bag from the floor, shielded my head with my hat, and made for the door. 'I'll see you around, Jack. Take care yourself.'

As I walked back to my car, Jack watched me through a cracked window, his face twisted in disgust. Not all was what he had hoped it to be. I looked back at Jack, staring me down from his window, and he shut the blinds, receding put of sight. It began to rain, and I pulled my hat low to shelter my bloody bandage, slid into the driver's seat, and switched on the engine, ready to go.

Still angry and dissatisfied, Jack stormed out the door, shouting towards me loud and obnoxious as I drove away. 'You are a damn coward, Father! A damn coward! You will regret this, you hear me?'

My journey brought me back into the city, heading towards my church in an effort to pay Father Franklin a seldom apology. I was greeted by blue flashing lights as I approached the church. I was stopped short by a male officer in his rain jacket standing beside his cruiser. Caution tapes, police barriers, and ambulances lined the street. Obviously something was wrong.

One look at my bloodstained bandage was enough to alarm the officer, who drew his pistol and aimed it towards me. 'Keep your hands where I can see them!' he shouted.

'This is my church! What the hell is going on?' I asked worriedly, ignoring the trigger-happy officer.

'Shut the hell up and step out of the vehicle, now!' the officer demanded, waving his gun at me.

I stuck one arm out the window, opened the door, and stepped out with my hands held high. The officer slapped his cuffs on me, walked me aggressively towards a group of officers busy at the scene, and slammed me face down onto a police cruiser just outside the church's access.

'Please! Listen to me! It's my church! What's going on?' I yelled frightened and frustrated, raging against the arresting officer-Another male officer on scene immediately jumped at me, offering his assistance.

'It's my church too, asshole!' the officer said, breathing down my neck as he forced my head back down.

The officer's 'blend was quickly recognized, and I called to him, 'Mr Shepherd? It's me, Father Brown!'

'Yeah, yeah, of course it is!' Officer Shepherd replied sarcastically as he and his fellow officers restrained me face down in the rain.

Detective Carl Brooks saw the commotion as he exited the church. 'What's going on here?'

'Caught him trying to sneak by, with his face all tied up and smeared in blood. Concealed identity! That was all I needed to bring him down', the arresting officer boasted.

'That's Father Brown! This is his church!' Carl cleared the crowd, allowing me room to breathe, and unlocked the cuffs.

'My apologies, Father Brown', Officer Shepherd apologised. 'Hope this doesn't affect our relationship.' He was again a humble churchgoer, slightly built, with a smooth face and dark hair, pushing forty.

'It's OK. You're only doing your job', I replied peaceably, still worried and baffled about what was going on. I pulled myself together and followed the detective into the church.

'Follow me, Father. You're not going to like this', said Carl, escorting me through the yellow tapes and into the church.

'What's going on, Detective? What happened here? Is Father Franklin around?' I was desperate for answers.

Carl sighed and looked at me with sympathetic eyes. 'There's been a shooting. Six church members were shot dead and four injured with bullet wounds!'

I was overwhelmed by the grim report, and my heart sunk. I had to have some answers, so I asked, 'Father Franklin? Is he all right?'

Carl went quiet. As we walked down the aisle, workers kept wheeling bodies out one behind the other with patches of blood soaking through the white sheets. The sight of bullet holes along the inside walls and the punctured and broken seats suggested an act of terror. At the altar, a team of paramedics huddled tending to a viciously wounded man. Looking closer, I saw it was none other than Father Franklin.

'Father?' I cried out aloud, shuffling towards the altar.

The medics held me back while they tried very hard to stabilize Father Franklin and save his life. A knife was wedged between his ribs, and he had a bullet wound in each leg. I could see he was bleeding heavily.

'Who did this? Who did this?' I bellowed, shedding tears beneath my bandage, falling to my knees.

'Let's get him out of here! He's losing blood, fast!'

The paramedics placed Father Franklin on a stretcher and wheeled him down the aisle and through the doors. I followed on at his side, holding his palm in reassurance.

'What happened, Father? Who did this?' I asked, jogging along in the rain to keep pace with the medics.

'Sir! It's best if he doesn't talk!' said one medic as they rolled the stretcher into a waiting ambulance. I tried hoisting myself into the back of the ambulance.

'Sir, I'm afraid you can't ride along!' said a male paramedic, blocking the doors into the ambulance.

'Like hell I'm not!' I growled, forcing my way into the ambulance despite the medic's effort to stop me from entering.

The medics fought professionally to keep Father Franklin alive as the ambulance raced through the lit streets bound for Carol City General Hospital.

'Come on, Father! You can fight this! Don't give up on me!' I pleaded into Father Franklin's ear as I tried to feed him constant reassurance.

Within moments we arrived at Carol City General Hospital. Doors flew open, and the stretcher was wheeled out of the ambulance into the rain and into the hospital where a team of doctors were on standby. I followed on, hoping for further reassurance and possibly some answers.

'Not allowed in the emergency room, sir! Please wait outside!' a female doctor insisted, cutting my journey short.

I stayed outside the room, pacing, restless and anxious. I sat down, took the load off my feet, placed my hat on my lap, and tried to ease the tension. Faces glanced and stared at a broken, empty man wrapped in bandages as they passed up and down the corridor.

'Can I get you some help, sir?' A female nurse approached with a mystified look on her face. She was slender and blonde, no more than thirty years old, about five-seven, with blue eyes and a sweet smile.

'I'm all right, thanks', I replied sympathetically.

'Are you sure? Your bandage looks like it may need a change', she persisted, and with nothing else to do but wait, I agreed.

'I guess you may be right. After all, I've got nothing but time.'

'Come on! Let's get you cleaned up!' said the nurse with a happy smile as she led me away from my lonely seat.

Without another word, I followed her into a room and sat down as she prepared a set of fresh bandages. She began cutting the filthy bandage from my face, damp with blood and discolouration, unaware of the horror that lay beneath.

'You might want to look away', I sincerely cautioned the nurse.

'Why? Is something wrong?' she asked politely, still smiling despite her ignorance.

'You might not like what you are about to see', I replied calmly.

'I've seen a lot worse. It's all right', she said, beaming with confidence.

Quietly and slowly she unwrapped the bandage and unveiled the horror. Then she stumbled backwards, frightened and petrified by what she saw, knocking her tools and equipment from her metal tray. 'What in God's name happened to you?' she gasped.

'Life happened!' I grunted in embarrassment and turned my face away, greeting the wall over my shoulder.

'That's too much for me to look at! I'm sorry!' said the nurse, fleeing the room in horror.

I took my time, neatly wrapped my face in a clean bandage. Then I hurriedly exited the room into the corridor towards the emergency room, where I stumbled upon Dr. Ramrod, who appeared to be in a great hurry.

'Father Brown! I've been looking for you! It's about Father Franklin', said Dr. Ramrod, breathing a sigh of relief.

'Please, Doctor, is he going to make it?' I asked with a burst of pure hope.

'We've stop the bleeding, but his condition is still critical', the doctor explained.

'Is he going to make it?!' I repeated, looking in on Father Franklin from behind closed doors.

'It's hard to say. He's in God's hands now!' Dr. Ramrod replied, not giving much away.

I slowly entered the room. I pulled up a seat beside Father Franklin and sighed in discomfort. Father Franklin lay helplessly upon his bed, eyes closed, wired to various monitoring and life support equipment.

'You can fight this, Father … you can. Just hang in there', I whispered quietly at his ear, hoping to reach him.

I began pleading in silence for a miracle. 'Please, God! I've already lost my family. I can't lose him too!'

Before long there was a cough. Father Franklin was awake, and with his eyes barely opened, he acknowledged me. 'Arthur? Arthur, is that you?'

'Yes, Lenard! It's me, Arthur!' I scrambled to my feet and grasped his hands in mine.

'Come closer. You need to hear this', Father Franklin whispered weakly.

I leant over and placed my ear next to his mouth, waiting for whatever he was about to say. He grabbed my collar and whispered into my ear. I became speechless, overwhelmed, lost for words. I staggered from his grasp into the seat before me, petrified by what he had told me. The heart monitor began to beep and then squeal steadily. He was flat lining—something was wrong!

'Help! Somebody help! I need a doctor!' I cried aloud down the corridors.

Within seconds, Dr. Ramrod came rushing into the room with his assistant. They asked me to leave whilst they did their best to save Father Franklin's life. I stood watch from the outside, still hoping for a miracle. Hurt and shrouded in sorrow, I slid down the door onto the hallway floor, burying my face in my hands in despair whilst I waited on the doctors.

Minutes later, Dr. Ramrod came before me. His face spelt sympathy and grief, and he was quiet.

'Is he all right? Did you save him? Tell me! Darn it! tell me!' I yelled, shaking Dr. Ramrod by his collar.

'I'm sorry. There's nothing more we could have done. He's passed on.' Dr. Ramrod broke the news as best he could.

I released his collar with tears rolling from my eyes and soaking into my bandage. I could not accept it. I didn't want to believe he had gone. I stormed into the room and pounded desperately on Father Franklin's chest.

'Wake up! Wake up! You can't leave me like this! God damn it, Franklin, wake up!' I cried like a madman, thumping on the dead, refusing to accept my loss. Dr. Ramrod and his assistants dragged me away, out of the room, and into the corridor, trying to ease the tension.

Days later, at the old Carol City Cemetery, the church bell ringing from the steeple echoed in the distance. Church members, along with close friends and distant relatives, all with grieving faces, turned out to stand under their umbrellas in the pouring rain to pay their respects. I stood before Father Franklin's casket bedded with dozens of red roses ready to give my last blessings. I was smartly dressed in my full clergy suit and a long black overcoat, with my felt hat seated nicely on my head sheltering my bandages. Officer Shepherd sheltered me with an umbrella held over my head.

With a sad tone and tearful eyes, I began. 'He was great man! A friend and a mentor! … There was nothing he wouldn't do for his church, his people! His flock!'

I started sobbing, fighting the rain behind my eyelids as I continued. 'He was all I had left! They took him from me! From us!' I cried out in tears, sympathetic, emotional, and hopeless.

Officer Shepherd rested his palm on my shoulder, letting me know all was well. 'It's OK, Father Brown. We understand your pain.'

Across the road, Detective Carl Brooks watched from the comfort of his cruiser. I began speaking of the good deeds, the righteous acts, and everything else that Father Franklin had stood for. Then after a prayer, the casket was lowered into the grave as the grieving audience laid even more roses on it as it sank into the earth.

At last the burial drew to an end, and Detective Carl Brooks appeared in his rain cloak and greeted me across the open grave. 'Hope this is not a bad time, Father. We need to talk', he said with an urgent tone.

'Now is not the time, Detective!' I replied, grieving and uninterested, turning to head towards my car parked along the side road just off the cemetery.

'Where were you the night of the incident?' Carl called out as he followed on behind urgently.

The whole scenario depressed me beyond description. 'I was finding myself, Detective. I was somewhere I should not have been. Do us a favour and find the monsters responsible', I replied and climbed into my car.

'I will find them, not to worry!' Carl replied, standing firm in the pouring rain.

'Your job just got a heck of a lot tougher, Detective. God be with you!' I switched the engine on, ready to pull away from the kerb.

'Where's God in all this, Father? Where is he?' Carl replied loudly over the heavy downpour.

'You tell me, Detective!' I replied with little faith as I drove away.

Carl stood and watched me drive away in the blistering rain. Sensing a hint of defiance, he took himself back to his cruiser and quickly left the cemetery.

The night had fallen, and the city was at its best, with drugs passing from palm to palm like legal tender as pushers hustled and exchanged hands in secret from street to street in all corners of the capital city. Raoul's latest 'sleep aid drug' was part of the traffic, hitting the volume he had suspected, slipping under the cops' noses in plain sight whilst they patrolled the streets.

Parked anonymously in the dark across the street from a local nightclub called Toxic was our wanted detective Craig. He sat behind the wheel keeping a low profile in a hooded top, shielding his face from unwanted eyes. He noticed a pair of male pushers on the sidewalk in shady outfits, popping pills in the open close to his car.

Craig became nervous and called to the pair of pushers urging them to mind their personal affairs. 'Hey! Try not to get yourself arrested!'

'Not with these we won't!' came one pusher's bold response as they secretly slid the sleep aids into their pockets.

'What's that you're holding?' Craig asked, noticing the disappearing packet of pills.

'This right here? This is some new shit!' one of them answered, and they drifted towards Craig's car.

'Let's have a look', Craig said.

The pushers passed him a tray of pills from the packet.

'What the hell is this?' Craig asked, glancing at the packet of pills in his hand.

'Crush that shit up, and bam! Instant cocaine!' the pushers happily explained.

Craig was impressed after the pushers demonstrated the sleep aid drug, crushing a pill on the hood of his car and snorting it up their noses.

'Whoa! Take it easy! Eyes everywhere!' Craig said, keen to avoid unwanted attention. 'OK! You pair of slime have just bought my interest. How much?'

'This shit doesn't come cheap!' the pushers claimed, willing to negotiate a handsome deal.

Craig lost his patience and snapped, 'Name your fucking price!'

'Two grand!' came the bold answer.

'Are you fucking kidding me? Two grand?' Craig wasn't too keen on the price.

'That's the price. Take it or leave it!' The men shrugged, driving a hard bargain.

Sitting impatiently in his car, Craig took a moment to contemplate the price, shaking his head in disagreement. 'You know what? I'll take it!'

Craig pulled his pistol with a suppressor attached. Then he emptied it into the pushers' chests through the open window of his car. He quickly got out, scraped the drug packets from the ground, and emptied the pushers' pockets. Then he jumped into his car and sped away.

Inside Club Toxic, music was blaring. Men and women were raving, kissing, and grinding, many women flaunting their boobs. The sleep aid was circulating on the dance floor and within the VIP booth.

Upstairs, Raoul, the club's owner, stood in his large office, bare-chested underneath his red silk shirt, black trousers and a pair of crocodile shoes, looking down on the audience through a giant soundproof window, smiling as his latest drug dominated the life of the party. 'Looks like we did it! The drug is a success!' He banged his fist on the desk in excitement.

'Yes! You've pulled it off, and not a moment too soon!' said Gosnell, lurking with his brother around Raoul's office.

Raoul snapped his fingers at a male employee standing at the door. 'Get us a champagne bucket! This calls for a celebration!'

He turned to the Logans and threw his arms wide. 'What did I tell you? We're rolling in money!'

'What can we say, Raoul? Your strategic idea took us by storm!' said Johnathon as they seated themselves on a black leather Italian sofa.

Just then, the male employee returned with two club staff, both females in skintight skimpy dresses exposing butt cheeks. They bent over, showing their thongs, and set the champagne onto a centrepiece before the brothers. Then they poured glasses and distributed them with a smile before leaving the room.

'Now if that's not good service, I don't know what is!' said Raoul, smiling proudly. 'A toast to success gentlemen! This city is as good as ours!' he said as they raised their glasses high.

After a sip, Johnathon walked to the window to take in the scene, one arm behind his back, 'Don't count that dying fool out of this arms race just yet', he said with a hint of scepticism.

Raoul smashed his glass of champagne as his anger became aroused by Johnathon's remark. 'What? That piece of shit and his son might as well quit while they can! This city is ours! His buyers are ours! Soon that fine piece of ass he's got changing his nappy will be mine! So let's just shut the fuck up and drink merrily! Fuck Mr Sullivan! Fuck him and his son! Fuck his bitch too! Fuck them all!' Raoul was shouting, angrier and more aggressive by the second.

'Raoul is right', Gosnell said calmly. 'It's all ours now. Let's enjoy this success!'

'Now that's the spirit! Let's drink some fucking champagne and be merry!' Raoul answered, rudely celebrative.

Later that night, in the large study of Mr Sullivan's mansion, a handful of his trusted men and three of his business associates lingered, drinking cognac and chatting. Amongst these men were Maxwell, Rick, and Paul Sullivan, present and accounted for.

Mr Sullivan entered the room, wheeled in by his carer, in his expensive robe dragging his oxygen tank along. All went quiet as he approached with a bitter expression on his face.

'Somebody tell me why have we just lost ten mil in our recent operation!' he shouted, angry, coughing. 'Tell me why our buyers and profits are way off! Tell me!' he demanded in the most authoritative tone-

Everyone was quiet, speechless. They were afraid to voice their opinion, fearing they might suffer the same fate as and fearing that the yacht incident might happen again—to them.

'I can tell you why!' A voice came from outside the room, and Craig stepped into the light. He tossed a handful of sleep aid packets onto the floor beside Mr Sullivan's feet-Mr Sullivan looked down at them, puzzled, and everyone looked at each other in confusion.

'What the fuck is this?' said Mr Sullivan. 'You trying to insult me? Is that it?'

'That right there is our problem!' Craig replied. 'This is why you've been losing!'

'You telling me our problem is a couple packs of sleeping pills?!' Paul asked in disbelief.

'They are not sleeping aids. Go on, try it!' Craig replied.

Maxwell picked a packet off the floor and opened it cautiously. He removed a few pills from the tray, looked at them, and crumbled them in his hand. Then he opened it and showed the room: powder!

'Well, fuck me sideways! We got ourselves cocaine!' said Paul after noticing the white powder drizzling from Maxwell's hand.

Intrigued by what they had seen, everyone scrambled for a packet off the floor, sampling it for their own satisfaction, confirming it was pure grade A cocaine.

'Who's responsible for this?' asked Mr Sullivan, very concerned.

'Who else would it be? It's the Logans!' said Paul confidently.

'Your son is right', Craig answered. 'The Logans are one step ahead of us. They need to be stopped.'

'I want their operation shut down!' said Mr Sullivan, furious. 'I want their drugs off my streets! I want them out my city! Get it done!'

Everyone dispersed at his command without a word or question.

CHAPTER 10

Late the next afternoon, the sounds of walls being smashed echoed along the now empty, dusty hallways my home. Upstairs, inside what used to be Lauren's and my bedroom, I was balls naked, my face clothed in bandages, hammering down the walls with a sledge. Crying my eyes out with every swing, I was desolate beyond repair, empty and heartbroken.

These walls carried memories, painful memories I could not bear. I wanted it to stop –the voices, the flashbacks, the screaming. I lowered the sledge, sweaty and tearful, and fell to my knees. 'Why? Why have you forsaken me?' I screamed at the empty walls. 'I've done nothing but been a faithful servant!' I pleaded to God. 'My family! You took them … you took them away!' I cried.

'Father Franklin? … what's he ever done to deserve his fate?' I muttered to myself like a madman.

Among the crumbled walls and debris, I noticed a family photo lying intact upon broken shards of mirror. I scrambled for the photo like a madman, cradling it on my chest, feeling helpless and emotional, contemplating death.

'Don't worry. I'm coming to meet you. I'm coming to meet you!' I chanted to myself repeatedly, rocking back and forth on my knees as my sanity dwindled away.

Darkness came and with it thundershowers. Night was here, cut by the sound of a shovel piercing wet earth. I was out in the backyard, vigorously digging, butt naked, shedding tears as I drove the shovel. On the lawn lay a black casket with a rope tied into the handle.

'Just a foot closer, Lauren!' I cried aloud as I reached the final depth. 'I'm coming! Tell the kids I'll be home! Daddy be home soon!'

At last, it was ready, six feet deep and waterlogged. I tossed the shovel aside, took hold of the rope, and dragged the casket into the grave. I opened the casket, sobbing as I climbed inside, and lay upon my back, out of breath.

'This is it, Lauren! I'm coming!' I bellowed from the grave.

I slowed my breathing down, caught my breath after my mammoth task, peeled my bandages off, and closed the casket tightly. Inside, I sighed with relief and closed my eyes.

The thunder banged, and the rain continued to pour, washing the bank of dirt back into the open grave. Later that night, the grave was filled, and the casket was consumed by the earth. All was quiet; in roughly five and a half hours my oxygen reserve would be consumed. Then my troubles, my misery, and my suffering would be over.

That night Paul Sullivan, along with a handful of men armed to the teeth, invaded an old warehouse on the southern edge of Carol City. This was supposedly an old drug farm of Raoul's, but it was empty, abandoned, and long since taken to pieces, they clearly saw.

Pail took out his mobile and called. 'It's me, Dad. There's nothing here. It's all gone!' he said, agitated and annoyed.

'Move to the next location', Mr Sullivan replied from the comfort of his bed as his carer massaged his privates under his linen sheets. 'I want these bastards found and taught a lesson!' Then he rudely hung up.

'OK, let's move out!' Paul called to his men as they mounted their SUVs and drove off into the rain.

After roughly two hours, I'd already began to feel agitated. Oxygen was depleting, but the dying process was slow. I was dizzy, and numb limbs were already turning blue, yet I showed no sign of remorse towards my dreadful act. I stayed put as the rain polished the surface above me.

Downtown Lismore, Carol City, there was a standoff between a batch of police officers led by Captain Walter himself and the Logan brothers' henchmen –eight strong. A drug deal had gone sour, and the men had the officers under suppressing fire from within the old public library.

'Where the hell is my strike team, for God's sake?' Captain Walter cried out aloud, taking cover behind his cruiser from the barrage of bullets.

Inside the library the men were priming smoke grenades and preparing and quietly laying explosives at both entry and exit points within the library.

The strike team at last arrived, a team of six specially trained officers. One by one they exited their armoured transport and stacked up safely behind it. With his head down, the lead officer, Darren Stein, rendezvoused with Captain Walter behind his cruiser. 'What's the situation, Captain?'

'We got eight fully armed dealers on the inside', Captain Walter reported.

'Weapons? Motives?!' asked Officer Stein.

'All weapons fired appear to be fully automatic. Nothing above range. They've got money and shitloads of drugs. The only motive these scumbags have got is that they want out of here. Neutralize the threat, now!' Captain Walter said as the bullets kept coming in.

Officer Stein rallied his team. In two sections they secured the front and rear of the building, ready to pounced. Inside, the dealers watched and waited. Then the strike team launched gas into the building; the dealers endured briefly.

On a three count, the team bashed the doors in. The explosions took out the entire strike team, scattering limbs and body parts among the debris. The dealers use the distraction of the blasts to shoot their way out of the building, lugging their drugs along as they escaped into a nearby van, leaving behind dead and critically wounded cops. Captain Walter was left to count the dead and tend to the wounded.

Meanwhile I was drawing closer to my last few hours of breath. My heart and lungs were on their final leg. I was hallucinating, envisioning a tunnel as I felt drawn towards the light.

'So this is it! You're finally moving on!' said a man with a familiar voice behind a desk, his back to me.

'Father Franklin! Is that you?!' I asked, confused but hopeful.

'More or less, I should say!' he replied, turning to face me in his clergy uniform.

'I … I don't understand! Am I dead? … Is this heaven?' I was puzzled.

'This isn't heaven! You're not dead, not yet', he replied, to my disappointment.

'What do you mean? What's all this?'

'In an hour's time you'll be dead. This is just a mirage conjured by your subconscious. This is what you wanted, isn't it?' he asked me, sounding doubtful.

'It's the only way to end the pain, the suffering, and everything else that comes with it!' I replied, agitated and looking away in shame.

I suddenly felt worried and disturbed, realizing I was in our church office. I was wearing my clergy uniform, my face was restored, and I felt at peace but somewhat guilty. I heard singing—the church choir was warming up the audience, I looked beyond the door, and as the singing stopped, a man approached the altar.

He stood before the audience ready to delivery his sermon. Father Franklin, whoever he was, noticed my curiosity and warmed my shoulder with his palm. 'Notice anything, Father Brown?' he asked gently.

Frightened, I did notice something that captured my attention. The man beside the altar was me. Sitting up front were my wife, Lauren, and our sons. My heart lurched at the sight.

'I don't understand! Help me understand! What does all this mean?!' I pleaded to Father Franklin.

'Don't you get it? This is everything you ever stood for!' he cried, leaning over me, holding me by the sleeves. 'The church, the people—the city that once believed in you! God, I hope they still do', he said, shaking his head in disappointment.

'I'm sorry! I never wanted it to come to this!' I shouted back, pulling myself away shamefully.

'Sorry? Is that it? You're about to die, and for what? Nothing!' I hung my head, facing away from Father Franklin's anger.

'You may have lost your family, but there's still hope', he said.

'Not for me, Father! I'm nothing without my family! I'm lost!' I protested.

'That doesn't mean you can't find your way! The church needs you,

Arthur. The city needs you too!' Father Franklin cried out in anger. 'This church used to be a powerful influence. Now look at it! Look at you', he said in disgust.

'Not anymore', I cried. 'Not since the drugs, the crime—all of it!'

'Then do something, for God's sake! Don't throw it all away by being a coward!' Father Franklin slammed his fist down on the desk and turned his back on me.

'I can't! … I can't. It's too late', I replied sadly.

Father Franklin turned to me with a worried look. I was fading, turning pale, my veins turning blue, my breath growing cold. I was on the verge of dying.

'I'm sorry. I really am'. I whispered.

'It's not too late! You can still turn this around!' a voice said with a note of hope.

I turned around. Someone stood before me … my own self, no longer present at the altar. He grasped me firmly by the collar, and his face changed. Mangled and disturbing, this was the image of who I was. 'Go! Go now! Make this right!' he shouted into my face.

Suddenly I realized what I must do, what was expected of me. He pushed me out the door, and I woke up, about to die. I began hammering my fist against the casket, using every ounce of energy I had left. As I punched viciously, desperate for survival, my fists began to bleed, but all of a sudden, life mattered, and I wasn't going to stop.

I punched and punched some more, and the casket showed signs of a facture. I continued as my fists became numb, and flesh tore away, exposing bone. By then the pain was behind me. I clenched my teeth and punched a hole through the casket and ripped away the splintered pieces of board. Then the earth came caving in, plunging me into cold, wet, and total darkness.

The thundershowers persisted through the night, an d the surface above the grave slowly began to sink. Then an arm with a clenched fist penetrated above the surface, then another—followed by my head as I desperately climbed from my own grave. Finally free and out of breath, on my knees I greeted the storm!

Weak and exhausted, I threw my head back and opened my mouth, tasting the rain, struggling for breath. Overwhelmed by the near-death experience, I growled into the air and grunted as the rain washed the dirt from my naked body. I gained my feet and staggered like a drunkard towards my broken home.

At first light, another anonymous tip led Detective Carl Brooks to Montgomery Funeral Parlour. He pulled up around back quietly and killed his headlights Then he called in on his radio, waited a moment, and then exited the cruiser with his gun drawn.

Inside, in the basement, six of Mr Sullivan's men, included Montgomery Daniels himself, were in the middle of loading cocaine into the dead corpses. Carl tried the rear door, which was locked. A window was open, so he climbed into the back room filled with empty caskets. He looked around, scanning room after room but tripping over a metal tray lying carelessly upon the floor. This simple error drew unwanted attention from below.

'You hear something?' whispered Daniels, looking around in confusion.

'I'll go check it out', replied a male colleague. He slide his gun from his waistband and carefully climbed the stairs.

Upstairs, realizing his error, Carl was on guard, backed up against the wall behind the doorway, waiting.

The man approached cautiously and entered the doorway. Carl knocked his gun onto the floor and shouldered him against the wall. The man fought back, kicking the gun from Carl's hand into an open casket.

'What's going on up there?' another called from the basement.

'Go check it out. We don't need any surprises', said Daniels, concerned.

Everyone else stopped what they were doing and made their way upstairs. Unaware of what was happening, they walked foolishly into the middle of the brawl, causing a distraction.

'Shoot him now!' the man yelled to his colleagues, trapped in an armlock.

Shots were fired, and Carl released his grip and dived across the room, landing in an open casket. He'd been lucky: he found one of the other guns and returned a few shots from the safety of the casket, causing the men to take cover. The walls echoed with gunshots as bullets flew across the room.

Downstairs Daniels was on the verge of freaking out, shaking as he hurriedly tried to stitch the dead filled with cocaine back together.

Two men were down, shot dead in the chest by Carl, whilst the other two engaged. The dead clicks of empty guns soon followed. The two were both out and eagerly tried to replace their empty clips –but too late.

Carl was already standing over the two with his gun to their faces. 'Put it down! Or I'll put you down!' Carl barked, a look of loathing in his eyes.

The men slowly lowered their guns.

'On your feet! Slowly now! Nice and slow! Keep those hands where I can see them!' Carl was cautious, unwilling to take any chances.

Both men slowly climbed to their feet from the corner they had occupied during the standoff, holding their hands high in submission.

'Now what, hotshot?' asked one of the men, reckless with luck.

'*Now* you do as I say! Turn around. Let's see what's going on down those stairs. Move it!' Carl nudged their backs with his gun.

A hammer cocked, and a pistol pointed to the back of Carl's head. He'd let his guard down too soon; someone had got the drop on him. All his hard work was now undone.

'Not so fast! Lower the gun slowly, and turn around!' Craig had silently appeared just in time to dismiss his former partner.

Carl put his gun down on the floor gently. One of the men grabbed the gun while the other seized him, whipped him around to face Craig, and put him in an armlock.

'Craig! You finally decide to show your face!' Carl faced him down furiously.

Craig pointed his gun at Carl's face between the eyes. 'Looks like you still don't know when to quit! I should have ended this when I had the chance!'

'What are you waiting for? Now's your chance, you scum! You never did deserve that badge! You're a piece of shit, just like the rest of these scum!' Carl shouted. The man restraining him gave him a punch to the ribs, but Carl took it like a man and held firm.

'You don't get it Carl!' Craig yelled. 'This is bigger than me! Bigger than us!' He was getting emotional, waving his gun about carelessly.

'No, Craig. You made this call. You should have fought these bastards. This isn't the way, and you know it!' Carl yelled back as he wrestled against the armlock, unable to cut loose.

'There's no fighting this, Carl. The city is lost. I'm just along for the ride. You should have stayed away!' Craig continued to yell and then knocked Carl out with a pistol butt to his forehead.

My heart racing, breathing rapidly, I awoke in a state of panic, naked. I lay on a mattress on the floor in the midst of my trashed bedroom, broken furniture and pieces of mirror all around me. Daylight pierced through the broken windows.

I had awakened from one nightmare into another: this new life I was driven to live on my own. I sat up, catching my breath, and noticed the family portrait lying right next to me beside the mattress. I reached out and took the photo from the floor. Feeling nostalgic, I wiped the dust from the frame to reveal their faces. I smiled a sad smile, whilst I held back the rain.

'I'm going to make this right, don't you worry', I whispered to the family portrait, gently rubbing the frame.

There was work to be done. Taking back the city would be a mammoth task. I wasn't prepared for the role, but I would be. I needed to learn a lot before journeying into hell. Conflicting thoughts played on my now twisted mind as I stood in my bedroom, clothed myself in my clergy uniform, and applied clean bandages to the fiendish face staring into a broken mirror at my toe cap. Then I placed the felt hat on my head and picked up the duffel bag at my feet. I went outside and placed it into the boot of my car parked off the drive. Then I got in and pulled away in a hurry.

My journey saw me through a long, winding country road, all quiet, heading outside the city. Later I found myself pulling off the main road into a narrow trail, just wide enough to fit the car with a wooden barrier posted '*DANGER—KEEP OUT*'. I pushed the barrier open, climbed back into the car, and carried on down the trail until I came to an old cottage partly consumed by thorn bushes directly ahead of the trail.-I pulled up outside the door and shut the engine down.

'Franklin, you bastard.' I fumbled in amazement, looking up at the cottage, and slung my bag from the boot.

I shouldered the door open after fighting my way past the cobwebs that decorated the entrance. My bag hit the dusty floor, and I set my hat neatly on a rack near the door. A spider crunched beneath my boot as I strolled about the cottage. It was filled with hunting antiques hanging from the walls. I took a moment to look around. There were no photographic memories, only hunting trophies. The cottage was now home to spiders crawling along an empty old wooden table set.

I suddenly felt that I was meant to be looking for something. I stopped and pondered for a second before noticing a latch above my head. My curiosity led me to pull the latch at arm's length, and out came a ladder into an attic. I was amazed. Up the ladder I went and into the attic. It was immense, empty except for a large wooden chest sitting in the middle of a finished oak floor covered with cobwebs.

I took a knee before the chest and closely examined the handcrafted woodwork from corner to corner. It was beautifully decorated, with crucifixes on all sides and the face of Jesus carved in the midst of the top.

I sharply exhaled as I flipped the rusted padlocks open with a trusted key from my pocket. My eyes went wide; I was overwhelmed by the arsenal stacked in the chest. Lost for words, I stood up and took a step back, passing my hand down my face, suddenly doubtful about what I was about to indulge in.

Looking across the attic, staring mystified at the chest, I fiddled with my chin, tapping my feet anxiously, thinking about it ... decisions, decisions. I could feel a sudden thrill rushing down my spine. Never had I seen so many guns in one setting; never had I touched or fired a gun. I had a lot to learn and fast. My days at the altar were now behind me. I felt different, reborn, with a sole purpose: to rid my city of the filth that polluted the streets and avenge my family. It was not God's way; God was sitting this one out. The old me was no more.

'Rest in peace, Father Brown', I whispered to myself. Then I took a knee and reached into the chest grabbing a pair of 12-gauge Taurus

Raging Judge revolvers, long barrels, semi-automatic fully chrome with an oak-finished pistol grip.

I rose to my feet with both pistols in my hands, taking a shine to them, murmuring these few words to myself: 'Godspeed, Arthur Brown … godspeed'.

Late afternoon, back at Raoul's drug lab at the boneyard, George Marcus had held up his end of the deal. A convoy of four trucks were being loaded with kilos of cocaine and numerous branded class A drugs from the doors of the aircraft. Raoul supervised from the roof of a commercial jet in plain view, his two dogs at his feet. He was bare-chested in his open velvet shirt with trousers and his feet inside a pair of Versace slippers.

The drivers were handed a set of fake consignment notes. Then with a tap on the doors, they were off on their journey out of the boneyard.

'It's done', Raoul said into his phone with Gosnell on the other end. 'The packages are on their way as we speak.'

Gosnell stared at the city from the balcony of his luxury condo in the middle of the capital, Lismore, smartly dressed as usual.

'Is it done?' asked Johnathon, appearing from inside wearing a white tailored robe with his initials inscribed on the left chest.

'It is done. Our biggest payoff in history!' Gosnell replied proudly whilst they both took in the panoramic view and smiled heartily. The city was within their grasp.

Somewhere across town, in a dark basement with dim, sputtering lights, a pair of legs were dragged along a wet concrete floor. The man's hands were chained together and slung over a meathook screwed into a ceiling beam. Carl, already beaten, cut, and bruised, now hung by his hands. Craig and two others from the funeral parlour stood before him, one with a chain wrapped around his fist and the other bearing brass knuckles whilst Craig held his gun firmly across the crotch of his pants.

'If you're going to kill me, you'd better finish the job', Carl grunted, spitting blood from his busted mouth.

Craig chuckled and jammed his gun up against Carl's chin. 'You really are a piece of work, aren't you? You are going to die—but not now, not just yet!' he said, putting his gun away.

'Waiting for the welcome party, are we?' said Carl, resilient despite his pessimistic circumstance.

'You worry about what's going to happen next. Don't say I never warned you, Carl!' Craig replied, threatening his former partner.

Just then, footsteps were heard approaching along the wet floor. Mr Sullivan himself, wheeled along by his carer, accompanied by his trusty entourage—his son Paul, Maxwell, and Rick—all emerging from the dark of the room semi-casually dressed in shirts and blazers. Carl mustered a disgusted expression at the dirty bunch.

'So, Detective! We meet again! This time, on bad terms!' Mr Sullivan groaned disappointedly.

'Screw you, you piece of shit! You think you own this city, do you? Huh?' Carl shouted, helpless but defiant.

'Everyone knows that I own this city! Too bad you and your friends in blue won't see the truth!' Mr Sullivan boasted, with pride dancing all over his wrinkled face. 'This time I'm afraid you have taken a step too far. I've come all this way just to see you, Detective!' Mr Sullivan vented his unhappy feelings towards the repugnant detective.

'I'm flattered!' Carl replied sarcastically and turned his eyes up at the audience who stood waiting to see him suffer.

'You think this is a joke, Detective?!' Mr Sullivan replied, nodding towards the pair that had grabbed Carl back at the funeral parlour.

Carl received a brutal jab into his left chest with a chained fist and groaned in agony.

'Now I've got your attention! I'm afraid your persistent ways end here, Detective', Mr Sullivan threatened with a businesslike ring to his tone, nothing personal.

'Go on, do your worst!' Carl cried out in pain from his cracked rib, grinding his teeth as he gave way to the pain.

Mr Sullivan twitched his index finger at Craig, beckoning him closer. Craig leant forward with his ear next to Mr Sullivan's mouth. A few words were muttered into his ear, and he nodded in assent.

Satisfied, Mr Sullivan called aloud to his carer, 'Get me out this filth!'

His carer wheeled him away, and the others followed on, leaving Craig and his two colleagues behind to handle this unfinished affair.

'Sorry, Carl! This needs to be done!' Craig spat into Carl's face without sympathy, borrowed the brass knuckles from his colleague, and knocked the detective cold with a single blow to the head.

Later that day back at the Cottage, I sat behind the old wooden table in jeans and a tank top stained with gun oil. On the table lay a nine millimetre pistol, a semiautomatic revolver, an assault rifle, and my two favourites, the 12-gauge fully revolvers. All were fully stripped and laid out before me. I'd been busy, and it was time to prove myself. There were a lot of guns and not much time on my hands; I needed to kick things up a notch.

'OK, Arthur. This is it', I urged myself in a strict voice.

I stood up, set an old kitchen timer, and began reassembling the rifle, racing against time. Second after second I put the pieces together, and ding! The clock stopped. CLICK went the trigger, and it was done! Nine seconds flat, a record time! I smirked beneath my bandage, self-satisfied, and then quickly reassembled the rest of the guns.

I picked up a book, *Stripping and Assembling for Beginners*, and went to the bookshelves, where I slid it neatly back in its place. My phone buzzed on the old wooden table amongst the guns—an alert, notifying me that a package had been left waiting at the end of the road down the cottage trail. I laid the phone back down, shrugged into a trench coat and my hat, and left the cottage on foot.

At the end of the trail, sitting beneath the wooden barrier was a parcel, a small box neatly wrapped, which couldn't have arrived any sooner. With little time to waste, I took the box and returned to the cottage. At the wooden table I opened the to reveal another prized book, *Marksmanship Principles*. My phase two appointment awaited me before I could feel ready to face the treacherous role that awaited me.

CHAPTER 11

At night fall, the trucks carrying the Logan brothers' class A drugs came upon a roadblock on route out of the city via the Interstate. Four police cruisers were dark, with no blue lights; all officers had been shot dead, some hanging from their doors, others face down on the street—a massacre. Just beyond the dead police vehicles parked in an interlocking formation, were a gang of unarmed men, all casually dressed and patiently waiting.

The trucks stopped, and the drivers grew fearful, slamming on their brakes, jackknifing to a stop. One driver boldly decided to reach for his long range radio just above his head; he was shot dead with a bullet to the head by a rifleman standing in the midst of the gang resting calmly on the bonnet of a car. The rest of the drivers reached for their shotguns, but they too were wasted with bullets pouring from automatic weapons as they dismounted their lorries to face off against the gang.

'Quick! Secure the trucks! Let's get the hell out of here!' bellowed one man with a big beard and a man bun, wearing a long leather jacket and a shiny pair of black shin-high boots and holding a .45 Magnum pistol in his hand.

The dead drivers were hauled from their lorries and the trucks were taken away. The man with the big beard and the man bun returned to his vehicle with the rest of his men and immediately left the scene.

The following day saw Mr Sullivan and his men down at the old rail lines on the far side of the city, out of public sight. The rails had been out of service for decades and sported urban art. Parked along the tracks, Mr Sullivan sat in the back seat of his car next to his carer with her hand on his thigh with the windows down. He was musing on the old trains when Maxwell approached him from the vehicle alongside his car.

'You sure about this place, sir?' Maxwell asked, gazing into the window of the car.

'Yes, I'm sure. We need to relocate, thanks to Detective Brooks', Mr Sullivan snarled with contempt.

'Right, Sir. I'll get the process moving at once', Maxwell replied and headed back to his vehicle.

Somewhere in a basement room, the sound of muffled grunts echoed within the darkness. Carl, chained up by his wrists and ankles, his mouth taped shut, and his clothes covered in filth, was on his back with rodents pestering at his feet. With no one to hear him scream, Carl was left to his own fate.

Across town in the capital city, Lismore, the Logan brothers sat at a fancy restaurant called Exotic Cuisine. The place was fairly busy, and they were in the middle of a celebration. With the brothers sat Raoul, and a handful of men, all smartly dressed, sat close by at their own table. An armed entourage waited outside in their vehicles in case of an unwanted guest.

Inside were laughter, smiles, toasts, champagne bubbling, and a couple of paid ladies in their circle enjoying the spoils, giggling and acting friendly; all was merry. Raoul stood up in the midst of the restaurant half-drunk, holding a bottle of Ace of Spades, causing a scene.

'Everybody, listen up! Stop whatever the fuck you're doing!' he shouted, drawing everyone's unhappy attention.

'For God's sake, Raoul!' snapped Johnathon, annoyed. 'Sit the fuck down! You're embarrassing yourself!'

'No! These people need to show some respect!' Raoul refused to pipe down, waving his bottle frantically. Then he pointed at a man two tables away, enjoying his pricey meal with his wife and kids. 'You! You right there, stuffing your stupid face! I'm talking here!'

'All right!' Gosnell broke in. 'You've had enough! Somebody get him out of here!' He wanted to end Raoul's antics, and they needed him to leave peacefully.

Two men stood up from the table, courtesy of Gosnell. They took Raoul by the arm, about to drag him out the restaurant. Raoul fought against the men, tearing away from their grasp and pulling a pistol from his waistband, under the blazer. Everyone panicked, holding on to their partners and loved ones in fear of what might happen next.

'Nobody fucking move! Raise your fucking glasses! We are here to celebrate greatness!' Raoul bellowed through the restaurant, firing a couple shots into the ceiling for emphasis.

'Put the gun away before you do something stupid!' Gosnell ordered, rising furiously to his feet.

'Fucking lighten up! We're all having a good time!' Raoul continued despite the effort to calm him, waving his gun around, drunk and excited.

Just then Lady Casandra walked in, unexpected, unannounced and unnoticed. She saw the commotion and shook her head, disgusted by Raoul's crude display. 'Sorry, kid. I'm going to need that'. She grabbed a baseball from a kid sitting at a nearby table who was latched onto his mother's arm in fear of Raoul behaviour. With Raoul still unaware of her presence, she hurled the ball at Raoul's head, knocking him cold to the ground. Everyone was relieved and resumed their business.

The Logans were remarkably pleased to see Casandra for the second time. 'Well done, Lady Casandra!' Johnathon said, standing to greet her. 'Not a moment too soon! If you hadn't walked in, I'm afraid my brother would have shot the poor brute!'

'Please, Lady Casandra, have a seat. Join us!' Gosnell interrupted, showing her to Raoul's empty chair. 'Get that evil mess out of here!' Gosnell called to his men, and they scooped Raoul from the floor and carried him away.

'I'm afraid I'm here on business', Casandra said. 'Hate to spoil your little party, but you've got trouble!' She had their full attention.

'Trouble? What trouble might this be?' Gosnell, about to sip some champagne, froze in mid-gesture.

'Let's just say someone jacked your shit!' she replied.

'In English?' Johnathon asked, not quite understanding the sour news.

'Your mountain of blow was taken, got that? Am I clear?' Casandra replied bluntly, agitated by Johnathon's ignorance.

'What? Tell me I didn't hear what I think you are saying!' Gosnell slammed his fist on the table, drawing attention once again from all around. 'What the fuck you all looking at?! he yelled at the nosy customers.

The ladies at the table abruptly grabbed their purses, excused themselves, and took off.

'You heard right!' Casandra replied with a stern look.

'This must be dealt with immediately!' Johnathon said, slinging his coat onto his back angrily, about to leave. 'Let's get the hell out of here!' he straightened his coat and rushed towards the door whilst his brother happily trailed behind in the company of Casandra.

'Er … Sir? You haven't paid for the meal!' A male waiter cut Johnathon short at the door, bravely grabbing onto his expensive coat.

Johnathon stopped, turned, and looked at the waiter with a foul expression. The waiter had barely flinched at the sight when Johnathon grabbed him by the hand and twisted his arm, shoving him to the floor. 'Pay this man his money!' Johnathon called to the men accompanying him out the door.

A wad of bills was tossed at the waiter crouched up on the floor, holding his arm in agony, belittled by the Logans' carefree ways as they took their leave.

'You do know who our first point of contact will be, don't you?' said Johnathon to his unhappy brother as they sat in the back of their limousine facing Casandra, about to be chauffeured off.

'Trust me, brother. That old fart will answer to us', Gosnell replied, setting himself into a foul mood.

'What are you proposing then?' Johnathon asked.

'We send him a message', Gosnell replied, looking grim.

'I'll make sure the message is delivered', said Lady Casandra, keen and willing to undertake the dirty work.

'Good! Get it done. This one's off the books, to be clear!' Gosnell emphasized.

'But of course! Free of charge!' Lady Casandra replied with a not-so-pleasant smile as the chauffeur drove the limousine through Lismore.

Late one afternoon a week later, a series of gunshots echoed amongst a clump of forest trees just beyond the Cottage. With bullet after bullet, I was blasting coins and empty water bottles from a tree stump at a hundred metres range, using an assault rifle and several pistols. I sat on a log, making use of what little time I had. Besides my face bandage, I wore only jeans, a pair of black mountain boots, and a red flannel shirt over a grease stained white T-shirt.

I had mastered the marksmanship principles, and hours of clockwork had paid off. I laid the rifle down empty at my feet and swapped it for my favourites—the pair of long-barrel fully chromed 12-gauge Taurus Raging Judge 28 revolvers, fully loaded.

I carefully set a few acorns out at a mere fifty metre range on an overhanging branch. Pacing myself backwards, shot after shot I delicately trimmed the acorns from the branch in front of me. The pistols smoked, and shells tumbled from the cylinders as they flipped open. Pleased with my progress, I spun the pistols around my index fingers, smiling under my facial bandages. It was time to make a move. I was quickly back to the cottage. I grabbed my duffel bag and tossed it into the boot of my car, slammed the door, and fired up the engine, and off I went.

With the Logan brothers' major setback, Mr Sullivan was filling the void; his drug operation was in full swing. At the old rail lines, at nightfall, cart after cart, the dead were lined up on wheeled tables, cut open, and stuffed with kilos of cocaine.

Under Montgomery Daniels's direction, the operation ran like clockwork with half a dozen men working on corpse after corpse. After they were stuffed and stitched closed, they were then wheeled into a separate cart at the rear of the train. Each one was suited up and placed inside a designated casket, marked by a special number code tagged to a buyer. Finally they were loaded down a ramp into the back of each waiting hearse.

That night, Paul was stumbling into his new penthouse in downtown Lismore, drunk, faffing around his jacket pocket trying to find his keys for the front door. Then his keys fell at his feet, and when Paul stooped down, he noticed blood seeping through beneath the door. Shocked and frightened, he nearly fell backwards in the hallway.

Panicked, he wandered around quietly, both hands on his head, contemplating his options whilst he sweated repeatedly. 'Fuck sake! Fuck! OK, OK … I can handle this! Fuck it!' Paul muttered continuously pacing up and down the hallway.

He pulled his gun from the back of his waistband. Then, with a grunt of effort, he shouldered the door open, carelessly slipping in the pool of blood, and landing on his back next to his glass centrepiece in the living room. He scrambled to his feet at the sight of a man hanging from his ceiling fan. It was one of his father's employees, no one unimportant—but the message was clear. The man's bowels were spread across the marble floor, and the blood that had poured from his slit throat was congealing on the marble floor.

Paul gagged. 'Fuck!' he shouted, vomiting into the midst of the unholy mess. Then he looked up and suddenly recognized the man hanging from his ceiling fan. He stood up, and after a closer look he began to grieve. 'No. No! Not you, Johnny! Not you!'

Still drunk, paranoid, and disorientated, Paul staggered about the room, trying to make sense of what had happened. He saw a note stuck to Johnny's back; it read: 'You fucked with the wrong family'. Lost for words, he snatched his phone from his pocket and called his father.

Mr Sullivan, accompanied by Maxwell, Rick, his carer, and a handpicked entourage was just leaving the Aqua Sushi restaurant in formal attire after a well prepared meal. Outside in the rain, umbrellas were deployed while Maxwell and two others escorted Mr Sullivan into a waiting limousine, taking their time with his wheelchair.

'Hurry up! It's pissing down, for God's sake!' Mr Sullivan called to his men impatiently as they carefully seated him in the back of the limousine. Just as Mr Sullivan was settling in comfortably, his phone rang within his coat pocket. Paul was on the other end eagerly awaiting a response.

'It's late, son! What is it?!' Mr Sullivan answered his phone with a stern approach.

'It's Johnny! He's fucking dead! They killed him!' Paul cried, sounding drunk and frantic.

'What? What the hell you talking about son? What the fuck happened?' Mr Sullivan asked, suddenly interested.

'Everything all right, sir?' Maxwell asked, looking into the limousine from underneath his umbrella.

'Just get the fuck over here now!' Paul cried out in anger and tossed his phone across the marble floor and held his head in a panic.

'Get me over to Paul's place, now! Let's go!' Mr Sullivan yelled in urgency.

Maxwell, Rick and the rest of the men quickly mounted their vehicles and took off into the pouring rain. Moments later, Mr Sullivan and his men were at Paul's penthouse, banging on the door. Paul opened up in a hurry, and four of Mr Sullivan's men came storming in, hands in their waistbands, ready to draw. They also threw up at the gruesome sight. Maxwell wheeled Mr Sullivan inside, both covering their noses gagging uncontrollably; the mess was unsightly.

'What the fuck happened here Paul? Who did this?' Mr Sullivan grunted.

'I don't know, Pop! Whoever it was, they left a note!' cried Paul, drunk and on the brink of tears. He passed the note to Maxwell.

Maxwell looked at the note, and his face twisted with hatred. The answer became clear as he passed the note on to Mr Sullivan. He too had a look of suspicion as he took the note; he read it and flicked it aside disgustedly.

'You know who this is, don't you, sir?' Maxwell whispered closely to his boss's ear.

'Who the fuck is it? I want to know!' Paul cried, flipping a lip throwing a tantrum.

'It's the brothers! The Logan brothers!' Mr Sullivan replied, worried for his fragile empire.

'Well, Pop! Is there something we should know? Like why the fuck they killed poor old Johnny? Huh, Pop?' Paul approached his father, boldly shouting in his already crestfallen face.

Mr Sullivan wheeled himself across the room in silence. He sighed, looking rather uncomfortable whilst taking a careful thought to himself.

'I was afraid this might happen.' He spoke quietly, refreshing his sick lungs with a breath of fresh oxygen from the tank at the back of his chair.

'Afraid what might happen? Dammit, Pop, what the fuck is all this about?' Paul yelled at his father impatiently, eager to know what was on his mind.

'They've lost millions worth of drugs! Their cargo was hit, hijacked! They stole it all. Cocaine, crystal meth, you name it. They took it all!' Mr Sullivan explained in the most dramatic voice, gripping the attention of his men.

'How long have you known this? What does any of this have to do with us? Answer me, Pop—answer me!' Paul yelled, breaking a few of his valuable ornaments in anger, startling his already frightened father clutching his oxygen mask.

'I heard about it from an old friend! It's nothing to do with us! You must understand we are the only ones they can suspect!' Mr Sullivan replied, wheeling about the room anxiously.

'Your father is right. We're their only rivals in this city. This is their reason!' Maxwell made a valuable point.

'So what the hell are we going to do about it?' Paul asked, anxious to get into a fight, shifting restlessly from one foot to the other.

'Keep the drugs going', Mr Sullivan ordered.' Have everyone on lookout. Nobody does anything without me knowing. Now clean this mess up! Get me out of here!' Maxwell wheeled him away whilst a few others stayed put to dispose of the body.

'Well? Let's get a move on!' Rick took charge, flicking a knife from his pocket, about to cut the body from the ceiling fan.

At home back in Carol City early the next morning, the daylight beamed through my broken windows onto my face like a spotlight. I rose from the mattress on the floor, where I'd slept in only my jeans, slipped into a flannel shirt, and found my way to the bathroom. There I trimmed my old bandages in a broken mirror and replaced them with a clean spread.

There was more work to be done, I needed the city's attention; it was time for another public appearance. I unfolded my laptop from the kitchen drawer and sat down behind the kitchen table. I typed an email to my contacts and the members of my beloved church. Sirens wailed past in the street. The cops were still trying hard to keep the streets clean, but it was too late; their efforts had been futile.

The city had already been lost to the kingpin, Mr Sullivan, ever since he'd set foot in town ... If only people could see the truth. The radio that sat before me on the kitchen table was busy with the day's latest report. A standoff in the middle of downtown Lismore between Mr Sullivan's men and their rivals, the Logan brothers, was the live report. With the emails sent, immediately I went outside and removed a medium-size crate from the boot of my car. I had brought it from the cottage. It had been concealed beneath the wooden floor by Father Franklin, another dark secret of his. I set it in the middle of my dismantled living room and cracked the lid open using a crowbar. Inside was a hefty amount of trinitrotoluene or TNT—all part of my grand agenda.

Downtown Lismore, mid-afternoon, a group of men courtesy of the Logan brothers came storming into a local dry cleaner, armed and looking for answers. The employees and customers fled at the sight of guns as the men forced Dale Rogers from his office. He was a client of Mr Sullivan and the proud owner of the establishment, a scrawny-looking man in his late fifties, short and bald, wearing a floral unisex shirt and long pants with a pair of square tip boots.

The men hung him by his coat onto the conveyor. 'Start talking!' Matt Wallis ordered. He was one of the Logan brothers' hired thugs, six feet tall and well built with a beard and dark hair, in his early forties, and very aggressive—just as evil as Raoul himself.

'I don't know what you are talking about! What the hell do you want with me?' Dale Rogers panicked, shielding his face with his hands from Matt's temping fists probing at his head.

'Your boss stole from my boss! Now my boss wants what's his, and I'm going to do whatever it takes to get it!' Matt threatened.

'I swear, I don't know shit! I pay my commission, and that's as far as my business with Mr Sullivan goes! I swear!' Dale replied, honest yet frightened.

'I think you are lying, and I'm going to find out the hard way! ...

Get him down!' Matt, determined to get what he came for, refused to accept Dale's honest words.

His men removed Dale from the conveyor. Matt grabbed him by the throat and dragged him towards a steam press. There he forced the man's head underneath the hot steam, about to scald the flesh from his face.

'Please stop! I don't know! I don't fucking know, I swear!' Dale cried out, pleading for mercy.

'Wrong answer, Dale! Wrong fucking answer!' Matt shouted in his face. Then he closed the steam press on Dale's head, scalding the flesh from the side of his face.

Dale screamed, pleading for the pain to stop. 'Please stop! I'm telling the truth!' he cried in agony.

'Not good enough, Dale! Not good enough!' Matt shouted back, applying the hot steam once more against the already burnt face, inflicting further injury.

Dale cried out, badly hurt, his flesh burnt and his ear scalded. But the infamous Matt Wallis offered no mercy. With the help of his men, Matt flipped Dale over, looking to scald the other side of his face.

'Last chance, Dale! Last fucking chance!' Matt shouted, about to slam the steam press down onto Dale's face.

Dale, already in shock, fumbled to get his words out, but nothing was clear.

'Sorry, Dale! Can't hear you! You're sleeping on me! I'm going to have to wake you up!' Matt snarled loudly, clamping the steam press down onto Dale's face.

Dale passed out during the continuous burning and battering of his face. They tossed him to the ground like a worthless pile of junk.

'Looks like Dale didn't know anything after all.' Matt straightened his coat, feeling proud of his actions, and the men saw themselves out.

At the Carol City docks late at night, two rows of headlights faced each other as Mr Sullivan and the Logan brothers turned out in their numbers, just as they did back at the old Carol City bridge. They were trying again to set aside their differences, reach a mutual understanding, and bury the hatchet.

'You Logans are making a grave mistake!' Mr Sullivan's voice shimmered calmly, as he sat in his wheelchair in his long overcoat, a flat cap, and a scarf. 'You're barking up the wrong tree!'

'I'm afraid we have to disagree, Mr Sullivan!' Gosnell replied, impatient but anxious. 'You should make it easy on yourself! Tell me, where's the cargo?'

'There's no cargo! This has nothing to do with me or my men, I assure you!' Mr Sullivan answered sternly and as genuinely as he could.

'A cargo that big doesn't disappear like that, Mr Sullivan! Tell me, where is the bloody cargo?' Gosnell replied, grinding his teeth, keeping his temper in check.

'I gave you my word, Gosnell! This has nothing to do with me or my men! I suggest you try looking elsewhere!' Mr Sullivan, annoyed, started coughing and resorted to his oxygen mask.

'This night doesn't have to end on a sad note', Johnathon interjected, trying to be the voice of reason. 'All we need is what's rightfully ours!'

'You heard the man! This is not on us!' Paul shouted with his ill-tempered attitude. 'Now! One of you assholes killed Johnny! I'm not going to let this go, you hear me?' Paul hinted at a threat, risking the Logans' temper.

'Easy, Paul! This isn't the time and place!' Mr Sullivan was trying to ease the tension and avoid another bloodfest.

'Your son's got a mouth on him. You should keep him on a short leash. Hate to teach him a lesson!' A voice came from the back of the gang—Raoul, once again making a grand appearance.

'Well, if it isn't the traitor himself! Might want to look a bit closer to home, Logans!' Rick boldly commented, standing proud next to Maxwell, arms across his body above the loaded piece inside his waistband.

Raoul's anger was immediately aroused. He didn't took too kindly Rick's remark, he drew his gun, and everyone instantly followed suit—excluding Mr Sullivan and the Logans who remained confident amongst their men. The groups pointed their guns at each other, ready to paint the night red.

'You accusing me of something, little boy? Huh? Are you?' Raoul growled in the foulest of tones, his face creased with resentment.

'Enough!' Gosnell barked, suddenly read to deal. 'We are all civilized beings here! Let's just come to an agreement, shall we?' Gosnell was surprised at his own sudden change of heart.

'What are you proposing?' Mr Sullivan sounded intrigued.

'You're not seriously considering a deal with these scumbags, are you?' Paul was concerned; he sought blood rather than peace for the good of his father's empire.

'You recover my loss, and we stop killing your men and your business! How does that sound?' Gosnell made the unusual offer as he hoped to buy Mr Sullivan's trust in return for letting his crippled empire thrive peacefully.

'If you are proposing to make me your bitch, you can go fuck yourself!' Mr Sullivan replied arrogantly.

'You know we have the resources to turn the tables! I suggest you take the offer!' Johnathon added, making a valid point but testing the patience of the trigger-happy men itching to get a round off.

'My brother is right!' Gosnell said. 'I'm afraid you don't have much of a choice!' What do you intend on doing? Mowing each other down, right here, right now? Or will you cooperate?' Gosnell closely evaluated the stakes at hand, trying to force Mr Sullivan to make an irrational decision.

'I'll get back to you. We're finished here!' Mr Sullivan replied with a hint of cooperation. Everyone turned and got into their vehicles, leaving on reasonable terms.

Across town, that same night, inside Denny's Diner, approaching midnight. Captain Walter sat, still in his work gear, cradling a cup of Joe in the company of a familiar face.

'The cargo is stored in the location you requested!' It was the man from the Interstate, with the big beard and his man bun, sitting before Captain Walter with a flat cap low over his face and his collar turned up, looking shady.

Ray Sutherland was his name. The man who had led the assault on the cargo up the Interstate sat conferring with Captain Walter, drinking an ice cold beer.

'Thanks for taking care of this', Captain Walter said, tired and exhausted with a can't-be-both attitude.

'Anything else I can do before I leave town?' Ray asked, with a smooth, cautious tone.

'No. You've done enough. I'm grateful. Here, take this', Captain Walter replied wearily, sliding a briefcase underneath the table towards Ray's feet.

'A man of your word. I like that.' Ray grinned with satisfaction as he nestled the briefcase close to his black leather boots.

'You can count it. It's all there. Ten mil, just like we agreed', the captain assured him, finishing his coffee.

'I trust you—and I know where to find you if you're short', Ray replied with a snide look. He took a swig and set the bottle down emphatically. 'So, Captain, how did you find the money? I'm curious to know.' His piercing eyes searched the captain's weary face.

'You've been paid. That's all that matters', Captain Walter replied, a bit unsettled.

'Don't make me ask twice, Captain. I hate to repeat myself!' His tone was foul as he hunched forward on the table, looking the captain dead in the eyes.

'It's all evidence! It won't be missed, trust me!' The captain hung his head, intimidated and ashamed, unable to meet Ray's burning stare.

Intrigued by the captain's honesty, Ray flopped back in his seat with a chuckle at the captain's expense.

'If you would excuse me, I think we are finished here!' Captain Walter stood up and straightened his coat, about to leave.

'See you around, Captain. Pleasure doing business with you!' Ray calmly bade the captain farewell with a suspicious smile still lingering about his face.

Without a word, Captain Walter quickly saw himself out of the diner, bringing their brief encounter to an end. Ray looked on through the window as the captain wearily got into his car.

CHAPTER 12

Two weeks later, somewhere in the dark, a squeaking Carl was somehow unchained, on his knees in filth, feasting on a rat that had blindly stumbled across his fingers. He had been forgotten, starved, and mentally crippled: time and hardship had turned him into an inhuman remnant of his former self. He stumbled about the dark like an animal, salvaging any life that dwelled within his reach. He had lost his spark and long since embraced his fate.

He banged against walls in the darkness, indicating that he was enclosed in some sort of steel chamber. It was futile to attempt escape. The shredded coat on his back, a rough stubble, and cracked, filthy nails were signs of abandonment. He slid his back down the dark wall and curled quietly into a ball.

Four weeks went by. There I was, running through the forest just behind the cottage, ranging into the denser woods, carrying a forty-four kilo backpack, shirtless, wearing only long cargo trousers and a pair of mountain boots. I was toned, in peak physical condition, my abdomen and chest glistened with the sweat running down my body. I had been busy. The old me was no more, no longer a coward, no longer weak but focused, strong and driven with a burning desire to finish what had started.

My trail brought me back at the cottage's door, where I threw the backpack onto the ground. I began stacking a small pile of boulders near the cottage, filling a gap in the broken stone wall; it was as if every activity made me more robust. I felt great, fit, and pleased with the new man I'd become. Inside, I wiped the sweat from my body and tore the sweaty bandages from my face, gazing at the monster in the mirror above the fireplace.

I sat down at the table with the laptop I had retrieved from my home and checked my emails. At last, success! I had numerous responses, almost enough to launch my final phase. All my correspondents were happy to rally in favour of my motion toward an anticrime/drug campaign.

Satisfied, I shut down my computer and headed for the antique bathtub, where I soaked right next to the chest filled with guns open beside me in the middle of the open plan living space. Pleased with the contents of the chest, I slid myself deep into the tub burying my body beneath the murky water for a full body soak.

Early the next afternoon, Captain Chris Walter stood in his office at the CCPD looking out the window. He was anxious after his meeting with Ray at the diner. His door swung open, and a female officer entered. Walter flinched, caught off guard and feeling on edge. He yelled, 'Damn it! Doesn't anyone know how to knock?'

'Sorry, sir. You've got an urgent call on line two!' she humbly let him know.

'What are you waiting for? Patch it through!' the captain ordered, planting his rear end into his seat behind his desk and answering the call.

He heard a female voice on the other end of the line, distressed and panicky. Detective Carl Brooks's wife, Miranda, was in her bedroom unpacking her luggage with the phone tucked into her shoulder at her ear. 'Captain Walter?' she asked, to make sure.

'Speaking. Who might this be?' Walter asked, feeling suspicious, still on edge.

'Oh thank God! It's Miranda, Carl's wife!' she said, slightly less worried.

'Mrs. Brooks? How may I help you?' the captain asked, loosening his tie and getting comfortable in his seat.

'It's Carl. He's not been home in weeks! I've tried calling, I've tried everything! I had to cut my trip short. It's not like Carl to do this!' Miranda stressed her heartfelt emotion towards the already worried captain.

'OK, Mrs. Brooks! Calm down!' the captain replied as he tried to make sense of what was going on beneath his nose. 'What exactly are you saying? I've got an email telling me your husband is on temporary leave. He took some time off, said you two were going through a rough patch', the captain explained, still somewhat boggled by Carl's sudden disappearance.

'That's not my husband, Captain! Everything is fine! I've been holidaying with my mother in France!' Miranda said through her tears, sinking onto the bed.

'Don't worry, ma'am. We'll find him. Try not to do anything foolish in the meantime.' The captain hung up, thinking hard. *First the mayor and now Carl! What the hell is going on?*

Captain Walter rushed towards his office door and shouted across the room, 'Officer Shepherd! Get in here, now!'

Officer Shepherd hurried in. 'What is it sir!' he asked, keen as ever, fixing utility belt around his waist.

'Detective Carl is missing. Last place he made contact was the Montgomery Funeral Parlour downtown. I want every officer on the street on the lookout! Gather a team and infiltrate that parlour. Keep an eye out for Mr Sullivan and his gang. Now go!' His orders were loud and clear, but he thumped a fist on his desk to make sure.

'Right away, sir!' Shepherd replied, bolting eagerly out the office door.

Still trapped inside his darkened prison, Carl was down to his last strand of hope. Slowly and calmly he tapped his head against the wall as his sanity dwindled away.

Meanwhile, at the boneyard the Logan brothers were doing their part to find who was responsible for their lost cargo. They had found a man who might have been involved and might just have some answers. Tied to an old aircraft seat in the middle of the boneyard was a man called Steven Walker.

He was an average-looking man with a touch of grey hair and a clean-shaven face, He wore a greasy overall with his name tag patched into the top left of his chest. Walker happened to know someone who knew someone who may have played a role in jacking the cargo.

Standing before him were the impatient brothers, Gosnell and

Johnathon, along with Raoul, his two dogs thirsting for a kill, four other handy men, and of course the infamous Matt Wallis, all intrigued to get some answers.

'Tell me what you know. That's all I'm asking', Gosnell tried being reasonable with a calm, collected approach. 'Tell me who took my cargo, and you walk out of here alive: simple.' He reasoned with Walker, hoping to find common ground.

'Like I told your men, I don't know who took your shit!' the man replied, a foolish response for someone whose neck was on the line.

A punch to the gut by Raoul shook him up, a wake-up call. Walker gasped with pain.

'Spare me the empty chat!' Gosnell raised his voice as his patience wore thin. 'You were overheard discussing the contents of my cargo! Tell me what you know!'

Walker spat at Gosnell's feet, scowling disgustedly at the audience before him, refusing to crack. As a sign of goodwill and respect to the Logans, Matt pulled a knife from his coat pocket, snatched Walker by the jaws, and held the knife pointing at his eyeball. Walker flinched, frightened, for his life.

'You heard the boss! Tell us what you know! Don't make me ask twice! ... I never ask twice!' Matt threatened intensely, inching his knife towards Walker's watery eye.

'Get that fucking knife away from me! Like I said, I don't know shit!' Walker yelled, standing his ground.

Without a word, Matt sliced the ear from the man's head like a butcher. Walker screamed horrifically, a savage price to pay for his insolence.

'I think you can hear very well with one ear, Steve! What do you think?' Matt toyed with his victim, hoping to hit the breaking point. 'You going to talk to us, or do I need to prove another point?' Matt got louder, waving his knife at Walker's throat.

The man was too busy screaming to think of an answer. The pain was paralyzing. He could only clench his lips in an effort to endure it.

'Come on, Steve! Talk to me! Can't hear you with all the screaming! Talk to me!' Matt called to Walker impatiently, circling him with his knife like a boxing referee.

Just when Walker thought things could not get any worse, Matt sliced his other ear from his head. Walker's pain became utterly unbearable, and he writhed in torment. The audience looked on, enjoying the bloody spectacle.

'I can do this shit all day, Stevie boy! You want to be talking right now!' Matt urged, with a fire in his eyes, passionate about his torturing methods.

'I'll talk! I'll fucking talk!' Walker replied, yielding at last to Matt's demands.

'That's the spirit! I'm listening!' Matt answered, folding his arms.

'I only have a name! That's all I know! Nothing else, I swear!' Walker showed signs of cooperation as he tried to cope with the agonizing pain pulsating on both sides of his head.

'It's about time this piece of crap start talking!' Gosnell was annoyed that it took so much effort to get the answers he needed.

'A name? Is that all?!' Matt asked, still prodding for answers.

'Yes, just a name!' the man replied faintly, weary of his pain.

'I hope you are not pissing me about, Steve! You know what's going to happen if you do!' Matt warned, brandishing his knife once more, this time directly over Walker's heart.

'I'm not! I swear!' His fright seemed genuine.

'Good. Now talk! I'm listening!' Matt demanded.

'His name is Arthur Brown, I was told. No one knows what he looks like. He keeps his face hidden. That's all I know!' Walker said, just doing his part, a favour for an old friend yet to be revealed.

Matt grabbed him by the neck, angry and frustrated that he might be lying. 'Is this a joke? A man without a face? This your way of screwing with me?'

'No! I'm telling you the truth! That's what I've been told! Nothing more!' Walker pleaded his honesty, holding fast to his words.

'Where is this man? Where can we find him?!' Matt shouted in Walker's face.

'I don't know! I wasn't told much! That's all I know!' the man pleaded desperately.

'You buying this crap?!' Matt asked the brothers, looking for confirmation.

'He seems very much convinced. Find out who this Arthur Brown is, and bring him to us!' Gosnell ordered.

'And him?' Matt asked, pointing his knife carelessly at Steve.

'I'll leave him to you', Gosnell replied, leaving the boneyard with his brother whilst Raoul and his dogs followed on, leaving a handful of their handy men behind, should Matt need a hand.

'Please! I've told you what I know! Let me go, I'm begging!' Walker shamelessly pleaded.

'Don't worry about that. I'm going to cut you loose. But first, I'm going to make sure you never get involved again. Hold him down!' Matt was about to perpetrate another remorseless act of violence. His men grabbed Walker and held him firmly against the seat while Matt prepared to conduct his blood work.

'No! No! Please don't!' Walker cried out in terror.

Matt took his knife and dug the man's eyes from their sockets. The other men then forced his mouth open, and Matt plunged his hand into Walker's mouth, seized his tongue, and sliced it from his throat, leaving him in hellish pain, gagging on his own blood. It was a gruesome fate, a hefty price to pay for a favour owed to a man he had deemed a friend.

'Take him away! I'm done here', Matt said, wiping his blade clean on Walker's greasy overalls. They untied him, threw him in the back of a pickup, and took him away. Raoul's dogs came racing around the corner of the boneyard and fought over the severed ears and tongue.

Later that afternoon the Logans pulled up at their mansion in the limousine. 'Arthur Brown. What a very profound name. It's as if I've heard of the man'. Johnathon sat in the limousine next to his brother, pondering upon my name.

'I do share the profound feeling you are having, brother', Gosnell replied suspiciously, rubbing his chin.

'Something tells me Mr Sullivan may just know exactly who this so-called Arthur Brown is, the man without a face. Have the men look into it, immediately!' Gosnell became obsessed at the thought of my name, impatient for clarity.

Downtown that afternoon, outside Montgomery Daniels's funeral parlour, Officer Shepherd and four other officers were about to enter the parlour's front door. They walked in, casually looking to get some information, and approached Daniels inside his office.

'Can I help you, officers?' Montgomery asked, springing to his feet nervously.

'You the owner of this establishment?' Officer Shepherd asked with a poised, professional attitude.

'Uh, yeah, that'd be me. Is something wrong, officer?!' Montgomery asked, nervously scratching his head.

Downstairs, in the basement, the conversation between the officers and Montgomery was overheard. Craig, with a group of six men, was in the process of cleaning up any trace of evidence that might link to their drug operation.

'Quiet. Hold still. You hear that? Think we've got unwanted company'. Craig alerted the men, who quietly eased their guns from the backs of their trousers.

'We need to have a look around. Standard procedure.' Officer Shepherd handed Daniels a warrant.

'May I ask what this is about?' Montgomery replied, feeling on edge. After all, his neck was on the line.

'Police business, I'm afraid!' Shepherd replied sternly, about to set off down into the basement.

'This is a respectable establishment!' Montgomery raised his tone, looking shifty, hardly conveying innocence.

Craig killed the lights. The men took firing positions in the event that Shepherd and his team should approach.

Officer Shepherd shrugged. 'I'll have to withhold judgement on that, sir. We need to have a look around, like it or not!' He turned to his men. 'Spread out and search this place!'

The officers immediately fanned out towards every part of the place. Fearing what was about to happen, Montgomery panicked and quietly let himself out the back whilst Officer Shepherd and his men searched.

'Over here!' one officer called out. 'Think I've found something!'

Shepherd and the rest of the team closed in. The officer pointed to the basement door.

Craig switched off his safety and waited in the dark with the men in his company.

Shepherd didn't hesitate. 'Looks like this might be interesting! Open it!'

The officers nudged the door open and saw only darkness. They tried a switch at the top of the staircase …nothing, it was blown. Using their torches, the officers slowly descended into the basement, carefully and quietly. They saw nothing but empty operating tables. In the dark corners behind the tables, Craig and his men waited anxiously.

'Looks clean down here!' Shepherd allowed, already satisfied.

One officer went farther and nudged a table aside. As he looked around, he stepped on something a bit pliable and unsettling. He aimed the torch at his feet and discovered blood.

'What the hell?' he whispered, suspicious, caressing his holstered gun.

There, off to one side, lay a human heart. Stunned, the officer stumbled backwards. Who would think Montgomery was up to no good? Who would question his work? *It's a funeral parlour, and may Montgomery just got sloppy—even unprofessional.* Still, something didn't feel right.

'Hey, I've got something!' he cried out, alerting the others.

Craig and his men took no chances. They emerged from the shadows firing upon the officers, starting a heavy exchange of gunfire. One officer was shot in the throat by Craig; another two were fatally wounded.

'Officer down, officer down!' Shepherd shouted over his radio, as he shot his way up the stairs and out of the basement, with one other officer.

Craig's men finished the job, making a mess of the fallen officers, emptying their clips. After reloading, Craig and his men followed Shepherd and his partner up the stairs, firing rapidly at the two officers upstairs in the arrangement room. Shepherd's partner was shot in both legs and fell behind the cover of a file cabinet. Sirens wailed in the distance just as Craig was about to close in and finish Shepherd and his wounded partner; backup was coming, the cavalry was near.

Craig had no choice but to flee the scene, leaving the officers to their fate. 'Let's get the fuck out of here!' the men shouted, panicking at the sirens, though Craig regretted not finishing the job, and they left the parlour in a hurry.

Officer Shepherd breathed a sigh of relief, lucky to be alive with an empty gun. Cavalry came, with not a moment to spare. Officers swept the scene for remaining threats and secured the parlour. Shepherd along with his wounded partner were immediately evacuated.

Late the following night, another cargo was hijacked outside the city on Highway 52. Blood trails, body parts dragged along the road, corpses crushed beneath a hearse, dead men hanging in blood from the front seats—a disturbing sight. A headlight approached, a vehicle stopped, and a pair of crocodile boots hit the tarmac. Ray had turned up.

He strutted along the road inspecting the scene, making sure there were no survivors. A driver in the front seat of a hearse, barely alive, reached for a gun in the passenger foot well. Ray put a bullet in his head and then slid his phone from a coat packet to make a call.

'It's done! The job is taken care of', he reported. Without waiting for a reply, he cut the call short and replaced the phone in his pocket.

That afternoon, at Mr Sullivan's mansion, the word was out. Mr Sullivan was in his study surrounded by his son Paul, Rick, Craig, and Maxwell, watching the game on the big screen mounted on the wall. The phone on a nearby corner table rang, and Rick answered.

Montgomery Daniels was on the line, calling from a pay phone on the sidewalk in the middle of town. 'The cargo is lost! We've been hit bad—it's all gone! Everything!' Montgomery, panicking, looked around restlessly over his shoulders.

'Calm the fuck down! What happened?' Rick quickly tried to make sense of Montgomery's words. The room went silent everyone directed their attention towards him.

'Can't talk! They might be after me. I'm out of here!' Montgomery bailed, hanging up in a hurry, and running across the street through the traffic, missing a few horns and bumpers.

'What the hell was that?' Mr Sullivan asked.

'It's Montgomery sir. I think we had our cargo jacked, just like the Logans did!' Rick answered with a blank empty expression.

Mr Sullivan was enraged, shouting, 'Someone is playing games—first the Logans, now us! I think relocating was smart. Make sure the rest of the cargo is ready to move!'

'Maybe the Logans hit us', Maxwell suggested. 'Maybe they think we hit them too!'

'You may be right. You might be onto something!' Mr Sullivan said.

'I beg to differ, gentlemen!' came a voice from outside the study.

The Logan brothers appeared. They had invited themselves into the mansion. In their company were Matt, Raoul, Lady Casandra, and four other men. Guns were drawn all around; their entrance had triggered another standoff.

'Now, now, gentlemen! That's no way to greet each other!' Johnathon cheerfully bellowed across the study, feeling thrilled to be back.

'What the hell is this? How did you get past my security?' Mr Sullivan was annoyed, in no mood for such surprises.

'Let's just say my brother can be very persuasive', Gosnell replied, smiling mysteriously as he wandered about the study.

'Give me one good reason why I shouldn't kill you and that traitor you're lugging around!' Mr Sullivan groaned an unhappy note.

'Such sharp words from a dying man!' Raoul boldly interrupted.

Paul stepped forward. 'You want to watch the words that come out of your mouth!' He felt trigger-happy and defensive about his father's honour.

'Cut to the chase! Why are you here?' Mr Sullivan demanded.

'We know who stole from us. We got a name', Gosnell answered with a smug look.

'Who? Who dared to cross paths with me?' Mr Sullivan roared angrily, groping for his oxygen mask.

'I've been told that he goes by the name Arthur Brown ... called him a man without a face. My brother thinks that you may know this man, hence our unexpected arrival', Johnathon explained, casting my name at familiar faces.

'What? You can't be serious! Tell me you're joking!' Rick could not believe a word of it. He knew the kind of man I was. If only they knew what loomed on the horizon.

'I'm afraid we are dead serious. It's straight from the source's mouth!' Johnathon insisted on foolishly believing I was behind the hijacking.

'There's only one Arthur Brown in town—Father Brown, to be precise. Trust me, that Bible-thumping coward couldn't possibly do this', Rick grunted, convinced the Logans had got their sources wrong.

'You know this how?' Gosnell was intrigued to why he thought they had it all wrong.

'Because we had someone do a number on that asshole! He was jacked up real good!' Paul insisted.

'Sounds personal. Sounds like this man has every reason to put you and me out of business!' Gosnell said.

He got more reason to believe I was the man they needed to confront. A live news report interrupted their debate on the television. A female reporter stood in front of City Hall and announced, "We interrupt this program to bring you a live broadcast. A crowd has turned out to protest the ongoing drug and crime related issue affecting the city. Here to address the public is none other than Father Brown himself. After a life-changing incident that drove him to the brink of his religious career, he has summoned the courage to unite the people of Carol City here outside City Hall.'

CHAPTER 13

A public announcement outside City Hall was the final phase of my strategic plan. I had the numbers I needed to address the city and draw the unwilling attention I needed, thanks to my devoted church colleagues and my email correspondents who turned out in their numbers. The local press and the police were present, standing behind me on the high stairs outside City Hall. Captain Walter and a squad of officers were here to ensure all went peacefully.

All eyes were glued to the television on the wall of Mr Sullivan's study and the homes across town.

'What's this low life think he's doing? What's all this about? Turn it up!' Mr Sullivan grunted arrogantly, intrigued to hear the broadcast.

'This ought to be interesting!' Gosnell muttered quietly to himself.

I anchored the felt hat over my face bandage, straightened my windbreaker over my clergy uniform, and began to address the mass gathered around the concrete stairs and lining the sidewalks. 'People of Carol City! I brought you here today to let you know that all is not lost. The city is in chaos, turmoil, with crime, drugs, murder. It's time to put it all to bed! It's time we take our city back! Back from the clutches of these so-called kingpins, drug lords, and cartels!'

'Be careful what you're saying. These people need help, not false promises!' Captain Walter quietly whispered in the background.

'Help is what I'm here to offer! You had your chance Captain! You failed the people!' I whispered back as the audience cheered on excitingly.

'What makes you think we can save this city?' A middle-aged man standing in the audience posed a valid question. 'The cops aren't cutting it! How are we going to do it?'

'I believe in each and every one of you, the people of this city! Together we can make a significant difference. Believe in yourselves! Believe in each other! With my help we shall bring about a new dawn', I replied with strong conviction, passion in my voice. The crowd cheered again in support of my heartfelt speech.

An elderly woman near the back of the crowd posed another question. 'How are you planning on bringing about this so-called change, this new dawn you so proudly speak of?'

'The same way Jesus did, my friend. Jesus himself walked through hell, unlocking doors and cages, freeing souls! Same way we shall free this city!' I stated loud and clear with confidence, and the crowd cheered, feasting on my solid truth.

'Father Brown? Do you have anything to say to those responsible for this dreadful ordeal?' the female reporter asked, standing up front with her camera crew, prodding her microphone in my direction.

'Choose your words carefully, Father!' Captain Walter slyly mumbled in the background.

'I want them to know I'm coming! And hell's coming with me!' I replied powerfully, tearing the bandage from my face and tossing my hat to the floor, revealing my hellish face. The crowd gasped, shocked and stunned by my marred face, sympathizing.

All eyes were glued to the television in Mr Sullivan's study, and all turned away, sickened at the sight of my face. All except one, Rick, who proudly admired his work—to him a job well done.

'Looks like you boys just brought hell to our doorsteps!' Johnathon became deeply concerned.

'He's a coward and a fool. I assure you he is no threat', Rick declared.

'Rick is right! Those were nothing but blind words! The man is a sham! A religious loon!' Mr Sullivan growled, refusing to take heed.

'This is not a chance we can afford to risk! We take care of him now and carry on with our business as normal!' Gosnell sternly refused to stand by Rick's solid words.

'Fine! We'll handle this! All will be resolved by tonight!' Mr Sullivan took charge of what he deemed a minor setback.

'I'll send my men along—just to make sure your men finish what they start!' Gosnell made the offer to satisfy his own doubts.

'We don't need your services! My men are very professional and capable.' Mr Sullivan rudely refused the brothers' help.

'This so call Arthur Brown, Father Brown, or whatever the fuck he calls himself is still breathing! I say you got no choice!' Gosnell shouted, very unhappily.

'Fine. Rick? Get the men ready. Clean your mess up for good. No fuckups!' Mr Sullivan ordered, acceding to the Logans' wishes.

'Let this day mark a new chapter. For this is the day we receive that change we've long awaited!' These were my last words as I finished addressing the crowd. There was another loud cheer as I parted the audience down the stairs, with the captain escorting me to my car parked up behind the crowd outside the local city bank.

'I hope you know what you're doing, Father! If you ask me, I say that was a foolish move! You may of just signed your death warrant!' Captain Walter vigorously breathed down my neck from outside the window of my car-feeling threatened by my speech.

'I know what I'm doing Captain! Wished I can say the same for you! Besides, I'm already dead!' A brave response as I aroused the Captain's shifty emotions.

'you listen! I am doing my part! Like it or not! You may be an upstanding member in this City! But that doesn't make you God!' Captain Walter replied aggressively, sensitive, on edge and emotionally disturb.

'No Captain! I'm not God! Just a man looking to make a difference!' I growled vigorously at the Captain, pulling away in a hurry-staying true to my words and my firm belief should he believe me or not.

Jack quietly sat in his caravan in front the television drinking a beer, having a dramatic moment. 'So, Father, I see that you've won the audience. You just may prove to be a formidable adversary!'

CHAPTER 14

Night came. I sat and waited in my car, parked on my street two blocks down from my home. I waited comfortably in my long trench coat, felt hat, and fresh bandages with my two fully chromed 12-gauge revolvers on the passenger seat. I checked my watch; the hour was growing late. Then, at last, headlights approached.

Three vehicles quietly pulling up, one on the far side of the street and two across the street from it, just short of my home. The word was out: they were here to finish their sloppy job. Rick stepped out the vehicle, him and one other—Matt, the stranger that I would come to know. With them came a gang of eight men, exiting the vehicles heavily armed.

'All right! You know what to do! Get in there and bring me his head!' Rick ordered his trigger-happy men.

'Make sure it's done right! No screw-ups!' Matt strictly warned the others on behalf of the Logans.

I watched as the men poured through the front door and the back entrance into my house. Rick, along with Matt, stayed back to await the news from inside. As one, the men trampled my already trashed rooms, the upstairs and the downstairs filtering into the kitchen like sardines looking for me. Instead, they found something else sitting on the kitchen floor: bombs, trinitrotoluene set for remote detonation. I held the triggering device with my finger ready to press the button.

'Get out! Get out! This place is going to blow!' They yelled their lungs out, scrambling for their worthless lives.

It was too late, I depressed the button on the detonator, setting the bombs off, and blew my home to pieces. All eight men were eliminated. The blast drove Rick and Matt behind their vehicle, where they shielded themselves from the concrete debris.

'Tell me that did not just happen! What the fuck is going on, Rick?' Matt shouted in confusion.

'He knew we were coming! Let's get the fuck out of here before someone sees us!' Rick replied. Both men jumped into their vehicle and took off, fleeing the scene.

I followed on behind, keeping a safe and reasonable distance. Not long after, they returned to Mr Sullivan's mansion, driving through the large metal gate, cleared by two armed security men. I waited out of sight as Rick and Matt headed into the mansion. Then I got out of my car and snatched a bag from the rear seat, scanning the heavily armed mansion yard from my car. Motion sensors, four armed men roaming the yard, dogs barking, more armed security on all four corners—but I had to get in there. I opened the bag, which held a disassembled dart gun amongst a varied arsenal. I quickly assembled the gun.

Inside, Rick and Matt brought the bad news home, ready to brief Mr Sullivan and the ever-present Logan brothers within the study on their failed operation.

'Well? Is it done?' Mr Sullivan growled impatiently.

'Our guys are all dead. Son of a bitch blew the entire house down! I think he was expecting us', Rick reported, feeling disappointed, anxiously rubbing his chin.

'That fucking nut job needs to be dead! I want him dead!' Mr Sullivan shrieked and began a coughing fit.

'This is getting out of hand. I thought you said this would be easy!' Johnathon was annoyed with Rick's and Matt's futile attempt.

'It is! It's just a minor setback; he got lucky, that's all.' Rick was set on maintaining the brothers' confidence.

Carefully and silently I scaled the mansion wall. One by one I quietly put the dogs to sleep as well as the guards patrolling the rear of the mansion, using the dart gun. All clear, I packed the gun away into my bag of supplies and swapped it for my two 12-gauge revolvers.

'Looks like you gentlemen just raised hell! I think it's time to raise the bar! Get out there and find this lunatic, now!' Gosnell shouted, sternly insisting on my death.

Across the lawn, evading the motion sensors. I dragged the sleeping guards out of sight to avoid suspicion. I headed towards the back door, which was unlocked, and nudged it open with my shoulder. Once in the kitchen, I heard the noise of footsteps as Rick and Matt came rushing by, intent on their business I plastered myself against the wall and watched them leave.

'Let's hope for your sake this doesn't blow our plans wide open', said Johnathon, having a rant in the study with Mr Sullivan, his son Paul. and Maxwell about their ongoing issues. 'This Father Brown is a menace, a nuisance. He must be controlled; above all, he needs to be illuminated!'

I navigated deserted corridors until I could listen in from the room facing the study. I noted the Logans as a new threat while taking my time to memorize the mansion layout. The silence was broken by Raoul and number of men patrolling the halls, so it was time to see myself out. All clear, I returned out the back, across the lawn, over the fence, and into my car. I was empty-handed, having left my bag stocked with explosives behind in the gas mains, vanishing without a trace.

The following night-at the Aqua Sushi restaurant, it was near closing time. I was on one knee, wearing my felt hat over my bandages with my windbreaker over my clergy uniform, sharing a few tins of all-day breakfast from my duffel bag with two homeless men, Rupee and Dale Murray. They were twins of average height and scruffy appearance, approaching forty. I was plotting my next step into dissolving the Sullivans' empire with another bag at my feet primed with explosives.

At last, the sound of the trash being dumped out back and the gloating tune from Paul and his gang of merry men, laughing and pinching the bums of the ladies who strolled by, signalled it was closing time. After a few drags on their cigarettes they took off in their cars, leaving Chen, the head chef, to lock the doors. After locking up, Chen looked around as if he knew someone was watching. He then climbed onto his motorcycle, parked across the street, and rode off. It was time to act.

'Catch you fellas later', I said to Rupee and Dale.

Wrapped up in cardboard and the local news, snuggling in for the night, they nodded in acknowledgment. 'Catch you later, Father Brown!' they said as I disappeared from the alley. My character and image had preceded me. Everyone knew who I was.

I went in the back, dodging the cameras. I kicked in the door and let myself into the kitchen Looking around, I softened my footsteps and gently placed a stack of ticker bombs between the ovens just as I did at Sullivan's.

Somewhere downtown, riding along, Chen had that feeling in his gut that something was wrong. He slammed on his brakes, spun around, and headed back.

Out in the dining area, the sharks and the collection of rare marine life wandered effortlessly beneath and above me as I carefully inspected table after table. Minutes later, just as I was letting myself out the back, a kick to the face greeted me in the doorway, driving me backwards against a refrigerator. Chen appeared, looking to draw blood.

'Thought I'd find you here! Say your prayers, asshole!' Chen was cocking his fist, ready for a fight.

'Fate led you back, my friend. It must be your time. I'll save the prayers till after you're dead', I replied calmly and unfazed. I laid down my half-empty bag and waited, looking at my watch. 'What are you waiting for? I've got a lot more of you to purge; I'm on a tight schedule, I'm afraid', I said to Chen, toying with his mind.

Angry,-Chen threw a left and a right hook; I barely flinched. He looked at me, surprised. 'Try again', I said, calm and poised.

Grinding his teeth, he upped his stakes, throwing me against the oven and landing a spin kick. He then grabbed me by the back of my coat and worked me over with punches. I grabbed his fist, held his arm, and threw him over the kitchen counter, burying him under falling pots and pans. He got up bearing kitchen knives, feinting and threatening with them.

I defended myself with the nearest baking tray, running towards Chen. He intercepted with a kick. I blocked it, twisting his leg. He began limping and went for another punch. I blocked that, broke his arm in two places, and turned his face into a punching bag, tossing him about the kitchen.

Chen got up, battered and in bad shape, studying me in disbelief.

'You are just a priest! This cannot be happening!' Chen murmured, embarrassed, with blood streaking his face.

A cleaver lay right next to my fingertips on the countertop. I fiddled with its blade, passing my thumb up and down its length like a butcher. 'I'm a lot more than that, I'm afraid. Give my thanks to Rick when he joins you in hell', I replied dramatically.

'Screw you, asshole!' Chen grunted in anger, spitting blood and charging me. He tackled me with his broken arm and injured leg. I shifted my body, evading his attempt and then slamming his head against the freezer. Holding Chen by the neck, I took hold of the cleaver and raised my arm, ready to put him down. Chen grabbed on to my arm, trying to hold the blade back. I head-butted him, breaking his concentration, and chopped his arm off at the shoulder. Then I split his head open with a single stroke—no remorse!

To avoid detection I cleaned the kitchen immaculately. Then I hoisted over my shoulder, with my half empty bag in one arm, and walked back into the alley, calmly strolling past Rupee and Dale. 'Some night, huh?' said Rupee. Both had satisfied smiles, already knowing what I was up to and somewhat pleased.

'Here, you might want to hold on to this. Keep it safe', I said, dropping my half-empty bag at their feet as I carried on.

'Hey, Father?!' Dale called out, and I looked back over my shoulder. 'Give 'em hell!' Dale showed in gratitude in a most unusual way; it felt right to me. With a nod, I acknowledged their trust and carried on. Rupee placed the bag under his news blanket and snuggled up to it like a baby going bye-bye. I laid Chen's body in the boot of my car, slammed it shut, and headed off into the night.

My phone rang inside my coat pocket, and I answered. 'What is it, captain?' I asked with an undisturbed voice.

'You know exactly what I want. Your home was blown to hell, and you are nowhere to be found. What the hell are you playing at? Where are you?' His tone was strident as he sat behind his desk burning the candle from both ends.

'Don't worry about me and where I am. I'm doing God's work!'

'You want to stop this madness before you get yourself killed, you hear me? You are digging your own grave!' Captain Walter shouted.

'I'm already dead, Captain! I've been there! I've dug that hole myself', I snapped and hung up on the raging captain.

Next day-at the Carol City Landfill, a bagged body was uncovered from the trash heap when a bulldozer driver was in the middle of his morning routine. He quickly shut down the engine and investigated. Within minutes Captain Walter and his team were on the scene. The captain unzipped the body bag and turned away from the horror show within.

'God darn it, Arthur', Walter muttered to himself.

Maxwell walked in on Mr Sullivan in the middle of his afternoon massage with his carer, at the indoor pool. 'Sir, I'm afraid we have bad news!'

'What exactly is this bad news?!' Mr Sullivan mumbled face down with his carer's elbow in his back.

'It's Chen. He's dead. Someone hacked him to death!' Maxwell spilled the news.

'What? How the fuck did this happen? Chen was one of the best!!' Mr Sullivan shouted, sitting up and donning his robe.

'You don't thinks this is the work of the priest, do you?!' Maxwell asked.

'I don't think! I know it is! He's onto us, and he's not going to stop till he's got his vengeance!' Mr Sullivan replied, enraged. 'Get me the Logans on the phone. Now!'

Riding along in their limousine were the Logan brothers, accompanied by Raoul and his two Rottweilers. The limousine phone rang. 'Now, who could this be?' said Johnathon indifferently and answered the call. 'Who dares ring me at such inconvenience?' he said into the phone

'It's me! We have a problem that needs addressing!' Mr Sullivan replied from his private quarters, already clothed and being wheeled out by Maxwell towards the driveway.

'By problem you mean the priest, Father Brown? The man that took care of your beloved chef?' Johnathon replied irritably but wanting to pass along his mood.

'How did you know?' Mr Sullivan asked, already sitting in the back of his limousine with Maxwell at his side.

'News travel fast! Besides, he's your problem! Why should we help?' Johnathon asked, unwilling to be reasonable.

'He's your problem too now! You heard his speech! He's coming for all of us!' Mr Sullivan insisted, as he was driving out the mansion gates.

'You created this brute of a man! I suggest you contain him!' Johnathon retorted and hung up his phone.

'Inconsiderate pile of shit!' Mr Sullivan grunted, throwing his phone aside.

'Has he got the message?' Gosnell asked.

'I think I was quite clear. He's got the message, all right!' Johnathon answered with a smooth tone, firmly fixing his tie up his collar with his legs crossed.

'Any changes, I'm ready to act.' Raoul offered his loyal service to the brothers, ready to draw blood at their command.

'Let's hope it doesn't have to come to that', Gosnell replied, cutting the conversation short on their way downtown through the city of Lismore.

That afternoon, at the cemetery. I stood before my family head stones- both kids at their mother's side. I laid roses at their feet, crouched down on one knee, thinking how much I've missed them, holding back the rain as I reflected on our last night together-it was my first vista since awaken from the coma and I was lost for words, only my grieving tears beneath my bandage could have expressed my heartfelt emotions.

'I'm sorry ... Sorry I could not protect any of you. I spend every day blaming myself ... I was weak. Very weak. A coward! ... I'm better now. I'm better!' I took my hat off placing it across my weeping heart.

'You may not like what I have become. I had to change! This path I've chosen is unrighteous ... I'm afraid I'm not the same man I use to be. I've lost myself in that hole that night! Now I'm just a shadow of my former self. There's a lot of bad people out there, and they need to be stopped! They need to answer for what they've done! I'll find my way when it's all over ... I promise!' These tragic, painful words I whispered over their grave as I fought fruitlessly to restrain the tears.

Enough said! I straightened my coat, affixed my hat, and returned to my car, breathing a sad sigh of discontent. The clouds broke down in tears as I drove away. Five miles into the cross-country road, all quiet and peaceful, I switched the radio on, tuned to the local station, and picked up the news report.

'Earlier today, the police recovered the body of Aqua Sushi Head Chef Chen Wang at the city's landfill. Sources reveal that the chef may have been personally involved with Carol City kingpin Richard Sullivan; the police have stated that this may related to a war on drugs!'

Underneath my bandages, I expressed a heartless emotion: no hard feelings, nothing personal; to me, a job well done. Suddenly there was a loud crash and bang. A large Ford pickup truck drove into the passenger side of my beloved '69 Volvo 122, shoving me off the road into a ditch. Shaken and thrown off balance, with cuts on the left leg, I managed to stayed focused: the driver had five male passengers, one up front, two in the back seat, and another two riding in the rear cargo hold. Trouble had found me.

I was just about recovering from the impact they had purposely caused. I reached into my glove compartment and snatched my pair of 12-gauge revolvers, fully loaded. The men climbed from their truck, closing in to finish the job. All of them were wearing flannel and jeans shirts with long cargo trousers. They were tattooed and hairy, ranging in age from forty to late fifties, carrying automatic weapons. I kicked my dented door open and fired a round, a bullet to the head, taking half his skull. One man down.

They sprayed a burst of rounds, driving me into cover, low behind my car, while one pair raked the sides with bullets. I had nowhere to run, and all five men began to advance. By a stroke of luck, they ran dry of bullets and paused to reload. Too late, I broke cover, rising to my feet, and let loose another head shot, blowing his skull from his shoulder: one more dead.

Realising the tables had turned, one decided to try reasoning with me and buy himself time as I held them at gunpoint. 'Listen! Take it easy! Just doing our job!'

'So am I!' I replied, blowing their heads off, one by one in quick succession.

It was over. I took no prisoners. With my car scrapped, I limped towards the boot and removed my duffel bag. Then I climbed into the truck on the side road and peacefully resumed my journey.

Soon I was back at the cottage. I flung the door open and dropped my bag, stumbling around the old cupboards seeking out a first aid kit. Successful, I sat down and ripped open my pants leg, revealing the wound: deep, nasty and pissing blood.

I strapped my belt around my leg to stop the bleeding, drew the cork from a whiskey bottle with my teeth, and poured it into the wound. It burnt like hell. I then began stitching my wound, closing the flesh into place, grunting painfully with every stroke of the needle as I successfully sealed the wound. Weakened and exhausted, I climb the wooden stairs to call it a day. I collapsed on an empty bed in the attic, breathing a sigh of relief. *Today I rest; tomorrow I act.*

A few hours later two vehicles approached the roadside where I was almost killed. The vehicles pulled over and stopped. Maxwell, Rick, and Paul along with several men stepped out of their vehicles and gazed around at the dead and the wreckage. They inspected the scene.

Paul whistled in amazement, running his hand through his hair in disbelief. 'Fuck me, Max! Looks like this guy made a mess of things!'

'He's made a mess, all right. This isn't just some priest we are dealing with. He's coming for us, and he's not going to stop till we are dead!' Maxwell replied with a deep ominous tune to his words.

'So the victim became the monster; how ironic. He must be controlled', Rick murmured carefully among the others, proud of the fein he had created.

'Look around, Rick!' Paul was annoyed at the trouble his companion had brought to their door. 'This shit is already out of control, thanks to you!'

'Hey! I was just doing your old man's job that night! Don't point any fingers!' Rick replied, standing his ground.

'This is not the time and place! Let's get out of here!' Maxwell shouted, as he tried keeping both men in line.

'Let's clean this mess up before the cops come snooping around!'

Maxwell whistled to the group of men they had tagging along on the sideline waiting for orders.

They loaded the dead corpses into my old Volvo. Then Rick soaked it inside and out from a can of gasoline. Finally, with a stroke of a match, Paul set the car ablaze, leaving the dead to be consumed by the flames.

Chapter 15

At the deserted rail lines, the evening was still young. Busy men with the help of Montgomery Daniels were fast at work cramming the dead with cocaine. A car came screeching in outside the rails, and a casually dressed man rushed into the cart with news for Montgomery. The man stood still, tapping his fingers anxiously on the worktop next to the dead, waiting for acknowledgment, looking concerned.

Montgomery worked on until, annoyed by the tapping, Montgomery decided to ask, 'Well, is the route secured or not?'

'You are not going to like this. The cops are raiding every funeral parlour in town. Worse, they got the streets on lockdown. We are grounded! These bodies aren't going anywhere in a hurry!' the man explained, frustrated.

'Inform the boss!' Montgomery ordered. 'Make sure he understands!'

'All right. Your call. Don't think he's going to be happy!' the man replied, walking away. He pulled out his phone and made the call.

'Talk to me! Make sure it's good news!' Mr Sullivan answered from his living room sofa, sipping red wine with a selection of imported cheese, with his carer beside him.

'I'm afraid it's not, sir!' the man replied, frightened.

'Explain!' Mr Sullivan snapped.

'Roadblocks! The cops are on to us!' the man quickly explained.

'Organize the convoy! Stick to the plan; the bodies will be moving tonight as scheduled!' Mr Sullivan insisted. He cut the call short and resumed his leisure activity.

On the streets of downtown Lismore, Captain Walter and a large number of officers were in the middle of setting up another roadblock in the pouring rain. They set it up in two stages-one just a few miles outside the heart of the city on the main route, labelled checkpoint one, and the other, checkpoint two, serving as the last line of defence leading into town.

'All right, men, this is it! Every route in and out of town is now secured! Nothing gets in, nothing gets out. Hearses are the main priority. Stay sharp, stay focused! Let's shut these bastards down!' Captain Walter loudly briefed his men as they waited out the night, hoping for something.

A mere two hours later, a convoy of four heavily armed pickup trucks appeared, heading into town, all mounted with .50-calibre guns. Bringing up the rear were the hearses. This was Mr Sullivan's desperate attempt to clear the route for his hearses into and out of the city.

'We got a heavily armed convoy closing in from the north!' an officer announced over the radio, from his cruiser behind the barriers of checkpoint one, his lookout point.

'This is it, men!' Captain Walter bellowed after receiving the news. 'Prepare to open fire on my signal!'

The officers at checkpoint one tried slowing the convoy down with a series of rapid gunfire; they failed. The .50-calibres on the pickups made a mess of the officers, leaving body parts spread along the streets, destroying everything in their line of fire.

Alive, lying on the ground bleeding out from his gut, was the officer who'd made the call. He was trying to radio in his last report when Maxwell jumped from his truck, put shotgun to the officer's head and silenced him, leaving his body unrecognizable.

It wasn't long until the convoy got close to the captain's last line of defence. The convoy stopped short a few blocks short of the roadblock. Captain Walter with his men hung low behind the armoured personnel carriers, waiting for a reaction.

'Okay, you're up!' Maxwell said to Paul, sitting in the passenger seat beside him.

Without a word, Paul exited the pickup, opened the rear door, and drew out a rocket launcher. Within seconds he was joined by three other men from the convoy, all bearing rocket launchers. It was a heck of a standoff.

The captain was overwhelmed by the arsenal at the dealers' disposal. He shouted to his men, 'Well, I'll be damned! Open fire, now!'

The officers opened fire, and the convoy retaliated with their mounted .50-calibres, providing Paul and the men with cover protection. Rockets away! The police and their armoured carriers suffered a death toll and a number of wounded.

Unable to hold their ground, Captain Walter issued a withdrawal. 'All officers! Fall back! I repeat: fall back!' he yelled into the radio.

All officers including Captain Walter retreated in their vehicles into an alley, evading the explosive firepower. The convoy roared through what was left of the blockade, heading out of the city, leaving the streets in shambles.

The hidden police watched helplessly as they drove past. 'I'll get you bastards. I'll get you', Captain Walter mumbled to himself, disheartened about his failure to stop the convoy.

I tossed and turned, groaning in my nightmare. Screams, cries, and gunshots echoed in my head. I sprang upright in the bed, out of breath, panting like a racehorse. I peeled the woolly blanket from my naked body and climbed out of bed, managing carefully on my wounded leg. I drew a curtain and saw only rain. There was more work to be done.

Soon I was banging metal against metal, shaping a blade on an anvil salvaged from beneath the cottage floor. I had turned the fireplace into a furnace, a blacksmith's workplace. Clad only in my underpants, I was forging iron, sweating and making use of the night.

Time was of the essence. I needed something special, something that would make a mess of things. I shaped the metal into a twenty-four-inch ribbed blade, perfect not only to cut but to disembowel—perfect for my line of work. The handle I fashioned into a silver crucifix only to remind me of what I stood for.

With the job done, it was time to get into character. My all-black clergy uniform, a set of black steel-toed boots, a utility belt around my waist loaded with rounds and magazines, and Point Blank body armour over my clergy shirt with the collar showing. Over my shoulders I strapped a pair of leather holsters with my two 12-gauge Taurus Judge revolvers strapped inside. A set of fresh bandages on my face and my black felt hat down to my forehead topped off a black cashmere knee-length coat and a pair of black leather gloves. I picked up my duffel bag from the dusty wooden floor and headed for the pickup. It was time to go hunting.

The evening brought me a few miles from town along the main road heading into the city. A siren wailed, and blue lights shone behind me. I pulled the truck onto the verge and stopped. The unmarked cruiser pulled up at rear. Suspicious, I kept a hand on my holster just in case.

The unknown officer stepped out of his cruiser and carefully approached the pickup. I waited anxiously, gazing at him from my wing mirror as he reached down and unholstered his gun. He stopped and called, 'Sir? Please step out of the vehicle with your hands up!'

I had a busy night ahead of me; last thing I needed was a trigger-happy cop getting in my way. I cooperated, exiting the pickup with my hands up and turning my back, blowing a sigh of frustration.

'Keep your hands where I can see them!' the officer ordered, his gun still aimed at me and keeping his distance.

'If you're dirty, walk away now!' I warned him in a calm, reasonable tone.

'Dirty? Just who the hell do you think you are?' the officer replied loudly, clearly feeling insulted.

'No one you need to know!' I replied calmly, still reaching for the sky.

'Shut the hell up and turn around, now! Keep your hands where I can them!' the officer commanded with a vigorous tone.

I turned around, and we recognized each other. A look of relief painted our faces. I then approached the captain halfway along the verge. 'What the hell are you doing out here, Captain? You could have got yourself killed!'

'I'm no easy target, Father! What are you doing, driving around in a marked vehicle?' He sounded concerned.

'It's all I could salvage', I replied quietly.

'Hmm. Salvage, huh? Looks like you're off doing another one of your famous deeds!' the Captain replied, gazing at the guns peeping from my coat.

'Well, you know what they say. Jesus walks!' I replied boldly, full of determination.

'You've got to stop this, Father!' the Captain carefully advised, about to give another lecture which I quickly interrupted.

'Don't go there, Captain! This has to be done. It needs to be done! There's no stopping it!' I emphasized my point to the captain once more, for the last time. 'They've taken everything from me! I'm just repaying a debt!' I grunted, turning towards the pickup and walking away.

'I already lost a great detective. I'd hate to see you end up that way, Father!' the Captain yelled.

He had my undivided attention. I stopped. 'What are you saying, Captain? What happened?!' I stared at him, anxious and confused.

'Detective Brooks is missing! Hasn't been seen in weeks!' Captain Walter answered.

'Did something happen?' I asked, struggling to grasp the grave circumstances.

'Carl must have found something he shouldn't have at the Montgomery Funeral Parlour. Last report received before he went AWOL, he was there but that's the last we've heard of him', Captain Walter explained with a weary, sorrowful expression.

'They must have got to him'. I said. 'Don't worry, I'll find him.' I was more than ready to repay an old favour.

'Since I can't stop you, go get these bastards! Do what you must!' Captain Walter gave his consent, seeing me off to my unholy duties.

I tipped my hat and returned to the pickup. As I headed off into the city, the captain stopped and watched me vanish in the distance.

Somewhere, in total darkness, Carl was scraping his fingers against the wall. His fingers bled, nails and flesh all but gone, and a full beard hung from his hollow face. His health was already deteriorating as he dully made one more futile attempt to escape his dark prison.

Early evening the same day, I pulled up outside the Logan brothers' mansion, making a quick stop on my way to the Aqua Sushi restaurant. Parked within the trees at the end of the street, I took up my duffel bag from the seat and headed towards the mansion's gate.

'Who the hell does this guy think he is?' one guard at the gate whispered to the other.

'Let's get him out of here.—Hey, you there! Get lost, this is private property! Scram!' the guards shouted as I stood there minding my business.

I didn't budge. I stared into the mansion, one arm leaning against the gate and the other tipping my hat, covering my already concealed face. The two guards suddenly grew annoyed, opened the gate, and approached me—a grave mistake, just as I'd expected.

'OK, asshole, you had your chance. Now we are going to really hurt you!' The guards advance, and one grabbed me by the collar about to lay down a beating.

Hammers cocked, my guns were up their faces ready to shoot at a moment's notice. The guards were stumped and both lifted hands, a sign of surrender. But I took no prisoners in my line of work. Still, I needed to keep thongs quiet; a single shot, and the entire guard team would be alerted. I dropped both guns, and the guards reached into their coats. I drew the blade from my waist, sliced their throats open, and left them for dead.

I raised an arm from the guard lying on the ground, slowly dying, and used his palm print to unlock the gates. Inside the mansion gates I marched, my bag in one hand and a gun in the other. Two armed men approached when they saw me heading up the path. I wasted no time delivering two head shots. Then a number of men stormed out of the mansion in reaction to the sound of gunfire. I dropped my bag, drew my second gun, and began firing from cover behind a water fountain.

As I reloaded my revolvers, a man drew near, sneaking up behind me. For his trouble he got one shot to the knee and another to his head. I lifted him by the collar as he was about to fall and used him as a human shield as I laid waste to the entire guard force. Finally it was over—all quiet all dead. I dropped the dead man, picked up my bag, and approached the front door to the mansion.

As I entered I was confronted by another guard coming down the stairs. He drew and fired, grazing the wall above my head. I returned two shots, one to the kneecap and one through the eye. I carefully made my way up the stairs and shot my way into an office. All clear, I set my bag down, holstered my gun, and took a seat comfortably behind a desk, waiting with the doors shut.

Outside the office, two men quietly approached the door, one on either side, carrying automatic weapons. With a nod at each other, they sprayed the door with gunfire in hopes of killing me at once. Then they kicked the door down and stormed in but saw no one. When they turned around, there I was, sweeping my blade across their necks with a single stroke, dropping their heads to the floor. I slipped the bloody blade back into my waist.

'Hold your fire!! I just want to talk', came a voice from outside the office. Matt and what was left of the security team were outside the door.

'Show yourself!' I called from the office, guns at the ready.

Matt ordered his men to lower their guns as a precaution while he entered the office. There he found me calmly sitting behind the desk calmly. He studied my bag on top the desk. 'So you must be the infamous Arthur Brown. Heard a lot about you!'

'What can I say? My reputation precedes me', I replied calmly yet fully aware of my surroundings.

Matt paced about the room slowly, touching a few objects on the wall and bookcases as he aimlessly wandered past the desk.

'You're quite right! Such a shame you weren't this man before your family got murdered—brutally, I might add!' Matt responded, touching a nerve. Though his back was turned, I saw a smile raise his cheek.

'I wouldn't go there if I were you!' I replied coldly.

Matt turned around with a smile as if he'd intended me to react this way. 'My apologies! How insensitive of me! May I ask why you're here? After all, your beef is with Mr Sullivan and his men ... Rick? Am I right?!'

'My beef is with those who are poisoning my city! As for Rick— he's got it coming! I'm here to deliver a message from a dying man; then I'll be on my way', I replied, getting straight to the point.

'Well said, Father, well said! May I call you Father?' Matt was trying hard to divert my attention with his charismatic gestures.

'Just Arthur Brown. That's all I am now', I replied. Then I stood up, turned my back, and looked out the window empty-handed.

Matt saw but kept wandering the office, keeping a close eye on me and especially the bag lying on the desk.

'Well, *Arthur Brown*, I'm afraid I can't let you leave here'. With those foolish words, Matt had made his bed and was about to lie down in it. 'If you're lucky, you just may get to deliver that message!'

'Now, why is that?!' I asked calmly, facing the window, looking out into the yard and the dead bodies strewn here and there.

'You came in unannounced, uninvited! Killed my men—a lot of men! Mostly, you have proven to be quite a nuisance-a pain in the ass. It's part of my job description, you know, to handle men like you. I'm sure you understand!' Matt ranted on, trying to get his point across and trying to tick me off, looking to force my hand.

'I perfectly understand, I do', I replied in a reasonable tone, looking across at him through the peepholes of my bandages.

'Good! It's hard to tell if the information is sinking in. There's no expression. All tied up behind that mask of yours! Rick must have done quite a number on you, huh?' Matt smiled, purposely testing my patience.

I kept it together, though I was rather impatient. I straightened my coat. 'I read you loud and clear. Now what?'

'Now, Arthur Brown, I'm going to put a bullet right between your eyes! Right there!' Matt pointed closely at my forehead, invading my personal space.

'First, I need to see what's in that bag of yours. Go on. Go ahead and open it right up.' He seemed frankly curious about the contents of my bag.

He whistled, and the rest of the security team filtered into the office—perhaps ten men carrying guns, waiting for orders. I was out gunned and outnumbered, or so it appeared.

'This is it, Arthur, boy! Road ends here! Get me his bag!' Matt was determined to find out what I had brought into the mansion. My bag was his main priority.

His men took the bag from my possession and passed it onto Matt before resuming their firing positions. I kept quiet, waiting for Matt to satisfy his curiosity.

'Let's see what you brought to the party, shall we?' Matt hastily unzipped the bag. Immediately, he was caught off guard by the trap laid out inside the bag. He had triggered the spring release pressure pad filled with nails, which was my cue to react. Like bullets, the nails flew from the bag, Matt lost his left eye, and his face and body were dotted in nails.

He dropped the bag and crumpled to the floor in excruciating pain, screaming to his men. 'Arrrrgh! Kill him! Kill him now! Fucking bastard!' Matt cried out from the floor, holding his bleeding eye.

What Matt didn't realize, due to his state of shock and distorted vision, was that his men were all casualties, with punctured arms, legs, and necks—bleeding out. I rose from my cover behind the desk. With a flick of my coat, I drew my revolvers. It was time to make a mess of things, finishing what Matt had started.

CHAPTER 16

The dead were jumbled together like sardines. Except for Matt—he was lucky. He shuffled himself up against the bookcases, fumbling around his jacket and drawing his gun. I shot his gun hand, and he dropped his firearm.

'You think this is over! You think you've won, huh? Is that it?' Matt yelled at me as I approached him, step by step, emptying the spent cartridges from my revolvers and reloading the cylinders from the utility belt strapped to my waist.

'It's not over, not yet, but soon', I replied peacefully, as I reloaded.

'Go on, kill me! That's what you want, isn't it? Kill me. Go ahead!' he shouted arrogantly, biting back his pain, holding his punctured wounds, trying to stop the bleeding.

I took a knee in front of Matt and spoke quietly into his punctured face. 'I'm not finished with you just yet. You've still got a message to deliver, so listen carefully! You tell the brothers: Get out of my city and leave, while they still got their legs. They have forty-eight hours. You know what happens next.'

I had delivered my message, said my piece. It was time to wrap things up.

'Screw you, you piece of shit! You're nothing, you hear me? Nothing!' Matt shouted continuously.

I remained quiet: took my bag from the floor, checked the rest of the contents, and closed it up. 'Look after yourself. I have a feeling we'll see each other again.' With those careful words, I was about to see myself out the door. I stopped at the doorway and looked back at Matt covered in blood and hanging on by a thread. 'Just remember, you got lucky. Next time it'll be different!' With those last words, I left Matt on his own.

Back at the truck, I climbed in empty-handed, leaving the bag behind—another surprise, should anything go bad. There was more work to be done; I was in for a long night, chasing bad souls. This night brought me back at the Aqua Sushi restaurant, no later than 9 p.m. There, I watched from the truck across the street with my hat down over my face, making myself less noticeable.

On time, the same time they emerged every night, Paul Sullivan, Detective Craig Bollington, and Rick Lawson himself appeared outside. The rage I felt gazing at Rick from across the road was enough to burn holes in my boots. *His time will come, not today, not tonight, not yet.*

I watched and I waited. A vehicle turned up, they got in, and I followed. For ten minutes I followed until they made a turn for the deserted rail lines. *What the hell are they up to?* I asked myself, killing my lights before pulling in on the far side of the rails out of sight and shutting my engine off.

They quickly exited the vehicle and walked towards the trains. There, they were met by another of Mr Sullivan's men, who opened the cart doors. I got out of my truck for a closer look, quietly moving through the dark between the sleeping trains. There they were, inside. I spotted Montgomery Daniels with two armed men, handing Paul a large carrier bag.

'Is it all here?' Paul asked, unzipping the bag and looking inside.

'It's all there, a hundred and twenty-five large!' Montgomery confirmed.

'Good work, Montgomery! Keep it up! I'll let the old man know how well you're doing!' Paul looked pleased with Montgomery's efforts.

'Just doing my part', Montgomery replied modestly.

'Yeah! You do that! We'll see you around!' Paul and his colleagues ducked out the door.

My interest was aroused. I stayed behind to take a closer look. Then I heard footsteps; someone was approaching. I hid between the carts from two men, armed of course, who were roaming the rails. I watched as they carelessly drifted past. Then I climbed into the cart, letting myself in. An empty passenger cart, this one nothing but broken seats, empty cabins, and cobwebs. Through and onto the next cart I went—into an armoury. This cart appeared to be a weapons hold, with guns, ammunition, and a supply of explosives.

Then I heard chattering; I had company. I hid behind the cabin's door. The two men who earlier had been parading the rails entered the cart. My blade went through the first one's gut from behind. Alerted rudely, the last man in tried for his gun. I took his arm off and then his head before his scream could draw more unwanted attention. Just that quickly and easily the job was done.

The next cart was as grim as death's home. There were dead spread everywhere, up one side of the cart and down the next, lying on operating tables with their chests cut open. I looked around the grisly affair and saw that some of the corpses were being filled with cocaine. My heart sank with a taste of disgust. 'This is inhuman. It has to stop', I whispered to myself as I stumbled around the cart inspecting the dead.

Montgomery Daniels appeared through the next door. His eyes locked on me from across the cart, and he ran. I chased him down through the carts, through door after door.

'He's here! He's here! Stop him!' Montgomery cried to the group of four men who sat ahead, reading the paper.

They stood up, discarding their paper and opening fire. I was stopped in my tracks, seeking cover behind the broken seats as bullets whistled by. Then I rose and introduced my revolvers to the gunfight, returning fire.

Montgomery made his way to a sleeping cart where he hid himself away, shaking in fear. He fumbled around in his pockets looking for something—empty, nothing. 'Shit! My phone! Where's my phone? Fuck!' He panicked, afraid to come out of hiding. He locked himself away inside the toilet and stayed put.

Before long another three men climbed on board the train, joining the gunfight and adding their firepower. There was no way of getting past the men, not without a quick-thinking strategy. I shot the lights out, and the cart went black. The shooting stopped as there was no way to get a clean shot. I used the darkness to draw closer to the men, replacing my guns with my blade and stroking an arm off; that was one man down. Blind and terrified, the men began shooting wildly into the dark. The muzzle flashes revealed bodies lying on the floor with missing body parts as I worked my way through the cart, slashing throats and ripping the guts from torsos. It was over in a flash.

Montgomery had locked himself away hoping not to be found. The gunfight over, my blade dripped with blood. I thrust it through an empty seat to wipe it clean and then set out after Montgomery. Cart after cart, there was no sign of him. At last, looking around a sleeper cart, I sensed it was quiet—too quiet. Montgomery had to be around, and he probably had held onto a gun, just in case he needed it.

'Come on out! Don't make this hard on yourself!' I called calmly, having a hunch he wasn't too far.

Montgomery was panicking, not sure what his options were. I thought about looking into the toilet, with no idea what was waiting for me. I waited, took my guns from their holsters, and cocked the hammers. I was ready.

I pushed the door open to reveal Montgomery, holding a gun, pointing it at me, afraid and full of self pity. 'Move and I'll shoot!' he said. 'I mean it!' Even his arms were shaking.

I looked at him, noticing something familiar. All this man wanted was to do the right thing, live a peaceful life, and pay his dues. I sat down, laid my guns on the table, and took my hat off. 'Go ahead. Shoot me', I said calmly, calling a bluff.

'I never asked for this! I wish they had just left me alone!' said Montgomery in a quavering voice.

'I know. I can see. Put the gun down!' I replied with a voice of reason.

'No, no! You're not talking me down!' Montgomery stammered, trembling with the gun in his hand.

'Don't do something we'll both regret. Walk out of here alive. Don't be crazy now', I said calmly, sitting comfortably with my arms crossed.

All quiet, Montgomery wasn't too sure what to do next.

'Let me guess. You are afraid. I get it. I used to be like you—afraid of my own shadow, not sure if what I'm doing is right or not. But it doesn't have to be that way. Walk away. Now', I urged him, trying to ease his troubled mind.

'No! You're wrong. It's too late. They made me do some things I will live to regret. Look around. You've seen the horror show! Even if I walk out of here, they will have me killed!' Clearly he was worried and afraid of what would happen if he abandoned his duties.

'What's your next move? Enlighten me', I said, carefully watching the gun in his hand.

'I'm not going to jail! And you are not going to kill me! I'm going to have to shoot you! Sorry!' Montgomery made his call, aiming his gun at me.

I sharply exhaled with a sigh of disappointment, stood up, donned my hat, and straightened my coat. I looked at Montgomery and shook my head disappointedly.

'Stay where you are! I'm warning you!' Montgomery commanded, waving his gun at me.

'You are not going to shoot me. Not now, not ever', I replied confidently.

'You are wrong!' Montgomery replied, pulling the trigger. The gun failed to fire. He tried the trigger a few more times; nothing. 'Stupid pierce of crap!' he yelled and tossed it down.

'Safety is on, asshole!' I said with a disappointed tone. My roundhouse to the face knocked him cold. I reached into my pocket to retrieve my phone and dialled a number.

Captain Walter sat alone in his office on the graveyard shift. His phone rang, and he answered. 'Talk to me!'

'Captain, it's me', I said.' I'm at the old rail lines downtown. get here now, and bring a sense of humour; you are going to need it!' Then I hung up.

The captain put his phone down, grabbed his coat from the back of his chair, and stormed out the door. Soon the rail lines were crawling with cops, flashing with blue lights, and festooned with yellow crime-scene tape. I watched from afar as they wheeled bodies into the backs of coroner's vans. Local news crews were on the scene, digging around for answers.

'Captain Walter? Captain Walter? Can we have a word?' a female reporter asked, poking her microphone at the captain across the yellow tape.

'Now's not the time. Sorry', the captain replied. He was too busy to be bothered.

'Was this another anonymous tip? How long has this operation gone undetected?' she persisted, tailing the captain along the rails behind the yellow tape.

'This was no anonymous tip! This is months of hard undercover work paying off! Now get out of here!' the captain replied as he ducked inside the train.

Overseeing the scene from a distance, out of sight, Ray sat in his vehicle on high ground on the far side of the rail lines. His right hand man beside him, Richie Austin, was of average height, clean-shaven, and well built. They had come in hopes of making another hit.

'Looks like we missed the party', Richie indicated, lighting himself a cigar.

'Don't worry. All is not lost. I'll give the boss a ring', Ray replied, taking his phone from his pocket.

At the Riders Bar, in a place called Wroughton, just outside the capital, on the rough side of town, this was where the roughest types hung out—ex-cons, roughnecks, hooligans, and thugs roughhousing and stirring up trouble.

Inside, a man shooting pool with a friend answered his phone and walked away, turning his back to avoid unwanted attention. He was dressed in outdoor camping gear with a rather scruffy appearance as seen from the rear. His friend waited by the pool table; half-naked women paraded about, serving drinks and lap dancing.

'Talk to me!' the man said to his caller.

'We got cops all over the place. Looks like something went down', Ray told his so-called boss.

'That's not good enough, Ray. This puts a dent in our plans', the man replied evenly, not happy.

His friend fiddled with the balls as he took his eyes off the pool table, keeping it quiet amongst the spectating customers.

'Don't worry. I'll take care of it', Ray replied, accepting his boss's disapproval.

'Give our friend Walter a ring! Remind him where we stand!' the man ordered and cut the call short. 'Now, where was I?' Back in the game, he chalked his cue as he leaned forward, about to shoot. Then he noticed the balls had been moved. He stood up and looked at his friend—not angry but sceptical.

'Something wrong?' his friend asked, scratching his head, looking mystified.

'You fuck with my balls, John? Huh? Did you?' The man was seriously irked.

'Hey, man! I don't know what you're talking about!' John replied, denying the obvious.

The man studied John from the other side of the pool table. Then he raised his cue stick and thrust it into John's eye and out through the back of his head. He pulled the stick from his head, retrieving John's eyeball, and John sank to the floor, dead. Everyone minded their own business, looking away, saying and doing nothing.

'Well, look at this! Got myself an eight ball!' The man laughed. He laid the eye on the table, took aim, and knocked it into a pocket. He picked up his shot glass from the edge of the table, necked the shot, and slammed down the glass. 'Damn, that's good whiskey! Who's next?' he roared with glee, looking for his next challenger at the table. Everyone edged away peaceably.

I had left the cops behind at the scene, calling it a night. Halfway out of town, I pulled over and exited the pickup. I opened the cargo bed and dragged Daniels to his feet.

'This is where you get off! You are alive for one reason!' I growled firmly into his face, holding him by the collar.

'What's that?' he asked, shaking like a coward dog.

'You are going to let them know. Now run! Run, I say!' I shouted, drawing my gun.

Montgomery took off down the road the way we had come, fading into the dark. I got back in the pickup and continued my journey.

Inside the train, Captain Walter was looking around the scene, stepping over body parts on the floor, trying hard not to gag.

'What the hell happened here, Captain! Any ideas?' Officer Shepherd asked, unable to look away from the floor, painted in blood.

'Looks like a goddamned slaughterhouse! Looks like someone took justice a bit too far, that's what it is!' the captain replied.

'You don't think this is what Father Brown meant by taking back the city, do you, Captain?' Officer Shepherd hesitantly.

The captain looked at him. He thought for a second, considering how to respond. Then his phone rang, breaking the silence. 'I have to take this call!' the captain replied, moving away into an empty cart.

'This is not the time!' Captain Walter answered the phone, feeling very uncomfortable.

'You had a job to do, Captain—a very simple job! What the hell Is going on down their?' Ray expressed his ingratitude from the seat of his vehicle.

'Someone got here before you did and made a mess of things', Captain Walter replied, on edge looking over his shoulder.

'Well, that someone just cost us a lot of money and valuable time! Do your job and make sure the load ends up where it should! Got it?' Ray breathed down the phone loud and unhappy.

'Listen, asshole! You can't talk to me like that!' Captain Walter replied, angry.

'Got a problem? Take it up with the boss!' Ray snapped and hung up.

'Fucking shit! Shit!' the captain grunted, angry and frustrated, feeling his hands tied.

'You all right, Captain?' Officer Shepherd asked, appearing outside the cabin door. 'Heard some yelling.'

'Nothing to worry about. Let's wrap this up!' the captain replied, walking away in a disturbed mood.

At Mr Sullivan's mansion, near midnight, all of Mr Sullivan's associates and business partners were drinking champagne and mingling. A pianist sat in the middle of the room playing a sophisticated piece.

Mr Sullivan, in tuxedo, was being wheeled about by his carer, shaking hands and showing his appreciation. A waiter weaving through the room passed a glass of champagne to Mr Sullivan who then cleared his throat. 'A toast!' he called to gain everyone's attention.

Montgomery stumbled in, out of breath, frightened, and exhausted. Rather than cause an immediate interruption, he held himself up against the fancy wall pillars at the rear, scanning the crowd, and trying to make eye contact with Mr Sullivan.

'Gentlemen! A toast to our successful operation! May you raise your glasses!' Mr Sullivan made his toast with a broad smile on his face. Everyone cheered with their glasses raised high.

Montgomery cut through the audience, shouting at the top of his lungs. 'It's all gone! It's gone! Everything's gone!' He paused to draw breath. 'The entire operation was blown wide open. The drugs are gone, the men are all dead—there's nothing left!' Montgomery drooped as he arrived and stood before Mr Sullivan.

The audience stopped and stared, the music died … all went quiet. Maxwell, Rick, and Paul appeared, ready to hustle Montgomery from the floor and remove him from the worried guests.

Maxwell apologized for the commotion. 'Sorry, sir! We tried to stop him on the way in! Thought the news could have waited!'

Mr Sullivan glared at Montgomery. 'What is the meaning of this! Explain yourself!'

'Mr Sullivan, are we to be concerned?' asked a man in the crowd.

'No! No need for concern. Everybody out! This party is over. Out! Now!' Mr Sullivan yelled, chasing his audience away. With the room cleared except for the gang's hangers on here and there against the walls, he redirected his attention to Montgomery, handing his champagne to the carer and waving her away. 'Pull yourself together and explain to me what the fuck is going on!'

Montgomery was being held on his weary feet by Maxwell and Rick. 'That Arthur Brown—the priest—he came. He found us … not sure how, but he did!' Montgomery panted, sweating.

'What's he done? I demand to know!' Mr Sullivan growled, out of control, snatching up his oxygen mask.

'He made a mess of things! He … he saw what we were up to! He killed everyone—it was a slaughter! Then he got the cops involved! It's all gone. The cops … they cleaned the place out! I'm only alive because he wanted you to know everything!' Montgomery, feeling pathetic and utterly useless, started to cry.

Mr Sullivan-unable to bear the news, began to hyperventilate and struggled to fit his mask to his face with the help of his carer, who was suddenly back at his side.

At last he faintly spoke. 'Find him. I want him dead. I want him dead. I want to see his face before I put a bullet in his head.'

'That makes two of us!' came Gosnell's loud voice. Suddenly guns were drawn all around, as both sides got excited. It was another standoff. The lingering guests were spooked and slipped out.

Gosnell and his brother Johnathon had invited themselves into the mansion once again with the company of Raoul, Matt, and a small entourage of men. Matt was patched up with plasters, an eyepatch, and his hand in bandages; his appearance was questionable.

'Please!' Gosnell said in his charismatic way. 'Let's be civilised! Lower the guns! We all got the same problem on our hands!'

'What is it this time? To what pleasure do we owe this surprise?' Mr Sullivan asked, struggling to catch his breath.

'Looks like someone isn't doing too well!' Gosnell replied. 'I'm here to assist with this menace, Arthur Brown!'

'Why the sudden change of heart! You've turned down my father's request!' Paul expressed his ingratitude towards the brothers.

'We had our reasons', Johnathon explained. 'Things are different now!' He was looking to negotiate.

'How?' Paul replied, intrigued by Johnathon's response.

'Let's simply say he's made his point quite clear! Just look at poor Matt here!' Johnathon said, shaking his head pitifully.

'Thought you were meant to be some kind of tough guy!' Rick said, mocking Matt in his defeat.

'Watch your mouth! You got us into this mess to begin with!' Matt grunted angrily.

'Enough tough talk!' Raoul interjected. 'This needs to end right now! I say we find this priest and finish him!'

'As much as I hate to admit it, he's right'. Mr Sullivan replied, still shaken by the loss of his operation. His carer continued to feed him oxygen.

'So what's the plan?' Maxwell asked, feeling keen and expectant.

'The plan is simple', Gosnell said. 'We hunt him down—together! But first he must suffer! I want to see that bastard's face before I put a bullet in his head!' He was just as angry about my supreme motives as Mr Sullivan was.

'Remember. We cannot afford to make any more mistakes', Mr Sullivan added, sitting there looking ill.

'Don't worry, Pop!' Paul assured him. 'I'll make sure it's done right!'

'Now, let's have a drink for old time's sake, shall we?' Johnathon said, boldly grabbing a champagne flute from a nearby table.

CHAPTER 17

Still stuck in a dark place and barely hanging on to his life, Carl sat with his back against the wall, mumbling a form of gibberish. His hair had taken over his already dim appearance. Then there was chattering, laughter—male and female voices outside the walls that enclosed him.

'Hey! Don't touch that! That's mine! We here to work, not fuck around, got it?' shouted a male voice.

'What? Come on! We are not starting for another hour! Chill the fuck out!' another male replied.

Carl immediately struggled to his feet. Through weak, dry lips, with a sore voice-he called out, 'Help me. Help me … Help, please', he cried out faintly, tapping on the wall.

'Listen, guys! Listen!. I think he's still alive!' a female voice quieted the ones who were arguing.

A loud bang on the wall drove Carl into the corner. Scared, he scrunched himself into the dark where he remained.

'Shut the fuck up in there!' an angry mail voice called. 'You should be dead! Don't make me come in there!'

An hour passed. Suddenly, loud noises filled the space outside his walls: music, and the sound of men and women partying, breaking things, and fighting.

A few days later, I was downtown behind the wheel of the pickup, next to a local locksmith's shop. There I'd noticed my next target, Paul, Mr Sullivan's golden child, leaving a tailor's shop, checking himself out in his fancy suit in the shop windows, and then climbing into his vehicle.

With no time to lose, I followed him through the town, shadowing him all the way to his penthouse. There I waited out of sight across the street and watched as a valet—a young male no more than twenty-two years of age—escorted Paul from his car and drove his car away. Not long after the valet returned, I headed across the street, making my way towards him at the entrance of the penthouse. 'Hey! You're that Father Brown! Saw you on the news; that was a cool speech, man!' The valet immediately bombarded me with enthusiasm before I had a chance to address him.

'I'm flattered, kid, real flattered. Robbie, is it?!' I replied in a rush, having noticed his name on his name tag.

'Yeah, yeah! Robbie all the way, friends call me Rob!' he replied excitedly.

'Well, Rob, maybe you can do your part in helping your city by telling me the number to the man's apartment whose car you've just parked!' I asked nicely with a very persuasive tone.

'Er … yeah! Sure thing, Father Brown. That's Paul Sullivan, and he lives in apartment twenty eight', Robbie willingly told me.

'Thanks, kid. Look after yourself!' I stuck a hundred dollar note into his pocket, a sign of goodwill and appreciation, and left the kid to his job.

'Hey, man, thanks! See you around!' Robbie smiled, fluffing the banknote he had just received.

Back on the road, on my way out of town I took a quick stop at Rosemary's Diner, one of my favourite spots, sitting just outside the Capital off the highway. Parked up, I walked inside. It was quiet as I parted the door, drawing attention to myself. My striking appearance bought me unwanted attention—strange looks and foul expressions strained the atmosphere. I kept my hat and coat on, pulled up a seat at the window, and unfolded the menu.

'What can I get you, Father Brown?' the waitress asked nicely, already knowing who I was. Aside from my recent notoriety, I'd long regularly entered these familiar premises.

'I'll have the number five special, as always!' I answered with an unseen smile beneath my bandages.

After taking my order, the waitress poured me some complimentary coffee with a drop of milk and a pinch of sugar on the side.

'Hey, Dad. Is that man a mummy?' a little girl asked her father. A family of four sat at a table in front of me.

'No, honey. That's Father Brown', her father replied quietly.

To pass the time, I indulged myself in the daily newspaper placed onto my table with a number of headlines: 'PA Angela Windsor replaces Reed as New Mayor to the City'; 'CCPD biggest drug bust'; 'Captain Walter suspected of foul play'; Detective Carl Brooks still missing, grieving wife seeks answers'.

My order was placed on the table, so I folded the paper and laid it aside. 'Thank you, ma'am', I said to the waitress with a humble smile beneath.

'Anything else I can get you?' she asked nicely.

'That'll be all. Thanks', I replied, sipping my coffee.

It wasn't long after when two four-wheel drive vehicles turned up outside. A group of four tough-looking men emerged from the vehicles. They lurked around the truck I was driving and then came inside the diner and they stood around, intimidating the customers with their silence.

'We are looking for a man by the name of Arthur Brown, supposedly a priest!' one man asked with a loud voice, standing out from his group.

He wore a holiday shirt underneath his blazer—a Cuba link around his neck, gold watch, smart shoes and trousers, and a shaved head rough around the edges. He appeared to be in his late forties, well built, with a sense of professionalism written all over his manner.

Everyone kept quiet. The family of four grabbed their kids and tried to leave the diner. Their attempt was foiled by the four.

'Just where do you think you are going? No one leaves until I'm finished! Sit the fuck down!' the man grunted fiercely, scaring the family back into their seats.

They knew who I was; they stood looking at me, waiting patiently for a reaction while I ate my meal. The men wondered around the diner, provoking the customers. While the group stood around keeping a close eye on me, their leader sat down across from an older man. 'Tell me, old-timer. You don't happen to know who this Arthur Brown is, do you?' he politely asked as if he had no idea who I was.

Afraid and fearful for his life, the old man trembled, looking across the diner at me. The other man noticed and smiled fiercely at me. 'Well, thanks for the chat, old-timer. I'll let you be!' Reaching across the table, he patted the old man on the shoulder firmly.

Meanwhile, I continued to sip my coffee, finishing up the last scraps on my plate. The lead ruffian stood up and wandered towards the counter. There the manager spoke up: 'Listen here! I don't want any trouble! Why don't you leave these nice folks alone and be on your way?' He raised a shotgun and held it to their faces.

'Well, look at this! Someone with balls!' The leader smiled, cheerful and unfazed by the gun pointing at his face. Then his tone shifted to a solemn threat: 'You going to use that thing, old man?' he asked, pointing at the shotgun. 'Don't make me set an example with you!'

The manager stood down, lowered his shotgun, and backed away—a coward in a pinch.

'That's what I thought! Anyone else want to play hero—anyone?' The man looked around the diner.

He noticed the family of four-a couple with two kids, boy and girl. He walked over and loomed above the table. The family felt intimidated, the parents holding their kids close. The man looked at them and then smiled at the little girl. I watched carefully, pushing my empty plate aside.

'Tell me, little girl. Do you know who I'm looking for?'

The girl held onto her mother's arm tightly, turning away from him. I had seen enough. I pushed my chair back, breaking the silence as I stood up. The men looked at me, reaching into their waistbands, ready to draw.

The lead ruffian turned to me. 'I was beginning to think you were going to just let me kill all these nice people, while you sat there enjoying the show. Nice of you to join us! Where are my manners?' He walked slowly towards me; I stayed put, unshaken, unmoved. 'Name's Ferguson, first name Fred. I'll be your undertaker today', he said stepping close to my face.

'I'm afraid you are a bit late. Death already claimed me', I replied calmly.

Ferguson and his men looked at each other in confusion, as if unsure whether I was kidding. 'You are a very funny man, Father Brown!' Ferguson replied.

'Please, call me Arthur Brown', I asked nicely while the customers looked on in fear.

'Look here, asshole! I'll call you whatever the fuck I want!' Ferguson growled at me.

'I suggest you watch that mouth of yours. There are children around', I replied in the most reasonable tone. The four laughed in scorn, elbowing one another with mocking looks at me.

'I'm going to enjoy putting you down—courtesy the Logan brothers on behalf of myself and good old Mr Sullivan!' Ferguson ominously unbuttoned his blazer, revealing two guns tucked inside his waistband.

'Before I make a mess of things, why don't you let these nice folks go?' I bravely requested, unfazed by my opponents' numbers.

'No, they will be my witnesses. I love witnesses, and there's a lesson to be taught here. They're staying', Ferguson replied, threatening the safety of the customers.

'And the Lord said to Pharaoh, "Let my people go!" I'm asking you nicely. No one needs to get hurt.' I spoke out sternly, hoping Ferguson would let the costumers leave peacefully.

The men laughed louder. It was quite clear that I wasn't being taken seriously.

Ferguson gave me a scowl. 'Spare me the Bible nonsense, Father. I think that bandage of yours is on too tight. No one leaves!' he yelled, scaring the kids.

'I suggest you cover the children's eyes', I said to the family sitting before me. 'They do not need to see what's about to happen.' The parents sheltered the children in their arms.

The men gathered around, ready to react. *A lot can go wrong*, I pondered, looking around to assess the grave situation. *All these innocent people's lives at risk … one false move may have serious consequences.* The last thing I wanted was to see the children hurt, caught in the crossfire. *I have to think fast, I need to be quick.*

'I believe we both know how this is going to end, Father Brown!' Ferguson slowly grasped his two guns, watching me closely.

Moments later, I stumbled from the diner alone, straightening my hat. My bandage and coat were smeared in blood, and there was a bullet in my left arm. Today was a good day to wear my concealed body armour; it could have ended much worse. I climbed into my truck with a painful grunt and saw myself off.

Back inside the diner, blood streaked the windows and the floor; the tables and counter were decorated with arms and limbs. Two bodies were sprawled on tables with holes in their heads; another hung over the counter. Blood dripped from their throats; all were dead. As for Ferguson, he rested peacefully against the jukebox, which was playing a funeral hymn; his severed head lay at his feet. The customers and employees had survived; frightened, they quietly skipped over the dead and fled the diner.

Home at the cottage, I dropped my coat, removed my hat, and tore off by body armour, along with the bloodstained bandages. I sat down at the table with a strap and a pointed pair of pliers. Blood streamed from my arm. With heart pounding in my chest like a battering ram, I fastened the strap around my arm and dug into the wound with the pliers. Painfully, I yanked the bullet from my arm and dropped it on the table. After cleaning and dressing my wound, I threw myself onto the old settee and closed my eyes.

Deep in my sleep, I heard voices, screams, whispers, cries, gunshots; my most painful memories began to plague me. Blood, so much blood—I killed them … I killed them all; they left me no choice. They washed their hands in the blood of the innocents; they had to die, they had to!

My thoughts haunted me. Surely my passion for justice justified my actions, but so much was on my mind, I felt as if I'd lost my sanity. I knew I wasn't the same ever since I rose from the grave. I rarely slept; I was afraid to—afraid of what I might see. I married the night; she was my bride. I stayed awake for her, preying on the unjust. There was nothing left to do but stare at the empty wooden walls until the night embraced me.

CHAPTER 18

As night fell, the Aqua Sushi restaurant was busy, filled with customers of every kind. It was a time of celebration for the Sullivans: Paul's birthday. His father had arranged a feast in his honour, with a table large enough to seat Mr Sullivan, his son, and the rest of their most favoured companions and colleagues.

The table was centred in the midst of the restaurant. Paul sat next to his father (whose carer hovered nearby) and Maxwell, while the others such as, Rick, Craig, and a few hand-picked men filled the rest of the seats. Together they dined merrily on food spread across the supine naked body of a young female, no more than twenty-eight years of age, dressed with food from her shoulders to her shins.

They weren't the only ones celebrating. That night the Logans were out at their newest establishment, the Modern Art Gallery in the heart of the city, celebrating its opening with a number of guests and partners, mingling and laughing heartily with one another, drinking fine wine and admiring contemporary art.

Paul returned to his penthouse early in the company of a lady, leaving his Father and the rest of the men to enjoy what was left of his party. He unlocked his door, and they stumbled around in the dark kissing and touching each other intimately, rough and aggressive, eventually making it to the bedroom.

She ripped his shirt open and unbuckled his pants. Shoving him onto the bed, she dropped her thong to her ankles on the floor and climbed onto Paul in the moonlight that shone through the window.

I sat quietly in a comfortable armchair in a dark corner of the room. I could end him right there, right now, but I let him enjoy his moment. I could let him have that before I took his wretched life.

She rode him vigorously for no more than ten minutes, after which he spilled his load.

Satisfied, pleased, and content, he pushed her aside, catching his breath. I flicked the lights on. Frightened, they scuttled up against the headboard, holding on to each other.

'You? What the fuck you doing in my home? Fucking spying on me? Is that it? You like to watch? Fucking freak!' Paul yelled. He scrambled out of the bed and looked around the bedside table for his handgun.

'I wouldn't bother. Whatever you are looking for is long gone', I replied, still sitting comfortably, arms folded, relaxed.

Naked as he was, Paul charged at me. I stood up and knocked him to the ground with a punch to the face. He shuffled towards the bed, digging through his pants on the floor. I pulled my revolver from its holster. 'Don't try anything stupid!' I warned, holding my gun over his head.

He pulled his gun from his pants, and I shot him in the wrist. He squealed, dropped the gun, and the lady in his bed shrieked. All she could think to do was cover her private parts with the Egyptian cotton sheets.

'You? Get out of here!' I said to her. 'You do not want see what happens next!'

She grabbed her clothes, slipped into her strappy heels, and took off naked out the door. I grabbed Paul by the neck and sat him down in the armchair.

'You should be dead! Ferguson was supposed to take care of you!' Paul growled unhappily, burning with anger.

The sound of gunfire echoed as my thoughts flashed back to the diner. I had shot a few of Ferguson's men and dispatched the others with my blade. Ferguson himself had shot me in the arm before I thrust my blade through his throat and twisted it, taking his head off.

'They tried. Sorry to disappoint you, but they failed!' I replied with a vengeful tone, staring Paul dead in the eyes.

'What the fuck are you? You're supposed to be a priest! You're supposed to be dead!' Paul raged, frightened and intimidated by my striking presence.

'I think you know just what I am!' I replied. I dragged him from the chair and tossed him to the floor.

'You can't kill me!' he cried, crawling towards the bedroom door.

'I'm not the one you want. I didn't murder your family. Rick did! He's the one you're after, he's the one you want, not me!'

I picked him up, threw a few punches, and tossed him about the room and out into the living room. Paul fought back, swinging weakly. I fractured both his arms, and a kick up the chin saw him onto a glass centrepiece, shattering it. He was out, naked, bruised, and full of glass shards. I stood over him and thought about finishing the job, clenching my fists, full of anger—yet somehow I managed to defer my anger.

Returning from a late night at the Aqua Sushi restaurant, Mr Sullivan was driven through the gates to his mansion. Maxwell rode with him as Sullivan sipped champagne with his carer, the two of them drunk and laughing in each other's face.

Outside the gates, across the street, I watched as Maxwell escorted Mr Sullivan and his carer into the mansion. In my back seat, Paul lay squirming on his back, tied up, with duct tape across his mouth.

'Save your energy', I said, 'it's going to be a long night.' With that, I slipped out of the truck.

After observing the mansion yard for some hours, I stationed myself at the gate, whistling. Two men appeared, poking their heads around, looking. A blade to the throat put them both to rest. I then took a hand from the arm hanging through the gates and placed it against the biometric keypad, letting myself in.

Across the yard I raced, quietly evading the roaming sentries. I slipped into the mansion and drifted past a group of men playing poker in the living room. Climbing the stairs swiftly with my blade at hand, I met with another of Mr Sullivan's men turning a corner on his way to the stairs. A flick of the wrist and his guts were in his hands. I caught him before he hit the floor and dragged him into an empty room. From there I observed the door to Mr Sullivan's private quarters; two armed men on security duty stood outside his door.

From my utility belt I took two knives and sent them through the air, striking both men's foreheads. They fell to the floor dead. Quickly I moved their bodies aside and let myself into the bedroom.

There he was, asleep in the dark wrapped up in silk with his carer sleeping on his chest. My hand itched at the handle of my blade hanging by my side; to slay or not to slay—a mammoth decision.

'Wake up, scumbag!' I grunted at him.

Sullivan's eyes sprang open; he was shocked, frozen in fear, and lost for words. I knocked him cold into his pillow. This woke the carer, and taken by surprise, she panicked and reached under her pillows, retrieving a gun. I grabbed her by the hands, restraining her, covered her mouth, and relieved her of the gun.

She struggled against me, trying to resist; her effort was futile. 'Sorry, lady. I'm going to have to keep you quiet.' I tied her up and gagged her, then locked her away inside the closet.

Soon, away from the mansion, strapped to chairs, unconscious, Paul, naked, and his pyjama-clad father sat side by side. A splash of water to their faces yielded signs of life.

'You have no idea what you're getting into!' Mr Sullivan shouted, furious. 'I suggest you cut me loose and run for your pathetic life!'

I took my blade from my waist and laid it on the table, creating a distraction. They looked at me as I strolled around the chairs. 'I'm done running', I announced. 'Running from myself, my pain, my troubles, my memories—from everything!' I lit a few candles on the tabletop.

'What are you doing! What are you going to do with us?!' Mr Sullivan asked, probing.

'He's going to kill us!' Paul yelled. 'What the fuck you think he's going to do? Look around!'

'Your son's right. You are going to die, all of you. First, some questions!' I replied calmly, taking my time, savouring the moment at the Aqua Sushi restaurant.

'You going to kill me in my own restaurant? Who the fuck do you think you are, you piece of crap?' Sullivan shouted, gasping for air. 'Let me out of here!'

'You should take it easy. Don't deprive me of the chance to kill you', I growled sternly, picking my blade up from the table.

Maxwell, strolling through the hallway, stopped at the sound of banging and rattling. He placed his ear against the door to Mr Sullivan's chambers. The banging continued. With a decisive kick, Maxwell cleared the door.

'Detective Carl Brooks! Where is he? I'm not going to ask twice!' I held my blade over Paul's head.

'I don't know what you're talking about!' Mr Sullivan replied, loud and obnoxious.

'Wrong answer!' I replied, raising my blade, about to remove Paul's head.

'No! Don't!' Paul cried. 'Please don't! Fuck's sake, Pop, just tell him!'

'Have some fucking balls, son! Have some balls!' Mr Sullivan shouted back, refusing to cooperate.

'Your call!' I replied and chopped the fingers from Paul's left hand.

Paul screamed, and his father panicked. This wake-up call left him speechless.

'Now I've got your attention! I'm going to ask one more time! Where is the detective?' I demanded, getting ready to take Paul's left arm.

Maxwell freed the carer from the closet and sat her down on the bed, while she eagerly explained what had happened.

'He took him away! I don't know where he's taken him—please find him!' she pleaded pitifully.

'Don't worry, we'll find him. Arthur Brown will be taken care of!' Maxwell assured her. Then he raced off to round up the men outside and brief them.

'Listen up! Mr Sullivan has been kidnapped! Arthur Brown paid us an unannounced visit. Let's find Mr Sullivan and take care of his problem, starting at the restaurant. Move out!'

Rick and Craig joined Maxwell on the manhunt. Together, they loaded themselves into their vehicles with guns and ammunition and took off.

'He's kept at a trap house!' Mr Sullivan answered involuntarily.

'Where? Tell me!' I grabbed him by the neck, digging my fingers into his throat.

'Out of town! Off the eastern highway ... Evington Road, the third street! It's the only house there, you can't miss it', Sullivan replied, barely enduring the force being applied to his neck.

'Let's hope for your sake he's there!' I tipped Mr Sullivan onto his back on the floor.

Outside, the sound of tyres screeching to a stop, indicated Maxwell and the gang arriving. Eight armed men, Craig and Rick included. I looked at my watch; they'd taken longer than I expected. They covered the exits, looking to box me in.

I slipped my blade back into my belt, read to go. 'Looks like it's time for me blow this hellhole—literally!'

'What you mean, blow this hellhole? What have you done? Answer me!' Sullivan shouted, on his back on the floor with the sharks prodding at his head through the glass.

'Like I said! I'm taking everything you've got!' I replied, heading towards the front door, both revolvers in my hands, loaded and ready.

'I'm going to kill you Arthur Brown!' Sullivan called out as I walked away. 'You hear me? I'm going to rip your fucking heart from your chest!'

Paul sat there, naked, wallowing in pain, delirious and about to pass out.

The men had already entered the kitchen from the rear, led by Rick, followed by Craig. Out front, Maxwell and four others waited, about to break in.

'In on three! Go!' Maxwell said, ready to enter the premises.

Both guns held high, I took a deep breath. Just as they were about to enter, I kicked the doors open, and the impact thrust the men to the kerb. With my revolvers I wasted no time, taking down four of Maxwell's men and forcing him into cover behind parked cars as we engaged in a gunfight at close range.

Rick and Craig stormed the dining area, finding Mr Sullivan and his son in jeopardy.

'What the fuck happened here?' Craig stared at Paul's naked body and missing fingers.

'Don't just stand there! Get us out, now!' Mr Sullivan yelled.

Outside, guns were blazing as I tried fighting my way from the restaurant to the pickup. Maxwell stood his ground, trying to pin me down from his cover. I was shooting my way to the pickup.

'You die tonight, Priest! This is it!' Maxwell was feeling lucky, keeping a low profile behind his vehicle, avoiding the bullets over his head.

I was running out of time. The fight could wait; there was a detective waiting to be saved and a bomb waiting to blow at any moment. Rick and Craig by now had no doubt extracted Mr Sullivan and his son out the back door. I somehow got to the pickup under heavy fire, with bullets penetrating the tailgate as Maxwell made his last attempt to stop me.

'Max! Get out of here!' Rick shouted. 'This joint's about to blow!'

The bomb I had planted during my encounter with Chen tore the Aqua Sushi restaurant apart. The walls and the roof caved in, and all of Mr Sullivan's ill gotten gains were destroyed as he and his men watched from across the street.

'This ends now. Gather the Logans and all their assets. We got a war to fight!' said Mr Sullivan, loud, angry, and bitter, looking at his restaurant in flames from the back seat of his vehicle.

In the alley across the street, Rupee and Dale had been observing the chaos. They overheard Mr Sullivan's goal and nodded at each other. Knowing what was beyond the horizon, they quickly faded into the dark alley with the bag I had left in their care.

I raced up the eastern highway, swerving between the late night commuters. I pulled off onto the side road and plunged down the dark country lane known as Evington Road, seemingly heading into the middle of nowhere. I saw nothing but trees and heard only owls hooting from the treetops.

Ahead of me an old five-storey building appeared. I took it to be a deserted hotel with broken windows and tattered walls partly covered in vines. Lights and the loud noise of rave metal came from inside—a sign of life. I killed the headlights, pulled over into the bushes, and reached into a pocket for my phone.

Sleepless and anxious, Captain Walter stood outside on the terrace of his home in his trousers and a vest, wearing his holstered guns and contemplating his actions when his phone rang. 'Talk to me!' he answered.

'Evington Road, of the eastern highway! Get here now!' I gravely urged the captain. 'Bring all the firepower you've got—you'll need it!'

'What the hell Is going on, Father Brown?'

'No time for answers, Captain! You've got fifteen minutes, and then I'm going in!' I was keen to get going.

'Hold on, Father Brown! Don't do anything stupid! I'm on my way!' he replied.

'Hey, Captain? When this is all over, we need to talk!' I said in an ominous tone. I hung up and settled in to wait.

The Captain looked at his phone puzzled, noticing I'd hung up. He hurried inside, slipped into his coat, dashed to his car, and peeled out in a hurry.

Somewhere in a remote part of the city, outside an old deserted steel factory, Mr Sullivan and his men met with the Logans. They all stood in the dark around their vehicles, lights on, discussing tactics. Mr Sullivan sat in his chair with his son Paul, Maxwell, Rick, Craig, and the rest of the gang at his side. The Logans again had the services of the deadly Lady Casandra, in full latex with pistols on either hip. Raoul, his dogs, Matt, and a number of hired gunmen loyal to the Logans were all ready for the fight to restore their precious empire.

'Glad you could join us!' Mr Sullivan said, keen and impatient.

'We won't miss this chance to terminate this infamous priest! No way in hell!' Gosnell declared, fiddling with his cufflinks.

'Tonight Arthur Brown dies for the last time!' Johnathon bellowed. 'Let's finish him so we can get back to business as usual!'

'OK, boys!' Lady Casandra chimed in. 'You heard the man. Let's load up and move out!'

They opened the boots of their vehicles, passing each other guns and loading ammunition. Raoul herded his two dogs into a vehicle, after which they saw themselves off.

Meanwhile my patience was wearing thin in the pickup, Captain Walter was running late.

'Sorry, Captain. Guess I'm going in', I muttered to myself.

I put on my hat, exited the pickup, and opened up the bed. There I flipped open the wooden chest with the last of my guns and ammunition reserves. I slipped my loaded revolvers into their holsters, nestled the knives in my utility belt next to the formidable blade, and put additional cartridges into the side pouches strapped to my legs.

I was up the devil's alley and about to enter the belly of the beast. Taking no chances, I scouted the building and its surroundings Only one way in, and that was the front—a large wooden double door with a lot of history and graffiti. Revolvers out, I eased the creaking doors open.

As I set foot inside, the music stopped. Everything went quiet as if someone knew I was there. I investigated cautiously as I moved past broken old furniture in the dark, dusty graffitied hall, which appeared to be the lobby.

Above me, up the stairs, someone was watching, armed and looking to take a shot. No more than two armed men stood in hiding, savouring the moment. They leant over the stairs in shadows, about to shoot, when a rat scampered past. I instantly reacted, plastering myself against the wall beneath the staircase. The shot missed, scratching the cracked floor beneath my feet.

Bullets began to rain down the stairs as the two men heavily suppressed me. Drug pushers, punks, social outcasts—men and women joined the fight from every corner of the staircase, armed with fully automatic rifles and 9-millimetres.

From wall to wall I fought against these drug-ridden hooligans, taking them down as they descended from the stairs and appeared from doorways. My cartridges ran dry, so I retreated into cover between cabinets against a wall. The clatter of empty shells from my revolvers echoed amidst the suppressive fire.

I used the time reloading to talk the shooters down. 'I'm here for the detective! Give him up, and this all ends now! Nobody else needs to die!' I shouted, filling my cylinders.

The shooting stopped, I peeked from the wall in hopes that they had came to their senses. My voice had drawn the attention of someone familiar. Aron Carter appeared at the top floor, looking down at me, holding an AK-47 over his shoulder, clothed in a dirty tank top and ripped jeans. A man and woman stood to either side of him, aiming their guns in my direction.

'Well, if it isn't the infamous Arthur Brown!' Aron shouted aloud, mocking me in his arrogance. 'Or should I refer to you as the unrighteous Father? The man without a face?'

'Call me what you like, pilgrim! You know how I came to be; keep pushing!' I warned, knitting my brows beneath my bandages. 'Hand over the detective, and be spared the treacherous fate that awaits you!' I looked up, carefully scanning the stairs.

Aron raised his arm, quietly signalling to his men to close in and finish the job whilst he distracted me. They slowly descended the stairs, filtering out into the lobby, ready to kill. I stayed put, waiting for the right moment to strike gazing at their reflection off the broken glass spread across the floor.

'The detective stays!' Aron yelled down the stairs. 'I've got my orders! Besides, he's already good as dead!' He gave a ghastly laugh.

'Didn't think so!' I replied, dashing across the lobby.

Bullets began to fly like whistling wind, streaming past my coat. Aron and his two friends retreated out of sight. One by one, I worked through the gang of armed assailants, piling up the body count as I shot my way up the stairs, using the walls and rails as cover. I fought floor to floor, killing every shooter in my path, flooding the hallways with bullets and painting the dirty walls with their splattered blood. Out of bullets, I put away my revolvers and drew my blade. I chopped and hacked my way to the top floor as bodies fall down the stairs and over the banisters.

At last, I made it to the top floor. All was quiet –, too quiet. Walking through the corridor, the broken portraits, ransacked rooms, and dampened walls painted a long history. I kept my blade close-Suddenly gunshots came from six doors ahead. I was being engaged by Aron and his two friends. Their suppressive fire drove me into cover in a nearby room. There I took the time to reload my revolvers from my utility belt.

'You so much as put your head out that door, you are a dead man.

Come on, Arthur, think! Where the hell are you, Captain" You are running late!' I chanted quietly to myself.

On the eastern highway blue lights lit the night as patrol cars raced along in a hurry. Captain Walter, in his cruiser, brought up the rear.

Back at the old hotel, reinforcements had arrive. More armed assailants climbed the stairs and stationed themselves along the hallway. I pulled the ventilation shaft open, stood on an old file cabinet, and climbed inside. I crawled along, pointing the way with my guns.

I heard Aron frantically yell, 'He's around somewhere, and I want him found!' I followed the sound, heading for what must be the hotel's presidential suite. From the vents I saw a large room filled with more graffiti, video games, a leather sofa, and a mountain of cocaine piled onto a mattress on the floor.

Aron yelled to his friends, panicking with his hands on his head holding his rifle.

There Aron was, waving a rifle, screaming into the phone, and pacing the room restlessly whilst his two friends secured the doorway, leaving everyone else to the search. I saw no sign of Carl or where he might be held; not much to see from the vents.

'Where the fuck are you guys? This maniac is killing my men! Get here now!' Aron screamed into the phone desperately. I guessed he was talking to Sullivan's men, whose dirty work he was failing to finish. They were probably on the way here.

A group of assailants entered the room-I watched and waited patiently for the right moment to dispatch some of these no-good thugs.

'We can't find him anywhere! The rooms are empty!' one of them eagerly reported.

'What do you mean you can't find him? He was just here! Spread out and find him!' Aron demanded, panicking all over again.

The men fled the room at his orders, looking for me.

'Make sure no one gets in this room! He's out there somewhere, I can feel it! It's like he's right on my ass, waiting to pounce!' Aron moaned ridiculously to his two friends standing watch at the door.

I transformed Aron's imaginings into reality. I dropped from the vent, knocking him to the ground. With two single head shots, I quickly dispatched the two friends standing at the door. Aron reached for a gun lying on the floor at arm's length. I kicked the gun away and scooped him up by the neck.

'Where's the detective? Don't make me ask twice!' I grunted in his face, angry and impatient.

Three assailants stormed in, and I shot them down without flinching. Aron struggled to get his words out as I continued to fasten my grip. 'I can't breathe … You're killing me', he groaned, trying to tear my hands from his neck.

I loosened my grip and tossed him to the floor with my bare hands. There I held him at gunpoint whilst he contemplated his answer. 'Talk!' I shouted, waving a gun in his face.

More assailants turned up, recklessly rushing into the room, I shot them dead, making a mess of their heads. I then refocused my attention on Aron, dragging him towards an open window and hanging him outside by the leg as he shrieked.

'Last chance, asshole! Or your head's going to be plastered across the pavement!' I grunted, short on temper.

'OK! He's in the next room! Two doors down!' Aron squealed, giving up Carl's whereabouts.

Then I heard a convoy of vehicles-approaching the hotel—but no sirens, no blue lights. I smelt trouble. This would be Mr Sullivan and his gang, probably along with the Logans.

Aron chuckled at the sight of his cavalry. 'Looks like you're not leaving here tonight, Father! I suggest you put that gun to your head. It's over!' He smiled, celebrating early.

'You are not out the woods yet. You're coming with me!' I dragged him inside. The assailants kept on flooding the corridors as I shot our way out of the room and down the hallway, dragging Aron along.

Outside, the Logans and their men dismounted their vehicles and filtered inside, with Maxwell and the rest of Mr Sullivan's gang. They spread themselves out around the building and inside the rooms.

'Remember, Arthur Brown dies tonight., This is it!' Gosnell shouted to the men as they charged the old hotel.

Rick, Craig, Matt, Casandra and Raoul with his two Rottweilers all stood gazing up at the building. All had one purpose in mind, and a few had a personal vendetta—to kill me, poison my city with drugs, and flood the streets with crime and chaos.

I threw Aron through the door of the master suite. Outside in the hallway, dead bodies, missing heads, missing limbs … I had run short of ammunition and resorted to a more primitive task. Still, nothing could prepare me for what I was about to see.

'What is this? What's in here? Answer me!' I growled at Aron, standing over him with my dripping blade resting sharply at his neck.

I was standing in the master room facing a giant steel vault with reinforced steel doors. Corner to corner, wall to wall, the giant vault consumed half the master suite.

'That's where we keep him!' Aron answered frightened.

'Open it! Now!' I shouted, nearly blind with fury, dragging Aron towards the vault.

CHAPTER 19

Meanwhile, the Logans and Mr Sullivan's men were advancing through the hotel floors led by Maxwell and Paul—skipping over the dead, carefully scanning their way up the stairs, checking rooms working through the corridors. *Their arrival changes everything; I need to be quick and extract in good time.*

Using a set of keys from his pocket, Aron unlocked the steel doors, shedding light into the dark steel vault. Nervous, I suddenly feared what I might see. I gathered my courage and strolled into the vault. The stench was foul beyond description. I stepped on decayed rodents scattered across the floor. I held my breath and continued, keeping Aron close, dragging him along.

In the dark of the corner, Carl was scrunched up, shaking, emaciated, sitting in his own filth, with loose shackles around his arms and ankles like a wild beast grunting aggressively like a wild dog, shrinking away from us in terror. Carl was no more; he was gone. I barely recognized the man before me. He needed saving.

Angry, furiously outraged, I turned my attention to Aron. 'You animals! What have you done? *What have you done?*' I shouted at him, finally striking fear into him.

I grabbed him by the neck and thrust him against the inside of the vault. I shouted, 'You will die! You hear me? You will die!'

'Please, man! I was just doing my job!' Aron pleaded.

'So was he!' I replied, punching my blade into Aron and slicing him open from the gut up to his ribs, pouring his bowels out at my feet.

'He's here! Secure the exits!' someone called out to the rest of the group, gazing in from the doorway.

The gang had arrived, and I was boxed in. Bullets rained against the vault, trapping me inside, the only available cover. I checked my utility belt; just enough cartridges to fill a single revolver. I reloaded, chopped the shackles from Carl, and knocked him cold for a safer transit out of the hotel should he somehow resist.

'Sorry, Carl. It's easier that way.' I heaved him onto my shoulders in a fireman's carry, ready to move.

Maxwell and Paul entered the room. Maxwell threw his hands up, signalling a cease-fire, as they casually strolled into the room and stood outside the storage, out of sight.

'It's over, priest! Come on out; let's finish this!' Maxwell ordered, with his gun aiming at the entrance of the vault.

No answer; all quiet. Paul signalled to the gang, spreading them through the room for extra protection.

Outside, the Logans stood around the vehicles with Mr Sullivan wheeling around on his own, loitering in front of the building.

'What the hell is going on!' Mr Sullivan growled impatiently, cradling his oxygen mask.

'Patience, my friend. They will get the job done. Father Brown will die tonight', Johnathon confidently reassured him.

'Okay, Carl. This is it. We're getting out of here'. Pumped, slipping my blade into my waist-swapping it for a 12-gauge Raging Judge revolver.

'There's nowhere to run, priest! Come on out already!' Maxwell loudly insisted.

I needed a diversion, and I had one more trick up my sleeve—a frag grenade inside my utility belt just for this one occasion. With my gun safely in its holster, I firmly grasped the grenade in my palm, flicked the pin with my thumb, and tossed it into the middle of the room. The grenade rolled across the floor, stopping at Paul's feet.

'Grenade!' Paul cried loudly, throwing himself into cover behind the leather sofa.

Maxwell shielded himself behind the reinforced steel doors whilst everyone dispersed themselves, some heading for the door and others seeking whatever cover might prove to be safe. The grenade went, and the blast took casualties—my cue to react.

In the lobby, waiting in reserve, Raoul, Rick, Matt, and Casandra responded to the blast by charging up the stairs.

'Sounds like trouble! This has gone on long enough!' Mr Sullivan grunted arrogantly.

With Carl over my shoulder, I strolled out of the vault, opening fire to finish the job, dead men falling from the nearby windows to land on the parked vehicles. The rest of the gang retreated out the door. Paul stood his ground behind the sofa. Maxwell stood to my rear, quietly emerging from behind the door—an ambush I evaded with the help of a reflection from a broken mirror on the wall.

Quickly reacting with two single shots, I forced Maxwell to take a dive into cover, shielding himself amongst broken furniture. I shot my way out of the room, fighting through the hallways and corridors, blowing the heads from assailants who jumped from door to door whilst lugging Carl along on my shoulders.

At last, the stairs, where bullets greeted me as Raoul and the rest of the reserve gang approached, Casandra and Matt bringing up the rear. I had no way back and no way forward.

Dogs were barking. 'Get him, boys!' Raoul grunted, setting his dogs at me from beneath the stairs.

The dogs charged up the stairs towards me. Assailants led by Maxwell and Paul closed in from beyond the corridor. I was boxed in and out of ammunition. My blade was my last resort.

'This is it, Carl. This is it!' I whispered courageously as I braced myself for the worst.

Then by a twist of fate, an assailant hiding in a room nearby emerged with his semiautomatic rifle, ready to engage. This was just what I needed to turn the tables. With my blade I claimed his arm and then took charge of the rifle. With a dry powder extinguisher on the wall and a fire hose beside the stairs, I was set for a quick extraction.

I blew a hole into the extinguisher, shrouding the floor and stairway in a cloud of dry powder. The I grabbed hold of the fire hose, abseiling down between the stairs with Carl on my shoulder, shooting my way down into the lobby.

Then I heard distant wailing sirens! The captain was late but not a moment too soon. A few assailants loitering in the lobby I shot dead on my way out. The sound of the sirens forced the rest of the assailants to flee the scene.

'We got company! Let's go, move it! Get out of here, now!' Maxwell shouted to the others. Raoul, Craig, Matt, and Casandra regrouped on the top floor.

'The cops are here! It's time to go!' Gosnell quickly ordered, heading to his vehicle with his brother and leaving Mr Sullivan a sitting duck.

'What about Father Brown? What about me, you fucking cowards?' Mr Sullivan shouted to the brothers, frightened and angry.

'Looks like the priest lives another day! As for you, Mr Sullivan, I suggest you get a move on if you ever want to see tomorrow!' Gosnell replied with a foul grin before climbing in and driving off.

Mr Sullivan began to panic. Quickly wheeling himself to his vehicle, he muttered, 'Fucking bunch of cowards!' Then he shouted towards the building, 'Maxwell?! Get here now!'

He felt a muzzle pressing at the back of his head. I had caught his attention at the most unfortunate time, still standing strong with my hat still fitted to my head, Carl snoozing on my shoulders and my face bandage smeared in blood.

'Go ahead! Shoot me! After all, this is what it's been about, isn't it?!' Mr Sullivan seemed to show little regard for his own life.

'Not even close!' I replied. I knocked him cold where he sat, grazing his head with the rifle. The cops swooped in, but the rest of the gang had long since left the building. Rick and Matt were the last to leave, staring at me with a foul look from a broken window on the top floor.

'Drop the gun, and put your hands on your head!' the officers yelled, raising their guns from behind a cruiser door.

'It's OK! He's one of the good guys! That's Father Brown!' Captain Walter shouted to the officers, causing them to lower their guns.

'Spread out! Search the building—sweep this area clean!' the captain ordered.

The officers hurried along. Mr Sullivan was taken away, out cold. Captain Walter rushed towards me, seeing the detective passed out on my shoulders. He helped me lower Carl to the ground gently and looked him over.

'What the hell happened to him?' the captain asked with a look of shock at Carl's unhealthy appearance.

'No time to explain. He needs medical attention, now!' I replied urgently.

'Somebody get me an ambulance now! Hurry!' Captain Walter shouted.

'No time, Captain! We got to get him there now!' I insisted.

'Right! Let's move!' he quickly agreed.

With daylight upon us, we set Carl into the back seat of the captain's cruiser. Under the escort of four police cruisers, the captain and I took off for Carol City General Hospital. In the back seat of another police cruiser, Mr Sullivan sat stumped for words, being driven away. The captain swung a hard left, and the rest of the cruisers followed, leaving the highway for a quiet cross-country road.

'Where are you heading, Captain?!' I asked.

'it's a lot quicker! Trust me, I know!' Captain Walter replied as he raced along the road towered with high rock features, dotted with trees.

Out of nowhere, tailgating the cruisers, three SUVs fell in behind us, jammed with heavily armed assailants. Leading the chase was Matt, riding along with Raoul behind the wheel, his dogs and Lady Casandra. Bring up the rear were Paul, Maxwell, Rick, and Craig himself shifting the gears. The SUV travelling in the middle slingshotted itself to the front, taking over the chase loaded with assailants. I took a quick glimpse in the wing mirror, which was shattered by a bullet as the assailants began to suppress the cruisers with heavily repetitive gunfire.

'We got company! Looks like it's my lucky day!' I said to the captain as the bullets came rushing in the rare.

'It's over! You might as well hand me over before this shit goes downhill!' Mr Sullivan called out to the officers in his car, keeping his head down.

'We need to shake them, quick!' the captain replied, swerving and accelerating aggressively.

Paul and the gang closed in, ramming the rear cruiser up the bumper. Two assailants hanging from the doors opened fire on the cruisers, careless of Mr Sullivan's safety. The loud shooting and screeching of tyres woke Carl from his slumber, and he became hysterical, grabbing at the captain's shoulder, causing him to swerve as I tried to calm Carl's hysterical outburst.

'Keep him down! I'm trying to drive here!' the captain shouted anxiously.

I pulled the captain's cuffs from his side and slapped them onto the delirious detective, and forced him into the footwell. The shooters were closing in beside us, and one cruiser was lost to the barrage of gunfire with blown tyres, nosediving into the rocky hillside. Vehicles travelling by caught the flying bullets, forcing them off the road.

'I need ammo, Captain! Where is it?' I called to him.

'Take my gun!' The Captain replied, struggling to keep the dented cruiser stable at high speed.

'I only trust these, Captain!' I shouted, pulling both my revolvers out. 'Now where is the ammo?'

'In the glove box!' the captain replied, dipping his head to the sound of bullets grazing the doors and windows.

'What the hell is going on?' Paul shouted to the assailants from his window seat. 'Somebody kill these cops and get my father! Now, damn it!'

'Get me closer. It's time to wrap this up', said Lady Casandra, calmly loading a rifle and emerging through the sunroof. She took aim, setting her sights on the driver of the cruiser with Mr Sullivan in the back seat, holding his head, coughing, and hyperventilating. She took the shot, just as her driver swerved to evade oncoming traffic. The bullet claimed the head of the officer riding shotgun.

'Hold it steady!' she called to Raoul.

Meanwhile-I loaded my revolvers, filling the cylinders with hollow percussion rounds, and climbed out the door, heading onto the roof of the cruiser.

'What the hell you think you are doing?!' Captain Walter shouted.

'I'm going to wrap things up! Keep it steady!' I called back as I hurled myself to the top of the cruiser.

My coat dancing in the wind, I balanced on one knee, surfing the bendy road as the bullets raced by. Bracing myself, I returned fire, taking a shot through the windscreen into the head of an assailant that happened to be riding shotgun.

'What the fuck is this guy?' Paul yelled to the men in his vehicle. 'Why isn't Arthur Brown dead? Kill him, now!'

'All right, Captain!' I shouted, raining shots into the SUVs. 'Keep it moving; don't stop till I say you can!'

The captain floored the gas, and I stayed firm, bracing myself. I shot the tyres out on the SUV, and it tumbled alongside the cruiser leaking a trail of fuel. I finished the job, setting the fuel ablaze with a spark, destroying the SUV along with the assailants.

'That Arthur Brown is one tough guy. Starting to turn me on!' Lady Casandra whispered to herself, peeking through her rifle scope.

The fight wasn't over. The rest of the gang was bent on finishing what they had started. They accelerated, drawing closer towards the front of the captain's cruiser. Running alongside me, Lady Casandra snapped a series of shots, and I rolled across the cruiser to hang down the other side, evading her bullets.

Quickly checking for ammo, I saw I was out. At the rear, Paul and the others were trying hard to capture the cruiser carrying Mr Sullivan as the officers fought back, firing from their windows. Raoul pulled ahead of the captain's cruiser, bumper to bumper, but the captain rammed the SUV up the rear, throwing Casandra's aim off target.

Inside the SUV, guns were being fitted with full magazines. One assailant smashed the rear window open and aimed at the captain, who flinched at the sight of the gun pointing at him.

'If you got a plan, Father, now's the time!' he yelled out to me where I hung over the side.

'Don't worry Captain! Keep the speed up! Wait for my command!' I replied, climbing back to the top of the cruiser.

The captain continued to ram the SUV, breaking the shooter's line of sight, disrupting his aim. Craig tried following up the rear; his attempt was intercepted by the officers following along, swerving in and out between lanes.

'All right, Captain! Hit the brake, now!' I shouted.

He slammed on the brakes, and I used the momentum to launch myself forward, into the back seat of the SUV. My impact shoved Matt into the dashboard, knocking him cold and causing his hands to jam the sunroof. Raoul began to swerve, reaching for his gun. I thrust my blade into the shooter, ending him. The dogs began snapping, and they two were knocked cold, banging their heads together. Lady Casandra was stuck in the sunroof, struggling to free herself and losing her rifle in the process. She wrapped her legs around my neck, strangling me where I sat. My blade fell into the footwell. I tried reaching down, stretching my fingers at the tip of the blade.

'You are fucking dead! You hear me? I'm going to shoot you in that fucked-up face of yours!' Raoul shouted, reaching into the SUV centre box for his gun. He grabbed it and swung his arm over the seat, pointing it in my direction whilst he swerved about the road, throwing the oncoming traffic off the road into the rocky hillside. With a quick stroke of luck I got hold of my blade and sliced Raoul's wrist open. He screamed, losing his gun between the seats as he held his wrist in agony, trying to stop the bleeding. With Raoul distracted and swerving about the road, I turned the blade onto Casandra, who was still trying to twist my neck from my shoulders.

'I might be stuck, priest, but you are a dead man!' Casandra yelled from above the roof, tightening her legs around my neck. 'Such a shame ... I was just getting to like the man you've become!'

I punched my blade into her tendons, cutting them clean from the back of her knee joints. Blood sprayed all over my hat and bandage. She cried out in agony, waking Matt from his seat, soon to be his casket.

Without a moment to spare, I wrapped the seat belt around Matt's neck and secured it to the head restraint, strangling him. Raoul tried for his gun, freeing his hand from the steering wheel. I took his arm off with my blade, leaving it in his lap. A lorry approached, blasting its horn at the SUV, which was dead centre in the wrong lane heading for a collision.

'This is where I get off!' I growled and climbed out the rear of the SUV.

Captain Walter swung into action, cutting in behind the SUV to keep up the pace at the rare. 'Jump now! Jump!' he cried out to me.

I launched myself out the boot of the SUV onto the bonnet of the captain's cruiser. He immediately broke away, just in time to avoid the collision. Casandra looked towards her grim fate, fighting harder to cut loose from the sunroof. Matt fought futilely against the seat belt, Raoul, unable to use his arm, nudged his door open, about to jump. The dogs awoke and escaped out the door along with Raoul, tumbling along the side of the busy road into a ditch, unconscious, with the dogs sprawled over his body. The lorry collided with the SUV, crushing Matt beyond recognition. The impact forced the glass roof into Casandra's abdomen, slicing her in half. The SUV was thrown off the road into a rocky pit.

Paul and the rest of the gang were driven off the road, trying to avoid the collision. Their head-on crash into a boulder brought an end to their pursuit. The captain and I had a clean sweep getaway as we headed into the city.

Doors swung open, Carl was lifted out, and doctors rushed a gurney through the hospital corridors, the captain and I jogging alongside, following Carl as the doctors rushed him to the intensive care unit.

'Is he going to make it?' the captain asked, worried.

'He's in bad shape, Captain. He's in very poor health. We'll let you know soon as we are finished!' Dr. Ramrod replied, closing the door in front of us. The captain and I were left standing around in suspense while the doctors performed their duties.

A bit later, Carl's wife, Miranda, strode into the waiting room in a state of panic. 'Oh, Captain! Please tell me he's going to be fine!' she moaned, with tear-filled eyes.

'We're not sure about that, Mrs. Brooks. Your husband isn't looking too good', the captain replied, mincing no words.

'You have to pray for my husband, Father! Please!' Miranda pleaded with me.

'That's not who I am anymore, ma'am. Not even sure if God still hears me', I replied shamefacedly, feeling hopeless and pitiful about myself, turning away.

'You listen to me, Father Brown!' she said, grabbing hold my lapel. 'You might have lost your way, but that doesn't mean you've lost hope! Now you get in there, and you pray for my husband!' she demanded.

Just then, the door to the ICU opened, and Dr. Ramrod emerged, with a look of doubt. Miranda rushed towards him, pleading once more for some good news.

'Mrs. Brooks. Your husband is in critical condition, but he appears to be quite stable at the moment', the doctor reported.

Miranda began to cry, in panic mixed with relief. 'He needs to be fine. I can't imagine life without my husband.' I felt her pain and understood her emotions, for I too was in that dark place.

'I'm afraid all we can do is wait for him to pull through', the doctor insisted. 'There's nothing more we can do to help. Not only is his health compromised, but he also has been through a traumatic ordeal', Dr. Ramrod said, adding salt to Miranda's wounds but placing his hands on her shoulders to convey his sympathy.

'Have some faith, Mrs. Brooks, and hope for a tremendous breakthrough. You may see him now.' With those kind thoughts, the doctor saw himself off.

Heartbroken, Miranda threw herself against my chest, crying miserably. 'Please, Father, pray for him, please!'

Swallowing my pride and feeling reluctant, I reassured her. 'I'll do it. I'll pray for your husband. Anything to help', I whispered kindly.

'Thanks, Father. I appreciate your effort', came her soft reply as she wiped her eyes and headed into her husband's room.

Captain Walter looked at me with scepticism, hands on his hips. 'You sure you are up for this? No offence, but you are not the Father Brown we once knew'.

'None taken. All I can do is hope my faith sees me through', I replied calmly, looking through the doors at the grieving wife holding her husband's hands.

Detective Bill Chessington thumped his fist onto the wooden table. 'Tell me who the buyers are and where the hell we can find them!'

Inside the CCPD interrogation room, he and Detective Bobby Roland were in the middle of pumping answers out of Mr Sullivan, who sat in his wheelchair looking like crap and feeding his lungs with oxygen courtesy the CCPD.

'I need to speak with my lawyer', Mr Sullivan replied weakly.

Bill slammed his palms onto the table before Mr Sullivan, leering into his eyes. 'You listen to me, dirtbag! You are not going anywhere till we get some answers!' he growled.

Mr Sullivan's attorney, Mr Cartwright, walked in, his chest out, full of pride and confidence, his briefcase in one hand and a fancy stick in the other. 'I think you've said enough, Detective. My client leaves now!' he said, placing his briefcase firmly on the table.

'Who the hell you think you are?' Bobby grunted, with his arms folded across his chest.

'I'm Mr Sullivan's attorney, here to demand his release!' Mr Cartwright answered with a stern voice using his judiciary powers.

Bill took exception. 'I'm afraid that's not going to happen!'

Mr Cartwright placed his stick on the table and unlatched his briefcase. He drew out a file and flicked it across the table towards Bill, who opened the file with Bobby looking over his shoulder. They scanned through the pages with unhappy expressions.

'Now that I've got your attention, my client and I'll be seeing ourselves out.' Cartwright, with a dirty smirk on his face, wheeled Mr Sullivan out the door.

Captain Walter turned up just in time to see Mr Sullivan on his way out, scot-free. The captain stood in front of Mr Sullivan and his attorney, blocking their passage, looking disgusted. After a brief, awkward stare at each other, he stepped aside, and, Mr Cartwright smiled as they carried on.

'What the hell just happened, Captain? We had him!' Bill shouted, feeling dissatisfied and unhappy.

'It's not over yet, Detective, not by a long shot. His day is coming!' Captain Walter replied firmly, gazing at Mr Sullivan as he exited the building.

Outside, it rained. Waiting on the side of the street outside the CCPD, Maxwell waited with an umbrella to receive his boss. Paul, having taken charge of his father from the lawyer, Cartwright, wheeled him down the ramp along the stairs.

From a distance, I watched from behind the wheel of a pickup as Paul and Maxwell helped Mr Sullivan into the back of their SUV. My job was not over; I had yet to wrap things up. Inside the SUV, in the back seat, Paul acknowledged his father's presence with a pat on the shoulder with a few missing fingers and a happy smile.

'Good to have you back. Let's get you home', he said with a broad smile.

'He's right, sir. Thought we'd lost you back there.' Rick shared in the happy moment, sitting up front, with Maxwell behind the wheel.

'This isn't finished. Father Brown cost me a lot that night. First, get me to the Logans' place', Mr Sullivan ordered with an ominous tone.

The SUV pulled away with one other following on at the rear. I followed on for two miles through the city of Lismore in the pouring rain along Elmwood Boulevard. At a red light, both SUVs came to a standstill. With my gas pedal floored, I rammed into the back of the SUV sitting at the rear, forcing it into the front vehicle.

'What the hell was that? What's going on?' Mr Sullivan asked, looking confused, more paranoid than anything.

Craig, sitting in the passenger seat of the rear SUV, with four smartly dressed armed men, spotted me in my truck through his wing mirror. Maxwell identified me stepping out of the truck with my two revolvers, my hat down over my forehead, and my coat drenched in the pouring rain, strolling towards the SUV.

'It's that priest—Arthur Brown! He's onto us!' Maxwell replied, not so surprised, taking his gun from his waist.

I strolled along the street, my hat on my head, face bandage neatly wrapped, the rain pouring off my hat and running down my knee-length coat. I held my two revolvers diagonally.

'Stay inside the vehicles! His guns are useless!' Mr Sullivan ordered, feeling safe behind his armoured windows.

'We can finish him here and now! What are you thinking?' Paul replied, anxious.

'Ready your guns! We got a fight on our hands!' Craig quickly alerted the men in his vehicle.

They loaded their guns and jumped from their vehicle, about to engage. I fired, blowing a hole the size of an orange through the head of the gunman hiding behind the door of the vehicle.

'What the hell is he doing?' Mr Sullivan shouted, noticing Craig acting without his consent.

With the bullets coming in, I rolled over the bonnet of a car that screaming commuters had abandoned on site. Whilst returning fire I'd noticed that the vehicle was armour plated. I lowered myself behind the cover of a car and began shooting my way back to my truck. Craig and his men kept the bullets going, pinning me behind the door of my truck.

As if on cue, the news helicopter arrived, gathering tomorrow's headline. Hanging out the door of the helicopter, the cameraman captured graphic footage beneath their spotlight, whilst the female reporter described the images on scene to the viewing public in homes and around town.

Back at the CCPD inside the coffee room the images captured the attention of Officer Shepherd and Detectives Chessington and Roland, with a number of officers catching a break. Whilst they watched, the captain walked in unawares, about to pour himself a cup of coffee.

'Hey, Captain, check this out!' Officer Shepherd said. 'Looks like Father Brown is going vigilante!'

Distracted, the captain scalded his tongue on the coffee as he glanced at the television on the wall. He stared at the footage for a few seconds. Across town in nearly every bar, food joint, business, and home, all eyes were glued to their television screens.

'It appears that Father Brown is engaged in a heavy fire fight, fending off what appeared to be affiliates of notorious crime lord Richard Sullivan, who was earlier released from police custody without charge', the reporter briefed the viewing audience across the city.

'I want every goddamned officer on patrol in that area, now! That goes for you slackers—move it!' the captain shouted, refusing to stand by while I took on the likes of Mr Sullivan and his men.

'Hey, fellas! My money's on the priest!' Officer Shepherd called after the officers as they raced out of the coffee room.

'I say we buy the priest some time', Detective Chessington proposed. 'What do you think, Captain?' He and Bobby Roland loitered in the corner sipping coffee, coats over their shoulders.

Lost for words, the captain scratched his head pondering. 'We all want these scumbags off the streets, so why not!' he replied.

CHAPTER 20

Paul was about to join the fight when his father grabbed his shoulder, yelling, 'Just what do you think you're doing?'

'Arthur Brown dies! Remember!' Paul replied loudly.

'There's too much at stake! We have to go!' Mr Sullivan said.

Meanwhile, I opened my glovebox, emptied the cylinders of my revolvers, and reloaded with armour-piercing rounds. I was back in action, bullets from my revolvers slicing into the doors of the SUV. Just like that, three men were down. Craig, realizing that he no longer had the protective cover in his vehicle, retreated inside the other SUV, looking to drive off.

'Get us out of here Max!' Mr Sullivan cried loudly, banging the headrest.

Both SUVs were about to take off. I shot the tyres out on both vehicles. In the pouring rain I stood still and took aim. Two shots from the barrel of my revolver went through the window and doors of Craig's SUV. The bullet passed through the seat and penetrated Craig's side, entering his abdomen.

Paul had his right arm placed against Maxwell's head restraint looking out the window for clearance. He received a bullet in his right arm, and the bullet travelled down his bone, out his palm, and through the head restraint to graze the back of Maxwell's head, rendering him unconscious on the steering wheel.

Another two bullets through the reinforced windows hit Rick's shoulders, leaving him in excruciating pain as he bled. Mr Sullivan was lucky, shaking and cowering in his seat.

Sirens wailed in the distance; I had to hurry.

I pulled the door open and hurled Mr Sullivan from his seat. In pain, immobilised by the gunshot, Paul made an effort to raises his gun. I could have killed him there and then, but the cops were closing in. I shot him in the other arm. Then I looked at Rick, paralyzed in his seat, with both arms decommissioned and bleeding out. I raised my gun to end him where he sat, but the sound of cops nearing drove me on to a greater deed.

'You are a dead man!' Mr Sullivan yelled. 'You hear me? Dead!' He was gagging as I dragged him by the back of his collar along the street towards my truck.

'Justice isn't yours to command! Your foul acts end today. You are coming with me!' I growled, angrily yanking him along the wet tarmac with the news catching it all on screen.

Craig staggered from the seat of his vehicle, one hand applying pressure to his bleeding abdomen and a gun in the other, about to take a shot. With a flick of my wrist I shot the gun from his hand and then shot him in both kneecaps, sending him face down onto the wet tarmac.

'Father Brown seems to have neutralized the assailants and taken his prized asset, Mr Sullivan, into the back of his pickup! It's not known if this is part of his antidrug-and-crime campaign or if it's an act of retaliation against those responsible for his loss.' The reporter vectoring above was carefully observing my actions.

'Get in!' Holding Mr Sullivan by the collar, I tossed him in the cargo hold, climbed in the cab, and drove away.

The helicopter followed on from above, but I skilfully evaded the news cameras, cutting through a series of alleyways, parting the crowded back streets, and manoeuvring around vending stalls. Unable to identify my whereabouts, the news gave up their search, heading back towards Elmwood Boulevard. Out of sight, I pulled out from a narrow alley cloaked with washing lines and overfilled dust bins.

Back on Elmwood Boulevard, not long after I'd vanished, another vehicle appeared, tyres squeaking, brakes screaming as it pulled up at the chaotic scene with the news crew lingering above. Doors were flung open, and Raoul—alive, with a few scratches—and four others, armed with automatic guns, swept the scene in search of survivors.

'Hurry up! Move it, now!' Raoul ordered his men, scanning the SUV in the pouring rain.

The news crew continued to silently broadcast the feeds as the men hurriedly dragged Paul and Maxwell from the vehicle and carried them into their waiting car. The cops were blocks away and closing in. Crawling face down towards Raoul's car, hauling himself along the wet tarmac and bleeding out, was Craig, seeking Raoul's help.

'What about him?' asked one of Raoul's men, pointing at Craig with his gun.

'Leave him! He's the cops' problem now. Let's move!' Raoul ordered, leaving Craig to his fate.

With the cops now in sight, Raoul and his men opened fire, slowing the cruisers' approach. They drove away rapidly, covering themselves by firing bullet after bullet, and disappeared in the distance.

One by one, the cops came racing in, skidded to a stop, and cornered Craig. Doors opened, boots hit the tarmac, and guns piled in as cops surrounded the scene.

Standing behind the safety of the cruiser door was Officer Shepherd, shouting in disgust, 'Freeze, sucker! Don't move!' with his gun aimed at Craig.

Craig was barely hanging on. He looked up at Officer Shepherd as if to have a word but unable to speak, he dropped his head flat onto the wet tarmac, passing out.

Three days later, at Peeks Hill, a local hangout in the countryside overlooking the capital city, Lismore, in the dark in an open track tucked away from the public eye, Captain Walter stood next to his unmarked cruiser, leaning against the trunk, tapping one foot anxiously. With him, Detectives Bill Chessington and Bobby Roland wandered around in the open, smoking cigarettes.

'What the fuck is taking these assholes so long?' Bill was impatient, flicking his cigarette butt to the ground.

Then headlights peered through the bushes. A vehicle drove in and parked right next to the captain's cruiser. A door opened, and a pair of leather boots hit the dirt. Ray had arrived, sporting a leather jacket, jeans, and a turtleneck shirt. With him came four others, three males and a female, all casually dressed, bearing a tough appearance.

'Nice location, Captain! You sure know how to pick the spot. You cover your ass well, I like that!' Ray smiled and shrugged elaborately, straightening his jacket.

Ray acknowledged Bill and Bobby. 'I see you brought company.'

'Everybody needs company around here!' the captain replied.

'Right about that, Captain', Ray agreed, calmly stroking his beard.' These are mean times; got to have someone to watch your back!'

The captain approached Ray with confidence, holding his chin high. 'I got what you need. Let's get on with it!'

Ray looked the captain dead in the eyes, with a blunt stare. 'Straight to business. I admire your spirit Captain! Let's get this over with!' Ray was equally keen to transact their personal affairs.

The captain opened the boot of his cruiser. Ray and his men gathered around, looking in. 'Not who we were hoping for, but he'll do. Load him up!' Ray called to his men and then headed back to his vehicle.

His men reached into the boot and grabbed what appeared to be a man wrapped in a body bag. He was wriggling and making muffled sounds, giving signs of life. They loaded the body into the back of their vehicle and joined Ray inside.

'See you around, Captain! Pleasure doing business as always!' Ray cheerfully bade his farewell and drove away into the dark.

'What you think their plan is?' Detective Bill asked.

'Doesn't matter. Just another scum taken care of, that's all that matters', the captain answered with a carefree tone. Together, they mounted the cruiser and departed the hill.

One early afternoon a month later, at Carol City General Hospital, Detective Carl Brooks was awakened—a bit confused and paranoid but in far better shape than expected. Clean-shaven and back to his former appearance, he sat comfortably in bed watching the afternoon news broadcast on the CCNN. An anchorwoman was reporting alongside her male colleague, both smartly dressed, whilst recorded footage of the Elmwood Boulevard shooting ran on the corner of the screen.

Anchor Darlene May was about to make her presentation. A

thirty-eight-year-old woman with long dark hair, of average height and fairly good-looking, she smiled as she presented the news.

'It's been weeks since the shooting downtown on Elmwood Boulevard. No one has seen or heard from public icon Father Arthur Brown since his last confrontation with notorious kingpin Richard Sullivan. The people of his local church and the general public are beginning to fear the worst.'

Darlene turned her attention to her colleague, Mason Green, a fifty-five-year-old man with slightly grey hair, tall and clean-shaven, with thick brows. 'Is there anything you'd like to add, Mason?'

Clearing his throat, Mason began his commentary. 'Well, Darlene, I think it's clear what's happening. Father Brown has once again taken justice into his own hands, as a one-man antidrug-and-crime campaign. Can we really blame him? No—this is what the city needs. CCPD needs to pull their thumbs out of their ears and follow his lead.'

'Strong words, Mason!'

'Right they are, Darlene! Crime lord Richard Sullivan and his followers must be eradicated. Same goes for his rivals, the Logans. This city needs to be drug and crime free!' Mason forcibly expressed his thoughts to the viewing public.

'It seems that the locals share your opinion of Father Brown's campaign. Let's go to Kelly, our local correspondent in downtown Lismore with the latest. Kelly, what's the latest in downtown Lismore, here in Carol City?' Darlene introduced her with a smile.

Kelly, the local news correspondent, stood downtown on the sideline where a large group of protesters were rallying. The police had turned out as a show of force in effort to maintain the peace, armed with riot shields, batons, and guns loaded with rubber bullets holding the line as the vigorous protesters expressed their views.

'Darlene, as you can see, many locals have turned out to express their concerns about the Elmwood shooting. Some aren't too happy, while others favoured the outcome', Kelly reported. She turned to an angry protester holding a placard that read, 'Father Brown is a lie!'. 'Excuse me, sir. Would you mind sharing a few words?' she asked, poking her microphone into the man's face.

'Father Brown has no right to take justice into his own hands! He's not the law around here. I say, let the Cops do their job!' the unhappy protester loudly responded.

Kelly turned her attention to another man waving his placard excitedly, chanting, 'Father Brown seeks justice for all!'

'Sir, anything you would like to add?' Kelly asked.

'I've got kids that are scared to walk the streets! Where's the cops when you need 'em? I say yes to Father Brown!' he replied, with a large group of protesters cheering him on.

'There you have it, straight from the source. Back to you, Darlene!' Kelly said, tossing it back to the studio.

The report caused Carl to become restless, tossing about in his bed. Trying to get to his feet, he fell to the floor.

His wife, Miranda, walked in, carrying some fresh flowers. She dropped them on the bed and scrambled to Carl's side when she saw him struggling to his feet. 'Oh my God, Carl! What were you thinking?' she gasped, helping him back onto his bed.

Carl began muttering indistinct words to his wife, trying to make sense. 'Father Brown. Father Brown', he mumbled.

Tucking Carl gently back into bed, Miranda replied in a caring voice. 'Oh, honey, Father Brown isn't around. He left just as he prayed for you.'

Carl went on mumbling persistently, throwing his hands up at the television. 'What happened? What happened?' he finally asked.

His wife looked up at the television, saw the news, and then responded, 'Oh Carl, you are not going back on the streets in a hurry. Doctor said you need plenty of rest. I'll water the flowers and make it a bit more homey for you!' She carelessly disregarded Carl's futile words, kissing him on the head as she began watering the eight vases of flowers already sitting in the room.

Carl looked over at her, annoyed and irritated. Unable to get his words out, he rolled his eyes at Miranda and then curled up under the sheets and went to sleep.

Late that afternoon, in the living quarters at the Logans' mansion, Paul, Maxwell, and Rick were all patched up and making good progress after the injuries they had sustained. They stood around debating and plotting their next move with the Logan brothers, who were refusing to cut their losses.

'Why are we standing around? We should be out there looking for my old man, not sipping fucking Scotch!' Paul yelled arrogantly at the brothers.

Gosnell sat peacefully in an armchair, dressed to the nines, nursing a glass of Scotch. Johnathon stood pouring himself another glass.

'Your father is probably dead already', he rudely remarked. 'After all, we're dealing with a deranged priest!' He then took a slow sip of his Scotch.

'You are not wrong, my brother', Gosnell replied. He turned to Paul. 'Maybe it's time you think about stepping up, filling your old man's boots—if you have it in you!' He savoured another sip of his Scotch.

'This is Mr Sullivan, our boss, you're talking about here!' Rick pointed out. 'We need to do something, and fast!'

'He's right', Maxwell said. 'Let's stop wasting time here; we'll handle this on our own!'

Together they saw themselves out of the Logans' living quarters. Paul followed them but turned around to say, 'Screw you sons of bitches! I wouldn't get too comfortable if I were you!' Then he stalked out.

In the back seat of their limousine, Paul was upping his game, making a move, tasking Maxwell and Rick. 'I want the word on the street. A hundred grand for the whereabouts of my father. Make it happen!'

Meanwhile, dangling upside down from a chain somewhere in the dark, unable to see or hear anything, not knowing what was about to happen, Mr Sullivan was terrified, panicking and hyperventilating. Feeling his shirt being ripped from his back was enough to scare the crap into his pants.

'You already took everything away from me! What do you want?' he cried out.

'Not quite', I said in a tremulous voice.

'For God's sake, I didn't kill your family!' Mr Sullivan protested weakly.

'This is not only about my family. This is about my city. I want you out!' This time my voice echoed in the dark.

'This city is as much as mine as it is yours! You represent the hope!

I represent the unjust!' Mr Sullivan shouted back. 'You are no different from me! You are unholy and unrighteous, and you've got blood on your hands!' His weak lungs had him gasping.

'Right you are. But, I'm not here to judge. I'm here to clean up the mess', I replied calmly, in a reasonable tone.

'You want to clean up the mess? Then you kill the man who murdered your precious family! That's your fucking mess!' Mr Sullivan shouted, coughing and wheezing.

'He's got a fate waiting that's worse than death, I assure you.'

I held the mask to Mr Sullivan's face, and he began inhaling some charitable oxygen I had provided. 'You are not dying yet', I said sternly.

'Show yourself! Why is it dark in here?' Mr Sullivan sounded worried.

'You are about to find out what pain and darkness really are', I replied ominously. 'Agree to my terms, and you just might walk.' I offered a life line, slowly pacing about the dark with echoing footsteps.

'You can try, Father, but you won't break me! You won't!' Mr Sullivan yelled dramatically, full of anger and confidence.

'Leave the city, you and your men', I continued, as if he had not spoken. 'No one else needs to be killed, As for the Logans—I'll dispose of them my way!'

'Screw you, Father Brown! Screw you!' Mr Sullivan cursed, blindly spitting into the dark.

He began to scream as pain was inflicted upon him. Blinded by the dark and confused by the silence, he knew not what method of torture might follow the last. His mind was all I needed to break.

Four days later, early in the morning, Paul, with the help of Maxwell, Rick, and a body of men were still busy searching every occupied or deserted building, home, safe house and underground lair they knew of in town. Building after building, they stormed in, disrupting the peace, causing a stir.

Inside the local steelworks on the western side of Carol City, the workers huddled together in a gang, ready to be interrogated. 'If any of you know anything,' Paul demanded, waving his gun about, 'I suggest you talk now!'.

The workers were frightened, and their lips were sealed. One of them, Brian Middleton,-pushing his late forties, whispered to a colleague nearby, 'What the hell is this asshole screaming about?'

Paul took notice and pointed his gun at Brian. 'Hey, asshole? Got something you want to tell me?'

Brian looked puzzled. 'Who, me?'

Paul marched up to him and grabbed him by the hair with his gun to his temple. 'You mind telling me what the fuck you're whispering to your friend, huh?' he grunted, tugging Brian's hair, poking his head forcibly with the gun.

Brian stammered, nearly lost for words. 'Nothing! Nothing, I swear!'

'You fucking with me, huh? You fucking with me?' Paul persisted, belittling Brian before his colleagues.

'Please, I don't know anything– I don't!' Brian pleaded, flinching away from Paul's gun.

Paul pointed the gun at Brian's colleague. Bernard Young was a fuzzy-looking man in his late fifties, about five-eight, and he flinched. 'You know something? Do you?' Paul asked, viciously poking his gun into his chest.

Startled, Bernard stuck his hands up in submission, stammering on his words. 'No, no, nothing. I know nothing.'

'Looks like a lesson needs to be taught here!' Paul shouted at the frightened workers. He kicked Brian to the floor, and his colleagues helped him to his feet. Paul tucked his gun away and straightened his jacket, whilst he approached his armed men standing by, waiting for orders.

'Take care of this. I want him dead', Paul closely whispered to his men, looking slyly at Brian's colleague.

'Let's get out of here', he called to Rick and Maxwell, leaving his shooters behind.

Now realising what was about to happen, the workers pleaded for mercy. Brian approached the gunman, holding on to his arm, trying to talk him down. 'We don't deserve this! Please, you got to let us go! Don't do this, I'm begging you, please!'

The gunman knocked him to the floor with a gun butt to the face, breaking his nose. No one knew who was about to die or what the shooter's intentions were; they only knew something unpleasant was about to happen.

The shooters—eight of them—emptied their guns into Bernard's chest. Screams and panicked moans filled the ghastly atmosphere. After finishing the job, the shooters walked out the door, leaving Brian and the rest of the shaken co-workers to pick up the pieces and mourn their loss.

Waiting outside, smoking a cigarette, was Paul. He flicked the butt away as the shooters approached him at the vehicle. 'It's done', they reported.

'Let's get the hell out of here.' Paul climbed into the back of his vehicle, which took off in a hurry.

Inside, Brian moaned over the death of his colleague. 'I'm sorry, I'm sorry', he stuttered in tears, on his knees cradling the dead man.

A circle of sad, angry, and outraged workers gathered around the bloody affair. With the blood of his colleague smeared on his greasy workman's shirt, Brian looked at the blood dripping from his right hand and clenched his bloody palm as tight as a steel trap. Furious, he silently contemplated vengeance.

On the way back to the mansion through the streets of Lismore, Paul's phone began to vibrate inside his coat pocket. Paul checked the caller: *ID UNKNOWN*.

Still in a foul mood with his father missing, he answered the call. 'Who the fuck is this?'

'Son, it's me! Your father!' a faint voice replied.

I stood behind Mr Sullivan and held the phone to his ear. He sat in the dark, chained naked to a steel chair, his bruised feet in a metal basin of water.

'Pop?' Paul replied, shocked and overwhelmed. 'Stop the car now!' he shouted to the driver.

Immediately the vehicle squealed to a stop, pulling up near a kerb outside a row of shops.

'Where are you, Pop? We've been looking everywhere!'

'Son, listen. I haven't got much time. You need to hear what I'm about to tell you. You need to prepare for what's coming', Mr Sullivan whispered weakly, seizing his son's heart with suspense.

Early the next day in Carl's room at Carol City General Hospital, Captain Walter stood at his bedside catching up with him on current affairs. on current affairs. Carl seemed to be making remarkable progress.

Still a bit halting in his speech, Carl opened his mouth. 'Have you found them?' he asked the captain.

The captain hesitated in his response. 'Darn it, Captain, talk to me!' Carl demanded.

'No, we haven't found them. Father Brown made a mess of things; it wasn't pretty', the captain replied quietly with a note of embarrassment.

Carl turned a sour face to him. 'Yeah, I've seen the news. At least someone's doing something. What the hell are we doing, Captain?'

'We're doing everything we can. Craig is in holding … you should be happy—it's not all bad!' the captain replied defensively.

'Let me guess. All thanks to Father Brown.'

The captain went silent, looking away, lowering his head in shame. 'Father Brown doesn't know when to quit.'

'Why not slap a badge on his chest and give him the keys to the city?' Carl responded, annoyed.

The atmosphere was getting tense. 'He got you out that shit of a mess; why not show some gratitude?'

'I'm grateful, Captain, believe me, I am! But Father Brown needs to understand he's going overboard. He's too reckless!' Carl expressed his deep concern about my actions.

'He'll find his way back. Let's hope it won't be too late', the captain responded quietly.

'I hope you are right, Captain. Let's hope', Carl muttered.

CHAPTER 21

Two weeks later, on an early evening in Demolition Town, I stood on a rooftop, one foot on the ledge, arms crossed, silently scanning the filthy streets from the peepholes of my face bandage. My shredded cashmere coattail surfed the cool air that drifted quietly by.

Previously known as Thomsonville in the southernmost part of the city, Demolition Town was a ghost town dotted with burnt-out apartments and abandoned homes and businesses. Old cars decorated the trash-filled streets, wind whistled through the broken windows, and door hinges creaked tunelessly in the midnight air.

Coughs broke the silence. Sitting behind me was Mr Sullivan, chained to a metal chair, his face covered in scars, and his mouth bubbling with blood down his chin and onto his dirty torn shirt. His fingers, clotted with blood, showed signs of missing nails; his bare feet were bleeding from the toes. He had lost considerable blood in my vicious attempts to force his hand to agree to my terms.

'You are wasting your time. You won't get out alive', Mr Sullivan mumbled through his bare gums.

I turned towards him and stared into his face. I replied with an ominous tone, 'I'm not planning to walk out of this alive! It all ends here. This is it, all or nothing!'

Mr Sullivan chuckled, spitting blood, bitterly mocking me. 'You are going to die in vain! You won't accomplish anything here tonight! You are just a man, and you stand alone!'

With an unscrutinized look, I stared into his eyes. Then I grabbed him by the chin. 'Don't be too sure about that!'

My attention was diverted by the sound of engines roaring up the sleeping streets breaking the silence. They were here; message received, and not a moment too soon. A convoy, three SUVs and three pickups, filled with shooters ready to be dispatched at Paul's command.

Paul was riding mid centre rear inside an SUV. With him were Maxwell and Rick, loading their guns. I watched in anticipation as they filed down the street, carelessly kicking aside or crushing the trash in their path. The convoy stopped in the middle of the street in a staggered formation, next to the old long-abandoned Sam and John's Firearms.

The assailants poured into the street, dispersing themselves around the vehicles with the headlights on, holding their guns ready. Paul, Maxwell, and Rick stepped out of their vehicle. Paul buttoned his blazer and looked around observantly, scanning the empty buildings and rooftops.

'Sure knows how to pick the place, I'll give him that', said Paul with a suspicious tone as he thoroughly admired the abandoned scenery.

He turned to his cohorts, alerting them. 'All right! I need everyone on standby. This man's not to be taken lightly; you've all witnessed his work. I need all weapons ready to fire should this go south. Stay sharp!'

Paul then began shouting in the distance, seeking me out; e was ready. 'All right, asshole! We're here, just like you asked! Show yourself!'

The rooftop on which I had last stood was now deserted. A gust of cold wind blew down the street as I approached from a distance, strolling towards the gang of trigger-happy assailants with Mr Sullivan naked over my shoulder and a 12-gauge Raging Judge revolver in one hand.

'Here he comes! Everybody stay sharp!' Paul alerted his men, holding their guns ready. Then he called, even louder, 'Hold your fire! Nobody shoot without my say-so! He's carrying my father!'

I stopped in the middle of the street, shy of the convoy. All was quiet, as everyone stood around waiting for something to happen. Then, with a twist of my shoulder, I heaved Mr Sullivan to the ground, unconscious.

'You hurt him in any way, and you are good as dead', Paul threatened with an evil snarl.

I replied, in a sombre bellow, 'You know the terms! You take your father, and you and your men leave the city as agreed! There's no need for blood tonight! All you have to do is leave quietly!'

Paul, Maxwell, Rick, and their men all looked around at each other as I were insane. They laughed, mocking me.

Paul chuckled, shaking his head disappointedly. 'All right, Father Brown! I think we can do that. Hand my father over, and this all ends now, as agreed!' he replied, with a hint of deceit upon his filthy tongue.

Knowing how it would all end and where the road would lead, I backed away from Mr Sullivan, sprawled in the street. 'There he is! Take him and leave!'

Paul waved a hand signal to his assailants standing at his side. Two men shuffled in, scooped Mr Sullivan from the ground, and took him to his son. 'Is he all right!' Paul asked with concern.

The men checked his pulse for confirmation. 'He's alive!'

'Get him in the truck!' Paul ordered.

I watched as the two men loaded Mr Sullivan into the pickup. With his father now presumably safe, Paul then turned his attention towards me. 'Thanks for holding up your end of the deal!' he said, with a suspicious smile on his face.

'Now it's time for you and your men to leave quietly. You've done enough!' I replied, loud and calm, hoping they would heed my peaceable words.

'I'm afraid that's not going to happen!' Paul said. 'I've got my father back, and everything is right where it should be!' he boasted.

'Is that right?!' was my doubtful reply.

'Sure looks right to me! All I have to do is kill you right here, right now, Father Brown!' Paul growled, grinding his teeth in hatred.

'So! You won't leave?' I said calmly, looking around as if assessing the odds.

'Why leave when we've got this city by its balls? We kill you, and everything goes back the way it should be!' Paul continued to boast; full of pride he was.

'Killing me won't change anything! I can promise you that!'

'Oh, I'm sure it will! Look around! You are outgunned and outnumbered. It's over!' he gloated.

'I thought you might say that. Looks like we have blood on our hands tonight!' I shouted loudly, full of passion, smiling all the while behind my bandage. 'You hear that, Carol City? They want blood!' I called out loudly across the abandoned town.

'Just when I thought you couldn't be any crazier! I'm going to enjoy finishing you!' Rick slurred at me with an angry tone.

My bellow had brought the street to life. Door after door flew open, and every abandoned building came alive as men in their numbers gathered and marched up the street behind me, bearing arms, ready to stand tall at my side in defence of their city.

Paul and his assailants looked on in astonishment, overwhelmed by the mob marching up the street. Leading them was Brian, with the rest of the factory workers. At their side were my Church followers led by Officer Shepherd, with a number of morose locals, cheated vendors, and angry businessmen rallying around me—all outraged and thirsty for justice.

'I told you before! This is my city! Leave now while you can!' My angry voice echoed along the street.

Paul looked around and saw that he still had the numbers and the guns. He chuckled with pride. 'You think a bunch of lowlife factory workers and a handful of Bible thumpers are enough to stop me?'

'Look again!' I bellowed with all my strength.

The buildings, doorways, and rooftops were suddenly thronged with armed allies. Men hung from broken windows, peeped from doorways and alleyways, all with guns at the ready. Rupee and Dale, my two homeless colleagues, had rallied their comrades to assist in the grave effort to drive Paul and the rest of his gangs out the city. They gave a thumbs-up from the rooftop they occupied; I acknowledged them with a tip of my hat.

Paul and the rest of his assailants shook in silence, lost for words as the odds turned against them. His men began to look dispirited and ready to retreat.

'Stand your ground', Paul shouted, trying to bolster their faith. 'We will not be intimidated! We stay and we fight! This city is ours!'

Maxwell and Rick stood firm, ready to buck the odds, cocking weapons and holding their ground. 'This ends tonight!' Rick shouted with conviction. 'Father Brown dies by my hand!'

'Have it your way!!' I cried aloud. Paul and his assailants wouldn't surrender the city; they refused to take their leave. I was ready to put an end to the mayhem that was crippling my city.

Suddenly, everyone who stood with me began donning respirators- Paul and his gang became concerned. Officer Shepherd handed me a GSR Mark One respirator, which I immediately secured to my face. Then I donned my hat again.

'What the hell is this? What's going on?' Paul shrieked in confusion.

'This doesn't look good!' Maxwell called out. 'Let's fall back! Now!'

From the rooftops gas pellets began to rain onto the street, shrouding Paul and his assailants in a cloud of smoke. Shots began on both sides as Paul and the others fell back into cover, shielding their noses, trying to resist the gas. I opened fire, and two assailants went down. I led the mob in advancing towards the convoy as we suppressed the assailants, keeping them at bay.

Paul had taken cover behind his vehicle with Maxwell and Rick, coughing and choking. 'My father! My father! Secure him now!' Paul cried out in desperation.

'We have to move now! There's no time! Let's go!!' Rick insisted, snatching Paul by the arm dragging him into the old asylum behind them.

The convoy was stormed and overrun. A few assailants had their throats slashed; some were shot dead. I smashed the window to the vehicle in which Mr Sullivan lay helplessly waking up to his fate. I dragged him out by the scruff of his neck and, fed him to the angry mob surrounding me.

'Take him away! Let justice be done upon him!!' I roared to the mob as they dragged Mr Sullivan away, crowd surfing him along into the depths of the mob with him moaning in terror all the way.

'No! No! Don't do this to me, don't!' Mr Sullivan begged, drowning, disappearing into the mob.

The rest of the assailants made it into the old four-storey asylum behind the convoy. Those left behind had to confront the mob. It was chaos in the streets. Amidst the roaring mob I stood and observed the asylum, assessing the situation. Brian and Officer Shepherd stood by me awaiting orders. 'What's the plan, Father?' Brian asked with expectancy.

'Shepherd? Have the mob secure the parameter! Nothing gets in or out of the asylum; have the shooters on the roof on standby! Brian? You are coming with me!' I ordered. Thanks to the gas mask, my tone was deep and dramatic.

'Gas the asylum! We're going in!' I called to the angry mob around me.

'You heard him! Let them have it!' Officer Shepherd called to the mob with a loud echo.

The mob fired their gas pellets into the asylum, gassing each floor with tear gas, creating a defensive smokescreen in and around the asylum. Somewhere inside on a middle floor, Paul, Maxwell, and Rick occupied a safe zone—a treatment facility inside the asylum with air-sealed vents—buying themselves time.

'We'll hold them off from here!' Paul ordered, panicking silently yet still looking for a fight.

'This room isn't going to last long!' Maxwell pointed out. 'We'll have to fight our way out soon as the gas fades!'

'Max is right!' said Rick, stumbling around broken appliances, looking for a way out. 'It's a matter of time before they find us. We need to find a way out of here, and fast!'

Meanwhile, on the ground floor, six assailants lay amidst the debris of broken furniture, already shot dead. Brian reloaded his shotgun, and I replenished my revolvers.

We carefully and tactically made our way towards the stairway, where we were confronted with two assailants. Brian employed his shotgun, making a mess of their heads. 'Clear!' he reported to me, standing at the rear.

We filed up the stairs and onto the middle floor. Potshots landed at our feet and whistled past our ears as six assailants held the line. We evaded the bullets, taking immediate cover near a concrete pillar.

The bullets kept coming, and I grew annoyed. 'We don't have the time!' I called to Brian at my side.

Brian dipped his hand into his pocket and drew it out with a grenade. 'This should buy us the time we need!' he replied. He pulled the pin and blindly tossed the grenade over his shoulder, hoping for the best.

The grenade landed between the nearest assailant's feet. 'Grenade!!' he cried and scampered away.

The grenade went. Two were dead, and four were stunned, wounded, and disorientated. Quickly, Brian and I closed in to eliminate the threat. The gas had long since dissipated, so we removed our masks and discarded them.

I looked around, scanning floor to ceiling. The path to the next floor up was sealed shut, tightly packed with fallen debris and building materials. We were stuck.

'There must be another way!' I said, considering the options. 'Otherwise this is it!'

We noticed a room with reinforced metal doors in the far corner of the middle floor. A burst from Brian's shotgun and the door was blown wide open.

'Empty!' I acknowledged with disappointment.

'Hey! Over here … found something!' Brian called.

He had discovered a hatch in the side wall. It was completely dark inside. 'This must be how they got out!' he said.

I began climbing into the hatch. 'What are you doing?' Brian asked in surprise.

'Finding out where this hole leads. Come on!' I replied, anxiously making my way into the hatch.

'Hell with it! Let's go!' Brian happily obliged.

I slid down into the dark hatch and found myself in a tunnel. Brian followed.

Outside, in the alleyway Paul, Maxwell, and Rick were still in danger from the mob. The crowd had flocked around the front and side of the building, with shooters patrolling the rooftops. There was only one way to safety: to head up the dark alley, using the dark as cover if lucky.

'Let's keep moving! He's onto us!' Rick insisted.

'My father! They got my father!' Paul replied, hesitating, stalling behind.

'He belongs to them now! Come on!' Maxwell replied, determine to push on despite Paul's lack of effort.

Brian and I appeared in the alley fifty metres shy of Paul, Maxwell, and Rick. 'He's here!' Rick called out, opening fire.

Brian and I immediately took cover behind the heavy metal bins within the alley. Paul and company took off, escaping under fire, with our allies on the roofs involved, laying down fire to buy Brian and me time to pursue our targets.

'Come on! They're getting away!' I called to Brian, running along keeping pace.

We quickly picked up their trail. Farther along the alley, they approached a three-way crossroads, and Maxwell made an executive decision. 'Split up! Hold them off!' he ordered.

The allies on the roof had lost our targets in the dark of the alley, but Brian and I headed up the trail, carefully scanning defensive arcs and watching our rear. Paul, Maxwell, and Rick had dispersed in different directions. Arriving moments behind, the crossroads halted our chase.

I quickly made a dead-on decision. 'I'll head right!'

Brian instantly acknowledged my decision. 'Watch your back, Father! I'll head left!'

Running along up the right-hand alleyway, my chase brought me towards a metal door in the wall that appeared to be part of an old medical treatment facility joined to the far end of the asylum. There was nowhere to retreat; I could only go through the door that stood before me. Someone was inside, maybe all three, I wasn't too sure, but it didn't matter. I checked my ammunition: both guns were half loaded and my blade was tucked into my waistband in reserve. I kicked the door in off its rotted hinges. Inside, I went up a set of stairs, keeping my guard up around every bend.

Brian made his way into an old underground basement beside the alley, dropping beneath the asylum. It was dark and dingy, with dim moonlight seeping in from the broken foundation. He carefully investigated, making his way across the open floor cluttered with dismantled fixtures and fitting equipment left to cobwebs.

Anxious and keen to kill, he drew attention to himself, calling his man out of hiding. 'Come on out! I know you are here! Show yourself, you scum!'

'If you think you're going to kill me, you are wrong!' Paul's voice echoed through the darkness.

'Only one of us will to be leaving here alive! Show yourself! Let's finish this!' Brian responded with pure hatred and aggression.

Paul stepped out into a narrow beam of moonlight with a deep chuckle, smiling at Brian. 'So, you came to avenge the dead.'

Meanwhile, my trek up the stairs brought me to a floor eight storeys high. There he stood, his back turned, facing a large murky window, arms at his sides, and a pistol in the right hand tapping nervously, as if he had expected me. Unfazed, unintimidated, with both revolvers ready, I quietly observed his manner.

'So, Father, we meet again. But on different terms.' Rick spoke with confidence, calm as ever and ready for what was coming.

I remained silent and still.

'You've changed. You've changed a lot. That's good', he remarked, referring to my new-found character.

Burning with rage and the desire to end his worthless life, still I waited quietly—thinking, planning, assessing, not knowing what trickery he might be up to. I needed to be ready.

'Go on, pull the trigger. I can feel the urge burning down my back. Go on; go on!' Rick shouted, trying very hard to force my hand.

I said nothing. Rick got annoyed, he flipped, losing the plot just as I was hoping.

'You ignorant swine! I'll kill you one last time! Right here!' Rick shouted in disarray.

He turned, making a quick draw, and we began exchanging shots, pitting and scarring the jagged walls of the already dismantled building.

Brian and Paul were already engaging in an intense gun battle, shooting at each other from behind broken appliances and tables. 'You shouldn't have come! Now you are going to die like your friend!' Paul cried out, sneaking closer in, using the broken furniture as cover.

Brian stayed put, refreshing his shotgun with fresh cartridges. 'Not if I kill you first, you piece of shit!' Brian growled loudly, unaware that Paul was closing in.

Brian began shooting. Using the loud exchange of gunfire to his advantage, Paul began to close in on Brian's firing position, step by step, keeping a low silhouette.

'This is it, Father!' Rick shouted, glancing over a fallen concrete post. 'Today you die! Just as you should have back then!'

With my back plastered to a solid wall partition, I checked the last four cartridges in my revolvers. *This is it; every shot must count.* Rick emerged, guns blazing, hitting the wall behind me. I broke my cover, returning two shots to buy myself time as I reoccupied cover behind a concrete pillar.

Rick carefully strolled around, looking for me. Then he figured it out. He stopped, chuckling. 'You are out of ammunition! It's over!' he yelled, unaware he was standing within my reach.

'Not quite!' I replied, quickly revealing myself.

I put two shots into Rick's feet and then an elbow to his face. He lost his gun, which slid away beneath a set of fallen shelves. He shrieked with agony, stumbling backwards over broken objects. He began crawling, making his way towards his gun. I grabbed him by the collar throwing him around.

Brian wasn't having much luck on his side of the fence. He sat comfortably in cover firing away, while Paul quietly invaded his cover. Then Brian heard a hammer being cocked. Paul stood over Brian with a gun to his head.

'Move and I'll blow your head off!' Paul towered above Brian, taking charge of the gunfight. 'Not very good at this, are you? Stick to your day job!' he mocked, about to pull the trigger.

Unwilling to admit defeat, Brian knocked the gun away, thrusting Paul to the ground with both legs. He wasted no time before trying for a shot, but Paul kicked the gun from his hand. Both began to engage in hand-to-hand combat pummelling each other like the men they were.

Rick, on his back after being thrashed about, sat up with his back against a broken wall, badly beaten and bleeding from his busted mouth as I stood over him with my fist, bruised and bloody.

'Go ahead! Kill me!' Rick wearily offered his life to me.

'No, not yet! I have something planned for you!' I growled, snatching him by the collar.

I brought towards the window where he had stood awaiting me and dropped him to his knees. Outside, several storeys down, the angry mob stood waiting impatiently, holding their ground.

Looking down from the large open window, Rick flinched at the sight of the outraged mob. 'What? Don't have the balls to finish the job?' Rick eagerly tested my patience, as if to be disappointed.

'This was never about me! Now meet your fate!' I replied, tossing Rick out the window, watching as he fell the long way into the angry mob.

The mob softened his landing. Then, as one, they swarmed Rick with their terrifying presence. The roar of the angry mob drowned Rick's screams for mercy.

I didn't stick around for the aftermath. With a flick of my coat I was gone like the wind, off in search of Brian should he need my help.

Brian was at the mercy of Paul's ferocious attacks. He was being thrown around the basement, battered, with a broken collarbone and shattered ribs, lying helplessly against the wall. Paul grabbed him by the neck, wrapped an arm around his throat, and began to finish the job. Brian struggled to tear Paul's arm away from his neck.

'Time for you to join your friend!' Paul grunted aggressively in Brian's ear, about to snap his neck.

Two loud bangs, and Paul dropped flat, shot in the back of both knee joints. 'Correction! It's time you join yours!' There I stood with two smoking barrels.

'What the hell kept you?' Brian panted exhaustedly, on his ass twisting his neck into shape.

'You think you've won! This isn't over, you hear me! This isn't over!' Paul shouted, crawling away helplessly.

I swung my fist and knocked him cold, face down on the hard dusty floor. 'You talk too much!'

Not long after, a pair of boots dragged along the road as we lugged Paul along, his arms over our shoulders. The loud roaring and protesting mob cheered us on as we tossed him at their trampling feet. They dragged him to his feet, passing him down the line, hand over hand, onto the back of a pickup with two armed allies taking him away.

Officer Shepherd approached me with a satisfied smile and a pat on the shoulder for a job well done. 'We did it! It's over!' He smiled proudly.

'There's one more thing I must do', I replied with a hint of defiance thinking of the bigger picture.

'Yeah? What's that?' Brian asked, curious to know what was on my mind.

'Have them ready to move. Clear the mob out and meet at Harbour!' I courageously ordered the men that stood before me.

Three miles out, fleeing Demolition town up a back street, hurrying along on foot, was Maxwell, gun in hand. He was making a break for it, continually looking over his shoulder in fear of me. Then suddenly a set of headlights switched on before him, Maxwell stopped, frightened. He turned around –to face another set of headlights, freezing him in his tracks.

Maxwell stopped, he was cornered, trapped, surrounded like a rabbit in the headlights. Blinded, he struggled to identify the group of men jumping and climbing from the pickup trucks encircling him. Amongst them, Ray emerged in a military type black parka coat, jeans, and hard boots with a group of tough-looking men and women.

Their piercing gazes intimidated Maxwell. 'What's the meaning of this?' he growled, swinging his gun from left to right defensively.

'You might want to holster that thing before someone gets hurt'. Ray admonished him. 'By "someone", I mean you.'

Maxwell, realizing he was outnumbered and the jig was up, tucked the gun into the rear of his pants.

'I'm going to need that gun. Hand it over', Ray calmly insisted, keeping his cool while he had the upper hand.

Maxwell meekly obliged, slipping the gun from his pants into Ray's hand quietly. 'Mind telling me what this is about?' Maxwell asked, alarmed.

'You are about to find out. Someone wants to have a word', Ray answered calmly with a dirty smirk on his face.

CHAPTER 22

A pickup truck door opened. A pair of shiny black boots hit the ground, topped with black stonewashed jeans and finished with a red afflicted T-shirt, the whole cloaked with a black knee-length wool coat, above all that sleekness a quiff and a neatly trimmed beard. The man from the Riders bar, the man behind the hijacking, the man responsible for Captain Walter's shifty actions, the man who sold me out to the Logans using his friend Steve, was the man who'd once sat outside the doors of my church: Jack Wielder, finally showing his true identity.

He was smooth and slick as a greasy tin, looking brand-new with a whole new attitude. Jack casually approached Maxwell with a swagger in his step, cheerful and quite pleased for some reason. Maxwell's face cringed at the sight of Jack. 'Should have known you were behind this! Got your stink written all over it!' he grunted, with a hateful look.

Jack, shaking his head with a smile of disappointment, lit a cigarette. 'Max! Max! Max! Been a while! How are things?' He calmly blew his smoke into the air. Maxwell kept quiet.

Jack beckoned with his cigarette. 'Let me guess. Not so good, huh?' Jack smiled with a happy chuckle. But no answer from Maxwell.

'I understand Father Brown has got you boys by the balls! He wants you out of town, gone like the wind. What a man!' Jack ranted with excitement.

'Well, that's not going to happen!' Maxwell spouted boldly.

Jack's happy face suddenly crumpled to a frown. He lowered his cigarette. 'I'm afraid it is', he replied firmly.

'Let me guess. We leave, you take over?!' Maxwell inquired, hitting the mark.

Jack threw his hand up in celebration, happy again, and spun around merrily. 'Somebody give this man a medal! Damn, you are good!' Jack pranced about his men excitedly.

'Even if we leave –', Maxwell began.

Jack quickly interrupted. 'You are leaving! Don't make this hard!'

'The Logans! What about them?' Maxwell asked out of pure curiosity.

Jack flicked away his spent cigarette and looked at Maxwell, surprised. 'What about them?'

'They control the supply chain, the routes, the customers, the logistics! They owned most of the high paid buyers you can think of, if not all! They've got the highest quality drug trading on the market as we speak! They've got the guns and the numbers to do as they please. You don't stand a chance!' Maxwell carefully highlighted all the logic that defied Jack's opposition.

Jack began to laugh, looking around at his men, all with a stony expression about their faces. 'This piece of crap thinks we don't stand a dying chance. I'll be damned! Those pair of spineless balls are already dead, they just don't know it yet!' Jack smiled a satisfying smile, happy to boast about his horizontal success.

Maxwell looked at Jack, concerned and curious. He asked, 'Oh yeah? What makes you so certain?'

Jack shortened the gap between him and Maxwell with a straight look on his face and piercing eyes. 'Let's just say I've got my ways of getting things done!'

He whistled and gave a hand signal to his men. Two of them went to the back of the pickup. They dragged Craig from the cargo hold. He was busted up, bruised, and beaten, with swollen eyes and a limp. They shoved him to the ground on his knees in the midst of the watchful audience. Maxwell looked stumped for words; he'd thought Craig was dead.

'See, Max? We got intel—sources—rats in the pipes—you name it!' Jack roared boastfully, pacing around in excitement with his arms flung wide.

'How?' Maxwell loudly demanded answers.

'Let's just say your friend here has been a big help! We are utterly grateful!' Jack replied with a smile and an insane laugh. 'Nothing like a dirty cop who knows his shit, right, Max? Trust me, I know!' Jack chuckled, strolling about Ray's side.

'So the long-forgotten Jack of Carol City, dirty DEA, wants back in.' Maxwell put two and two together, knowing Jack's secret past. 'Let's hope Father Brown doesn't catch on. He seems to think this city is already his, so good luck to you, Jack!' Maxwell calmly said his piece.

'You hear that, Ray? Maxi here thinks the infamous Father Brown is going to drive us out of town like dogs, our tails between our legs!' Jack, loud and humorous as ever, spread laughter amongst Ray and his gang.

'The Father is doing my will! Best part is, he doesn't even know it!' Jack continued to boast. 'In fact he's on his way to put the Logans out their misery as we speak! That's how good he is. Man of his word!' Jack laughed, pleased with himself and how far he had gotten with his clever plans to rise above all the rest.

'Soon he will be cutting the head from the snake! That's when good old Jack of Carol City, myself, takes his throne once again! This city won't know what hit 'em!' Jack proudly proclaimed his unseen future.

'Love to stay and gloat, but we've got work to do. Ray? Take care of the Father's unfinished work; I'm sure he'll be pleased!' Jack saw himself off to his pickup, leaving Ray in charge of his work.

Maxwell suddenly became worried. He stood his guard, watching carefully. Ray and the gang began chanting ominously, 'Death! Death! Death! Death!'

One by one they drew chains with jagged spikes from their trucks. Ray kicked Craig to the ground. Maxwell, realizing the danger, began to fend off the gang, throwing his fists around. Jack watched from the comfort of his pickup in the back seat. He chuckled, shook his head with pity, and smiled, lighting another cigarette, enjoying the gruesome spectacle from his window seat.

The gang overpowered Maxwell, Craig already helpless on the ground. All as one, Ray and the gang began swinging their chains, whipping the clothes from the two men's backs, shredding the skin from their flesh. It was a bloody affair. From Craig, they whipped the life away, and he gave up the ghost.

Maxwell, on his knees, drenched in blood, stripped of his dignity—he was last to go. Two chains came looping around his neck, one from either side. Two men fiercely tightened the chains, popping the veins in

Maxwell's eyes as he struggled to hold on to his last breath. Ray stared him down with a smile in his red bloodshot eyes.

Unable to talk or breathe, Maxwell, with his last ounce of energy, lifted his middle finger to Ray. Ray looked over at Jack, who nodded back at Ray. Ray then nodded to the men holding the chains. Then, with all eyes on Maxwell, with a forceful yank of the chain, they ripped his head from his shoulders. Swift as the wind it was over.

Nothing was left. The gang saw themselves off to their vehicles, climbing into the pickup trucks.

Jack looked out the window at the mess he had orchestrated. 'Let's see what Father Brown is up to. It's time for the final phase', he said to Ray, who sat in the driver's seat. Jack rolled up his window as they drove away.

After a clean sweep of Demolition Town, we drove along the deserted street; I rode shotgun with Brian behind the wheel of the pickup. We came upon Maxwell's and Craig's mangled bodies lying in the middle of the street. Brian stopped the truck. We quickly got out with our guns in hand, taking precautions. Standing in blood, we looked at the mess before our eyes.

'Looks like someone finished our job.' Brian turned up his nose at the gruesome sight at our feet.

I crouched down over the dead, carefully scrutinizing their bodies. 'Whoever did this to them, they haven't been here long. The blood's still fresh!'

'You don't think the mob did this, do you?' Brian worried.

I stood up and looked around the old buildings and the surroundings, just in case someone was watching. Then, with my head high towards the rooftops, I answered Brian. 'No, this is the work of another. I've seen this before, years ago, on the news. Let's get out of here', I replied, a bit concerned.

We got back in the pickup and drove away. Late that night Brian and I arrived at the Carol City dockyard, parking amongst the containers with the headlights on. Not too far ahead, another set of headlights flashed, signalling at us. We exited the truck and approached an SUV parked between two containers. There we met with Captain Walter and Officer Shepherd, who had already rendezvoused ahead as scheduled. They stood waiting in front of their SUV, looking to go ahead with our final plan of action.

'Is it ready?' I asked urgently.

'It's ready. Let's load them up', the captain quickly replied.

Officer Shepherd unlocked an empty miscellaneous container. Together, all four of us we offloaded three wooden crates labelled *FRAGILE*. Then we unloaded Mr Sullivan, his son, Paul, and Rick from the SUV, while they slept unconsciously. We loaded each of them into a wooden crate, replaced the crates in the container and sealed it tight.

'Right! We're done here! Let's get a move on!' I said to the others, walking back to the pickup.

I was stalled by the captain upon approaching the pickup. 'Hey, Father?'

I looked back at him in acknowledgment. 'Captain?' I answered quietly.

'What about the Logans?' he asked worriedly.

'Let me worry about them; you keep your end of deal', I replied, calm as a judge.

After that, Brian and I disappeared into the night, leaving the dockyard in the rear-view. Later, after dark, sitting alone in the pickup after seeing Brian off, I was looking in on the Logans' mansion from across the street. It was quiet—no security, no armed sentries around the yard—a perfect opportunity to finish the job.

Further up the road, under cover of darkness, an SUV lay in hiding. Inside, Ray and three others watched in silence, making sure I was going through with my plans. Ray's phone began to vibrate on the dashboard; caller ID displayed as 'The boss'.

Ray answered. 'Talk to me!'

'Is the task being carried out as planned?' Jack was calling from inside the Riders bar with a drink in his other hand.

'As we speak!' Ray replied, short and precise.

'Good. Make sure it's done', Jack ordered and hung up the phone, carrying on with his drink and grabbing a waitress by the bum as she strolled past.

From the comfort of their vehicle, they carefully watched as I skilfully evaded the gate cameras to the mansion, picked the locks, and let myself in. The place was awfully quiet, and something didn't seem right. Inside the mansion I was being watched by the Logans and a group of armed assailants from inside a room equipped with closed-circuit television.

'Wait till he's inside. Then bring me his head!' Gosnell yearned for blood.

'Spread out inside the mansion, and await orders!' Johnathon called to his assailants loitering in the background, fully armed.

Immediately the assailants dispersed themselves throughout the building and waited in silence. Calm and collected, I stood out before the mansion doors and looked up at the camera zooming in on me. The Logans stared an evil stare, waiting for me to enter.

'Come on, Father Brown. Take the bait like the animal you are', Johnathon whispered aloud to himself.

'Don't worry, he will', Gosnell said. 'It's the only way in; he's got no other option.'

The door cameras went blank ... static interference. The brothers panicked. 'What the hell happened? Get him back on screen now!' Gosnell growled desperately at his man sitting at the console.

The man struggled to rectify the fault, but he stuttered without a clue what to do or what was going on. 'I-I can't seem to identify the fault, sir! There must be some kind of electrical interference!'

Furious, Gosnell drew his gun from his waist and shot the man dead, blowing his brains all over the camera panels. Johnathon looked on, unfazed by the gruesome assault.

'He got on my nerves', Gosnell casually said and tried assessing the cameras himself.

Suddenly the cameras were back online. 'there we go!' Gosnell said, pleased with his efforts.

He began flicking through the security feeds. There was no sign of me or my whereabouts. 'We've lost him! Where the fuck is he?' Gosnell shouted in frustration. He grabbed a walkie-talkie and immediately alerted the gunmen within the mansion walls. 'Everyone! Keep your eyes peeled! Do not let your guard down!'

All of them, lurking in the study, the living room, the hallways, the kitchen, and the bedrooms, had their ears glued to their radios and hands strapped to their guns, on edge and trigger-happy. Suddenly, quietly—like a cold chill, I came sliding down the chimney inside the living room.

Three assailants waited to react instantly yet were unaware of my presence. One stood guard within the archway, and two casually roamed the living space. Out I swooped with both revolvers in my hand, catching the assailants off guard. A bullet to each of their heads, and the living room was cleared.

Alerted by the sound of gunshots, the Logans quickly alerted the rest of the assailants. 'He's in the mansion! Everyone to the living room, now!' Gosnell shouted into the radio.

I looked up at the camera above the fireplace, picked up a radio from the dead man at my feet, and passed a daring message on to the Logans. 'Get out while you can, because I'm coming, and I'm bringing hell!' I growled into the radio.

Immediately, the lights and the power were shut off, the mansion went black, and the brothers panicked. 'He's somehow cut the power supply! He's blinded us!' Johnathon wailed.

'He's not getting in this room, not without a fight!' Gosnell drew his gun from his waist, already holding firm despite my message.

Meanwhile, in the dark of the mansion, in the hallways, I was killing the shooters silently, using nothing but my blade. I carefully went up the stairs where two gunmen were patrolling the floor. They had their backs turned, their guard down, leaving me a clear opportunity to strike. I took their arms off and buried my blade in their sides.

'It's too quiet, brother!' Johnathon complained, loading a full magazine into his gun.

'I think it's time we get out of here!' Gosnell replied, ready to flee the room in a hurry.

'I couldn't agree more. Let's get moving!' Johnathon fearfully tailed his brother, who left the room in a hurry.

Bloodstained coat, tainted bandage, and a thirsty blade pried from the body of its victim—one of the gunmen, dead at my feet outside the corridor upstairs. I was just about finished when the Logan brothers came running, fleeing for their safety up the corridor.

Seeing me, they opened fire, missed, and retreated into a nearby room. Then they were shooting from the open door within the cover of the room.

'You can't hide from me, Logans! Face me!' I shouted, slowly strolling down the corridor with my blade dripping blood.

They tried making deals, offering bribes, looking to buy me into submission. 'We can pay you!' Johnathon shouted back from their hiding place. 'Lots of money, lots of it! If you just walk away and forget this whole bloody vendetta!'

Meanwhile, I was removing a smoke grenade from the utility belt around my waist but kept quiet, making no response. Gosnell shouted in desperation, 'Don't be an arrogant fool, Father! Take the offer!'

I swiftly tossed the smoke grenade into the room, shielding my own nose as the gas amplified. I could hear the Logans coughing and struggling to stay put. Out of options and overwhelmed by the gas, they tried for a quick getaway, shooting blindly into the corridor as they made a break for it.

There was no sign of me. As the Logans hurried down the stairs, they froze in their tracks at the sight of me standing patiently, waiting with both my revolvers ready to be unleashed. They raised their guns, and I impulsively shot the guns from their hands. They retreated into the living room, but I was there already, one step ahead like a ghost moving amidst the dark of the mansion, playing their every move.

'How?' Gosnell growled angrily, annoyed at my persistent manoeuvres.

'Not how, but when! When you were busy owning the city, flooding the streets with drugs, I've had the time to study these walls like the back of my hand. There's nowhere you can run that I won't find you. The jig is up; come quietly!' I explained, giving the Logans a chance to surrender.

The Logans noticed a gunman quietly creeping up my rear. They felt lucky and stood bold, disregarding my protest.

'You may be holding the guns, Father Brown, but the game is far from finished!' Johnathon snarled with a hearty smile on his pompous face.

Immediately I tucked my revolver under my arm, the barrel pointing backwards, and potted two shots into the eyes of the assailant behind me. I finished the job by shooting the chandelier from the roof, crushing the assailant.

I then turned my guns onto the Logans. 'How about now?' I snapped aggressively.

Defused, disarmed, and outgunned, the Logans impatiently awaited judgement.

'Mark my words, Father Brown! You will pay!' Gosnell grunted angrily.

'What's your motive?' Gosnell asked. 'You got the man that took your family away! What the fuck do you want with us?'

I shook my head at their ignorance and holstered my guns. Then I calmly wandered about the Logans' presence, keeping a close eye, and began to list their wrongs.

'You've defiled my church in your desperate attempt to provide a safe house for your drugs. That's not all; it didn't stop there. You've killed a dear friend of mines—Father Lenard Franklin. Does it ring a bell?' I asked, glaring at the brothers through my bandage.

'That old fool had it coming! All he had to do was say yes, and all would have been fine! Too arrogant, too proud—that was his downfall!' Johnathon boasted, smiling, proud of his heinous actions.

'And all you had to do was leave!!' I shouted harshly, causing the pair to flinch.

Quietly, under my nose, Gosnell was fiddling with his hands behind his back, reaching down into his waist for a hidden gun. My back was turned, but my guard was up; I was still self-aware and fully alert.

Gosnell drew his firearm, hoping to put a bullet in my back. I reacted quickly, drawing my blade decisively and slicing his hand from his wrist. I finished the job by taking his other arm from his shoulder. Gosnell fell to the ground shrieking in agony, with blood spouting from his missing limbs. Johnathon plastered himself to the wall, shaking, with my blade at his throat.

'Any more bright ideas?' I growled, and Johnathon silently shook his head. 'That's what I thought. Now help him up! You are leaving town!' I ordered, my anger barely under control. It would have required only a flicker of movement to decapitate him on the spot.

With a mammoth effort, Johnathon helped his wounded brother onto his shoulder and began walking towards the door under my direction. 'Head for the pickup across the road!' I grunted with my blade pointed directly at Johnathon's back.

From the darkness, Ray and his men watched as I escorted Johnathon towards my pickup with his brother over his shoulder, barely conscious and bleeding out.

'Well, I'll be damned! Just when I thought he could not get any colder!' Ray said to himself aloud, looking on from behind the wheel.

'He didn't finished the job. The boss won't be happy!' Ray's companion retorted.

'Right you are, Smith, right you are!' Ray replied as he scrutinized my actions from the dark of his front seat.

'Toss him in the back!' Johnathon placed his mangled brother into the cargo hold of the pickup. 'Give me your belt. Now!' Johnathon handed it over. 'And the tie! Take it off!' I ordered as Johnathon unwillingly obliged. 'Don't stand there looking stupid. He's bleeding out!'

At once Johnathon caught on and strapped his belt and tie around his brother's missing limbs under my watchful eyes. After he was finished, I slapped a set of chains from the cargo hold onto his wrists and ankles. 'Now get in! We're going for a ride!' I ordered, holding my blade at his neck. Johnathon stood firm, looking at me with devilish eyes and an angry face, showing signs of resistance.

'Don't make me ask twice!' I snatched him by the jaws with a fierce grip. 'You haven't seen the worst yet!'

He acceded to my demands and grudgingly loaded himself into the back of the pickup with his brother. I got in the cab and drove the brothers away into the dark of the night, past the watchful unseen eyes of Ray as I drove past. Ray then took it upon himself to follow me along, keeping a safe distance.

Later that night I returned to the docks. This time, alone. I pulled up beside the shipping container and killed the headlights. I got out and pulled the cargo hold open, dragging Johnathon out by his shackled feet to sprawl on the pavement.

'Stand up! It's time to send you packing!'

Johnathon scrambled to his feet. 'Where the hell are we?' he stammered, looking nervously around the docks.

'This is the last place you'll ever see!' I replied with an ominous tone as I unlocked the container.

Frightened and confused, Johnathon made a break for it. He took off into the dark, shuffling between the containers. I immediately headed him off before he could escape. Shuffling along in the dark, he stumbled into my fist, which threw him onto his back, out cold.

Again dragging him by the shackles, I got him back to the pickup towards the container. Gosnell was awake and groaning in agony. I took the time to treat his amputated arms with bandages and a shot of morphine from a first aid kit stashed away in the back of the pickup. I was still being watched secretly by Ray, sitting behind the wheel of his vehicle in the dark of the dockyard.

'This isn't over, Father. Mark my words', Gosnell groaned softly into my ear as I shot the morphine into his shoulder.

I grabbed him by the collar aggressively. 'I tell you what! You ever get out of this, you come find me!'

Angry and disturbed, I set my hat aside and ripped the bandage from my face, unveiling the horror beneath. Gosnell, startled, shook in terror at the sight of my fiendish appearance.

'Remember this face! This is how it all started, and so it shall end!' I growled angrily into Gosnell's terrified face.

I dragged him feet first from the cargo hold of the pickup and into the container as he pleaded for mercy. I loaded him into an empty crate and his brother in another, out cold and unaware of what fate had bestowed on him.

'Please! Don't do this, I'm begging you! Please!' Gosnell cried out from the crate.

'You had your chance. You chose your fate. Now live with it!' I replied and knocked him cold with a blow from my fist. Then I sealed him and his brother away.

Outside the container, at my feet, lay my bandages. I looked down at them and decided to carry on without them for the rest of this dying night. Then came thunder, and I raised my gaze to the sky as it pissed all over my mangled face. The I straightened my coat, loaded myself into the pickup, and drove away. Ray and his men quietly watched as I slipped past, retreating from the dockyard.

'It's done. He took care of our problem', Ray immediately told Jack on the phone.

'Good. It's time to cut the head from the snake. Meet me at the safe house!' Jack sat behind a polished oak desk flanked by Raoul's Rottweilers and petting the head at his right arm.

Early the next afternoon, pickups and motorcycles decorated the empty space inside an open warehouse. Jack, Ray, and their gathered body of men waited patiently.

'Where the hell is he? He knows better than to keep me waiting!' Jack said, annoyed and extremely agitated.

'I'll get the boys on it', Ray replied.

'No, give it another hour. I'm a patient man', Jack said, stalling Ray's hasty impulse.

Meanwhile, at Carol City General Hospital, Detective Carl Brooks was being discharged from the hospital's care. Inside his room he was in the midst of straightening his tie and keen to get away. With him stood Captain Walter, waiting to escort the detective and Dr. Ramrod himself with the patient's chart in his hand.

'Well, Detective, I must say you've made a remarkable recovery! Your vitals are in good shape, and you appear to be mentally and physically stable!' Dr. Ramrod proudly gave the all-clear.

Happy with the good news, Carl was eager to leave. 'If that's all, Doctor, I'll be on my way!' He slipped into his overcoat.

'Come on, let's get you home.' Captain Walter seemed just as eager.

'See you around, Dr. Ramrod! Thanks for the hospitality!' Carl acknowledged the doctor on his way out the doors that had sheltered him during his recovery.

Outside the hospital, the captain's cruiser was parked in the handicap area, the only available space. Yet the captain seemed blasé about it. Carl took notice and looked at the captain cautiously.

The captain looked back. 'Yeah, yeah, I know! Let's just get the hell out of here!'

Driving through the city, they me a set of traffic lights. The captain waited impatiently, tapping the steering wheel, looking at his watch.

Carl took note of his shifty antics. 'You all right, Captain? Seem a bit anxious.'

'Just trying to get you home to your wife. It's been a long day.

Besides, she's dying to see you', the captain replied with confidence, putting Carl's mind at ease.

Carl chuckled, shook his head, and laughed. 'I hear you, Captain, loud and clear!'

The lights went green, and the captain pulled away, turning left at the lights. Carl suddenly became concerned. 'Whoa, Captain! Right turn, remember?'

'Calm down. I've got something you need to see', the captain replied, carrying on along his uncharted route.

Carl wasn't having it. His gut was telling him different, that something was wrong. The captain wasn't being himself, and Carl wasn't about to take any chances. 'Whatever it is, I'm sure it can wait!'

The captain ignored him and drove on, heading out of the capital towards the outskirts of town. 'Trust me, Carl. You need to see this!' the captain insisted, again with a stern voice.

The situation escalated. Carl grabbed the steering wheel, trying to take control. The two of them struggled, and the cruiser began swerving about the street as drivers and pedestrians threw themselves away in fear of their safety. They finally crashed into a lorry emerging from a cross junction. The impact knocked the captain cold, and Carl was slammed with the airbags.

Alive, bruised, and disorientated, Carl pushed the door open and staggered to his feet. He took out his phone about to make a call for help, when he heard a hammer cocked. The captain was awake with a bump on the head and a busted nose holding Carl at gunpoint.

'Put the phone down, Carl! Don't make me shoot you!' the captain said, agitated.

Carl lifted both hands in submission and tried to talk the captain down. 'Don't do this, Captain! It doesn't have to end like this. Just put the gun down!' he pleaded with a loud voice of reason.

The captain thought for a second, seeming to have a change of heart. Then he quickly reverted back to his earlier stance. 'I'm sorry, there's no other way', he replied sadly.

Carl shouted to him, 'No!'

The captain pulled the trigger several times and shot Carl down, on the kerb at the roadside. The driver of the lorry and the onlooking public scampered at the sound of the bullets fired.

The captain exited the car, approaching Carl. He wasn't dead only wounded in both arms and legs. The captain looked down at him, shaking his head in disappointment, still holding his gun. 'This is just like you, Carl: it always has to be the hard way, right?' the captain yelled. He reached down, grabbed Carl, and dragged him back into the car. 'Father Brown won't be saving you this time, I'm sorry!' he ranted angrily as he got into the car and took off.

At the warehouse, still waiting anxiously, Jack was running short on patience. 'Okay, Ray, looks like we'll have to send the captain a reminder!' He was about to have a sudden change of heart.

'I'll round up the men', Ray happily obliged.

Suddenly they heard tyres screeching and revving roaring engine as the captain sped into sight and pulled his cruiser into the warehouse.

'Speak of the devil', Jack muttered to Ray.' Looks like someone had a bit of trouble.'

The captain jumped out of the car, leaving Carl to his agony whilst he awaited his own troubled fate. The captain hurried towards Jack, about to explain why he'd been kept waiting, when without warning Jack threw a punch, knocking the captain backwards against a pickup.

'That's for keeping me waiting! And this, Captain, this is for causing me doubts!' he grunted and began beating the captain harshly in his gut with his bare fists.

Then he looked into the captain's cruiser and noticed Carl passed out in the front seat with fresh bullet wounds. Jack laughed excitedly, poking his head into the passenger window to examine Carl, who looked back at him with a dismal expression. 'Looks like someone is having a bad day. It's about to get a whole lot worse!' Jack said with a gruesome smile.

'I remember you', Carl murmured weakly.

Jack grabbed the detective by the jaws. Then with an evil stare he leered into Carl's eyes. 'Course you do, Detective. Soon this city will remember me and what I stood for', he growled.

Carl passed out, and Jack tapped the roof of the car, drawing his men's attention. 'Get him out of there! Get him patched up; we have work to do!'

Carl was taken away into a room in the back of the warehouse. Jack looked at the captain with a trace of scepticism in his wicked eyes. The captain approached Jack to try again to explain why Carl was shot. 'I had to …!' he began, but Jack rudely interrupted.

'Whoa, now, Captain! Hold your horses! You don't have to explain. I know what happened. You tried talking him down, he wouldn't listen, shit hit the fan, you did what you had to do to get the job done! Am I right or am I right?' Jack smiled ecstatically at the captain, amazed by his own words.

The captain was puzzled and stumped for words but had to agree that Jack was right. 'Er … yeah, yeah, that's right!' he answered.

Jack patted the captain on the back and escorted him along into the back room of the warehouse. 'Come along now, Captain! We got a rogue priest to find!'

CHAPTER 23

After a long, bloody, restless night, I woke up in a cold sweat in the room of a local motel half a mile from the edge of the city. I sighed with discontent, weary of another nightmare. The horrors kept on coming—the pain, the blood, the heartache, and my loss all added up to my own personal hell. I drew the certain, greeting the daylight as it poured into the room.

A quick wash and a change of clothing from the night before, and I was ready to see my troubles off. Looking across to the bedroom sink, I noticed my filthy bandages lying there, stained from last night's antics. I pondered: should I? I shrugged and put on a fresh, clean bandage. Then I pressed my hat down onto my forehead and was soon behind the wheel, engine roaring, and I was off.

Not long after, I pulled up outside the city dockyard, where I was greeted by Officer Shepherd in uniform. 'The container leaves as we speak. It's all taken care of', he whispered secretly, maintaining his professional air.

'Good job. I'll see you around', I replied, shifting into gear, about to pull away.

Shepherd waved; he had something more to add. 'Hey, Father Brown? Just want to thank you for what you've done!'

'Way I see it,. I was just doing God's work. It's Arthur Brown now; I'm not the man I used to be.' It didn't seem right to take any credit for a job well done.

Shepherd was a bit surprised. It was not what he wanted to hear, he still believed in what was left of the man I used to be. 'You will always be Father Brown to me. Take it easy out there', he said with a satisfied smile.

'I'll see you around. Look after yourself', I replied kindly, appreciating Shepherd for his bold efforts.

I headed out of town on the winding country road, back towards the cottage. The journey was quiet and peaceful, giving me a chance to think and even do some soul-searching, letting my mind roam freely. Suddenly the quiet was broken by the sound of a gang of bikers speeding by, overtaking me around the bend.

Ignoring the riders, I carried on and soon pulled off the road onto the dirt track towards the cottage. To my surprise, the bikers were there waiting, sitting on their bikes with guns in hand. I stopped and touched my revolver, which happened to be riding shotgun. I had no idea who they were, but clearly my troubles were far from over. I slammed the gear into reverse and started back up the tracks, where I was suddenly intercepted by a group of four pickups.

Trapped and boxed in like a rat, I had nowhere else to go. 'All right, Arthur, this is it. Live or die', I whispered to myself dramatically.

Looking in the rear-view mirror, I noticed the trucks were crammed with shooters. Ahead the bikers posed another deadly threat. It was obvious that I was outgunned and outnumbered. Releasing a deep, calm breath, I exited the pickup with both guns, all shooters aiming at me, and waited for a reaction.

Carefully I looked around, observing the unfamiliar faces—unaware I was being watched from behind the tinted glass of a pickup, Jack and Ray looking on silently.

'What now, Jack?' Ray asked, sitting behind the wheel.

'Let's see what happens', Jack replied, with piercing eyes and a suspicious tone.

'So! How does it end?!' I called to the men surrounding me, ready to die.

All quiet, not a word. Just as I was about to lift both arms and unleash the revolvers, a loud shout cut the silent air. 'Father Brown!' Jack emerged from the privacy of his pickup. 'I suggest you think about what you are about to do. Can't afford to let you die!'

I turned around, barely recognizing him in his new look. I struggled to understand what was going on and what Jack's role was in all this strange occurrence. 'Jack? Is that you?' I was confused, surprised, and definitely suspicious.

'It's me, Father Brown—the one and only Jack of Carol City, as once known!' Jack replied, his smile never wavering. He strolled over with a swagger in his step, happy to see me. His excitement had an odd note, and I held my ground, my revolvers pointing at him. He stood before me with a suspicious grin on his face. I looked him in the eyes with a grey expression.

'Why the long face, Father? This is a moment of celebration!' Jack roared merrily.

'What are you talking about, Jack? What is all this about? Answer me!' I demanded, gesturing with one revolver. The sound of cocking guns and thoughts of happy trigger fingers made me think twice.

Jack leered at my revolvers pointing dead at his chest and smiled a dirty cheating smile. 'Now, now, Father. I think you should lower those bad boys. They have served you well—loved your work. Well done, Father, for making my work a lot easier. I could not have done it better myself, much appreciated!'

I kept quiet, not saying a word, still trying to wrap my head around it all. Then it hit me. I remembered the news reports plastered across the walls of his trailer, the headlines the articles—and it was all clear. Jack noticed the look in my eyes through the peepholes of my bandage and chuckled, grinning away. 'You remember! Don't you, Father?'

Outraged, I shouted, 'You started it all, didn't you, Jack? It was all you, all along! You didn't just want me to avenge my family! You wanted me to clean up the mess, take out the trash!'

Jack twirled in excitement and howled, 'Amen, hallelujah, you figured it out! All it took was a dear friend of mine. Had old Steve to drop the dime on you. But the job's not quite done yet, I'm afraid. I'm going to need you to do one last thing for me, Father. Or is it Arthur now?'

With a feeling of hatred and disgust I burst out in anger. 'I'm done! My journey ends here. I suggest you leave now!'

Jack shook his head as if disappointed by my lack of cooperation. He turned his back but then seemed to have second thoughts and turned at me. 'You know what, Father? I think you are going to do exactly as I tell you!' he said with a confident smile.

'I've lost everything, there's nothing you can do to change my mind!' I shouted.

'Right you are, Father! Right you are! However, I've still got one last bargaining chip up my sleeve!' Jack whistled aloud at Ray, sitting in the truck.

Ray got out and walked towards the cargo hold. From it he dragged a man onto his feet with a sandbag over his head. The man appeared to have been beaten; judging from the bandages on his arms, he had been shot. I watched as Ray kicked the man to his knees and put a gun to his head whilst he mumbled as if struggling for words.

'How about now? Last chance before Ray puts a bullet in his head!' Jack tried inevitably to persuade me, hoping that I'd care for the life before me.

Deep down, I wanted to care, but my new-found hatred towards Jack dictated otherwise. Conflicting thoughts and emotions battled within me; what was it going to be? I pondered the obvious: *If I let him die, I die; if I give in and Jack wins, either way I lose.* Then I gave in, playing my cards cautiously and buying some time.

'All right, Jack, you win. What is it you want from me?' I holstered my guns and was quickly disarmed by Jack's gunmen and shoved towards the trucks.

'Let's go for a ride!' Jack said gleefully, walking me along.

As I was pushed past him, the man on his knees began to mumble louder, rustling against Ray, who grunted, 'Shut the hell up!' and knocked him cold with his gun to the back of his head.

My curiosity was aroused as to who this man might be. I stopped, facing Jack at the door of his truck. Boldly I asked, 'Who is he?'

Jack laughed and kept me in suspense, ignoring me and ordering his men to get moving. 'Load 'em up, boys. Let's ride!'

Eagerly they forced me into the back seat of a pickup and the man in another, and set out along the cottage trail.

What seemed like moments after we've left the cottage, I found myself strapped to a chair, my head covered, my vision blocked. Immediately the blindfold was unwrapped.

'Rise and shine, Father, it's showtime!' Another unexpected greeting by Jack himself.

I was in a reasonably large room that appeared to be a garage. Two armed men stood watch at the door; Ray along with three of Jack's men lingered about the room should my actions prove unexpected. Then there was Jack, leaning comfortably against a large, untidy oak desk, a cheerful smile on his face, stroking the heads of Raoul's Rottweilers at his knees, which were grinding their teeth at me.

Jack chuckled. 'I think you and my new best friends may have some history here, Father! Found them both wandering my warehouse, poor things; took them in like they were my own. Thanks to your excellent work, I found me a new pair of muscle! Very loyal they are, no different from the men standing with me.'

Jack was having a happy moment, gloating as he paced about the floor. Then he stopped and looked at me with a straight face. 'So tell me, Father, are you loyal?'

'Not to you Jack!' I answered with a scowl.

Not so keen on my response, Jack began to lecture me with his dark motives, raising his voice across the room ecstatically. 'Well, Father, today you are going to be as loyal as these two dogs before me, and I'm going to make sure of it. Whatever it takes, you will finish this blood campaign. You will kill one last time—for me. Like it or not, it will happen!'

My anger raged, and I began shouting at Jack. 'Damn you, Jack! Don't get your hopes up about it. I'm done!—it's over!—finished! You hear me?'

Jack stormed towards me and slammed a hand down on my chest. Pulling me into his face, e roared, 'This isn't finished, Father—not till I say it is. I've got too much riding on this. You will do exactly as I say!'

Through the peepholes of my bandages I peered into his eyes, and in the most intense voice, I spat my words at him. 'Hate to disappoint you, but I'm no killer.'

Jack looked stunned. He backed away with a puzzled expression. Then he laughed. 'I'm afraid you have already chosen that path, Father. After all, righteous kills, and this is who you are now!—Hey, Ray? Get me our bargaining chip. It's time to play hardball!'

Ray left the room along with another man. I insisted to Jack that his cruel intentions were futile, shouting my lungs out. 'You won't break me, Jack! You've tried before, and look what happened!'

Jack smiled a proud smile at me. He thought differently. He fed the dogs treats from his desktop and then began lecturing, using logic against me.

'Oh, I did try, all right. You went right ahead and made me proud, you did exactly what I had planned. I could not have asked for a better man for the job! Priest goes rogue, the righteous becomes the unrighteous—man of faith or man of vengeance?' Jack pranced about hysterically, loud as ever.

'The answer is easy: you will kill for me once more, for the last time before you hang up that dirty blood filth collar of yours to dry. Hell! I didn't think you had the balls to do what you did, but then you proved me wrong—a self-made killing machine! Such a shame I had framed you to get the Logans involved, but it was worth it. Cost me dear old Steve, but it was worth it! Like I said, Father, righteous kills!'

I was quiet, nothing more could be said. As much as I hated to admit it, Jack was right. His logic shot right through me like a bullet to the heart. The truth did hurt. Jack, watching my expression change, walked over to me. He leaned into my face and whispered, 'Kill for me, Father. Kill!'

Hurt and dismayed, with self pity, hatred, and guilt towards myself, I shrieked loud and painful. Let's just say emotions were running high. Jack was happy to see me at the pinnacle of self-destruction.

'That's it, Father, that's what I want from you! Just a bit of guilt stirred with anger!'

The back-room door opened. Ray and one other returned, shoving the man into the room with his hands and feet in locks and chains and a sandbag over his head. 'Just in time!' Jack greeted them. 'We were about to wrap things up!'

From a desk drawer he took a gun and placed it to the back of the man's head. 'Kneel!' he shouted at the man.

The sound of Jack's pistol cocking was a clear warning-Carefully, the man lowered himself to his knees in submission. 'Right, Father! It's time to make an executive decision: kill once more or be killed. Your call!'

I replied with a speck of resistance. 'You dragged me here, played a wild card, and made empty threats with a stranger. I'm afraid I'll face the music. Do your worst, Jack!'

Jack was suddenly annoyed by my lack of cooperation. In fact, his manner was hysterical, aggrieved, and irate. 'You want to see empty threats! I'll show you empty! Nobody fucks with Jack, nobody!'

Immediately, Jack pulled the bag from the man's head, revealing his identity. 'Still think my threats are empty, Father? Do you?'

Son of a gun. The bastards had Carl Brooks, gagged and muzzled like a dog in a kennel. I was caught—*He's got me*—stunned and lost for words Jack had played his wild card, and somehow he knew I'd care.

'Carl! How? How, Jack? How could you? Stop this madness now, I'm warning you!' I cried out angrily, trying to talk Jack out of his witless attempt to blow Carl's head from his shoulders.

Carl began to mumble, trying to get his words out. Jack nudged his gun at Carl's head. 'Shut the fuck up, Detective! You got ten seconds to decide, Father! Ten!'

Jack began to count backwards, and Carl began to murmur. Sympathetically, my heart began to race, pulse elevating, palms sweating. I needed to make a call; to do or to die was the only choice left for me to play.

'Nine! Eight! Seven! Six! Five! Four! Three, Two! One!! Goodbye, Detective!'

Jack was about to pull the trigger. I cried out, 'Stop! Don't … I'll do it.'

Jack held back, still visibly tempted to pull the trigger. 'I can't hear you, Father. Speak up before I blow his head off!'

'I'll do it! I'll kill one last time! I'll do it!' I shouted my lungs out for the safety of Carl's life.

Jack holstered his gun. 'Now that's more like it! It's time to go to work. Get him up. Our dear Father is about to do God's work!'

I was unstrapped from the chair and placed aggressively in front of Jack on my knees. Jack reached over his desk and grabbed a folder, which he then presented to me. 'Everything you need to know, right here!'

I snatched the folder from Jack's hand, after which his men unhanded me. Carl, on his knees, looked at me with painful eyes. It hurt to see him at his worst. I had to do this, one last time.

'I'm sorry, Carl. I can't let you die like this', I whispered aloud.

'He doesn't have to. Do your job, and he lives!' Jack was anxious and keen to see me off.

He called, 'Hey, Ray? Get the Father his guns; he's got a big day ahead!'

Ray quickly fetched my revolvers from the boot of his car. With them, he brought my utility belt, and my prized possession, my blade, laying them all down carelessly on Jack's desk. Quietly, peacefully, I began prepping my revolvers with cartridges from my utility belt and strapped on my holsters. Jack looked at me and smiled proudly with a deep chuckle.

'You sure look the part, Father! I'll give you that! Make old Jack proud!'

Focusing on the grim task before me, I ignored Jack's selfish ways. I picked up my blade, about to slide it down my side. Jack hastily intercepted, taking the blade from my hand. I looked crossly at him.

Jack then wandered about the floor admiring the blade at its finest, teasing it against Carl's face as he circled him like prey. Carl flinched at the sight of the blade against his face while I kept a close eye.

'This is one fine blade you got here, Father. Very creative, fine craftsmanship. You are good, real good! Maybe too good. I've seen your work—bloody, a bit like hell! Should I be concerned?'

'No, Jack. Be afraid', I warned with an ominous tone. Jack was both intrigued and somewhat concerned as to where my loyalty lay. He fiddled his chin, thinking.

'Striking words, Father! Very intimidating coming from behind that bandage mask! You may have strike fear into these men, right here, but not me, Father. I think I'm going to have to show you just how much I'm a man of my word, should you fail me!'

Jack whistled to his men pointing at Carl. As a joint effort, Carl was placed on his feet. Jack shouted. 'Unchain him!'

The chains were removed, Carl was about to be used as an evil example. Quickly I shouted to Jack, 'Jack, don't! Please!'

Jack wouldn't have it, not ready to cease his bloody rampage. I hurriedly reached towards him, trying to detain his foul act. Reacting simultaneously his men halted my attempt to do so, holding me at gunpoint, restraining me on the floor. The dogs began barking as the circumstances escalated.

Ray muscled Carl's palm onto the table. With a clean stroke of my blade, Jack sliced Carl's hand from his wrist.

Carl fell to his knees in agony. Shocked, stunned by Jack's cruel act, I turned away, speechlessly burying my face into my hand. After he had finished, Jack fed Carl's hand to the dogs clamouring at his feet. I watched helplessly as the dogs tore and devoured the hand.

'Get him patched up!' Jack ordered.

Carl was then taken away while Jack redirected his attention towards me. 'Now the message is clear! Nobody intimidates me!'

Jack then towered over me with my blade stained with blood. I looked up at him with a mountain of hatred, trying hard to retain that fiery rage beneath. He shouldered my blade and savoured the moment. 'I get it, Father; you are angry. Deal with it; get on with the job.'

Outside Jack's warehouse, eight or so of his men gathered around the trucks and bikes with their guns. Jack had me front and centre facing the gang with Ray at his side and my blade pointing into my chest.

'Take a good long look at these men, Father. They will be accompanying you, keeping a close eye, making sure you get the job done. It's time you were on your way, so move it!' Jack grunted, pushing my blade firmly against my chest.

I looked around, seeing no sign of my truck. 'Where's my ride?'

'That old pile of junk is long gone! Get yourself a bike!' Jack replied, grinning sharply at me.

Parked next to a four-by-four was a black V-Rod Muscle, set there for the taking. I bravely mounted the bike, staking my claim.

Ray wasn't too happy about my choice. His foul look was enough to burn holes in my chest. 'You scratch that bike, and you are good as dead!'

Without a word I cranked the bike to a start. I looked at Ray and replied, 'I'm already dead! Deal with it!'

'No Ray! Let the man be; it's only a bike!' Jack kindly eased Ray's burning temper.

Jack casually strolled towards my side. Leaning closely at my ear, he whispered, 'Twenty-four hours, Father, twenty-four hours. That's all you've got, and I do not need to tell you what happens if you fail'.

Without a word I revved the engine, taking Jack's words with a pinch of salt. Jack smiled and ordered the men to mount their vehicles, ready to move. 'It's time to go! Let's not keep the Father waiting; he's got his hands full. Move out!'

Jack's men, along with Ray and his company, mounted their trucks and followed on out the warehouse. Jack was as excited as ever. He folded his arms to his chest with my blade dangling at his side, smiling a grand smile while I rode on past.

CHAPTER 24

We were travelling along the eastern country road heading outside the city just as the sun touched the horizon, with Jack's gang bringing up the rear. According to the intel from Jack's folder I was after a man by the name of Ethan Charles. His people referred to him as Father Charles for obvious reasons. He was a sadistic drug lord, the head of the largest drug trade flooding into Carol City, and Jack wanted in; Jack wanted to head his empire. For that to happen, Ethan must die, and Mexico City was where I would find him. Carl's life depended on it.

Now here I was the next day. Hours after the sunrise greeted Mexico City, I was already sitting out in the Metropolitan Church square on the seat of the V-Rod with narrow eyes lingering from walls to walls, making sure that I was going ahead with Jack's plan. *Ten minutes ... anything beyond that window, and Carl is as good as dead.* So I fixed my hat firmly over my forehead, dismounted the bike, and made my way into the church, parting the large quiet double doors.

Inside, all was quiet—a pair of grieving members on their knees before the altar pouring their guilt before God, making the sign of the cross. They fled at the sight of me as I steadily walked the aisle. I saw no sign of the man I was looking for as I wandered the aisles. I took a seat gazing up at the magnificent structure and its religious monuments. I recalled days at my church, looking down from the altar at my family, smiling back at me. Secretly smiling beneath my bandages, I shed a tear.

Then, the curtains of the confessional shifted. Casting my memories aside, I noticed a penitent leaving in tears, taking little notice of me as she dried her tears with her bare palms. Wasting little time, I approached the confessional and drew the curtain, seating myself inside. My sigh of discomfort caught the attention of the man I had been sent to dispatch.

He cleared his throat. 'You sound troubled, my child!' Ethan called to me in a curious voice, heedless of any danger.

Just then, I was struck with a moment of silence, pondering and debating the mammoth task that I was about to undertake. My palms quietly settled on my revolvers on either side. This was it: Ethan Charles, the false priest, the man truly responsible for the poison that washed over my city. Worst of all, he sat beside me pretending to be the man I was; my heart wrenched with anger.

I broke the silence at last. 'Trouble I am, Father!' I said with a disgusted tone.

'Your voice says it all! I sense pain and guilt. Feel free to confess your transgressions. God forgives!' Ethan replied as if to show passion and commitment to his idle beliefs.

'First, let me tell you my pain!'

'Go on, my child! Let the Lord be thy judge!'

'My wife, my two sons … I lost them. They were my world. They are my pain, my cross to bear.'

'My deepest sympathy for your loss. They are with God now! Let God's grace ease thy pain!'

'I'm afraid it's not that simple.'

'Why is that, my child?' Ethan was intrigued and kept on digging.

'With my pain came my troubles—troubles that brought me to your doors!' I replied, calm, confident, and poised.

'What troubles do you speak of, my child?'

'The kind of trouble that brought me the pain I had to endure.'

'Well, my child, all that's left to do is to cast thy burden at Jesus' feet. Let him take care of all your troubles.' Ethan preached on, using biblical slogans, a sign that he was deep into character.

Looking at my watch, keeping check on the time, I said, 'I'm afraid it's not that simple. My troubles are too grave!'

'Tell me what exactly is troubling you. I'm here to listen and offer God's abundant grace.' Ethan continued, selling me this false idea of the man he was claiming to be.

'I'll tell you—but then you'll have to die!' I replied with an ominous tune to my words.

The priest Ethan Charles chuckled, finding me humorous,

disregarding my honesty. 'At least you've got your sense of humour. I'm listening; carry on!'

By then my hands were already locked to my revolvers with my thumbs massaging the hammers. It was that time. So I did him the favour of naming my troubles as his fate drew nearer by the minute. One by one I carefully named the dreaded things that had made me what I am.

'Drugs!' I highlighted-Ethan groaned a suspicious groan, his interest peeked.

'Crime! Chaos! Murder! Betrayal! And worst, blasphemy! Something you may know all too well—Ethan!' I called his name, exposing his cover; the devil was revealed.

He was lost for words. He had no idea who I was or how I knew his name. He wanted answers. He grunted desperately through the lattice, 'Who are you? How do you know my name? What do you seek? Money?'

'I'm just a man, doing the wrong things for the right reasons. A life for a life is all I seek—nothing personal, Father.'

'You came to the wrong place if you are seeking revenge! I own this city, and you won't leave here alive!' he snarled, trying to instil fear.

I aimed a lone revolver into the lattice of the confessional. 'This isn't about revenge. Your time has just expired.'

I pulled the trigger, leaving a hole in Ethan's head. His brains smeared the walls of the confessional, blood washed the curtains and drizzled across the floor, and it was over. With my guns resting quietly on my lap, I relinquished my hat to the floor and tore the bandages from my face, revealing the horror beneath. Sighing with some relief, I rested my head against the lattice next to Ethan's in the other half of the confessional and took a moment of silence.

There within the confessional I silently reflected upon my past, pondering the man I used to be and simultaneously hating the man I'd become. The irony was striking: I was a man who once spent his life saving others from the path I had come to embrace. Now look at me—far down the path of unrighteousness, stuck between good and evil. All the while I was waging war against the wicked, the real conflict was within myself.

As I was in the depths of my own inner evaluation, contemplating and reassessing my own self-judgement, Ray and his men appeared. They confirmed the death in the confessional booth. Ray looked at me, repelled by my hideous fiendish appearance. With Ethan dead, they departed without a word. I was left on my own, grateful, to take time to reconstruct my grand finale.

My phone rang—a minor interruption. I dug it from my pocket. Caller ID was Jack. I answered, hoping for good news.

'I hope you have kept your end of the deal, Jack!'

At his desk in the old warehouse, Jack sat with his feet up, laughing merrily. 'Well done, Father! Bravo, bravo! Thanks to you, I will once again rise to power!'

'Cut the crap, Jack. Release Carl, just as you agreed', I demanded, not caring to hear him gloat.

'Don't worry, Father, Carl is in good hands. I'll order his immediate release.'

'You want to hope, Jack, I do not need to tell you what my actions will be!'

'Oh, I think I know, Father. Before you think about heading home to your beloved city, you might want to think about surviving what you are about to head into. See you around, Father. Pleasure doing business with you!' He hung up, leaving me in suspense.

It was time to see myself off. Hat off the floor onto my head, revolvers away, a quick sign of respect to the dead sitting next to me, and I was off. Thrusting the church doors open, I was greeted by a torrent of rain. I hurried across the churchyard only to see that the bike was gone, Ray had taken his ride.

'Bastard!' I hustled across the road in the moving traffic trying to catch a ride. Horns blared, followed by a few swear words from the angry commuters. Brakes screeched towards me, as a car came fishtailing in, out of control. With seconds to spare, I jumped as the car plunged beneath my feet. I landed hard on the windscreen.

The driver stopped, and I pulled his door opened. 'I'm going to need this car!'

'Take it! Just take it!' Frightened, the driver scampered from behind the wheel at the sight of my foul stare and fiendish features.

Before I knew it, I was behind the wheel of the car, switching lanes,

A Righteous Killer

shifting through the gears, and fleeing the city, hoping to caught up with Ray and his gang. Ray had mentioned an old outpost just outside of town—a titbit he should have kept to himself, for that was where I'd be heading.

A mile short of my destination, the car died. The engine croaked—*she won't start, she's done playing*—but there was no time to waste. On my feet, I ran the last leg of my journey along the side of the road, pacing it out in the pouring rain.

Cutting my journey short, I headed off the road, into the bushes, hurdling fallen trees, dodging overhanging branches. Then there it was—the outpost, an old hut in the middle the of a rocky, deserted landscape. I stood back behind the bushes, making sure it was safe to proceed. I saw no sign of Ray and the gang; all clear. I broke cover, headed towards the hut, guns drawn, and kicked the door in.

All clear; they were long gone. I was too late. There was only the stench of cigars, booze, and leftovers sitting on a wooden table. In the middle of nowhere with no form of transportation, I was stuck and needed to play catch-up. I needed to know if Carl was still breathing, most of all. I had a war coming, and these two guns wouldn't be enough.

Eagerly I rummaged through the hut hoping to find guns, ammunition, explosives—anything that might help square the odds. But there was nothing. Angry and disappointed, I hurled an old cabinet to the ground, revealing a hold in the wooden wall. Hastily, I investigated and found a pair of fully chromed 12-gauge shotguns with a few cartridges lying beside them.

Coat off, hat set next to an old fireplace to dry, I was grounded. There was nothing left but to wait out the rain. I seated myself at the table and laid out my guns and ammunition before me. I carefully stripped down my revolvers amidst the shotguns as I made use of what hours I had to spare.

After careful thought I decided not to be hasty. I needed time to think before heading back to Carol City. *Jack will be expecting me. He'll expect me to be arrogant, giving him the edge, but it won't happen. I'll bunk here for the night; tomorrow, Jack dies!*

TO BE CONTINUED

Author Biography

Ellace James is a fiction writer whose imagination and creative mind give him the edge he needs to produce compelling titles such as this wonder masterpiece. His writing appeals to readers' imagination and visual senses, thus bringing his story to life through his in-depth descriptive approach. His inspiration is said to be spiritual—which also comes from his intensely active mind, which spontaneously erupts with interesting ideas—and the support of his family, which played a vital role in his aspiration as a fiction writer.

Printed in Dunstable, United Kingdom